# Poison Fruit

# Poison Fruit

AGENT OF HEL

JACQUELINE CAREY

RoC

A ROC BOOK

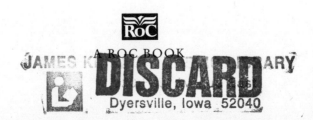

ROC
Published by the Penguin Group
Penguin Group (USA) LLC, 375 Hudson Street,
New York, New York 10014

USA | Canada | UK | Ireland | Australia | New Zealand | India | South Africa | China
penguin.com
A Penguin Random House Company

First published by Roc, an imprint of New American Library,
a division of Penguin Group (USA) LLC

First Printing, October 2014

LIBRARY OF CONGRESS CATALOGING-IN-PUBLICATION DATA:

Carey, Jacqueline, 1964–
    Poison fruit: Agent of Hel novel / Jacqueline Carey.
        p. cm
    "A ROC book."
    ISBN 978-0-451-46531-3 (hardback)
    1. Women detectives—Fiction. 2. Werewolves—Fiction. I. Title.
    PS3603.A74P65 2014
    813'.6—dc23        2014015080

Printed in the United States of America
10  9  8  7  6  5  4  3  2  1

Set in Stempel Garamond
Designed by Alissa Rose Theodor

# Poison Fruit

# One

Pemkowet in November is a study in neutral hues. Don't get me wrong—it's still a beautiful place, but you have to work a little harder to see the beauty. Except for the dark green pines, the trees are naked and barren. It's overcast more often than not, a sullen gray sky reflected in the gray waters of the Kalamazoo River.

Still, it makes you appreciate the subtler charms that it's easy to overlook on a bright summer day: the tawny expanses of marsh grass waving gracefully along the shallow verges of the river, the elegant yellow-gold traceries of willow branches draping toward the water.

And of course the dunes, the vast sand dunes, rendered more majestic without the foliage of cottonwood, oak, and birch trees that disguises their scope in the growing season. Those dunes are what make a little town in southwest Michigan such a popular tourist destination. Well, the dunes, the white-sand beaches on the shores of Lake Michigan, and the eldritch community—and, last month, the hauntings.

I was glad *that* was over. It had been a close call, but the gateway between the dead and the living was closed. The annual Halloween parade had been a debacle, but it hadn't turned into a cataclysmic bloodbath. Talman "Tall Man" Brannigan's remains had been laid to rest once more, and the local coven had sealed the mausoleum with all kinds of protection spells just in case.

And I was still Hel's liaison, authorized by the Norse goddess of the dead, who presided over the underworld that lay beneath the sweeping dunes, to maintain the balance between her rule of order and the mundane authorities. It helps that I work for the Pemkowet Police Department. Technically, I'm a part-time file clerk, but the chief calls me in to consult anytime there's eldritch involvement in a case.

That's me: Daisy Johanssen, girl detective.

Well, except that at twenty-four, I can't really call myself a girl. And, perhaps more significant, there's the fact that I'm only half human.

My mom's a hundred percent human and one of the nicest people you'd care to meet. No one here holds it against her that at nineteen years of age she inadvertently summoned my father, Belphegor, lesser demon and occasional incubus, with a Ouija board.

Obviously, she wasn't originally from Pemkowet. Well, obvious to anyone who was, at least. I consider myself a local, and no local would risk fooling around with a Ouija board. When you're sitting on top of a functioning underworld, there's just no telling what could happen.

The problem is that the Pemkowet Visitors Bureau promotes paranormal tourism while downplaying the possible risks, and as a result, we get tourists who are unaware of the very real dangers they might face—like the spectators at the Halloween parade last month, who weren't expecting to encounter the reanimated corpse of an infamous axe murderer.

Or like my mom, who was vacationing here on spring break with some college girlfriends.

If you're wondering what sort of special powers my demonic heritage gives me, the answer is pretty much none, which is because I refuse to claim my birthright.

There's a good reason for it. If I did, it would breach the Inviolate Wall, which separates the divine forces of the apex faiths—Christianity, Islam, Judaism, Buddhism, Hinduism, all the big -isms—from the mortal plane. And a breach of the Inviolate Wall could ultimately unleash Armageddon.

At least that's what I've always been told. It's conventional wisdom around these parts.

Oh, and two weeks ago, one of the Norns laid some major soothsaying on me and informed me that someday the fate of the world might hinge on the choices I make.

No pressure, right?

When I asked her for advice, she told me to trust my heart. The problem with that—I mean, aside from the fact that it sounds like a line of dialogue from a Lifetime movie—was that my heart was in a serious state of confusion, which is why I'd been spending an inordinate amount of time that November mooning over the subtle glimpses of beauty to be found in the bleak, dun-colored landscape instead of confronting actual issues. And if one of the issues hadn't decided to man up and acknowledge the fact that we had things to discuss, I'd probably still be mooning.

*Mooning*, by the way, is a particularly apt term when there's a werewolf involved.

I'd be lying if I didn't admit that my heart leaped when my phone rang and Cody Fairfax's name popped up on the screen. I hadn't seen him since Halloween night, and I was pretty sure he'd been avoiding me on purpose, not entirely without reason.

I let the phone ring a few times before I answered. "Hey." I kept my tone casual in case Cody was calling on a police matter. "What's up?"

"Nothing," he said. "I'm off duty today. And I just thought . . ." There was a long pause. "We need to talk, Daisy."

No kidding. It had been well over a month since we'd had what I'd categorize as earth-shattering sex. I hadn't made a secret of the fact that I'd had a crush on Cody since we were kids riding the school bus together. Cody hadn't made a secret of the fact that there was no possibility of a real relationship between us because I was an unsuitable mate for a werewolf. Kind of ironic, since he was in the eldritch closet, so to speak, but there you have it.

My temper stirred and my tail twitched. Um, yeah. I don't have any demonic powers, but I do have super-size emotions that occasionally cause bad things to happen, especially when I lose my temper . . . and I have a tail, of a more modest size. "Are we really going to have this conversation on the *phone*, Cody?"

"No, no," he said hastily. "I just wanted to see if you were free. Are you at your apartment? I'll come over."

"Yeah, that's fine."

"I'll see you in ten." He hung up.

I spent the next ten minutes tidying my apartment and, okay, checking my makeup. For the record, I mostly resemble my mom: fair skin, white-blond Scandinavian hair, a pert nose. The only trait I inherited from dear old Dad's side of the family—well, aside from the tail—is jet-black eyes, the kind you don't find in ordinary mortal humans.

Ten minutes later, I heard Cody's footsteps on the stairs leading to my apartment, which was located above Mrs. Browne's Olde World Bakery.

"I brought cinnamon rolls," he offered, holding out a bag when I opened the door. Mrs. Browne's cinnamon rolls were legendary. All her baked goods were. No one, human or eldritch, can bake a better brownie.

"Thanks." I took the bag. "Come on in."

I put the cinnamon rolls on a plate while Cody hovered in the living room of my apartment, which seemed smaller with him in it.

"Have a seat." I set the plate with the cinnamon rolls on the coffee table in front of my futon couch.

"Daise . . ." Cody stayed on his feet. His hands opened and closed in a gesture of frustration. "I'm sorry. This is awkward."

"Yeah." I blew out a breath. "Sit. Let's talk."

He sat on the futon, and I took a seat on the adjacent armchair. The cinnamon rolls sat untouched. Mogwai, the big calico tomcat who had more or less adopted me, peered warily around the door to my bedroom.

"How have you been?" Cody asked. "Since . . . ?" He let the sentence die.

"Okay," I said. "You?"

"Okay."

See, here's the thing. I'll spare the details, but the gist of the matter is that if Cody and I hadn't hooked up that first time—which was, by the way, completely spontaneous and unexpected—it's possible that we would have found the Tall Man's stolen remains; or at least Cody, with his werewolf-keen olfactory sense, would have. There's absolutely, positively no way we could have known it at the time, but the fact is that while we were lolling in the afterglow of earth-shattering sex, a thunderstorm washed away a scent trail we would have stumbled across in the course of duty, which would have meant no Halloween debacle, no axe-wielding zombie skeleton. All in all, a much better outcome.

I know Cody didn't blame me, but I knew he blamed himself for it, which made a situation that was already awkward even worse. And it frustrated me, because it gave him an excuse to avoid me.

Which is why I'd put a lot of thought into the matter while I was mooning over life's subtle beauties.

"It probably wouldn't have mattered, you know," I said to Cody. He looked blankly at me. "You and me? Delaying the investigation?" I shook my head. "It wouldn't have mattered, Cody. We spent a couple of hours canvassing the neighborhood around the cemetery that morning. Either way, the thunderstorm would have passed through long before we went to Brannigan's house. That scent trail would have been gone."

"Yeah." Cody ran a hand through his bronze-colored hair. "I figured that out after I had a chance to cool down. We still should have started investigating right away and I'm not letting myself off the hook for it, but . . ." He shrugged. "That's not why I'm here."

Oh.

"Why?" I asked softly, regarding him. He wore a worn flannel shirt and faded jeans, and it looked good on him. Unlike a lot of men, Cody Fairfax could pull off backwoods chic. "Are you here to give me the unsuitable-mate speech, Cody? Because I've already heard it."

A corner of his mouth twitched wryly, but there was regret in his topaz eyes. "Not the long version."

I said nothing.

Cody glanced around the living room, his gaze lighting on the small steel buckler leaning against my bookcase. "What the hell do you have a shield for, Daisy? Are you going to a Renaissance fair?"

"No," I said. "It's for practicing. It helps me visualize a mental shield."

While I don't have any special powers per se, it turns out that thanks to my outsize emotions, I do have an abundance of what Stefan Ludovic—hot ghoul, six-hundred-year-old immortal Bohemian knight, and the issue *I* was actively avoiding—informed me the ancient Greeks called pneuma, or the breath of life, and George Lucas called the Force, or midi-chlorians. Just kidding on that last part. I don't think Stefan's seen *Star Wars*, although he has surprised me before. At any rate, under his tutelage, I've learned to channel that energy into a mental shield, which is handy for warding off things like the emotion-draining ability of ghouls—more politely known as the Outcast—and vampiric hypnosis.

It can also be used as a weapon, which Stefan warned me was very, very dangerous, and that I should not attempt it before he gauged me ready. Given that I nearly got myself killed doing that very thing, I'd say he was right.

Anyway.

"Did Ludovic give that to you?" Cody asked me, an edge to his tone. His nostrils flared slightly, and there was a glint of phosphorescent green in his eyes. In the bedroom doorway, Mogwai hissed and bristled.

"Yeah," I said. "He did." My heart ached a little. "Goddammit, Cody! We've been over this before, too. You can't have it both ways. You can't tell me I'm an unsuitable mate, then act jealous. It's not fair."

"I know, I know!" Cody took a deep breath and wrestled himself under control. "That's why I'm here."

I swallowed. "Is this the long version of the speech?"

"Yeah," he said quietly. "It is. You know I haven't been in a relationship since Caroline died—"

"You've dated a ton of women!" Not exactly a considerate response under the circumstances since he'd just referenced his Canadian werewolf girlfriend who was tragically killed five years ago, but it was true.

"Human women," he said. "They don't count."

Being half human myself, I couldn't help feeling a surge of indignation. My tail lashed, and a few knickknacks on my bookshelves rattled in protest. "I'm sure it would warm their hearts to hear it."

Cody sighed. "I didn't mean it like that. But it's not the same, and you know it."

Unfortunately, I did. The intensity of what I'd experienced with Cody was unlike anything else I'd ever known.

He shifted on the futon. "That's why I never dated anyone for longer than a month. I never let it get serious. I never, ever misled anyone."

"I never said you misled me," I pointed out. "And you also never dated anyone longer than a month because they might start noticing a conspicuous pattern of absence around the full moon."

"True." Cody gave me the ghost of a smile. "But you . . ."

I waited. "What?"

His smile was gone. "You're getting under my skin, Daise," he said simply. "I wasn't expecting it, but you surprised me."

Oh, crap. My heart gave another painful hitch. "But."

"But I have a duty to my clan." Cody leaned forward and clasped his hands loosely between his spread knees. "I know it doesn't seem fair, but it's not just one of those arbitrary eldritch protocols. The entire survival of our species depends on our mating and breeding with our own kind."

"I know," I whispered. "But . . ." I didn't have a "but." There really wasn't anything to say.

"My family's given me a lot of leeway since Caroline's death," Cody said. "But at twenty-six, it's time I started thinking about settling down with a suitable mate."

"Are you sure?" I was just stalling now. "Twenty-six is still young."

"Not when you run a higher than average risk of being shot by a hunter or a game warden," he murmured.

That was how his Canadian werewolf girlfriend had died. "But . . ."

Cody's gaze was candid and human. "But it's not going to happen if we go any further with this, Pixy Stix."

Despite everything, I made a face at the nickname. "Oh, gah!"

"See?" His lips curved into a rueful smile. "That's one of the ways I know I'm getting in too deep. I find myself making up excuses to tease you."

"Yeah, if we were six and eight again, you'd be pulling my pigtails on the playground at recess," I muttered.

"Not at the risk of setting off your temper," he said. "That old boiler at East Pemkowet Elementary was awfully touchy."

"Don't make me laugh," I pleaded.

"Sorry." Cody rubbed his hands over his face. "I really am, Daise. But I have to try to do the right thing."

"So . . . what?" I asked him. "Does the Fairfax clan have someone in mind? Are you going to settle down with your second cousin?"

"No." He dropped his hands to his knees. "We're careful about bloodlines. With a relatively small gene pool, we have to be. Even wolves in the wild do their best to avoid intrafamilial breeding." He hesitated. "Sometime in the next couple of months, the Fairfax clan will host a mixer."

"A mixer?" I echoed.

"Yeah." To his credit, Cody didn't look happy about it. In fact, he looked fairly miserable.

"Okay." I stood up. "Well, thanks for telling me."

Cody stood, too. "Daisy . . ."

"What?" I spread my arms. "It is what it is, Cody. Like I said, you never misled me. I knew what you are."

"I wish I could share it with you, Daisy," he said to me. "All of it." A distant, slightly dreamy expression crossed his face. "The call of the full moon rising, all silvery and bright in the night sky, tugging at muscle and sinew and bone. The incredible release of shifting, the incredible freedom of casting off your humanity and hunting with your packmates; howling to each other, howling back at the moon, howling for the sake of knowing you're alive. The thrill of the chase and the glory of the kill, the scent of your prey's fear in your nostrils and the taste of blood in your mouth. I wish I could. Because you'd love it, Daise. You'd fucking *love* it. But I can't."

"I know." Well, I didn't know about the whole taste-of-blood-in-your-mouth thing, but I knew what Cody meant. I'd love it if I were a werewolf, but I wasn't and I never would be, which meant there was an intrinsic part of his life that I could never, ever share with him.

There was a moment of uncomfortable silence.

"So I guess . . ." Cody cleared his throat. "That's all I had to say. I'm sorry, Daisy. I really am."

I nodded. "Are you going to be okay if we have to work together again?"

"Are you?"

"Sure," I said. "It's my job. I've been doing it all along."

He nodded, too, and held out his hand. "Anytime, partner."

I gave him a look. "Jesus, Cody! A handshake? Really?"

Cody grabbed my hand and yanked me in for a hug, hard and fast enough that I stumbled into the embrace. I wrapped my arms around him, feeling his lean, muscled strength, my fingertips digging into his shoulder blades. I inhaled his scent of pine needles, musk, and a trace of Ralph Lauren's Polo mixed with laundry detergent from his shirt. He pressed his cheek against my hair, then let me go.

"Take care, Daise," he murmured.

I blinked back tears. "You, too."

On that note, Cody made his exit. I waited until the sound of his footsteps had receded to let my tears fall. If he'd just stuck with the unsuitable-mate speech, it would have been easier. Somehow, the fact that he'd admitted to developing feelings for me made it worse. Mogwai wound around my ankles and purred, trying to console me.

"Dammit, Mog," I whispered. "It's not *fair*."

He purred louder in agreement.

I got up and put Billie Holiday on the stereo to sing about heartache, then ate one of the cinnamon rolls. Neither did a whole lot to make me feel better, so I grabbed my phone and called my friend Jen.

"Hey," I said when she answered. "Any chance you're available to come over and get epically drunk with me?"

# Two

Everyone should be lucky enough to have a BFF. Jennifer Cassopolis has been mine since we were in high school. We knew each other's histories and secrets, hopes and fears and dreams. When you need to get good and drunk, that's the kind of person you want keeping pace with you.

"Okay, girlfriend," she announced as I opened the door. "I've got a bottle of Cuervo, a bag of limes, and a carton of Breyers cookies and cream, just in case. So go get your saltshaker and—" She cocked her head at my stereo. "Oh, hell no!"

"What?"

Jen thrust a shopping bag at me. "Put the ice cream in the freezer and cut some limes. I'm putting on some music from this century."

"Okay, okay!" I went into the kitchen. In the living room, the plaintive strains of Billie Holiday's voice gave way to the stomp-and-clap cheerleading beats of Gwen Stefani's "Hollaback Girl." "Hey, that's not our old high school playlist, is it?"

"Yeah. I plugged my phone into your stereo." Jen came into the kitchen. "Remember when you and I'd have our own dance parties in your mom's trailer?"

"Yeah." I smiled. "Good times."

"Uh-huh." Jen hopped up to perch on the counter beside my cutting board. Her dark, lustrous eyes were shrewd. "So, what's the damage, Daisy? Officer Down-low or the hot ghoul?"

I finished slicing a lime into wedges and fetched a pair of shot glasses from the cupboard. "Cody."

"Oh, Officer Down-low!" Jen shook her head. "What now?"

I sighed. "Let's move into the living room."

Over the course of a couple of tequila shots, I laid out my tale of woe. Of course, Jen knew the background.

"Damn," she said sympathetically when I'd finished. "I'm sorry, Daise. That's harsh."

I shrugged. "Like I said to Cody, it is what it is. I mean, it's not his fault. It's no one's fault."

"Yeah, but . . ." Jen licked the web of skin between the thumb and forefinger of her left hand and shook a judicious amount of salt onto it. "He didn't have to tell you that he was basically starting to fall for you. That just makes it harder, doesn't it?"

I salted my own left hand. "I know, right? It totally does! Do you think he did it to make himself feel better? Or me?"

By the time we'd finished giving my conversation with Cody the sort of thorough analysis and dissection that it deserved, the level in the bottle of Cuervo had dropped noticeably, and both of us were feeling the effects. Not exactly drunk yet, but sober was definitely in the rearview mirror. On the stereo, Outkast was telling us to shake it like a Polaroid picture, and after one more tequila shot, it seemed obvious that the thing to do was order a pizza, dance around the living room, and flirt with the blushing delivery boy when the pizza arrived.

Okay, maybe we were more than a little drunk.

One medium sausage-and-mushroom pizza, two beers I'd found in my refrigerator, and at least another tequila shot later, we were *definitely* drunk.

"Okay, Daise." Jen set down her empty shot glass with an emphatic thud. "What about the hot ghoul? Are we gonna talk about the hot ghoul?"

"Outcast," I said automatically.

She blinked at me. "You want to put it on repeat?"

I blinked back at her. "What?"

"Outkast?"

Oh, right. "Not the band," I clarified. "I mean Stefan's kind of Out-cast."

To be fair, I can't blame Jen for using the term *ghoul*. Everyone does it. I haven't entirely broken the habit myself, though I try to be respectful.

"*Outcast*, right. Sorry." Jen paused. "Did you ever find out what he did to get . . . Outcast?"

Here's the thing about the Outcast. The name, which is the name they call themselves, refers to the fact that they're formerly mortal human beings who've been cast out of heaven and hell alike and condemned to an eternal existence on the mortal plane, forced to subsist on the emotions of other humans.

Hence, the reputation as ghouls.

I admit, I'd found ghouls—the Outcast—pretty damn creepy myself before Stefan Ludovic came to town. If I've changed my tune, it's in part because I've gotten to know him, and realized that you don't get kicked out of heaven and hell without one heck of a tragic backstory. I'm not exactly sure how it works—even the Outcast themselves aren't certain—but essentially, a human soul becomes Outcast by dying in a state of commingled sin and faith and transcendently powerful emotion, which creates some sort of theological loophole that thrusts them back into their bodies in the mortal plane . . . over and over and over again.

Oh, they can die, all right; but they come back. Cast out again. It happens in the space of a heartbeat. I've seen it and it's profoundly unnerving. As far as I know, there are only two ways one of the Outcast can end his or her existence. One is to be starved of human emotions for a prolonged and agonizing period of time, until they consume their own essence and fade into the void of nonbeing.

The other is if I kill them, because I just so happen to possess a magic dagger that only I can wield and that's capable of killing even the immortal undead. It was given to me by Hel herself, and its name is *dauda-dagr*, which means "death-day" in Old Norse. Right now, it was in a hidden sheath in the custom-made messenger bag hanging from my coatrack. So far, I'd only had to kill two ghouls and dispatch one zombie skeleton with it.

"Daisy!" Jen snapped her fingers at me. "Daise?"

"Um, yeah." I poured myself another shot of tequila and downed it without bothering with the salt or lime. "Stefan's uncle killed his father and married his mother. He—"

"Wait." She interrupted me. "Isn't that the plot—"

"Of *Hamlet*," I agreed. "Only Stefan wasn't indecisive. He killed his uncle outright, and his uncle's guards stabbed him to death."

Jen shivered. "Damn."

"Uh-huh."

"Honor thy father and thy mother," she murmured. "That's the element of faith, right?"

"Right."

We sat in silence with that for a moment. On the stereo, Snoop Dogg advised us to drop it like it's hot.

"I think you should do it." Jen poured another shot for both of us. "One date. What do you have to lose?"

I held up my shot glass and squinted at the tequila it held. "Well, there is the small matter of one of the Norns warning me that the fate of the world might hinge on the choices I make."

She did her shot with salt and lime. "Do you *really* think the Norn was talking about your love life?"

"Probably not," I admitted.

"So?"

I pointed at her. "I can't believe you of all people would suggest I date an eldritch predator." That was because Jen's sister Bethany had spent eight years as a blood-slut in thrall to a vampire. Okay, she proved to be a surprisingly badass vampire in her own right when he finally turned her, but for eight long years, no one would have guessed it. Plus, her blood-bonded vampire mate was an insufferable prat.

"I know, I know! But . . ." Jen hesitated. "Daise, sometimes I forget that you're *not* human. If all you really wanted was a nice human guy—"

"I'd still be dating Sinclair," I finished for her, downing my shot.

She nodded. "You know what brought it home to me? When you told me that first time with Cody, he was a little . . . wolfy."

"Sorry." I grimaced. "I didn't mean to freak you out."

"I know." Jen refilled our shot glasses, her shiny black hair falling forward. She tucked it behind her ears. "I'm just thinking, you've spent your whole life trying to repress your inner nature. Maybe it's time to explore it."

Okay, this definitely wasn't a conversation we'd be having sober. I wasn't sure if that was a good thing or a bad thing. Jen was right. I *had* spent my entire life trying to contain my outsize emotions, especially anger and anything linked to the Seven Deadlies. I had an array of visualization techniques that my mom began teaching me at an early age. It kept me safe—safe from the prejudices of mundane humans, safe from the temptation scenarios my father, Belphegor, whispered to me when my unruly temper weakened the Inviolate Wall dividing us.

Too safe, maybe? After all, I'd recently indulged in some serious lust without any apocalyptic consequences. And when I'd nearly gotten myself killed using the pneuma as a weapon, it was my anger that had turned the tide.

On the other hand, unleashing Armageddon really wasn't something you want to take a chance on.

"You're the one I count on to keep me grounded," I said to Jen. "This is not exactly helpful."

She shrugged. "Look, the Norn said to trust your heart, right?"

"Yeah, but—"

"But you don't know what your heart wants." Jen pushed the full shot glass toward me. "How the hell else are you supposed to find out?"

I picked up the shot. "You have a point."

"And you know what else?" She was warming to the topic. "Stefan's *interested* in you, Daise. I don't know . . . I don't know exactly what that means for a ghoul, um, Outcast, and a hell-spawn, but . . . he's being upfront about it, you know? He's not dicking you around. What did he say when he kissed you?"

"He said he couldn't offer me eternity," I murmured, "but he could offer me the here and now."

"Right!" Jen gestured with her shot glass, tequila slopping over the sides. "He's not gonna sneak around on the down-low like Cody. He's owning it."

"He's sexy and he knows it," I said, paraphrasing the not exactly immortal lyrics of LMFAO.

For some reason—well, the obvious reason—this struck us both as hysterically funny, and we spent a solid minute laughing our fucking asses off. Which, under the circumstances, was appropriate.

"Oh, my God." Jen wiped away tears of laughter. "You know what, though? He really is."

"Mm-hmm." That was undeniable.

"You know what *else*?" She fumbled for the saltshaker. "I think Stefan actually respects you, Daise. Unlike some werewolves."

"Cody respects me!" I protested.

"Oh, fuck Cody!" Jen waved the saltshaker. "Because Cody . . . Cody . . . Look, it's not like plenty of couples don't struggle with fertility issues. He's willing to write you off just because you can't have his were-puppies. Who does that?"

"Members of a dwindling species fighting for their survival," I said. "Plus, there's that whole hunting-beneath-the-full-moon thing I could never share with him."

Jen made a dismissive sound. "Yeah, and if I was dating a guy who ran marathons, that's not something we'd ever share, no matter how much he went on about the endorphin high."

Again, she had a point. I'd never thought about it that way.

"So call Stefan." Seeing me weaken, Jen put down the saltshaker and looked around for my phone. "Here. Call him."

"No." I folded my arms. "I am *not* drunk-dialing a six-hundred-year-old immortal Bohemian knight."

"Text him?"

I hesitated. "No."

"You want to," Jen said. "You *so* want to. Fine. I'll do it for you."

"Don't you dare!"

Her thumbs danced over my phone's screen. "Too late."

"Jen!" I pleaded.

She put the phone out of my reach. "You'll thank me in the morning, Daisy. Trust me on this one."

After that, it gets a little blurry.

I'm pretty sure that Jen and I reached the maudlin stage of drunk, bawling along to a Kelly Clarkson song on our old playlist and declaring our undying friendship for the umpteenth time. I have a vague memory of the two of us digging into a carton of Breyers cookies and cream with a pair of spoons, talking about whether or not Lee Hastings would ever summon the courage to ask Jen out, and an even vaguer memory of ransacking the linen closet and dumping an armful of clean sheets and a blanket onto the futon for Jen before staggering to my own bed, where I collapsed in an unconscious heap.

All in all, a successful night.

# Three

I awoke with a hangover.

Not just any hangover, but an epic hangover—the kind of hangover they make movies about.

Unfortunately, I *did* remember the thing I'd rather have forgotten about last night, and it jolted me out of bed and in search of my phone. And when I found it, it was even worse than I'd feared.

"Jennifer Mary Cassopolis, what the fuck were you thinking?" I shouted at the figure buried beneath a pile of linens on my futon.

"Huh?" The pile stirred.

"The text," I said grimly. "The text you sent Stefan!"

"What?" Jen's head poked out of the covers. Her eyes were bleary and she looked as hungover as I felt. "Why?"

I showed her the message she'd sent on my phone's screen. UR HAWTT!! LETS DO THIS!!!

"Oh, shit!" Jen made a sound somewhere between a gasp and a laugh. "Daise, I'm sorry. Is there any coffee?"

I glared at her. "Seriously?"

She sat upright, pushing the hair out of her face. "I'm sorry! It seemed funny at the time."

"He's a six-hundred-year-old immortal!" I said. "You sent him a text from *my* phone that sounded like it came from a fourteen-year-old schoolgirl!"

"Look, just explain it to him. If he's got a sense of humor, he'll understand," Jen said. "And if he doesn't, you might as well find out now and avoid wasting your time . . . Daisy, what are you doing?"

I'd disconnected her phone from my stereo and was composing a message on it. "I'm returning the favor." Jen made a futile, blanket-encumbered lunge in my direction, which I dodged handily. "There." I finished and handed her the phone.

"Want to get a cup of coffee sometime this week?" she read aloud, then made a face. "You sent that to *Lee*? I just texted *Skeletor* for a date?"

Back in the day, I would have been surprised to find myself considering Lee a friend. He'd been a tall, painfully thin—hence the nickname—geeky kid who'd spent all his time hanging with a couple of other geeky kids, playing *World of Warcraft*. But things change. Oh, Lee was still tall and too thin, but he'd parlayed his love of video games and genius with computers into a successful career out in Seattle. Now he was back in Pemkowet, doing consulting work and caring for his ailing mother. And since Jen had given him a makeover last month, he was actually looking halfway decent.

Plus, he'd developed an awesome database that would let me keep track of the eldritch population in town, and he was doing some research on the side into a matter that Hel had asked me to look into.

"It's just coffee," I said to Jen. "And at least I had the decency to make you sound like an adult."

"Yeah, and I'll sound like a jerk if I try to explain it was just a joke," she grumbled. "Speaking of coffee—seriously, is there any?"

"I'll make some."

"Thanks." Jen began extricating herself from the tangle of sheets and blankets. "Hey, Daise? Did Stefan reply? You didn't say."

In my mortification, I'd forgotten to look. Now I did, and what I saw made me frown. "Yeah, he did."

"Well?"

"He says he needs to talk to me," I said. "And I should stop by the Wheelhouse today." Jen and I exchanged a look. "Do you think he changed his mind? Do you think he got sick of waiting for me to make up mine?"

Jen shook her head. "I don't think someone who's been alive for six hundred years loses patience easily."

I wasn't so sure. That text might have been enough to remind Stefan of the vast gap in age and experience that lay between us and convince him to change his mind.

Maybe.

On the other hand, thanks to the fact that I'd let him feed on my emotions last summer, Stefan had a direct pipeline into what I was feeling—a fact that I conveniently managed to ignore most of the time. At least that meant he'd know I was a little messed up last night. And today, for that matter. With the weight of my hangover crushing down on me, coffee seemed like a very good idea.

I shrugged. "We'll see."

In the kitchen, Jen shuffled up behind me, wrapped in a blanket. "I'm really sorry about the text, Daise." She rested her chin on my shoulder as I poured water into the coffeemaker. "Honestly, I don't know what I was thinking."

"I blame the playlist," I said. "We wouldn't have been acting like teenagers if you'd left Billie Holiday on."

Jen grimaced. "I blame the tequila."

"That, too." I turned to face her. "But you laid some righteous truths on me, too."

She gave me a wry smile. "Well, I hope I didn't undo whatever good it did."

"Eh." I waved a dismissive hand. "You're right about that, too. Screw him if he can't take a joke."

Half an hour later, fortified by coffee, we drove in separate cars to the Sit'n Sip; separate cars because I planned to stop by the Wheelhouse later and, no matter how hot she thought Stefan was, Jen had no intention of walking into a biker bar filled with ghouls; and the Sit'n Sip because when you have a towering hangover in Pemkowet, that's where you go for a gloriously greasy breakfast. I'm talking the equivalent of a Denny's Grand Slam, scrambled eggs, bacon, and hash browns, plus a side of biscuits and sausage gravy. It sounds disgustingly excessive— okay, it *is* disgustingly excessive, but there's nothing better for putting ballast in your belly to offset that queasy, acidic, roiling sensation.

By the time I scraped my plate clean, I felt marginally human—no pun intended. When it came to hangovers, apparently I was all human.

Of course, now I had to face Stefan, and despite what I'd said to Jen, I wasn't feeling all that easy, breezy, and carefree about it. For one thing, there was the lingering mortification. For another, there was the dawning realization that it really wasn't a good idea to respond to someone's interest in you immediately after someone else has . . . well, not broken your heart, but definitely dinged it.

Especially when that initial someone can read your emotions like a book and will know that's *exactly* what you're doing, which is why I entered the Wheelhouse with my mental shield blazing.

At this hour—it was around eleven thirty a.m. on a Sunday—it wasn't busy. Actually, the Wheelhouse was never really what I'd call busy for a bar in a thriving resort town. There just aren't that many Outcast in existence, and according to Stefan, far fewer of them are created in the postmodern era. But since their numbers barely dwindle, the small patronage that existed was stable.

And, of course, there were their . . . hangers-on, I guess. *Victims* is the word that comes to mind, but that's probably rude. The unhappy souls on whom the Outcast fed, and who relied upon the Outcast to take away their pain and misery.

Before Stefan came to town, that included a lot of drug addicts— meth-heads in particular. The Outcast did a lively trade in meth, perpetuating a vicious cycle of misery that gave them a constant source of sustenance. Stefan considered that particular flavor of wretchedness a kind of chemically induced poison and after establishing himself as the head ghoul in charge, he banned the drug trade.

But there are plenty of reasons why people can be miserable in this world, and some of the patrons, mostly women, came to the Wheelhouse for the respite they found there. For the record, the overwhelming majority of the Outcast I'd encountered had been men. The only female member of the Outcast I'd met was dead.

I know, because I killed her.

Anyway.

There was a little silence as I entered the bar, the Outcast assessing my psychic shield, the hangers-on evaluating me as a rival. Cooper, Stefan's chief lieutenant, peeled himself away from the pool table, where he'd been engaged in conversation with a woman who looked old enough to be his mother, and sauntered over.

"Hey there, Miss Daisy," he greeted me, looking a bit wary. "You're keeping well, I hope?"

"Well enough, thanks," I said. "And you?"

Cooper's mouth twisted as he regarded the mental shield I kept raised between us. "Well enough that you needn't fear me."

The last time I'd seen Cooper, he'd been ravening, which is what happens when one of the Outcast loses self-control, and pretty much what it sounds like. It wasn't entirely his fault—he'd been part of the ghoul squad that was providing emergency emotional crowd control at the Halloween parade, and had overestimated his discipline and stayed too long. But the upshot was that he'd completely drained a couple of mortal humans, a father and daughter, of their emotions, rendering them terrifyingly vacant. Stefan had assured me that they would recover in a week's time. I sure as hell hoped that they had.

At any rate, Cooper's pupils were steady and normal now, not out-of-control pits of blackness. I lowered my shield a measure. "Sorry. I didn't mean to insult you."

He shrugged his narrow shoulders. "Ah, you've the right to. It's you I'm owin' an apology."

"Accepted." I started to put out my hand, then thought better of it. When it came to me and my super-size emotions, Cooper preferred to avoid temptation.

"Hey, Coop!" His hanger-on joined us, carrying a drink with the exaggerated care of someone who's already had a few. Not that I was one to judge, certainly not this morning. "Who's your friend?"

There was a jealous note in her voice. At close range, she wasn't as old as I'd taken her for, probably only a few years older than me. Years of hard living had taken a toll, and her heavy makeup wasn't doing her any favors.

Cooper glanced sidelong at her, his pupils dilating slightly. The apparent age gap between them was still disconcerting, but then, it was bound to be. Cooper was over two hundred years old, but he had been seventeen when he was Outcast, and his body would never age a day.

The tense lines of the woman's face softened under his gaze, her jealousy vanishing.

"Daisy here is Hel's liaison," Cooper said to her in a surprisingly gentle tone. "The right-hand woman of the goddess herself. Go back to the pool table, Susie lass, and I'll join you in a tick."

She went, placid and obedient.

"Is she your . . .?" I didn't know what to call her.

"Source?" He shrugged again. "One of them, sure enough." The bleakness that lived behind his angelic blue eyes surfaced briefly. "Nothing more."

"I'm sorry," I murmured, painfully aware of the inadequacy of the words.

"I know." Cooper set aside his pain to summon a sweet smile. "So! Here to see the big man, are we?"

"We are," I confirmed.

He beckoned. "Come along, then. Himself will be tickled."

I hoped so.

Stefan was on a phone call when Cooper knocked on the door to his office at the rear of the bar, but he opened the door and waved me in. I took a seat and waited. Stefan paced as he spoke into his cell phone, unusually restless for him. I had no idea who he was talking to or what they were talking about, since he wasn't speaking English or any language I recognized. Not that I'm any great linguist—I've got two years of high school Spanish under my belt—but at least I have a passing familiarity with some of the biggies. I mean, I've seen foreign films. Whatever this was, not so much.

"My apologies," Stefan said after concluding his call. "So." He sat behind his desk and raised one eyebrow, the faintest hint of a smile hovering in the corners of his mouth. *"Haaawwwtt?"*

Oh, my God. Somehow, the way he drew the word out made it even worse. Although I kept my shield in place to deflect my emotions, a scalding tide of blood rose to flush my face. "Um, yeah, about that. I didn't . . ." I paused. Okay, I hadn't sent the text, but I hadn't stopped Jen from sending it. And middle-school language or not, the sentiment was apt. Stefan sat motionless, regarding me with the patience and discipline honed by centuries. His pupils were steady in his ice-blue eyes, a stunning hue you only see in Siberian huskies and the occasional supermodel.

Unexpectedly, I decided to own it. "Yeah," I said, lowering my shield. "That's what the kids called it back in my day."

Stefan's smile deepened and his eyelids flickered slightly. "Based on the chagrin I sense mingled with your embarrassment, I suspect you were not the author of the message, Daisy. But the fact that you were willing to allow me to believe it to be the case is . . . intriguing."

I squared my shoulders and raised my chin, ignoring the fact that my heart rate had increased. "I'm glad you think so."

A shadow of regret crossed Stefan's face. "Unfortunately, I asked to speak to you on a professional matter as Hel's liaison. A situation that requires my attention has arisen in Wieliczka."

"Wieliczka?" I echoed.

"The town in Poland where I most recently resided," Stefan said. His jaw hardened and his pupils waxed. "Apparently, the successor I appointed there is encountering some . . . difficulties."

"Oh." I found myself unreasonably disappointed by the news. "Do you have to go yourself? Can you send one of your lieutenants?"

He shook his head. "It is a delicate business that requires knowledge of the situation and the players. I must go myself. If there is aught that you require, Cooper will be in charge in my absence."

"Duly noted," I said. "Any idea when you'll be back?"

"No."

Ohh-kay. There wasn't a lot I could say to that, which seemed to be something of a theme to my weekend.

"I do apologize." Behind the desk, Stefan stood. "Having so recently established my authority among the Outcast in Pemkowet, I am reluctant to leave on such short notice. But this successor is a friend of long standing. And if I understand the situation rightly . . ." His voice turned grave as he rounded the desk. "I may have a favor to ask of you, Daisy. A very great favor."

I rose from my seat. "Care to give me a hint?"

He hesitated. "Lest what I fear not come to pass, I would rather not say."

"Okay." I shrugged. "Safe travels."

"Daisy." Stefan's voice dropped to a lower register, setting off butterflies in the pit of my stomach. He took a step toward me. I fought the urge to raise my shield, caught in the push-pull of conflicting emotions that his nearness created in me. He cupped my face, his thumbs caressing my cheekbones, and bowed his head toward me, his slightly-too-long black hair falling to frame his face. "Given the state of your emotions last night, perhaps it is for the best that we must continue this conversation at a later date," he murmured. "But do you agree that we *will* continue it?"

I raised my hands to grip his wrists—not to push him away, just to hold him in place. "Yes."

Stefan's mouth covered mine as he kissed me, hard. I kissed him back. I could feel the bond between us, feel a part of myself spilling into him. The two of us together was a dangerous proposition, which was what made it so damn exciting and terrifying. The last time he'd kissed me, I'd pulled away and raised my shield.

This time, I didn't.

It was Stefan who broke the kiss. He was breathing hard, his pupils dilated, a sliver of icy blue rimmed in black around them. His mouth stretched into a predator's grin. "I will count the hours, Daisy Johanssen."

I smiled back at him just as fiercely. "So will I."

What can I say?

*Hawtt!!*

# Four

On Monday morning, I arrived at the police station to catch up on filing, only to walk into a situation. I'd call it a domestic disturbance, except the wild-eyed guy and the skinny, bleached-blond chick screaming at each other weren't in their own domicile.

"—want to *file a report*, goddammit!" he yelled at her. "Some crazy old bitch breaks into our apartment in the middle of the night—"

"—need to go back on yer meds!"

"—fucking *sits* on my chest—"

"Yuh need to go back on yer meds, Scott!"

Behind the reception desk, Patty Rogan looked more annoyed than frightened, probably because Chief Bryant was in the process of lumbering out of his office like a bear disturbed from its hibernation.

"What seems to be the problem here?" he rumbled, hitching up his duty belt. "Oh, morning, Daisy."

"Morning, chief." I kept my distance. I'd rather face down an ogre than get in the middle of a domestic dispute, especially since the only ogre I know is a friend of the family.

The feuding couple began shouting at the same time again. The chief winced and held up one big hand for silence. It worked. For an ordinary human being, the chief has a lot of presence. He looked at Patty Rogan, who cleared her throat.

"Mr. Evans here would like to file a report regarding an intruder," Patty said in a neutral tone. "Mrs. Evans is of the opinion that there was no intrusion."

Chief Bryant pointed at the wild-eyed guy. "Scott Evans, right? Braden's boy?" The guy nodded, looking marginally less agitated. "You first."

"That ain't—" his wife began indignantly.

The chief silenced her with a look. "You'll get your turn, ma'am."

The upshot of Scott Evans's story was that he'd awakened in the middle of the night to find an elderly woman sitting on his chest—an elderly woman with skeletal features, glowing red eyes, and long, lank hair, that is. He'd been terrified and unable to move as she'd reached down and begun to throttle him, leaning over to inhale his breath. He was sure he was going to die, but then his wife, Dawn, rolled over in her sleep, and the scary old lady fled.

Somewhere in the course of Scott's less-than-coherent recitation, the chief gave me an inquiring look, which I answered with a slight shrug and head shake. I wasn't sure if a succubus was anything like an incubus, but it didn't *sound* at all similar to my mother's experience. Other than that, I couldn't think of anything in Pemkowet's eldritch population that would fit the profile.

"All right, ma'am," the chief said to Dawn Evans when her husband had finished. "What's your version?"

She sighed, her shoulders slumping. "There weren't no old lady, sir." There were dark circles under her eyes. "Scott's got the PTSD. Sometimes he sees thangs. And he ain't bin takin' his meds."

"It's got nothing to do with the meds!" he shouted. "She was *there*, dammit!"

"Oh, honey! Ah know yuh think so." Sorrow, a whole world of it, had replaced the anger in her tone. "But she weren't."

It was enough to convince Chief Bryant. "All right, here's what we're going to do. Scott, Mrs. Rogan here's going to take your statement, and I'll send Officer Mallick over to examine the apartment for any sign of forced entry. Meanwhile, I want *you* to go home and take your medication. Can you do that for me?"

"I guess."

"Is that an affirmative, soldier?" The chief pressed him.

Scott Evans stood a bit taller. "Yes, sir!"

"Good man." The chief nodded in approval. "All right, then. Carry on."

Feeling bad for Dawn, I sat with her while her husband repeated his story and Patty took down the details. "I take it you're not from here?" I said to her.

"No'm." She gave me a tired smile. "Is it that obvious?"

"Kind of, yeah," I admitted. "Where are you from originally?"

"Alabama," Dawn murmured, tears filling her eyes. She sniffled and knuckled her eyes. "Ah'm sorry. It's just that this is so *hard*. Ah love Scott, ah do, but this is so goddamn *hard*. His family tries to help as best they can, but . . ." A stifled sob escaped her, and she clenched her teeth on another.

"Hey, hey!" I put my arm around her shoulders. "It's okay. I mean, it's not, but . . . just breathe, okay?"

Dawn swallowed and nodded. "Thank yuh."

I found a tissue in my messenger bag and handed it to her. "So how did you end up here in Pemkowet?"

She blew her nose. "We met in Iraq," she said, pronouncing it "eye-rack." "Same ole story. Girl meets boy, falls in love and gits married, moves to his hometown."

"You served in Iraq?"

Dawn gave me a sidelong look. "Yes, ma'am. U.S. Army, maintenance and repair personnel. Ah drive a mean Humvee."

"I'm impressed," I said.

"Yuh mean surprised?" she asked wearily.

I was beginning to regret my initial assessment of Dawn Evans as "skinny, bleached-blond chick." Okay, I stand by the hair—it was pretty bad—but there was a lot more going on here. God knows, I knew what it was like to be underestimated because of my looks and age, and the thick Southern accent probably wasn't doing her any favors in these parts. "Look." I lowered my voice. "You're probably right about this whole thing. I mean, you know Scott. You know what he's been through. I don't. I can't even begin to imagine what you guys have seen and done and how you're coping with it. But just to be on the safe side, it wouldn't hurt to sprinkle your bed with holy water. And, um, hang some cold iron over your front door. An old horseshoe or something. It keeps away the fey."

She knit her brows. "Yuh think—"

"I just think it's worth taking the precaution," I said. "I'm going to look into it. And if it happens again . . . call me. Oh, I'm Daisy, by the way. Daisy Johanssen."

"Ah know who yuh are," Dawn said, fishing for her phone so we could trade numbers. "Yer the ghostbuster. Ah seen yuh on YouTube."

I winced. "Right."

"Ah 'preciate it," she said to me, direct and forthright. "And ah'd 'preciate if you didn't say nothin' to Scott 'lessen yer sure. He's got enough bad thoughts in his head. He don't need no one else puttin' none there."

I nodded. "Understood."

Dawn reached out to grasp my hand and squeeze it. "Thank yuh."

"Anytime." I returned her squeeze. "Seriously. Even if you just need to talk . . . call me."

Seeing Scott approaching, she stood. "Ah will."

Call me crazy, but I just don't get the whole concept of a war of choice. I mean, war's awful, right? I guess at some point there's a choice involved in everything, but when it comes to war, it seems to me it should be the absolute last resort. And it's a choice that should only be made for majorly compelling reasons, like defending your loved ones, or at least a grand humanitarian cause, not some trumped-up excuse to carry out a political agenda that turns out to be totally ill-conceived.

But hey, that's just the opinion of one lone hell-spawn. Humanity's been waging war against itself since the dawn of recorded history, so maybe I'm missing something. All I know is I'm glad it's a choice I'd never had to make.

Anyway.

I put in a couple of hours filing, then used the department's laptop and secure connection to covertly check the Pemkowet Ledger, which is the name of the top secret online database that Lee created for me. Covertly, because Chief Bryant was a little touchy on the subject of my refusal to allow anyone else in the department access to the ledger.

I felt a little guilty about that, but not enough to change my mind. For one thing, the eldritch code requires that I respect the privacy of members of the community, and as Hel's liaison, I had to honor it. For another, it turns out that the ledger was a valuable tool in terms of negotiating with the community. The eldritch have a healthy regard for the notion of favors and debts owed, and I'd realized that I could use my ledger to influence individual members who were eager to rack up favor points or have past transgressions erased.

The Pemkowet Ledger was a work in progress—I was still inputting data from the past few years—but I did several keyword searches to see if they turned up any cases I'd forgotten that involved a scary old lady sitting on someone's chest or attempting to throttle them in their sleep.

No dice.

I checked the Vault and the Penalty Box, which aggregated favors and transgressions. Nothing useful there, either, but one entry in the Vault gave me a pang.

*Jojo (nickname) the joe-pye weed fairy: One large favor owed for identifying a hex charm created by Emmeline Palmer.*

Jojo the joe-pye weed fairy never got to claim that favor. Talman Brannigan—or at least his reanimated remains—had cut her down in midflight while she was attempting to defend my ex-boyfriend Sinclair Palmer, whose secret twin sister had hexed me some weeks earlier.

Have I mentioned that my life is complicated?

I let the cursor hover over Jojo's entry, thinking I should probably delete it, then decided against it. Maybe someday I could repay the favor to one of her clan, assuming joe-pye weed fairies had a clan.

Since there was nothing of use to be found in the ledger, I elected to pay a visit to one of my favorite resources: Mr. Leary, my old high school Myth and Literature teacher, who knew more eldritch folklore than most members of the community themselves.

Mr. Leary lived in a charming old cottage in East Pemkowet, which is a separate governmental entity from the city of Pemkowet proper and Pemkowet Township; a distinction that often confuses tourists since the three are joined at the hip for all intents and purposes.

"Daisy Johanssen!" He greeted me effusively at the door, waving a mug. "Welcome, my favorite ontological anomaly. I hope you've brought me an interesting conundrum to ponder. Can I entice you to join me in a hot rum toddy on this dreary day?"

I considered the offer. After all, it was a dreary day, and technically speaking, I wasn't on the job. "You know what? That sounds delightful."

"Wonderful!" Mr. Leary beamed at me. Well, maybe *beamed* wasn't the right word. With his long, saturnine features and majestic mane of white hair, Mr. Leary wasn't a beamy kind of guy, but he definitely looked pleased. I guess when you're that passionate about your libations, it's nice to have someone to share them with.

He ushered me into his tidy bachelor's kitchen, where I perched on a stool and watched him set about making a rum toddy with all the ceremony of a priest preparing to offer communion. The teakettle was filled with fresh water. Once that reached a boil, Mr. Leary used a pair of silver tongs to place one sugar cube in the bottom of a mug. After dissolving the sugar in boiling water, he added two precisely measured ounces of rum, topped the mug with more water and garnished it with a slice of lemon.

"La pièce de résistance," he announced, retrieving a whole nutmeg and a microplane grater from the counter. With judicious care, he passed the nutmeg over the grater three times, studied the results, then took a final swipe. "One simply must use fresh whole nutmeg." He handed me the mug with a grave nod. "I consider that one of life's great truths, Daisy. Heed it well."

I hid my smile behind the mug. "I will."

In the living room, we followed our familiar ritual and took our seats on the overstuffed furniture draped with old-fashioned crocheted antimacassars. For the record, I had no idea what Mr. Leary's sexual orientation was. Although he always seemed pleased to see me, he also seemed perfectly content without companionship. I thought for a while, when he was spending time with poor old Emma Sudbury, that that might turn into something, but it appeared their friendship was purely platonic.

"So!" Mr. Leary set his mug on a coaster and rubbed his hands together in anticipation. "What do you have for me?"

I took a sip of my rum toddy—and he might be onto something with that fresh nutmeg, because it was delicious—and told him about Scott Evans's experience.

"Oh, dear." Mr. Leary gave a disappointed sigh. "I was so hoping for a good challenge."

"Not so much, huh?"

He gave me a look. "What an appalling colloquialism that is. The good news is that the phenomenon is easily identified." Rising, he perused his bookshelves and selected a volume of folklore. "In layman's terms it's called Night Hag Syndrome," he said, finding the page he wanted and handing me the book. "It's actually a common form of sleep disorder called sleep paralysis."

I skimmed the entry, which fit Scott Evans's description to a T. So did the accompanying illustration of a beaky old crone crouching on the chest of a nubile young woman. Well, the crone part, anyway. "So you're saying the Night Hag doesn't exist?"

Mr. Leary shook his head. "It's a hypnopompic hallucination. It's been well documented at clinics that specialize in sleep disorders," he added. "There's one affiliated with the hospital in Appeldoorn. You might suggest that the young fellow pay it a visit."

If Scott Evans wasn't even taking whatever meds he'd been prescribed for post–traumatic stress disorder, I doubted he'd be willing to go to a sleep clinic, but it couldn't hurt to suggest it to Dawn. Maybe he'd be amenable to the idea once his mood was stabilized.

"Thank you," I said. "I will."

Mr. Leary hoisted his mug. "At your service, my dear."

# Five

There was another line of inquiry I was planning to pursue regarding the Night Hag—it was good to have a name to put to her, even if she was a hallucination—just to cover all my bases, but I was distracted by a call from Lee Hastings asking if we could meet for an update on his investigation.

Long story short, there was a mysterious lawyer representing an unknown entity that was buying up large tracts of undeveloped land in Pemkowet. I'd caught a glimpse of him, and I was pretty sure he was a hell-spawn like me.

Not only that, I was pretty sure he'd claimed his birthright. Don't ask me how I knew, but I did. He *smelled* wrong. Well, that's not exactly right, but it was something like a smell; and since he'd handily persuaded a number of people to sell property that they'd cherished for years, I was willing to bet he had demonic powers of persuasion, which meant that he had to have invoked his birthright.

Which, of course, shouldn't be possible without breaching the Inviolate Wall. Like I said, mysterious. And it had Hel concerned enough to ask me to look into it. All I'd had to go on was a cell phone number and a Gmail address—again, pretty mysterious for a lawyer—on the card he gave Amanda Brooks at the Pemkowet Visitors Bureau after talking to her about purchasing some property that had been in her family for ages. When he didn't respond to my calls or e-mails, I asked our resident genius and computer whiz, Lee, to investigate.

At any rate, since a request from Hel took precedence over a sleep disorder in my book, I drove over to Lee's place to meet with him. He actually owns his own house, which given the property values around here is unusual for someone in their mid-twenties, but Lee made a lot of money in video games out in Seattle, where he was headhunted right out of high school. He moved back to Pemkowet to take care of his mother, who has severe rheumatoid arthritis, which is particularly admirable of him given the fact that she's a nasty, controlling old bitch. Hence, the purchase of his own house.

I suppose Lee could have rented, but privacy was important to him. Or, to put it less charitably, he had a paranoid streak. Either that, or the gaming industry is rife with corporate espionage like he claims. Or both. But at least Lee seems to trust me now, and I think he considers me a friend, too.

"Hey, Daisy!" he greeted me at the door. "Come on in."

"Thanks." I eyed him. "Hey, you got the cast off?"

Lee waved his right arm, which had been broken in an altercation with Jen's newly risen vampire sister, Bethany, earlier in the fall. "Last week."

"You look good," I said. It was true; he looked less gaunt, fuller in the face. "Do they have you doing physical therapy?"

"A little." He flushed with pleasure. "Mostly just some light strength training. And I, um, joined the gym."

"Good for you."

His flush deepened. It was sort of cute. "Thanks. Do you, um, want a protein shake? I was just going to make one for myself."

"I'll pass," I said. "But go right ahead. What have you got on our mysterious lawyer friend?"

Lee gave me the basics while he whipped up a vile-looking protein shake for himself in the kitchen.

In a nutshell, our mysterious lawyer, Daniel Dufreyne, was listed as a senior advisor at a financial services firm based in Detroit, although there was no direct contact information for him on the company's website. He was a member of the Michigan and International Bar Associations, and he owned a residence in Birmingham, a wealthy suburb of Detroit.

"That's as far as I've gotten on Dufreyne," Lee said, beckoning me over to the dining table where he had a laptop with a large screen set up. "It looks like he's gone out of his way to leave a light electronic footprint. I can dig deeper if you like, but I don't think he's the real story. Look." He called up a map of the Pemkowet area.

I peered at it. "What am I looking at?"

"See these properties in red?" Lee pointed. "Here, here, and here. Those are purchases that Dufreyne negotiated in Pemkowet over the past six months. I checked the current property records, and they're all registered to Elysian Fields LLC."

"Which is . . . ?" I asked.

Lee shrugged. "You tell me. It's a privately held company, and they haven't released a public profile."

I studied the map. "That's a lot of property."

He nodded. "It is."

"And it's adjacent to Little Niflheim, isn't it?"

"Uh-huh."

For the record, *Little Niflheim* is the unofficial—call it irreverent but affectionate—term for Hel's demesne, the underworld beneath the dunes. Once upon a time, back in the nineteenth century, it had been an actual aboveground community, a logging town called Singapore. After the terrain was deforested by the likes of Talman Brannigan and the other shortsighted lumber barons, the dunes rolled over the town and swallowed it. Hel, Norse goddess of the dead, took up residence here in the late summer of 1914, relocating her entire cosmology in advance of the tides of World War I in Europe. The most powerful earthquake ever to occur in Michigan was recorded when Yggdrasil II, a pine tree the size of a missile silo, erupted from the sands.

My skin prickled.

"This is the old Cavannaugh property that belongs to Amanda Brooks."

Lee pointed to a sizable green wedge on the map. "You can see why some-one would want to acquire it if they were looking to develop here."

I could. "What about Little Niflheim? Who owns *that* property?" Oddly enough, it had never occurred to me to wonder before.

Lee's cursor hovered over it. "It's actually owned by the City of Pemkowet."

I relaxed a little. "So that's not on the market."

"None of these were ever *on* the market," Lee observed. "At least they were never listed. Apparently Elysian Fields made them an offer they couldn't—"

"Dammit!" I didn't mean to interrupt him, but a thought had struck me. "I'm an idiot."

He blinked at me. "Any particular reason?"

"Yeah," I said. "I know how to get hold of Dufreyne."

"Well, you can try the general number for the investment firm," Lee said in a dubious tone. "I'm sure they'll get the message to him. But if he hasn't returned any of your other calls or—"

"Right," I said. "He's not going to return this one. Which is why I'm not going to call him. Amanda Brooks is going to call him to set up a meeting about selling the Cavannaugh property."

"You think she'd do that for you?"

"She'd better." I stood up and slung my messenger bag over my shoulder. "She owes me. Meanwhile, keep looking. See if you can find out anything more about this Elysian Fields outfit."

"Will do." Lee escorted me to the door. "Hey, did Jen happen to mention that we're getting together for coffee tomorrow?"

"Maybe," I said, playing it cool. "Why?"

A tinge of pink had returned to his face. "No reason. It's just . . . she probably wants to talk about my mom, right?"

Jen had been helping out with Mrs. Hastings while Lee's arm healed. She'd actually offered Jen a job as her full-time caretaker, and Jen had even considered it before deciding that the old crabapple would make her life miserable—which was saying something, since working for the Cassopolis family business cleaning houses wasn't exactly a bed of roses.

"Well, I don't think she's changed her mind about the job," I said. "And I doubt she's been missing your mom since you got your cast off."

He laughed self-consciously. "So you think it's a date?"

"I think it's coffee, Lee. Ask her out to dinner. Tell her you want to thank her for helping take care of your mom."

"Good idea."

"Just call me Cupid." Hopefully, Lee would never find out I was the one who had sent the text in the first place. Given his paranoid streak, he'd probably think we were making fun of him.

I drove over to the Pemkowet Visitors Bureau office to talk to Amanda Brooks. Somewhat to my surprise, her daughter, Stacey—also known as my old high school nemesis—wasn't working the reception desk. Instead, a pleasant young woman I vaguely recognized as being a couple of years behind me in high school informed me that Amanda could meet with me in ten minutes and offered me a cup of coffee. I liked the improvement, although in terms of people offering me beverages today, Mr. Leary won hands down.

Ten minutes later, I was sitting across from Amanda Brooks.

"What can I do for you, Daisy?" she inquired, almost sounding sincere. There wasn't a whole lot of love lost between us, but we both knew that if she'd taken my advice and called off the Halloween parade last month, hundreds of innocent spectators wouldn't have gotten injured. Frankly, we were lucky there were no fatalities. Oh, and I'd pretty much saved Stacey's life, although Stacey didn't give me the credit for it.

"Do you remember that lawyer who wanted to buy the Cavannaugh property?" I asked her. "I need you to call him and set up a meeting."

Amanda raised her brows, or at least tried to. Botox, I suspect. She was an attractive woman, in a brittle, highly groomed fashion, and she worked hard at maintaining her looks. "Why? I have no intention of selling it."

It hadn't looked that way to me—before I'd talked her out of it, she'd shown every appearance of considering it. "No, I know," I said. "I don't think you should. But I want to talk to him."

"Why?"

My tail twitched with suppressed irritation. Once, just once, it would be nice if she trusted me. "He's representing a company called Elysian Fields," I said. "They've bought up a good chunk of property around Hel's demesne."

She frowned—or again, tried to. "Are you sure? I haven't heard anything about it."

It wasn't just arrogance on her part. Pemkowet was a small town, and Amanda Brooks had her finger on every pulse. The fact that this was happening unnoticed was definitely strange.

"I'm sure." I played my trump card. "And Hel is concerned. That's why I want to talk to this Dufreyne guy and find out what's going on. But he won't return my calls."

Amanda drummed her manicured nails on the desk. "Well, that's highly unprofessional of him."

Duh. "That's why I need your help," I said. "There's something very odd about this whole business."

If you're wondering why I didn't tell her I suspected Daniel Dufreyne was a hell-spawn, there were two reasons. One, I had no proof. Two, when trying to obtain the cooperation of certain people, it's best not to remind them that I'm one myself. Amanda Brooks was one of those people.

"All right," she said reluctantly. "I'm not fond of the idea, but if Hel is truly concerned, I'll do it."

"Excellent." I made myself smile at her. "Let me know when the meeting's set up. Oh, and whatever you do, don't meet with him alone."

Amanda gave me a suspicious look. "Why? After all, I've met with him before."

Oops. "Just give me this one, will you?"

She hesitated. "Is he dangerous? Because I seem to remember . . . something."

"I'm not sure," I said honestly. "But as Hel's liaison, I'd like to take every precaution with him."

"Very well." She nodded. "I'll be in touch."

"Thanks." I stood to leave. "Oh, by the way, did Stacey take a job somewhere else? I was just wondering." Wondering if I could quit bracing myself for the encounter every time I entered the PVB, really.

"You might say so." A smile of maternal pride lit Amanda's face, softening her features. "She's our new head of online promotion. I suggested it after she did such a wonderful job with the video footage of our, ah, manifestations last month. The board approved the position last week."

Oh, gah.

# Six

I fell asleep that night thinking about the ominous blotch of red on the map Lee had shown me, encroaching on Hel's territory.

I didn't like the look of it, not one bit.

I woke up to my phone ringing at approximately six o'clock in the morning, which is never a good thing.

"Daisy?" a woman's voice rasped in a heavy Alabama accent. "Ah'm so sorry to trouble yuh, but it happened agin, and Scott's out on the balcony with a gun."

"What?" I sat bolt upright and fumbled for the lamp on my nightstand. Curled on the bed beside me, Mogwai let out a mewl of protest at being disturbed. "Dawn, what's happening?"

"He tried to strangle me in mah sleep." Her voice was thick with tears, and possibly the effects of an attempted strangling. "Now he's threatenin' to kill hisself."

My brain jolted into alertness. "Did you call 911?"

"Yes, ma'am, there's an officer on the way, only ah thought . . . yuh seemed to know things the police mebbe don't."

Shifting the phone against my ear, I rummaged for clothing. "What's your address?"

"Beechwood Grove," she said. "Apartment 207."

"I'm on my way."

Although I didn't have the first idea how I could help, I drove like a bat out of hell through sleet and darkness to Beechwood Grove, an apartment complex that had been nice enough when it was first built in the 1970s, but was now a bit run-down. There was already a police cruiser parked in front of the Evanses' apartment.

Dawn Evans opened the door before I could knock, clad in a ratty aqua-blue chenille bathrobe. Her eyes were red-rimmed and weary, her face was tear-streaked, and there were serious bruises already forming on her throat. "Thank yuh," she murmured. "Ah do 'preciate it."

"Scott's upstairs?" I asked.

She nodded. "On the balcony off the master bedroom. The officer's tryin' to talk him down. Ah best get back to him."

"Let's go."

In the master bedroom, a sliding glass door that led to a small balcony was wide-open, cold air and icy sleet blowing through it. Beyond the police officer blocking the doorway, I could see Scott Evans, wearing only a pair of drawstring pajama pants, the muzzle of a pistol pressed under his chin.

Shit.

I must have said it out loud, because the officer glanced back at me. It was Cody, his eyes grave and worried. "Daise. Do you think—?"

I knew what he meant and I shook my head, indicating that it wasn't an eldritch matter.

He blew out his breath. "Mr. Evans, just come inside for a moment, won't you? It's freezing out there. No one can think straight in that kind of cold. I'm freezing. You're freezing. Your wife's freezing. Just step inside long enough so we can all warm up."

"Lissen to him, Scott!" Dawn pleaded. "It's all right. Ah know yuh didn't mean to do it. We bin through way worse, yew and me."

"No, I don't think so." Scott bared his teeth in a grimace, but there were tears in his eyes, too. "Bitch nearly got me to kill you tonight, honey. We can't go on like this. We can't. I love you, but it's for the best."

His finger tightened on the trigger, knuckle whitening.

"Wait!" Cody spread his hands. "Okay, you don't have to come inside, but Mr. Evans, Chief Bryant's on his way. You promised me you'd talk to him. You promised me you'd wait until he got here, right? You don't want to renege on a promise, do you?"

Scott hesitated.

"He's right," I said. "The chief's going to be pissed as hell if we dragged him out of bed at this hour for nothing."

Beside me, Dawn let out a choked, hysterical laugh, biting down on her knuckle to stifle it.

"Okay, so we're all waiting for the chief to get here," Cody said in a calm, level tone. "No problem."

I had to give Cody credit—he kept up a steady stream of quiet, innocuous talk, keeping Scott Evans's attention engaged while we waited for Chief Bryant to arrive. It was likely a technique he'd learned in training at the police academy, but as far as I knew, he'd never had to use it before. Still, it felt like forever before the chief's car pulled into the parking lot, though it was probably only five minutes.

"Yuh promise yuh'll lissen to what the man has to say?" Dawn asked Scott.

The muzzle of the pistol remained firmly lodged under his chin, and the slow, steady tears that leaked from his eyes were half-frozen on his cheeks. He was shivering in the cold so hard I was afraid he'd pull the trigger by accident. "Said I'd give him the courtesy, didn't I?"

She nodded. "Yuh did."

Jesus fucking Christ, my heart ached for both of them, and I felt helpless; obscenely helpless.

"I'm sorry," I said to Dawn. "I'm so sorry. I wish I did know something that could help, but I don't."

"It means a lot that yuh came," she murmured. "Mebbe yuh could show the chief inside?"

I nodded. "Of course."

Chief Bryant's face was pouchy with sleep and his hair was disheveled, but his eyes were sharp and alert beneath their heavy lids. "All right," he said in a deep, reassuring voice as he entered the master bedroom. "Let's everyone just take this down a notch, okay? Mr. Evans, why don't you step inside so we can talk man-to-man?"

"No, sir." Scott shook his head. "I'm fine right where I am."

"All right, then, why don't you just hand the gun over to Officer Fairfax?" the chief suggested.

Scott wasn't budging. Well, except for the violent shivering. "No, sir," he said politely. "I can't do that."

"Sure you can."

Something caught my eye. Scott Evans wasn't the only thing shivering. The silver watch chain dangling from the chief's coat pocket was vibrating visibly.

"Son of a bitch!" I said without thinking. Chief Bryant shot me a look. "Chief, the watch, the watch!"

He glanced down. "Must have shoved it into my pocket on the way out. Force of habit."

"Take it out!" I said. "Hold it over the bed!"

"Excuse me?" Dawn said in a perplexed tone. On the balcony, her husband looked as bewildered as she sounded—bewildered enough that he'd involuntarily lowered the pistol a few inches.

I couldn't blame them, but I didn't want to take the time to explain. Chief Bryant fished the watch out of his pocket and let it dangle over the bed. It rotated in a circle on the end of its chain, the hands on the dial spinning backward.

"Son of a bitch!" I said again. That's what I got for lending too much credence to a mundane expert. I whirled around to face the open sliding door. "Scott, you're not crazy. She's real. The Night Hag's real."

He lowered the pistol a few more inches. "She is?"

"She is?" Dawn echoed.

"Yeah." I glanced at Dawn. "You didn't put a horseshoe over the door, did you?"

She shook her head. "Ah couldn't find one on short notice. Ah was gonna call yuh tomorrow."

I grimaced. "It's my fault. I should have figured this out yesterday. Scott, will you come inside now?"

He still hesitated. "This is a trick, isn't it?"

"No trick," I promised him. "The chief's watch is genuine dwarfish craftsmanship. It responds to the residue of eldritch presence."

Scott looked uncertainly at Chief Bryant.

"Crazy as it sounds, she's telling the truth, son," the chief said. "I give you my word of honor."

"That means we can catch the bitch." My tail lashed with vehemence, my temper surging. "She's not free to prey on anyone in *my* town."

"Hell, yeah!" For the first time, Scott Evans smiled, a tight, fierce smile as he lowered the pistol to his side.

Unfortunately, at that very moment the balcony gave an alarming creak. Scott took a lurching step, his bare feet slipping on the sleet-covered wood. His hand clenched on the trigger as he fell backward and the pistol discharged, the gunshot sounding like . . . pretty much nothing but a gunshot. A scream caught in my throat. Scott hit the railing hard, and the pistol fell from his hand. If the balcony had been up to code, it would have caught him, but the old 1970s-built railing was at least a foot and a half lower than current regulations required, and he began to topple backward over it.

Moving with inhuman speed, Cody let out a growl and lunged through the sliding glass door, catching Scott by the waist of his drawstring pajama pants. I'd like to say I was there in a flash to back him up, but it was Dawn who helped him wrestle her husband into the bedroom. Cody kept his face averted, and I hoped she was distracted enough not to notice.

"Are yuh shot?" she asked Scott with professional efficiency. "Lemme see."

His teeth were chattering. "I'm okay."

"It's all right," Cody said, his voice sounding muffled as he retrieved the pistol and examined the balcony. "The bullet went straight down."

"Yuh idiot!" Dawn clutched Scott's shoulders, tears in her voice. "Yuh goddamn idiot!"

"I know," he whispered, wrapping his arms around her. Oblivious to the world, they held each other.

"Well, then." The chief hitched up his belt. "Daisy, Cody, it looks like you've got yourself a case."

A few days ago, I would have been glad to hear it. Today, I stifled a sigh. Great.

# Seven

Cody and I took another statement from Scott Evans. It was identical to the first one, except that this time he'd broken the paralysis to fight back; or at least he thought he had, until he awoke to find himself throttling his wife.

"So what happens now?" he asked us, an afghan blanket wrapped around him.

"Ideally, I'd suggest you get out of town until we find the Night Hag," I said. "The eldritch need a functioning underworld to enable their magic, and she shouldn't be able to operate outside of Hel's territory. Is there anyone you can stay with well outside the city limits?"

Scott and Dawn exchanged a glance. He shook his head. "No one I can think of. I've got family, but they're in town."

"A hotel?"

"We're still waitin' on the VA to approve Scott's claim fer disability benefits," Dawn murmured in an apologetic tone. "Yuh said a horseshoe would do, didn't yuh?"

"Yeah, but it's just a general precaution," I warned her. "It might not be enough, and I need to do more digging to know exactly what we're dealing with. As far as I know, there's never been a Night Hag in Pemkowet before."

Scott grimaced. "It's probably my goddamn nightmares that brought her here."

"It's possible." I didn't want to lie to him. "Do you know the Sisters of Selene? The occult store?"

"By the coffee shop?" he asked. "I've seen it."

I nodded. "It opens at eleven. I'll call Casimir and give him a heads-up, tell him you need whatever he's got to ward off a powerful fey predator."

"A fey predator," he repeated. "All right."

"You should consult with your doctor, too," Cody suggested gently. "You're under a lot of stress."

"Yeah." Scott rubbed his eyes with the heels of his hands. "I know. There's a reason the bitch came for *me*, right?" Dropping his hands, he glanced up at Cody. "So what the fuck are *you*?"

Cody missed a beat. "Excuse me?"

"I saw your face, man. When you caught me." Beneath the afghan, Scott's shoulders rose and fell in a shrug. "Look, I owe you. I could have broken my neck. But either I'm crazy or I'm not, and either way, I'd like to know. I saw your face, and there were way too many goddamn pointy teeth in it. So what are you?"

A long silence stretched between them. I held my tongue and avoided meeting Dawn's inquiring look.

A muscle twitched in Cody's jaw. "Werewolf."

Holy crap, Officer Down-low had actually admitted it, out loud, to an ordinary human being.

"No shit!" Scott sounded admiring. "Does it run in the family? I went to high school with your brother Caleb. I always wondered what the deal was with that guy."

Cody didn't answer.

"Ohh-kay," I said. "Remember Don't Ask, Don't Tell? Stupid policy, I know. But the eldritch community has a code."

"So it ain't polite to ask questions," Dawn observed. "And yuh don't want us to say nuthin 'bout Officer Fairfax."

"Right."

Scott nodded. "No problem."

After finishing with the Evanses, Cody and I retreated to the parking lot. A few residents of neighboring apartments came out to ask about the gunshot. After reassuring them it was an accidental discharge and no one had been harmed, we took the opportunity to ask if anyone had seen a strange elderly woman in the vicinity. Unfortunately, no one had. We went door-to-door throughout the rest of the apartment complex, accomplishing nothing more than annoying anyone who hadn't been awakened by a stray gunshot at that hour.

"I'm not surprised," Cody said when we sat in his squad car to compare notes, strategize, and pretend it wasn't incredibly awkward to be working together this soon after he'd broken things off with me. "Whatever was in that bedroom, it didn't leave a scent." He glanced at me. "Are you sure about this, Daise?"

I shrugged. "*Something* was there. The chief's watch has never been wrong. Do all eldritch have a scent?"

"So far, yeah."

"Do I?" I couldn't help but ask. "I mean, other than an ordinary human scent?"

Cody gave me another sidelong look. "Yeah. Yeah, you do. There's sort of a . . . hint of brimstone."

"Oh, yuck!" I made a face. "Like sulfur? Rotten eggs?"

"No, no!" He shook his head. "It's not like that. You know how perfumes sometimes have those weird notes that might be unpleasant on their own, but—" I stared at him. He sighed. "You smell good, Daisy. Trust me."

"Thanks." Given the sort of odors that most dogs I knew found appealing, it occurred to me that Cody might not be the best judge. "I hope that's your human side speaking."

He flashed a grin at me. "Afraid you smell like something I might want to roll around in, Pixy Stix?"

"Something like that." Dammit, teasing wasn't fair! I managed to avoid giving him the satisfaction of a reaction. "Look, if no one in Beechwood Grove saw anything, I don't think there's any point in canvassing further, and your shift's probably about over. Why don't you let me do some research, and we'll talk later?"

"Deal."

I hesitated. "Hey, I'm proud of you for what you did in there." I nodded toward the Evans apartment. "Owning it like that."

"Thanks." That muscle in Cody's jaw gave another little twitch, but his gaze was steady and open. "Let me know what you find out."

Back in my own trusty little Honda, I called Casimir, aka the Fabulous Casimir. In addition to being the owner and proprietor of the Sisters of Selene, Casimir was also the head of the local coven. Despite the early hour, he was already up. I could hear him puttering around in his kitchen as we spoke, probably clad in something like an exotic caftan. Casimir claims his cross-dressing is part of a shamanic tradition, which very well may be true, but he takes a lot of pride and pleasure in it, too.

The good news was that Casimir was confident that he had charms and protection spells in stock to deter any manner of predatory fey. The bad news was that he didn't know anything about Night Hags in particular and could neither confirm nor deny their actual existence.

"Sorry, dahling," he apologized. "I've known more than my fair share of hags, but not this kind."

I smiled. "That's okay. I've got other resources. Thanks for taking care of the Evanses."

He blew me a kiss over the phone. "Anytime, Miss Daisy."

I tried calling Lurine, the resource I had in mind. When my call went to voice mail, I decided to drive over to her place anyway. I'd known Lurine since I was scarce out of diapers—she used to babysit for me when she lived two doors down from Mom and me in Sedgewick Estate—and I figured there was a good chance she was already up too, and simply not answering her phone. Of course, given the cold weather, there was an equal chance that she'd been asleep for several days. Lurine's schedule didn't exactly conform to mortal circadian rhythms.

Either way, it was worth a try.

Lurine's mansion out on Lakeshore Drive was a far cry from the mobile home she'd lived in when I was growing up. The sky was just beginning to pale in the east as I pulled up to the gated drive and pressed the button on the intercom.

"Yes?"

"Hi, Edgerton," I greeted her trusty and discreet butler or manservant or whatever the hell he was called. "It's Daisy Johanssen. Is, um, Ms. Hollister available?"

There was a pause. "Ms. Hollister is enjoying a swim."

"She's in the pool?" I didn't know why that would matter. I'd spent plenty of time poolside with Lurine. Never in November, mind you, but she could afford to keep her pool heated year-round. "Can you ask her if she'd mind if I stopped by?"

"I'm sure she would be delighted," he said in a formal tone. "But I'm afraid Ms. Hollister isn't in the *pool*."

Oh.

"Thanks, Edgerton," I said.

I put the Honda in park and got out, slinging my messenger bag across my chest. Lurine's place was on the east side of the road, situated inland in the woods and safely away from the eroding bluffs, but her property came with lakefront access. On the west side of Lakeshore Drive, a long zigzagging wooden staircase broken up by a series of platforms led to the beach below.

I crossed the road, turned up the collar on my black leather motorcycle jacket, and began the long descent, taking care on the sleet-slick steps. The wind was bone-chillingly cold, but at least it appeared to be driving away the clouds. Lake Michigan's iron-gray surface was ruffled with wavelets. I couldn't begin to imagine swimming in it on a cold November day, but then, I wasn't a lamia.

Halfway down, a distant glimmer of green and gold and blue caught my eye. I paused on one of the platforms to take in the scene.

Lurine was swimming some fifty yards from the shore, undulating coils gleaming with rainbow hues whenever they broke the surface. Pale, silvery forms darted around her—naiads or undines or nixies; I couldn't tell at this distance.

Whatever they were, it was an incredible sight. As the sun rose above the tree line behind me, laying a shining golden path on the gray water,

Lurine and her coterie of water elementals surfaced to greet it with a burst of song, a shimmering chorus that made me shiver to the bone with its unearthly beauty.

The bell-like notes hung in the morning air after they finished, fading slowly, until an aching sense of loss filled me. I found my feet moving unbidden, carrying me down the slippery stairs with reckless abandon.

Alas, the water elementals scattered, dispersing in silver flashes.

"Wait!" I cried out in despair. "Don't go!"

Out in the lake, Lurine cocked her head. "Daisy? Is that you?"

"Yeah! I'm coming!" I called to her, crossing the expanse of driftwood-strewn sand.

"Oh, for God's sake. Stay where you are, cupcake." Lurine plunged beneath the water, arrowing for the shore.

Ignoring her order, I kept going. I didn't have a single thought in my head beyond an overwhelming desire to hear those glorious voices again. I was knee-deep in Lake Michigan when Lurine surfaced a few yards away, water streaming from her golden hair and naked human torso.

"Okey-dokey, baby girl." The coils of her tail encircled my waist, plucking me out of the frigid water. "Snap out of it."

"I just—" I blinked. "Whoa. Did I just walk into the lake?"

"Mm-hmm." Lurine looked amused. "Now you know why thousands of sailors have plunged to their watery doom over the years." She gave me an affectionate squeeze, those sleek, muscular coils capable of crushing a grown man to death contracting around my waist with suggestive intimacy. "You should be more careful, cupcake."

"Lurine!" I protested. "Put me down, will you?"

She stroked my cheek with the tip of her tail. "Aw, you're blushing! That's just adorable."

Okay, so there are probably plenty of people in the world who have a little bit of a crush on their ex-babysitters—yes, fine, I'm willing to admit it—but I might be the only one whose attraction is only operative when said ex-babysitter is in the form of a millennia-old mythological creature whose lower half looks like the love child of an anaconda and a rainbow.

I closed my eyes, blocking out the sight of those iridescent coils and trying to ignore the fact that they were still firmly wrapped around my waist, smooth scales sliding against the leather of my jacket . . . damn.

"I'm here on business, okay?" My voice sounded feeble.

"Oh, fine." Lurine deposited me effortlessly on the shore. I cracked open one eye and watched her shift into her human form. She waded out of the lake, wringing the water out of her hair. "What is it?"

Now that I wasn't warm with inappropriate thoughts and embarrassment, I realized that my knee-high black leather boots—which had been a splurge purchase, dammit—were filled with icy lake water. My feet were freezing and my teeth were chattering. "Can we talk about it inside?"

"Of course." Lurine stepped into a pair of baby pink Juicy Couture sweatpants. "Hand me my jacket, will you?"

# Eight

Up at the mansion, Lurine turned maternal on me, wrapping me in a blanket and insisting I drink a cup of hot tea. She even sent my sodden boots off with her butler to be dried with one of those fancy Sharper Image–type appliances. I didn't know anyone actually bought those things. "What were you thinking, Daisy?" she chided me. "You shouldn't have been out there."

I sipped the tea. "Edgerton said you'd be delighted. I assume he didn't know I'd be crashing some sort of sirens' dawn choral practice?"

"True," she admitted. "My bad. But in all fairness, I wasn't expecting you."

"I didn't know you sang," I said. "Not like *that.*"

Lurine gave a modest shrug. "A girl's got to have some secrets, cupcake. So what's up?"

I told her about Scott Evans and his dilemma. "So what's your verdict on Night Hags? Real or not real?"

"Oh, they're real," Lurine assured me. "They're also part of humanity's collective unconscious, which is why mortals anywhere might think they've experienced an attack. But here in Pemkowet, yeah, it was probably an actual hag." She shuddered. "Nasty, smelly creatures."

"Cody said there was no scent," I said. "Which seems odd."

Lurine waved one hand. "Oh, you know those dreamwalker types. They have a complicated relationship with corporeal reality."

I did not, in fact, know those dreamwalker types. Being Hel's liaison came with a steep learning curve and a lot of on-the-job training. "Meaning . . . ?"

"Meaning the Night Hag only exists physically for the person whose dreams she enters, cupcake," she said patiently. "Or nightmares, I should say. That's what they feed on."

"Okay," I said. "So Night Hags are basically the Freddy Kruegers of the eldritch community?"

You might think a pop culture reference like that would be lost on someone whose origins date to the Bronze Age, but in Lurine's case, you would be wrong. In the current incarnation of her identity, she left Sedgewick Estate when I was in my late teens and attained B-movie fame starring in a couple of cult-favorite horror films. After that, she married an octogenarian real-estate tycoon who died within a year, leaving her the bulk of his massive fortune.

Hence, the mansion and the boot-warming appliances. Although to be fair, Lurine's probably thrown away as many fortunes as she's gained over the course of centuries.

"More or less," she said. "As far as I know, Night Hags don't have the ability to actually kill people in their sleep."

"Just to make them think they're dying," I said. "Or crazy."

Lurine nodded. "All good fodder for nightmares."

"Or suicide attempts," I noted.

"That, too," she agreed. "The mortal human mind's at once a powerful and fragile thing, baby girl."

"Okay," I said. "So how do I find and catch the bitch?"

"No idea, cupcake." Lurine shrugged apologetically. "Sorry, not my area of expertise. If I were you, I'd ask around among the fey. Night Hags are kin to bogles, if I'm not mistaken. I have a hard time keeping track of them all." She eyed the pendant around my neck. "You could ask *him*."

My right hand rose to close over the silver acorn-shaped whistle. "The Oak King?"

"Well, you might not want to start by pestering eldritch royalty," she said in a pragmatic tone. "But it's something to keep in mind."

"I'll think about it," I promised. "Thanks, Lurine."

She smiled at me. "Anytime."

Okay, so that boot-warmer thingy? Totally awesome. Plus, Lurine's butler/manservant Edgerton had waxed and shined them, so that they not only felt toasty warm but looked completely undamaged and as good as new when I put them on. He seemed embarrassed when I thanked him profusely.

Lurine escorted me to the foyer. "Hey, how's your love life, cup-cake?" she asked me. "Any less complicated?"

I hesitated. "You might say so."

"Cody?"

I shook my head, my heart aching a little. "Taking himself out of the picture."

"So who's still *in* the picture?" Lurine's gaze sharpened. "Stefan Ludovic?" I didn't say anything. She frowned at me. "You're walking on thin ice with that one, Daisy."

I temporized. "Well, he's in Poland. Outcast business."

She sighed. "Oh, baby girl!"

"I thought you were okay with Stefan." I was feeling a bit defensive. "Look, he's been a strong ally. You helped him rescue me last summer! And if it wasn't for Stefan, that Halloween debacle would have been a bloodbath."

"*I'm* fine with Stefan, but I can handle myself. It's you I worry about." Lurine's cornflower-blue eyes began to take on a stony basilisk stare. "Do you have any idea how dangerous it would be for you to consort with a ghoul?"

I kindled my mental shield between us, something I'd never done before. "Yeah. I do. Apparently, I'm drawn to dangerous things."

Lurine's expression was unreadable, and she held her silence long enough that I began to fear I'd crossed a line. But at last she gave me a rueful smile. "Touché." She nodded at the shield of energy I wielded, invisible to the mundane eye, bright and shining to the eldritch. "Just tell me you don't actually think you need that with me."

"No, of course not." I let it dissipate. "I just wanted to show you that I can take care of myself, too."

"Daisy—"

"Look, Stefan knows you've declared me under your protection," I said to her. "He knows you'd crush him to a pulp if he ever did anything to harm me."

Lurine folded her arms over her baby pink Juicy Couture jacket, managing to emphasize her admittedly spectacular cleavage in the process—maybe an attempt to distract me, probably just reflex. Lurine knows perfectly well that her human bombshell form doesn't faze me. But her real one . . . that's something else.

Perverse, but true. What can I say? Eldritch tendencies manifest in unexpected ways.

"I don't think he'd hurt you on purpose," she said. "But if you send him ravening, all bets are off."

"I know, I know!" I said. "Lurine . . . I've got to make my own choices. And you've got to decide whether you're going to treat me like a child or a grown woman. You can't keep doing both."

"Oh, cupcake." She laughed softly. "You can't tell people how to feel. You know, I like the young woman you've grown into very much. You're determined and brave and loyal. But you'll always be that impetuous, hot-tempered hell-spawn toddler I first knew, too, and I'll always worry about you. You'll just have to live with it. You and your mother are the first mortals I let myself care about in a long, long time."

It's kind of hard to argue with a declaration like that, especially when you're a bit misty-eyed.

"Thanks," I said. "And I'll be careful. I promise. Anyway, you don't have to worry about Stefan anytime soon. Like I said, he's off on some mysterious errand in Poland." I strapped my messenger bag across my chest. "And I'm off hunting a Night Hag."

"Good luck," she said.

"Thanks," I said again. At the door, a thought struck me, and I turned back in curiosity. "By the way, what were you and those undines singing?"

"Naiads," Lurine corrected me. "They're prickly little bitches, but they can sing. It was a hymn to Helios."

"Really?" I don't know why it surprised me. It's not like I ever forgot what Lurine *was*, but I guess sometimes I lost sight of exactly what it meant, and where and when she came from.

There was a faraway look in her eyes. "Some of us try to keep the old traditions alive, Daisy. At least when we can." Her gaze returned from the distance. "Off-season is the only time I can greet the dawn properly."

"It was beautiful," I said honestly. "Truly."

"Thank you." Lurine smiled, looking genuinely pleased. "Sorry about accidentally luring you into the lake."

I shrugged. "Totally worth it."

"Don't mention it to your mother."

"I won't."

# Nine

ack in my car, I checked my phone and saw I had a text from Sinclair inviting me to attend his ritual tattooing at noon today, which was perfect. Well, mostly perfect. If you wanted to talk to one of the fey, especially a nature elemental, without spending hundreds of dollars on cowslip dew, Sinclair Palmer was the man to see. He ran Pemkowet Supernatural Tours, and thanks to the generous support of the Oak King, there were almost always nature fairies along his route.

Obviously, there weren't as many around this time of year—it's a seasonal thing—but there were a few species hardy enough to endure the winter. Plus, it helps that nature fairies freakin' *love* Sinclair.

I can't blame them, since Sinclair's a great guy. He's also my ex-boyfriend. That would be the less than perfect part. Okay, it's not like we dated that long—it was only about a month—and I'm the one who broke it off, but still.

It's not that I *regret* ending things with Sinclair, but the relationship didn't have a chance to run its natural course. It's a long story, but suffice it to say that it involves his secret twin sister, obeah magic, and a Jamaican duppy.

Anyway.

Since I had time to kill, I drove over to East Pemkowet. Realizing I was starving, I got a cheese Danish to go at the Sit'n Sip and ate it on the way to the library.

Let me just say that for my money, the Pemkowet District Library is one of the best things about this town. Seriously, it's awesome. It's small and quaint—it's actually lodged in a charming old building that was a church in the 1800s—but the services it offers are huge in comparison.

The library was a big part of my life when I was growing up. Mom and I didn't have a lot of money, but as long as we could use computers and check out books and videos and music CDs from the library for free, it didn't matter that we couldn't afford cable or satellite TV or an Internet connection at home. Being a small facility, the library doesn't have an extensive collection, but it's good—you can also request anything you want from another library in the region, and they'll deliver it within days. Very cool.

Plus, there's the Sphinx, which is why I decided to pay the library a visit today.

The Sphinx is either an oracle or a very eccentric old librarian with an incredible memory and a penchant for riddles. I'm honestly not sure which, and I don't know how or when she became known as the Sphinx. According to Mr. Leary, whoever gave her the nickname was probably thinking of a Sybil instead, although he allows that the Sphinx was also known as an oracle.

Which, by the way, anyone who's ever seen *The NeverEnding Story* could have told him. That's one of the classic movies from Mom's childhood that we watched on loan from the library. I recommend it, although I'll warn you, unless you have a heart of stone, you *will* cry at the part where the pony dies.

There weren't a lot of patrons in the library at this time of day. I approached the Sphinx, who was puttering around behind the checkout counter, returning DVDs to their filing units.

For the record, the Sphinx's given name is Jane Smith. If you think that sounds too generic to be true, I'm right there with you.

Generally speaking, the eldritch always recognize one another.

Even if we can't identify the other's exact species, there's a telltale tingle. I have to admit, I'd never felt it with the Sphinx. Sinclair can see auras, and he says that hers is very muted, which means that either she's near the end of her life, or she's powerful enough to suppress it.

It's a tough call. The Sphinx has looked ancient since I was tall enough to see over the checkout counter.

"Good morning, Ms. Smith," I greeted her. "I'm looking for information on Night Hags."

The Sphinx looked at me without blinking. She couldn't have been more than five feet tall. Her shoulders were hunched with osteoporosis, and her skin was beyond wrinkled, etched with deep crevasses. We're talking apple-head doll territory here. It was impossible to determine her ethnic heritage. Egyptian, East Indian, Native American, light-skinned black—she could have been any or all of the above. I was pretty sure she wasn't Asian, anyway. Not only did her eyes lack an epicanthic fold, but they were disconcertingly round and an almost luminous brown, without a lot of white showing around the iris. Her eyes looked more like a monkey's or a chimp's than a human's, and I knew for a fact that she could stare an unruly child into silence in three seconds flat without a single "Shush!"

The memory made me wriggle my tail a bit.

At last the Sphinx did blink once with great deliberation, crepe-skinned lids closing and opening over those unusual eyes. She rattled off a string of numbers in her surprisingly deep voice, and went back to filing DVDs.

Luckily, I'd been braced for the possibility. When you asked the Sphinx for advice, she either posed you an impenetrable riddle or directed you toward the appropriate research materials.

I retained enough of the sequence of numbers she'd recited to plunge into the stacks in search of a particular volume. And yes, that does mean the Sphinx has the library's entire catalogue memorized by the Dewey Decimal System call numbers.

Unfortunately, the volume in question was a book on sleep disorders. I went back to the counter. The Sphinx ignored me. Her head, wrapped in a paisley scarf, remained bowed over her task.

"Excuse me," I said. "Ms. Smith? I'm sorry, I'm actually looking for Night Hags in folklore."

Her head came up. "Why didn't you say so in the first place?"

"I'm sorry," I repeated. "I'm trying to catch one. A Night Hag, that is."

"Ah." The Sphinx nodded sagely. "Some pass through the gate at dawn crowned; some do not. Some pass through the gate at nightfall crowned; some do not."

I waited to see if there was more.

There wasn't. Just a long, unnerving stare from those round, luminous brown eyes that set my tail twitching.

"Okay," I said. "Thank you."

I was halfway across the library when the Sphinx called my name. "Daisy Johanssen."

I turned. "Yes?"

The power of her stare didn't lessen over distance. "Learn to see with the eyes of your heart as well as your mind," she said, tapping her chest with one gnarled forefinger. "When the time comes, you will need it."

I hesitated. "Um . . . is this still about the Night Hag?"

The Sphinx made a shooing gesture. "When the time comes, you will know." She paused, then added, "Or not."

One of the library patrons, a portly gentleman who looked to be of retirement age, strolled past me to approach the checkout counter holding a book from the New Releases shelf. Pemkowet's resident oracle took his book and scanned it while he pulled out his wallet and fumbled for his library card.

Ohh-kay.

Clearly, I'd been dismissed. Well, as far as encounters with the Sphinx went, that wasn't entirely unproductive. At least I'd gotten a riddle *and* a piece of soothsaying out of it, even if I had no idea what either meant.

Next up, Sinclair's ritual tattooing.

If you're wondering what that's all about, Sinclair is apprenticed to the local coven. He's actually descended from a long line of obeah practitioners, but until recently, he'd been avoiding claiming his heritage—

which, now that I think about it, is something else we had in common. Well, except for the part where claiming it could breach the Inviolate Wall and unleash Armageddon.

At any rate, he's claimed it now, on his own terms. The tattoo isn't mandatory or anything, but according to Casimir, having a seal tattooed on your own skin is one of the most powerful protection wards you can obtain. And conveniently enough, two of the members of the coven, Mark and Sheila Reston, happened to own a tattoo parlor. Since the events of Halloween, they'd been working with Sinclair to develop his own personal sigil.

There were a fair number of people crowded into the tattoo parlor when I arrived. I wasn't surprised to see Casimir, since he was the head of the coven and his shop was right across the street, or Warren Rodgers, who owned a nursery and landscaping business and had taken Sinclair on as a mentee and part-time employee during the off-season when tourism was slow. I was a little surprised to see Jen and Lee—but then, Jen and Sinclair had become fairly good friends since she'd sublet a room in his rental house last fall.

Stacey Brooks, though . . . that I was not expecting. *At all.*

"Hey, girlfriend," I greeted Jen. "What are you doing here?" I lowered my voice. "And what the fuck is *she* doing here?"

Jen grimaced. "Yeah, um . . . Sinclair invited me, and since Lee and I were going for coffee, we figured we'd stop by. And . . . okay, they've been spending time together, but I was really hoping it wouldn't last and I'd never have to mention it to you."

"Son of a bitch!" My tail lashed, and the atmosphere in the crowded tattoo parlor crackled with rising tension. A set of chimes hanging over the front door, probably part of a protection ward, shivered and clanged unhappily.

"Daise, be cool," Jen warned me.

"I'm cool, I'm cool." I visualized stuffing my volatile mix of jealousy and profound irritation in a box, tying a bow around it, and setting it aside for later. Above the door, the chimes quieted.

"Hey, Daisy!" Sinclair threaded his way through the parlor to greet me with a hug. "Thanks for coming. Sorry about the short notice."

"No problem," I said. "I need to talk to you anyway. It's a professional matter. Will you have a minute later?"

"Sure." Sinclair nodded, the beads in his short dreadlocks rattling. "Stick around." Stacey Brooks came up behind him to slide a possessive hand around his arm. "You two know each other, right?"

I *want* to say Stacey gave me a simpering smile that did nothing to mask her gloating look, because that's what the Stacey Brooks I'd known since kindergarten would have done, but the truth is, she looked nervous—possibly because the last time we'd seen each other, I'd been dispatching the zombie skeleton that was trying to hack her into pieces, possibly because we were getting too old for all this adolescent bullshit. My money was on the zombie.

"Of course," Stacey said in a tentative voice. "Hi, Daisy."

"Hi," I said. "I saw your mom the other day. Congratulations on the new position."

"Thanks." She looked relieved. "I'm looking forward to taking on more responsibility."

"That's great." I turned back to Sinclair. "I didn't know you were allowed to let, um, civilians attend this."

"Oh, it's fine as long as they stay outside the ritual circle," he assured me. Flashing his infectious grin, he gestured at Jen and Lee. "Plus, they're your Scooby Gang, right? Of course they can be here."

I sort of wished I'd never made that joke, or at least never explained it to Sinclair, especially now that Stacey was apparently making a bid for the role of unlikely mean-girl ally.

Oh, well.

"People!" The Fabulous Casimir clapped his beautifully manicured hands for attention. "Let's get started, shall we?"

The ritual itself was simple. Sheila Reston drew a chalk circle on the floor of the parlor large enough to encompass her husband's tattoo station and sufficient room for the other members of the coven who were present. The rest of us squished ourselves into the outskirts while the coven called the four quarters and invoked the blessing of the Lord and Lady, bringing a charged sense into the space. The chimes hanging above the front door stirred and sounded again, this time on a harmonious note.

"This is fascinating," Lee murmured. Jen nudged him with her elbow to silence him. For being on a sort-of first date, they seemed more comfortable together than I would have expected.

After the invocation, it was pretty much just a matter of Mark Reston giving Sinclair a tattoo while the rest of us watched.

I have to admit, I drew a sharp breath when Mark applied the stencil to the upper part of Sinclair's left pectoral and I saw the details of the sigil. When we'd talked about it earlier, Sinclair had said he couldn't wait for me to see it, but he wanted to keep it a secret. The outer circle of the sigil incorporated the curving lines I associated with the split-tailed figure of Yemaya, the orisha to whom Sinclair was dedicated. I recognized some of the squiggly talismanic glyphs in the inner circle from the Seal of Solomon that Casimir had given me for protection. I wore it on a silver chain around my own neck, right next to the Oak King's token.

But nestled in the innermost circle of Sinclair's sigil was a stylized rendering of a stalk of joe-pye weed in full bloom.

Across the parlor, Sinclair caught my eye. I nodded my understanding, and he returned my nod with sorrow and regret.

Jojo.

Jojo the joe-pye weed fairy had been a foulmouthed, sparkly little bitch with a wicked crush on Sinclair. When the Tall Man cut her down, Jojo had been trying in her own ridiculous way to protect Sinclair from the death-magic his own mother had unleashed on Pemkowet.

The tattoo needle buzzed steadily as Mark Reston etched ink onto Sinclair's skin, until at length he announced, "Done."

The sigil didn't stand out vividly against Sinclair's cocoa-brown skin, but it was beautiful; and hopefully, effective. With one last invocation and a chorus of "So mote it be," the four members of the coven in attendance called a ceremonial end to the ritual. Sheila Reston swept the chalk circle away briskly with a broom while her husband swabbed Sinclair's chest with antibiotic ointment and applied an adhesive bandage.

"Cas!" I called to Casimir as he made his way toward the exit. "Hey, did the Evanses come in this morning? Were you able to get them set up?"

The Fabulous One pursed his carmine lips. "They did and I was, although I had to offer them most of it on account, which, I might add, I did for your sake, Miss Daisy, since you seemed so concerned." He shrugged. "Mr. Evans is strung awfully tight, dahling. You're sure he's not . . . ?" He raised his plucked eyebrows and circled one manicured finger in the vicinity of his temple.

"No," I said honestly. "He's pretty fucked up, and I don't blame him for it. But he's right about the Night Hag."

The shrewdness that lurked behind Casimir's false eyelashes surfaced. "You're sure?"

I nodded. "Do you have a lot of whatever charms and wards you sold them in stock?"

He shook his head. "Not a lot, no."

I laid one hand on his shoulder, which was draped in a vintage brocade kimono. "Time to order more."

# Ten

Jen and Lee's sort-of coffee date that afternoon turned into a group affair.

It wasn't my fault. Sinclair invited me to get a cup of coffee with him to discuss whatever was on my mind. Stacey decided to join us— and by us, I mean Sinclair—and Jen jumped in to suggest that we all go together. Lee looked a bit crestfallen, but I didn't want to take the time to argue.

Which is why the five of us were sitting at a table across the street at the Daily Grind—okay, not the most original of names, but since they do roast their own beans and grind them fresh to order, I guess they're entitled to it—making awkward conversation while we waited for our orders to be called.

"Why do you always carry that clunky old thing?" Stacey asked me as I adjusted my messenger bag over the back of my chair. I actually think she might have been trying to make small talk, not slam me, be- cause she flushed and backtracked, fidgeting with her ash-brown hair; which, of course, had expensive blond highlights. "I just mean . . . if it's about money, you can get really cute designer knockoffs these days."

Across the table, Jen raised her eyebrows at me.

"It's not about money," I said to Stacey. "I keep my magic dagger in here."

Her flush deepened. "I was being serious."

"So was I." I patted my messenger bag. "You ever try to find a purse that can hold a dagger the length of your forearm? This clunky old thing was custom-made. It has a hidden sheath."

"Oh."

The barista called our order and Lee jumped up with alacrity, not to mention more physical coordination than I would have given him credit for. Joining the gym was definitely having a positive impact on him. "I'll get it."

"I'll help," Sinclair added hastily.

Cowards.

"Okay," I said when the guys had returned and distributed our assorted beverages. "As long as you're all here, I actually *could* use your help with this. We've got a Night Hag on the loose." I told them what had happened, omitting the Evanses' names, and what I'd learned since from Lurine and the Sphinx, omitting Lurine's name.

"So you're looking for me to hook you up with one of the fey?" Sinclair asked.

"Yeah." I nodded. "It's a starting place, anyway. Can you do it?"

"Sure."

Lee frowned. "What about the Sphinx's riddle?"

"Knock yourself out," I said. "Got any theories?"

He shook his head. "Not yet."

"Well, let me know if you do. In the meantime . . ." I shrugged. "Keep your ears open. Ask around. If you hear of any likely Night Hag visitations, let me know. Oh, and send them to Casimir. He's going to lay in a stock of protection charms."

"Maybe you should write a letter to the editor, Daise," Jen suggested in a pragmatic tone. "Get the word out and warn people."

"Oh, please don't!" Stacey said quickly. The PVB's new head of online promotion looked pained. "It's just . . . after the fallout from the Halloween incident, we really, *really* can't afford any more negative press."

"Which is *soooo* much more important than the public safety of us ordinary citizens," Jen retorted. "Right?"

Stacey appealed to me. "You did say the Night Hag couldn't actually kill people in their sleep, didn't you? Just scare them?"

"Um, yeah. Possibly scare them to death." I sighed, turning to Jen. "Look, it's a good idea and ordinarily, I'd agree with you, but there are a couple of problems. One, Casimir doesn't have a whole lot of inventory yet. If there's a run on it, someone who really needs protection could be left in the lurch. Two, I don't want to start a panic. Apparently, this whole Night Hag thing is sunk deep in humanity's collective unconscious, and I'm afraid if people knew, it would trigger a lot of false alarms."

"And you just want to catch the bitch," Jen observed.

"Exactly."

"Gotcha."

Out of the corner of my eye, I noticed Stacey Brooks watching our exchange with a slightly wistful expression, and it occurred to me that she hadn't known what it was like to have a BFF since high school. The rest of the mean-girls coterie—which, by the way, was one of the vocabulary words Mr. Leary had drilled into me—had moved on without her, taking jobs outside of Pemkowet after college. All Stacey had left to cling to were the remnants of our juvenile antipathy, which was also another one of Mr. Leary's vocabulary words.

Well, that and apparently my ex-boyfriend. The clinging, that is, not the vocabulary word.

I finished my mocha latte. "Is now an okay time?" I asked Sinclair. "I'd like to keep moving on this."

"Absolutely." He glanced at Stacey as he rose. "I'll text you later, all right?"

Stacey lifted her chin. "Absolutely."

Oh, yuck. Just shoot me.

During the off-season, Sinclair only ran tours on Saturdays and Sundays. Since it was a weekday, the fairies were off duty at his regular stops, so he suggested that we rendezvous at his house instead. Mercifully, Stacey had to get back to the PVB, so it was just the two of us.

After accidentally crashing Jen and Lee's sort-of date, I'd insisted on buying them another cup of coffee—or more accurately, another short cappuccino and another cup of chai tea. Jen shot me an evil look behind Lee's back, which I ignored. I had the feeling she actually was interested in Lee, but she just needed a push to admit it to herself.

And if I was wrong, it was fair payback for the UR HAWTT! text.

I followed Sinclair out to his place, where the old double-decker tour bus he'd bought on craigslist was parked in the driveway, advertising PEMKOWET SUPERNATURAL TOURS in vivid red, green, and yellow.

"Come on out back," Sinclair said, heading around the corner of the house.

Since he'd begun working part-time for Warren Rodgers at the nursery, Sinclair had discovered an affinity for herbs and he had big plans for the backyard come spring, but right now, it was pretty sparse, mostly hard-packed dirt with brittle patches of dead grass and some weeds along the back fence.

"Ellie!" Sinclair called softly. "Ellie, can you come out for a minute?"

A clump of straggly dark green weeds stirred, and a fairy emerged from it. Her skin was a pale chartreuse, and a cape of pointy dark green leaves hung from her shoulders, trailing on the cold ground and concealing the translucent wings folded on her back. She narrowed cat-slitted yellow eyes at me with disdain. "Who is *she* and why hast thou brought her here?"

When it comes to Sinclair, fairies get a little possessive.

"Hi," I said, holding up my left hand so she could see Hel's rune etched on my palm. "I'm Daisy."

The fairy sniffed. "Thou most certainly are not."

Fairies also have a tendency to be very, very literal. "Not *a* daisy," I said to her. "It's a human name, too. I'm Hel's liaison. Will you answer a few questions for me?"

"Why?" Her yellow gaze darted back and forth between Sinclair and me.

"Please, Ellie?" Sinclair said. "It's just a few questions."

She hesitated.

"I'll record it in my ledger," I said. "One favor owed to Ellie the, um . . ." I had no idea what in the world kind of fairy she was.

"Hellebore fairy," Sinclair supplied.

"Right," I said. "One favor owed to Ellie the hellebore fairy, recorded in my ledger."

Ellie's yellow eyes glowed with avarice. I'm telling you, that ledger was a useful tool. "Very well. Ask."

"I'm trying to catch a Night Hag who's preying on humans," I said. "I was told to ask the fey. Do you know how I can do that?"

"Thou art asking one now," she pointed out.

Like I said, literal. Fighting the urge to grit my teeth, I rephrased the question. "Do you know how I can find and catch a Night Hag?"

Ellie shook her head, the leaves of her cape stirring. By the way, I don't know exactly what hellebore is, but if you ask me, it probably looks a little like a shaggy marijuana plant. "I do not."

"Do you know who would be able to tell me?"

"A bogle."

God, it was like playing a game of Twenty Questions. "Do you know where I can find a bogle?" There was another long pause. I flashed my rune-marked palm at her again and put on a stern voice. "Ellie, I'm working to uphold Hel's rule of order. If you're withholding information from me, not only will there be no favor recorded in my ledger, but there will be a transgression. A serious one."

The hellebore fairy blanched, her skin turning a paler hue of chartreuse. "A bogle haunt lies a league yonder," she said, pointing to the southwest.

Even if I had known how far a league was, that didn't exactly narrow it down. "Any chance you can be more specific?"

"Yes." Her pretty green lips curled in a smirk, revealing a glimpse of needle-sharp teeth. "There is a chance."

My tail twitched with irritation. "Where's this bogle haunt?" I said. "Please be as specific as possible."

Ellie's slight chest rose and fell in an aggrieved sigh. I knew how she felt. "The bogle's haunt lies in the woods," she said reluctantly. "It prowls the grounds of the abandoned encampment by night."

"The abandoned . . . Wait, do you mean the old Presbyterian camp?"
I asked her.

She shrugged. "I know not what you call it."

"Fair enough," I said. "Is there anything else I should know? Anything you're not telling me that would earn you a black mark in my ledger?"

"No."

"You're sure?" I pressed her.

Her yellow eyes flashed. "Dost thou call me a liar?"

"Hey, I'm just checking." I spread my hands. "No offense intended. Thank you, Ellie. I'll record the favor."

With another sniff, she vanished.

So goes the scintillating work of conducting a paranormal investigation. Actually, it's not that different from conducting a regular investigation, which is infinitely more tedious than it looks on TV. Lots of interviewing witnesses, sources, and informants, lots of paperwork, not a lot of chasing bad guys.

"Thanks," I said to Sinclair. "I appreciate it."

"Anytime," he said. "Do you want me to go out to the camp with you?" He thumped his chest. "I'm extra . . . ouch!"

I winced. "Sorry! Does it hurt?"

Sinclair coughed. "Only when I hit myself. It's a little tender. Do you want me to come with you?"

"No, thanks." I shook my head. "We couldn't go right now. Bogles only come out at night. Anyway, I'm working with Cody on this one."

"Ah." Something in his expression shifted. "Are you okay with that?" Damn, I didn't think Sinclair knew about me and Cody. He gave me a wry smile. "Sorry, sistah. Jen let it slip after your night of debauchery."

"It is what it is." I couldn't help an edge creeping into my voice. "What about you and Stacey?"

"What about us?"

"I don't know," I said. "Do you actually *like* her?"

"Maybe. I don't know—it's too soon to tell." Sinclair was silent for a moment. "I think she's lonely, Daisy. And sometimes I am, too. I mean, I'm glad to have made some friends here, I'm glad Jen decided to rent the spare bedroom, and I'm grateful for the coven, but I'm still the new guy in town. Look, I love Pemkowet—I really do. You know I've always been drawn to the place. But sometimes it seems like everyone here's known one another forever, and I'll always be the new guy."

"The new guy everyone likes," I pointed out.

"The new guy who got dumped by the first girl he liked," he said quietly. I flinched a little. "It's okay. I understand. Our timing was lousy. But that doesn't mean it didn't hurt, Daisy."

"I'm sorry," I murmured.

"I know." Sinclair shrugged. "What can I say? Stacey brought me cookies as a thank-you for saving her life. We got to talking. She's got an overbearing mother," he added. "I can relate."

"That's a bit of an understatement," I said. No kidding; Amanda Brooks might be a pit bull as the head of the PVB, but Sinclair's mom was a judge, an aspiring candidate for the Jamaican Parliament and a powerful obeah woman who'd unleashed the duppy that raised Pemkowet's dead and nearly got Stacey Brooks killed. "And you weren't exactly going it alone in the life-saving department."

"Yeah." He nodded. "I mentioned that to her. To be honest, I think she feels a little self-conscious about it."

It was on the tip of my tongue to say she damn well should feel self-conscious given the amount of shade she'd thrown my way over the years, but I figured there are times to take the high road, and this was probably one of them. "Just doing my job."

Sinclair smiled, a genuine smile. "You want to come in for a cup of coffee or something?"

I shook my head. "I should head down to the station and catch up on my filing. Thanks, though."

He walked me to my car. "Take care, Daisy."

"You, too." I paused. "By the way, your tattoo's really beautiful. It's perfect. Totally perfect."

"Thanks." Sinclair laid a hand over his heart; gently this time. "I think so, too."

The rest of the day proved uneventful, with one exception. I got a call from Amanda Brooks notifying me that Daniel Dufreyne was coming to town to meet with her tomorrow morning at eleven a.m. I confirmed that I'd be there well in advance, reiterating my warning not to meet with him alone.

I left a voice mail message for Cody telling him I had an update on the Night Hag case and to prepare for an after-hours jaunt to the old Presbyterian campgrounds, and spent the afternoon filing, as well as writing up a report for the X-Files, which I logged into my ledger, along with an entry for Ellie the hellebore fairy and the favor I owed her.

Shortly before five p.m., just as I was wrapping things up, Cody swung by the station.

"Hey," I greeted him, still trying to pretend things weren't awkward between us. "Did you get my message?"

"Yeah, about that." He perched on a corner of my desk. "I can't do it tonight, Daise. I'm on duty. I called around, but there's no one else who can cover my shift, and the chief doesn't want the only cop on call traipsing around in the woods looking for . . . What, exactly, would we be looking for?"

"A bogle," I informed him.

Cody blinked. "Huh. Okay." He nodded in the direction of the conference room. "Maybe you should give me the lowdown."

I filled him in on what I'd learned. "Don't worry about tonight," I added. "Sinclair offered to go with me. I'll just take him up on it."

Cody made a sound in the back of his throat that sounded a lot like a suppressed growl. "I'd rather you waited until I'm free, Daise. The Evanses should be safe now, right?"

"*Should* being the operative word, yes," I said. "But that leaves the rest of the town vulnerable."

"Yeah, well, the rest of the town isn't as unstable as Scott Evans." Cody rubbed the bronze stubble on his chin. "If you absolutely, positively insist on going, I'd rather you take Ludovic for backup," he said reluctantly. "I don't like him, but I'd trust him in a clinch over the fledgling Jamaican warlock."

"Stefan's out of town," I said. "I could ask Cooper."

"*No.*" Phosphorescent green shimmered in Cody's eyes and his voice was adamant. "No way."

I couldn't exactly blame him, since the last time he'd seen Cooper, Cooper was ravening. Still . . .

"You don't get to go all possessive alpha male on me, Cody," I said to him. "You just don't."

"I know." He looked away, his jaw tightening, then looked back at me. "Give me this one, Daise? We're talking about over a hundred acres of woods. You could look for hours without finding a thing. But if there's a bogle out there, I can track it."

He had a point.

"You can track a bogle?" I asked.

"Yeah." Cody nodded. "And I'll twist some arms to make sure I'm free tomorrow night. Deal?"

I hesitated. "Deal."

# Eleven

I found myself in a restless mood that night.

Part of it was the lack of action. I'd been planning on hunting a bogle, and I'd had to put my plans on hold. It made me apprehensive; worried that the Night Hag might find a way around the wards Casimir had sold the Evanses, worried that she might strike somewhere else, finding another unstable victim.

But if I was honest with myself, it had a lot to do with the fact that I'd be meeting with Daniel Dufreyne, possibly nefarious lawyer and suspected hell-spawn, late tomorrow morning.

Someone like *me*. Only . . . if I was right about him, he'd claimed his birthright.

It made me feel strange and shivery inside. I'd spent my whole life trying to avoid the Seven Deadlies, using the visualization techniques my mom had taught me to keep my outsize emotions in check, afraid that if I didn't, I might succumb to one of the temptation scenarios my father offered me and breach the Inviolate Wall in the process.

What if that was wrong?

It's not that I *wanted* to lay claim to my demonic heritage—or at least, not exactly. I mean, it would be nice to have powers of persuasion and all that, but I'd seen Daniel Dufreyne in passing and something about him felt downright icky. I didn't want to be icky. I just wanted to know. What if everything I'd been taught was wrong?

It was an unnerving thought.

I rummaged through my music collection until I found something that suited my mood: an old, scratchy recording of the mostly forgotten blues singer Clara Smith. Long ago, when my mom was dating a jazz musician, I discovered that there's something about the blues that always calms me down.

Tonight it was Clara Smith singing in a doleful warble about how she done sold her soul to the Devil and her heart done turned to stone, reminding me that whatever the truth, the bargain was never worth it.

Especially since, according to all the soothsaying that had been laid on me lately, it seemed that I was going to need to trust my heart or see with the eyes of my heart, whatever that meant.

"I'm pretty sure that's not going to happen if my heart done turned to stone, Mog," I informed my cat, who was purring on my lap. Mogwai liked it when I was in a blues-listening mood.

I listened to the track half a dozen times, letting Clara's mournful regret settle deep inside me, until my thoughts were quiet enough for sleep.

Speaking of sleep, the next morning I called Dawn Evans to make sure Casimir's charms had proved effective. Good news—not only had they worked, but the peace of mind they gave Scott had allowed him to sleep through the night for the first time in ages. I breathed a sigh of relief.

After running a few errands, I made a point of arriving at the PVB office a good fifteen minutes before the scheduled meeting time. Since my last visit, the lobby had been rearranged to incorporate an additional desk: a sleek, modern, minimalist number behind which sat Stacey Brooks.

"Daisy!" Stacey practically leaped from her chair as I entered the lobby, her eyes bright with excitement. "I figured it out!"

You know that thing in sitcoms where a character pulls a "Who, me?" face and looks around to make sure it isn't someone else being spoken to? Yeah, I actually did that before determining that it was in fact me that Stacey Brooks was addressing with animated enthusiasm. "Figured what out?"

"The Sphinx's riddle." She lowered her voice, twisting a lock of highlighted ash-brown hair around her fingers and giving me a significant look. "It's *hair*."

I stared at her. "Hair?"

"Some pass through the gate at dawn crowned, some do not, right?" she said. "She's talking about birth."

"And *hair*?"

"Haven't you ever heard that saying about a woman's hair being her crowning glory?" Stacey asked. "And the gate at nightfall, that's death, right? Well, some babies are born with hair, and some aren't. And some men go bald before they die, right?"

Now that I dredged my memories to recall Mr. Leary's old Myth and Lit classes, it did echo the original—or possibly simply the younger—Greek Sphinx's riddle, which was something about what goes on four legs at dawn, two legs at noon, and three legs at night, the answer being man, who crawls as a baby, walks on two legs as an adult, and uses a cane in old age.

But . . . *hair*?

"You know, that's great," I said to Stacey. "I think you might really be onto something with that whole birth and death thing. I'm just not sure how I'm supposed to use hair to catch a Night Hag."

She shrugged. "Look, that's your department. I'm just trying to help out."

"Thanks," I said, striving for sincerity and managing to get pretty darn close. "I appreciate it."

"No problem."

We had a vaguely uncomfortable frenemy moment, which was broken by Amanda Brooks poking her head out from her office and inviting me inside to wait for the lawyer Dufreyne.

I'll say one thing for the mysterious Mr. Dufreyne—he was prompt. He showed up at eleven a.m. on the dot, and Amanda's new assistant ushered him into her office.

My tail twitched in an involuntary response.

At a glance, Daniel Dufreyne appeared innocuous. Average height, early thirties, a decent build. It's fair to say that he was handsome in a bland, upper-middle-class Ivy League white-guy sort of way, and he looked like money, with an impeccably tailored charcoal-gray suit, expensive loafers, expensive briefcase, and a hundred-dollar haircut.

But then, there were those black, black eyes, which shouldn't have been disconcerting, since I saw the same thing in the mirror every day. Yet they were.

And then there was the smell. Except it wasn't a smell, not exactly. It was a sense *like* a smell, the olfactory equivalent of someone striking a hideously discordant note on a piano or screeching fingernails over a chalkboard.

All I know is that it made my skin prickle in a distinctly unpleasant way.

Dufreyne paused in the doorway, his too-black gaze skating over me. His nostrils flared slightly, and he permitted himself a faint smile.

"Mr. Dufreyne," Amanda said briskly. "I do apologize for bringing you here under false pretenses, but I understand you've been avoiding returning Ms. Johanssen's calls, and frankly, I'm a little curious myself about what the company you represent is planning to do with the property you're acquiring on their behalf."

"I'm sure you are." He had a smooth, mellifluous voice. I could see Amanda Brooks relaxing visibly at the sound of it, and if it hadn't been for that smell, which apparently was undetectable to mundane mortals, it might have worked on me, too. "I assure you, the party I represent has nothing but Pemkowet's best interests at heart."

"Which are?" I said bluntly.

His gaze lingered on me. "Daisy Johanssen, I presume?" He offered his hand. "A pleasure."

I didn't want to shake his hand. I really didn't. But my mother had raised me to be polite, and there was a part of me that was just plain curious, so I did. It felt like shaking any ordinary human's hand, but there was something about the press of his flesh against mine that gave me the creepy-crawlies. He smiled again without any warmth, and I had the impression of something unpleasant lurking behind his black pupils, like the flicker of a shark's tail in dark waters.

When he let go of my hand, I had to fight the urge to wipe it on my skirt. "So tell me about Pemkowet's best interests."

"All will be made clear in due time." Dufreyne took a seat uninvited. "Business deals are complicated. My employers are under no obligation to divulge their plans prematurely."

Ignoring a disapproving look from Amanda, I hiked my butt onto the corner of her desk so I could keep him in view. "Elysian Fields?"

His eyelids flickered with annoyance. "Yes."

Amanda cleared her throat. "Mr. Dufreyne, I must say, the sheer amount of property—"

Dufreyne held up his left hand to forestall her, then lowered it quickly, but not before I caught a glimpse of a symbol etched on his palm, the lines a golden shimmer. It was similar to the silvery lines of the Norse rune etched on my own palm, although it didn't look like any rune I'd ever seen. "Again, I assure you, there is no cause for concern," he said in that velvety voice. "I have no doubt that Pemkowet will be delighted when the plans are unveiled."

"I do," I said.

His black gaze flicked over me. "Then I look forward to your surprise when you find yourself convinced otherwise. Ms. Brooks, since I'm here, shall we discuss the offer on the table for the Cavannaugh property?"

"I really haven't any intention of selling." Amanda sounded uncertain and her features had taken on an unfamiliar vague look.

I kindled my mental shield, spinning it into a disk wide enough to encompass us both. "She really doesn't."

"I really don't," she repeated in a stronger tone.

"Interesting." Daniel Dufreyne arched one manscaped eyebrow. Goddammit, why was it that everyone in the eldritch community but me could do that? "Well, then." He rose. "I'm sorry we've wasted each other's time."

"That's it?" I let my shield dwindle. "You're just giving up? You're not going to pit your powers of persuasion against me?"

Another smile, this one condescending. "Powers of persuasion? What a quaint term for a modern young lady."

If my tail hadn't been tucked on account of the hard desk beneath my butt, it would have been lashing. "You know what I mean."

"I know the circumstances have changed since the initial offer was made." Dufreyne addressed Amanda. "And I will tell you this as a courtesy, Ms. Brooks. Eventually, you *will* want to sell that property, and if you choose not to accept this offer, the next one may not be as generous."

"Is that a threat?" I asked him, expanding the circumference of my shield to cover Amanda again.

"No, Ms. Johanssen." He leveled his black gaze at me. "A fact. Ms. Brooks, you have my number. Good day, ladies."

Swearing under my breath, I grabbed a pad of paper and a pen from Amanda's desk, sketching out my best approximation of the symbol I'd glimpsed on Dufreyne's left palm while he let himself out of the office.

"Daisy—" Amanda protested.

"Back in a sec." I followed Dufreyne into the parking lot. "Hey! I wasn't done talking to you. What do you mean, circumstances have changed?"

Standing beside a silver Jaguar, he fished out his car keys. "All I'll say is that according to the rumors I hear, a lot of people have been very busy since the events of Halloween." His black gaze with dangerous things swimming in it fixed on me and he smiled again, showing his very white teeth. "Why don't you ask me what you *really* want to know?"

That foul smell that wasn't a smell hit me, and the pit of my stomach lurched. I swallowed hard and took a deep breath. "How can you be? I mean, you did it, didn't you? Claimed your birthright?" I waved one hand. "And yet—"

Dufreyne leaned close to me, the reek of wrongness that hung about him intensifying. "And yet the Inviolate Wall still stands," he whispered in a silken tone, his breath hot against my face. "Is that it?"

I held my ground with an effort. "Yes."

He laughed. It wasn't a full-on villainous *mwah-ha-ha*, but it was close. "I don't know whether to envy you or pity you, Daisy Johanssen. You honestly don't know what the difference is between us, do you?"

I gritted my teeth. "Well, I can think of a few."

For a long moment, he just stood there, his gaze boring into mine, the stench of his existence surrounding me. "Your mother was an innocent," he said at length. "Foolish and ignorant, but innocent."

"I don't understand."

"Oh, it makes all the difference." This time Dufreyne's smile was bitter. "Only one of our kind conceived in innocence has the power to breach the Inviolate Wall and destroy the world as we know it. One such as you." He shook his head. "But you'll never use it, will you?"

"No," I said automatically.

"More's the pity," he observed. "I hope you appreciate the irony. You, possessed of world-shattering power, can never use it."

"Why the fuck would I?" I asked. "Why would you? Why would *anyone*?"

Dufreyne did the eyebrow-raise. "To reign over the resulting chaos?"

Beneath my skirt, I swished my tail back and forth. "Yeah, that's not really on my bucket list."

"No, of course not," he said. "Because you were raised to love and cherish this tiresome world, to live a tiresome mortal life and die a tiresome mortal death."

I eyed him. "If you're that bored, maybe you need a hobby."

"A hobby." The notion seemed to amuse him. "Yes, thank you for the suggestion. Perhaps when this business is concluded, I'll take a flower-arranging class." He beeped his Jaguar unlocked and turned to open the driver's-side door. "In the meantime, I have a vocation."

"Wait!" I called out. "Your mother . . . If she wasn't innocent, what was she?"

He paused, his back to me. "Complicit."

"I'm sorry." The words came unbidden.

His shoulders tensed visibly before easing, but the tone of his response gave no indication that my sympathy had struck a nerve. "Don't be. She was well compensated for it." He got into his car. "I may not be capable of destroying the world, but I can wield influence over it, and there are those who value my skills."

"Like who?" I asked him. "Satan's Planned Parenthood? Whoever's behind this whole Elysian Fields thing? What do you mean when you say a lot of people have been busy since Halloween?"

"Good day, Ms. Johanssen." Daniel Dufreyne closed his car door, cracking the window. "I'm sure our paths will cross again."

I watched him pull out of the parking lot. "No shit."

# Twelve

I ducked back into the PVB office.

"Wow, way to throw yourself at Mr. Brooks Brothers, Daisy," Stacey observed. "Not exactly subtle." I shot her a glance, and she had the grace to look abashed. "Sorry. Force of habit."

"Don't have anything to do with that guy," I said to her. "He's bad news."

"Like what?"

I hesitated, then flashed her the devil-horns sign with my right hand. As far as I was concerned, Daniel Dufreyne wasn't protected by the eldritch honor code. "One of my kind gone to the dark side."

Her face paled. "Are you serious?" She cast an involuntary glance upward, as though the Inviolate Wall were hovering above us. "I didn't think you could do that without . . . you know."

"*I* can't," I said. "But he can. Apparently, not all hell-spawns are created equal."

I knocked on Amanda's office door and went in to retrieve the sketch I'd made, apologizing for my hasty departure.

"That's quite all right." Amanda Brooks sounded shaken, which was disconcerting in and of itself. "Did you learn anything further from him?"

"Not really." Well, that whole only-one-conceived-in-innocence thing was a pretty big bombshell, but that wasn't what she was talking about. "I asked him what he meant by circumstances changing, and all he'd say was that a lot of people had been busy since the events of Halloween."

She frowned. "Meaning what?"

"I wish I knew." I held up the piece of paper with my sketch. "He had a mark on his palm. Like mine, only different. You wouldn't have been able to see it," I added. "It's an eldritch thing. It could mean that he's sworn to someone's service like I'm sworn to Hel's. Or it could be something altogether different. I'll see what I can find out."

"You don't know?" Amanda's voice took on an accusatory tone, which was annoying, yet reassuringly familiar.

"Look, it's not like my job came with a training manual," I said. "I'm just doing my best to figure it out as I go along, whether that means doing a Google search like everyone else, or bargaining with fairies and hunting bogles . . . Oh, crap."

She raised an inquiring eyebrow. Okay, so can *everyone* but me do the one-eyebrow-raise thing?

"Sorry," I said. "Just thought of something." I tucked the sketch into my messenger bag. "Thanks again for setting up the meeting. I appreciate it."

Amanda gave me a brusque nod. "I don't know where this is going, but I don't like it. Keep me in the loop."

"Will do," I promised.

Outside, I called Cody.

Investigating the suspicious purchases of large tracts of land in Pemkowet was something Hel had specifically asked me to look into, and it had occurred to me that since Dawn and Scott Evans were safely warded and there were no rumors that the Night Hag had struck elsewhere, reporting to Hel had to be my top priority.

And unfortunately, that could only be done after sunset, which meant our bogle hunt would have to wait until tomorrow night.

"Goddammit, Daise," Cody grumbled into the phone after I'd explained it to him. "I had to call in a favor from Ken Levitt to cover my shift tonight."

"Well, can he cover it tomorrow instead?" I asked. "I mean, I'm sorry if it inconveniences him, but it is a request from a goddess, after all."

Cody laughed. "Good point, Pixy Stix."

I sighed inwardly. "Well, let me know. If you can't get off tomorrow night, maybe we can go when I get back from Little Niflheim."

"Or I could go alone," he said. "I can track the bogle without you."

"Yeah, but you don't have Hel's authority to question the bogle," I said. "Believe me, it's hard enough to get answers out of the fey with it. Without it, you're screwed."

"Okay, okay," he said. "I'll see what I can do."

"Thanks."

I headed over to the Sisters of Selene to see if Casimir recognized the symbol, waiting while he assisted a couple of middle-aged shoppers poring over his selection of crystal pendants.

"Hey, I know you," one of them said to me as Casimir rang up the other's purchase. Her eyes widened, and she mimed a stabbing gesture. "You're the ghostbuster girl from those YouTube videos, aren't you?"

"Yeah," I admitted reluctantly. I'd tried to keep a low profile after the Halloween parade debacle, but a number of spectators had gotten footage of the incident, including me using *dauda-dagr* to dispatch the Tall Man's reanimated remains. "Guilty as charged."

The shopper shivered. "I have to say, that looked absolutely terrifying. Claire and I even considered canceling our annual holiday shopping trip, didn't we?" she said to the other woman.

"We did," Shopper Claire agreed. "But Pemkowet has the *cutest* boutiques with the most unusual items."

"Thanks ever so much, dahling," Casimir said to her, wrapping up the pendant she'd purchased and tucking it into a little cardboard box. "We do appreciate it, don't we, Daisy?"

"We certainly do," I agreed. "And I assure you, what happened on Halloween will never happen again."

"Well, I should hope not," the first shopper said in a tart voice. "If you ask me, it was irresponsible of the city to use all those dreadful ghostly appearances to promote itself in the first place. It's exploiting the dead, may they rest in peace, and putting the living in jeopardy."

I raised my hands. "You're preaching to the choir, ma'am."

That appeared to mollify her. "I'm glad to hear it."

I watched them make their exit, purchase secured. "Have you been hearing a lot of that, Cas?"

"More than I'd like, Miss Daisy." He tidied his counter. "What can I do for you today? Has the Night Hag struck again?"

"No, all's quiet on the Night Hag front. I'm here about something else." I gave him the background and showed him my sketch, which, by the way, looked like a capital letter *C* with a cross added to it.

Casimir studied it with a frown, pursing his carmine lips. "It looks familiar, but I can't place it. It's not one we use in the practice. Are you sure it's not a compound glyph? It could be the crescent of Islam combined with a Christian cross."

"I'm not sure of anything," I said. "Though I'm guessing he's probably not a Jihadist for Jesus."

"Here." The Fabulous Casimir emerged from behind the counter to peruse a shelf of books. "You can borrow this," he said, handing me a thick tome titled *Dictionary of Symbols*. "It's got everything from alchemical notation to hobo signs. Just be careful not to break the spine."

"Thanks, Cas."

As long as I was in the vicinity, I took the book over to the Daily Grind next door to get myself a mocha latte while I skimmed through it. With all the tedious investigation I'd been doing, I figured I deserved a treat.

I started out trying to actually read the thing, but it was pretty dense going, although I did learn that a cat chalked on a residence was a hobo sign indicating that a kind lady lived there. Go figure. I guess that was before the crazy-cat-lady stereotype was born. Or maybe crazy cat ladies were kind to hobos back in the day. Halfway through my latte, I gave up and just started flipping pages, looking for anything that resembled the symbol in my sketch.

Amazingly enough, I found it within ten minutes. "Gotcha," I murmured with satisfaction, flattening the page. "So what do we have here?"

I don't know what I was expecting, but it wasn't *Hades*; and to further confuse matters, the symbol didn't refer to the Greek deity. It referred to some hypothetical planet that probably didn't exist.

"Huh." I sat and thought about that while I finished my mocha latte. Okay, I didn't know any astrologers, but I did know someone with firsthand knowledge of Greek deities, so I opted to pursue that angle.

"Hey, cupcake!" Lurine answered her phone when I called. "You must have read my mind."

"I did?"

"I'm over at your mom's. We're talking about my spring wardrobe and looking at some *gorgeous* fabric. Can you get away to join us?"

In case I haven't mentioned it, my mom's a seamstress. She started sewing when I was a baby, altering my onesies—and probably diapers, too, come to think of it—because I couldn't stand to have my tail confined. It turned out she had a real flair for it, and years later, she managed to turn it into a full-time business.

"Sure," I said. "Can I pick your brain while we're at it?"

"Absolutely."

After returning Casimir's book, I drove over to Sedgewick Estate. It's a little mobile home community, which is a lot nicer than it sounds by virtue of being located right on the Kalamazoo River. I'd grown up there, and it was a pretty cool place to spend your childhood.

"Hey, Daisy baby!" Mom greeted me at the door of her double-wide with an effusive hug, then held me at arm's length to give me the maternal once-over. "Everything okay?"

"Yeah." I smiled at her. "It's good to see you."

"You, too." She patted my hand. "Come on in and see the embarrassment of riches that Lurine brought."

Mom wasn't kidding. The entire place was strewn with bolts and lengths of fabric. That wasn't unusual when she was in the middle of a commission, but this time the array was staggering.

"What did you do?" I asked Lurine. "Buy out the entire stock of Mood?" Mood, by the way, is a fabric store in New York where Tim

Gunn always takes the contestants on *Project Runway* to shop. Unsurprisingly, that's one of Mom's and my favorite TV shows, right up there with *Gilmore Girls*.

"Oh, I just ordered a few things." Lurine set a glass of champagne on our old Formica dinette and picked up a bolt of midnight blue silk shantung, beckoning to me. "C'mere, cupcake."

I let her drape a length of it over my shoulder. It had the subtle sheen and texture of a very, very expensive fabric.

"See?" Lurine cocked her head at my mom.

Mom did the make-a-picture-frame thing with her fingers. "Cocktail dress? Maybe a 1950s silhouette?"

"Exactly."

"You can't do that!" I protested. "You bought this stuff for *your* spring wardrobe!"

"Oh, just indulge me." Lurine tweaked a lock of my hair. "I ordered a lot of fabric that caught my eye for one reason or another. I must have had you in the back of my mind. This isn't a color for spring, anyway."

I stroked the silk, feeling the barely perceptible slub of the natural fibers under my fingertips. "You're sure?"

"Positive."

For the next several hours, Lurine and Mom and I delved into the treasure trove of fabrics that Lurine had purchased, fanning out glossy copies of foreign and domestic editions of *Elle* and *Vogue* and *Marie Claire*, sipping champagne and nibbling on canapés.

And okay, yes, I probably should have gotten straight to business, but there was a part of me that needed this. Daniel Dufreyne's revelation had shaken me, maybe more than I'd admitted to myself.

It made me look at my mother with renewed tenderness. I might have been conceived by accident, a horrible accident, but no matter what, I had never, ever doubted that she loved me. Not once.

I didn't think Daniel Dufreyne's mother had loved him. And yet she'd borne him on purpose.

*Complicit*, he had said. Complicit in his conception, complicit in his birth. And then she'd done . . . what? Raised him to claim his birthright? Handed him off to whatever creepy cabal had hired her to serve as a surrogate mother to a hell-spawn? Were there others? Was there a freakin' *breeding* program? Ick! The whole thing made my skin crawl, and there was no better antidote than an afternoon of old-fashioned girl time with my mom and Lurine.

But alas, all good things must come to an end. Before I knew it, it was almost four o'clock in the afternoon, and outside the windows of Mom's double-wide the world was beginning to look gray and murky. The sun wouldn't set for another hour and a half or so, but it was getting late.

I fished out my sketch of the symbol on Dufreyne's palm and showed it to Lurine. "Does this mean anything to you?"

She shook her head. "No. Why?"

I explained, although I left out the part about Dufreyne's birth. I didn't think Mom needed to hear that; not now, anyway. If we had that discussion, it should be just the two of us. "Casimir's book said it was an astrological symbol representing a hypothetical planet called Hades," I finished. "Which probably doesn't exist. So I was wondering if it might refer to the actual deity."

"It's possible." Lurine frowned in thought. "As far as I know, astrological symbolism is a bit of a mishmash developed over the ages. Back in my day, there weren't any graphic symbols that represented Hades, or any of the Olympians, for that matter. At least none that I was aware of."

"So Hades might have appropriated it?" I suggested.

"Maybe." Taking my left hand, Lurine turned it over and traced Hel's mark on my palm. "After all, this is just an ordinary rune, right?"

"Basically," I agreed. "I mean, it marks me as Hel's liaison, but it's part of the common runic alphabet."

Lurine shrugged. "So maybe Hades did the same thing. Your guess is as good as mine, cupcake."

"I was hoping you might have some extra insight," I said. "You, um, did mention something about keeping the old traditions alive the other day."

Her gaze turned flinty. "I wasn't talking about the Olympians, Daisy."

*Oops.* I had the feeling I'd unwittingly crossed a line. "I'm sorry. Did I miss something?"

For a few beats, the unexpected tension between us persisted, and then Lurine sighed. "No, I'm sorry. You touched on a sensitive subject." She paused. "What, exactly, do you think you know about me?"

I exchanged a panicked glance with Mom, who murmured, "Lurine . . . don't put her on the spot."

"It's all right, Marja," Lurine said to her. "I'm just curious."

Of course I'd looked into Lurine's origin myth. Who wouldn't? The thing is, there were several conflicting versions, the most common being that Lamia was a beautiful Libyan queen and a mistress of Zeus, caught out by a jealous Hera, who killed her children and transformed her into a grief-crazed monster that hunted and devoured the children of others . . . okay, I guess I was a little dense on that antipathy toward the Olympians. And then there was a whole other tradition regarding lamiae in the plural, casting them as seductive, bloodsucking succubi. Nothing I'd read seemed to depict an accurate portrait of the next-door neighbor and ex-babysitter I'd grown up with, so I'd quit wondering about it years ago.

"I don't know," I said honestly. "I mean, I know what the books say, but Mom and I always figured if you wanted us to know the truth, you'd tell us."

"Touché," Lurine said in a wry tone. "Let's just say history is written by the victors, and when the Olympians overthrew the Titans, a lot of their children got screwed in the bargain."

"So you were never a Libyan queen?" I said.

"Oh, I didn't say that," Lurine said. "But never a *mortal* one. And I certainly never devoured any children," she added.

"I never thought you did," my mom offered.

Lurine gave her an affectionate glance. "And I didn't think you would have trusted me with Daisy if you had."

"Okay, so about Hades," I said. "I take it you're not a fan?"

She shrugged. "As a matter of general principle, no, but I don't bear him a particular grudge, either."

"Can you think of any reason Hades would have his minions nosing around Pemkowet?" I asked.

"Honestly, no." Lurine looked genuinely perplexed. "He's got his own demesne in Montreal."

*"Montreal?"* Mom echoed. "Why on earth?"

"Oh, it was part of that whole eldritch diaspora of the twentieth century." Lurine waved a dismissive hand at the passage of time. "Hades probably foresaw the Greek economy tanking in this century. He's the Greek god of wealth as well as god of the underworld, you know. He must have seen an opportunity there."

"Yeah, he's spent the last fifty or sixty years behind the scenes building one of the world's biggest underground cities in Montreal." Underworld deities tended to be reclusive and keep a low profile, but I knew about Montreal because that's where Cody's late ex-girlfriend— and current sister-in-law—were from. With a pang, I wondered if the Fairfax clan would be importing more Québécois werewolves for the upcoming mixer. "From what I understand, it's the poshest underworld in existence."

"Maybe he's just looking for an investment opportunity," my mom suggested. "Property values *are* on the rise."

"It's possible," Lurine agreed. "I mean, no offense, but Hades is a lot more worldly than Hel. That's what comes of being a god of wealth."

I wasn't convinced. "Maybe."

"Do you want me to read the cards for you, honey?" Mom asked. "We can do it right now."

I glanced out the window, where the murky gray light was dimming. "I'd better not take the time. I need to report to Hel. Can I take you up on it later?"

She smiled. "Anytime."

At the door, I gave her an extra-long hug. My mom, the innocent. While Daniel Dufreyne's mother had been enjoying her compensation, mine had been waiting tables and sewing tail-slits into my onesies. I wished I could go back in time and protect her, even if it meant negating my own existence.

"Be careful out there, honey," Mom cautioned me. "Down there in Little Niflheim, too. Okay?"

"I will," I promised.

# Thirteen

By the time I sent my request for an audience with Hel, it was well after sunset.

The process was a simple one. An iron casket I'd stashed on the top shelf of my closet held a copper bowl, a box of wooden kitchen matches, and six massive scales of pine bark from Yggdrasil II that were densely etched with runic script.

There had been seven, but I'd used one a couple of months ago. Since then, I'd come to consider Lee Hastings a friend, but the initial price of his aid in developing a database for me was, as he put it, a single glimpse of Hel.

For this presumption, Hel offered Lee a terrifying demonstration of her ability to stop his heart with a thought; and when I took the blame for allowing him to accompany me, she generously included me in the demonstration.

Not that that was on my mind or anything as I took my gear out to the park next door.

Okay, it was totally on my mind, even though I felt a hundred percent confident in making this request. Having a goddess demonstrate her ability to stop your heart will do that to you.

In case you're wondering, I don't begrudge Hel the demonstration. I deserved the responsibility I took for Lee's transgression, and you don't say something like that to a deity without being prepared to accept the repercussions. You just don't. A deity will take you at your word. Hel could be cruel and Hel could be compassionate, but she was always fair.

Anyway.

Sitting cross-legged, with my shoulders hunched against the cold November wind, I placed the copper bowl before me, struck a match, and set fire to one of the six remaining scales, dropping it into the bowl. The dry, brittle bark burned briskly, crackling and snapping, flames devouring the runes. A thin trickle of fragrant piney smoke vanished into the darkening sky overhead.

I watched it go. When the scale of bark had burned to ashes in the bottom of the bowl, I retreated to my apartment to wait.

It took about fifteen minutes before I heard the familiar chugging rumble of Mikill's dune buggy pulling into the alley beside my apartment. To be honest, I'd been hoping Mikill drove something else in the off-season, maybe a nice warm SUV with all-wheel drive and power windows, but I guess that was a vain hope. If there's one thing a frost giant doesn't mind, it's a blast of cold wind blowing through his beard.

So I bundled up in a down coat that made me look like a miniature version of the Michelin Man, wrapped a wool scarf around my neck, and yanked an old Pemkowet High School knit ski hat over my head, making sure my ears were covered.

"Greetings, Daisy Johanssen!" Towering beside the dune buggy, Mikill raised his left hand in salutation to display the spear-headed rune that indicated he was one of Hel's guards. "Your request for an audience has been granted."

"Thanks, Mikill." I flashed my own palm in response before dragging on a pair of warm gloves. "Hey, you look good. This weather agrees with you."

It was true. In warmer weather, Mikill looked like an enormous ice sculpture in the process of melting. With the temperature hovering under freezing, he looked like a pristine ice sculpture.

A modest smile curved his blue lips, the rime of frost on his paler blue skin crackling. "It is kind of you to notice."

"How could I not?" I climbed into the passenger seat, fishing around at my feet for the loaf of bread that was the hellhound Garm's tribute before buckling my seat belt. "Okay, ready when you are."

Mikill gunned the engine in reply.

I hunkered low in my seat as we sped down the highway, tucking my chin into my scarf. Mikill's frozen hair and beard crackled in the wind of our passage, but at least they weren't shedding a hail of sleet like they did in the summer.

We turned off the highway and passed the darkened grounds of the Pemkowet Dune Rides, now closed for the season, which meant their trails weren't being maintained on a regular basis.

No matter how many times I'd made this journey, it never failed to be simultaneously terrifying and exhilarating. I'd learned to take Mikill's driving on faith, but my stomach still dropped every time we departed from the trails to plunge over the undeveloped dunes, the buggy bouncing, beams of its headlights jouncing wildly, cutting two narrow tunnels of light in the darkness.

And then there was Garm.

Unnerving as it was, there was something plaintive about the hellhound's howl as it echoed across the dunes on a cold November night. I'd imagine it probably *was* pretty lonely being Garm, whose sole purpose was to patrol Hel's territory aboveground and guard Yggdrasil II.

How and why that came to be, I couldn't say, any more than I could tell you why Garm can be pacified by a loaf of bread. When I asked the first time, Mikill's response was simply that that was the way it was, which is an annoyingly common response among the immortal members of the eldritch community. After his one and only visit to Little Niflheim, Lee theorized that it had something to do with bread being an ancient and universal symbol for life, and that it represented a symbolic sacrifice in order to pass over the liminal threshold between the realm of the living and the dead.

After I had Lee define the word *liminal*, which he admitted was more or less a fancier word for *threshold*, I had to agree that his theory sounded pretty good.

None of which was the slightest bit reassuring when Garm bounded out of the darkness, the size of two Volkswagen Beetles stacked atop each other, his eyes like twin saucers of yellow flame, his plaintive howl turning into a slavering snarl.

And this time, he had been lying in wait for us. He launched his attack just as we were cresting the rise of the immense sand basin from which Yggdrasil II emerged. Mikill had to veer sharply to the left to evade the hellhound. I let out a yell as the dune buggy teetered on two wheels, grabbing the roll bar with one hand and clutching the loaf of bread to my chest with the other.

The dune buggy thumped back to earth as Mikill threw his weight toward me and wrenched the steering wheel. Behind us, Garm let out a full-throated howl and reversed course. Mikill gunned the engine and sand sprayed under our oversized tires, the buggy sinking.

Uh-oh.

"Mikill!" I shouted in a panic. "We're stuck!"

"Yes." The frost giant reached across me with one long arm to un-buckle my seat belt. "Throw the offering, Daisy Johanssen. As hard and far as you can. Then be prepared to take the wheel."

"*What?*" I stared at him.

"*Now*, Daisy Johanssen!" he said impatiently. "The hound is upon us!"

Doing my best Major League pitcher impression, I stood up in my seat and hurled the bread as far as I could into the night. Garm checked himself in mid-attack, the claws of his massive paws plowing furrows in the sand.

For a moment his immense head hung over me, yellow eyes flaming, strands of drool hanging from his jaws, his panting breath hot on my face.

"Good boy," I whispered, my heart in my throat. "Go get it!" Garm's ears pricked up and he bounded away after the bread.

Mikill vaulted out of the dune buggy. "Drive, Daisy Johanssen! I will push."

I scrambled into the driver's seat. Son of a bitch, wouldn't you know it was a stick shift? I worked the clutch and the gas pedal frantically, yanking at the gearshift while Mikill set his shoulder to the rear of the buggy and heaved with all his might.

Given the grinding, thunking noises I was eliciting from the dune buggy in my desperate attempts to find a gear, any gear, if Mikill hadn't been a frost giant, we probably never would have gotten unstuck. Then again, if Mikill hadn't been a frost giant, I wouldn't have been there in the first place. With a groan of protest, the dune buggy lurched free. Out in the distance, Garm was making nummy noises.

Mikill yanked open the driver's-side door. "Take your seat and be quick about it!"

I scooted back to the passenger seat. "Sorry! I never learned to drive stick."

Mikill glanced at me. "So I noticed." Clearing his throat, he put the dune buggy in gear and uttered his usual warning. "Be sure to keep your limbs inside the vehicle during the descent."

We careened down the face of the sand basin, the buggy's headlights illuminating only a fraction of the vast trunk of Yggdrasil II. I held my breath as we approached the crack in the trunk that led to the interior. Even though I knew from experience that it was more than large enough to admit the buggy, it was always hard to wrap my head around the sheer scale of the thing.

Inside, I let out a sigh of relief as we spiraled down a ramp hewn into the interior of the trunk, Mikill reducing his speed. The temperature dropped as we descended, though not as markedly as it had on previous visits. Icy mists rose from the deep well-spring far below, beneath the immense canopy of roots that the Norns tended with loving care. I gave them a wave as we reached the bottom and sped past them, but they were busy with their buckets.

Other than the Norns' tireless activity, all was quiet in Little Niflheim as we drove down the dark, mist-shrouded street to the old sawmill where Hel reigned on her throne.

I snatched off my hat, shoving it into my coat pocket, as Mikill escorted me into the sawmill. I don't know for sure if wearing a hat in the presence of a deity is a breach of protocol, but wearing a knit ski hat with PEMKOWET HIGH SCHOOL emblazoned on it didn't exactly seem like a gesture of respect.

As always, Hel was seated on her throne, a massive affair that the *duegar*, the dwarves of Little Niflheim, had wrought from old saw-blades. And as always, the vastness of her presence struck me like a physical blow, even before my eyes adjusted to the darkness well enough to see her as more than a dim, imposing figure attended by the equally dim and almost as imposing figures of several frost giants.

I knelt, bowing my head.

"Daisy Johanssen." Hel's voice tolled out of the darkness above me. "Rise, my young liaison."

I stood.

In the faint illumination emanating from patches of glowing lichen creeping along the walls of the abandoned sawmill, Hel's image re-solved itself, the fair-skinned right half of her face grave and beautiful, the black and withered left side of her face skeletal and terrible. Both of her eyes were open. The right eye, the eye on the side of life, shone with a deep, luminous compassion, as ageless as a mother's love. On the side of death, her left eye in its charred, hollow socket glowed a baleful pits-of-Mordor red.

Needless to say, it takes a certain effort of will to look Hel in the eyes, but I'd had practice.

"So, young Daisy." The shriveled claw of her left hand stirred on the arm of her throne. "What compels you to seek an audience?"

Confidence notwithstanding, my heart skipped a beat, remember-ing the sensation of that hand closing around it with an iron grip the last time I'd requested an audience. "I have some information regard-ing a matter you asked me to look into, my lady," I said.

Hel inclined her head. "You may report."

I told her what I'd learned, omitting no details. When I'd finished, Hel gazed into the distance for a small eternity, her bifurcated face expressionless. That had a tendency to happen down here in Little Niflheim, where I'm pretty sure they have an entirely different rela-tionship with time than we mortals do. I waited patiently, shivering in my down coat as the cold sank into my bones. I was glad I'd left my gloves on.

By the time Hel's gaze finally returned from the unknowable distance, I was beginning to rethink the hat. She closed her right eye and uttered a single word, her ember eye glaring. "Hades."

Behind her, the frost giants murmured.

"So it's definitely him?" I asked her.

That evoked another long, fathomless gaze, at the end of which Hel opened her luminous right eye. "I do not know." Her brow—or at least the fair right side of her forehead—furrowed in perplexity. "All that you have told me, including the name Elysian Fields, suggests the possibility. And yet I cannot surmise to what purpose the Greek Hades would wish to acquire property in Pemkowet."

I was a little confused by her reference to the *Greek* Hades. "Umm . . . is there another Hades?"

Hel made a slight, dismissive gesture with her fair right hand. "It is a manner of speech, young one."

Ever get the urge to crack inappropriate jokes in a tense situation? I bit my tongue against a perverse desire to suggest that maybe he should be called the Canadian Hades now. "Maybe it's just an investment. Like my mom said, property values are on the rise."

"Perhaps." Hel didn't sound convinced.

"Do you think—" My mouth had gone dry. I licked my lips and swallowed. "My lady, do you think he's moving in on your territory?"

"No." Another dismissive gesture. "Despite his wealth, not even the Greek Hades can maintain two demesnes. It is an impossibility. And the gods of yore no longer make war on one another." She closed her right eye, sounding almost wistful as her ember eye continued to smolder. "We are too few and too diminished. Only those of us with ties to the deep places beneath the earth endure. Our age has all but passed, and our days of battle have ended."

"A pity," Mikill said in a low rumble. "It would have been a great battle."

Hel closed her left eye and opened her right to cast a sympathetic gaze on him. "Once, my friend. No longer. We are not what we were."

Mikill bowed his head in acknowledgment. "No, my lady. We are not."

Ohh-kay, call me a bleeding-heart pacifist, but I can't say I was sorry to hear that there wasn't going to be an epic Greco-Norse Supernatural Smackdown taking place in my hometown. "What would you have me do, my lady?"

Her gaze shifted to me. "Wait. Watch. Report aught of significance that you learn. Continue to uphold my order. I trust that all is well?"

"Um . . . mostly." I told Hel about the Night Hag, which brought on the baleful gaze of her left eye.

"I did not grant license for such a creature to prey in my demesne," she said. "Certainly not one so careless of the fragile mortal mind. You have my leave to banish her in my name, Daisy Johanssen."

Good to know, since that was pretty much what I'd planned on doing when I caught the bitch. "Thank you, my lady."

"Is there aught else?" Hel inquired.

I shook my head. "No, my lady."

"You've done well, my young liaison." Opening her right eye, Hel fixed me with her double-barreled gaze, the right corner of her mouth lifting in a smile. "And I am grateful for your service."

It's impossible to describe the effect of a goddess's approval. A warm glow suffused me, driving away the chill of Little Niflheim. Beneath my down jacket and the layers betwixt and between, I wriggled my tail with pleasure.

Hel's smile—well, her half smile—broadened. "You have my leave to go."

I bowed. "Thank you."

# Fourteen

The euphoric mood that Hel's approval had instilled in me lasted for approximately twelve hours.

Long enough for Mikill to drive me home, long enough to check the messages on my phone and confirm that Cody had gotten Ken Levitt to cover for him tomorrow night so we could go bogle hunting. Long enough to fill Mogwai's bowl with kibble, climb into bed, and fall into a deep, dreamless sleep.

Long enough to report to the police station the next morning to catch up on the latest backlog of filing.

And that was pretty much where it ended. At around nine thirty in the morning, Jen called me from the Reynolds place, one of the regular year-round customers of the Cassopolis family's housecleaning service.

"Hey, Daise," Jen said in a low tone. "I thought you might want to know that Sonya Reynolds kept her son Danny home from school today after he woke up screaming bloody murder in the middle of the night."

I swore. "The Night Hag?"

"Well, apparently he said that an evil old lady sat on his chest and strangled him."

Crap. I'd really hoped the Night Hag wouldn't find another victim that easily. "Does Sonya know you're calling me?"

"Yeah," she said. "I didn't give her any details, but I told her she should talk to you. I'm just being quiet for the kid's sake."

"I'll be right over." So much for euphoria.

Don and Sonya Reynolds had a house on the hill overlooking downtown Pemkowet and the river beyond. I'm not sure if it qualified as a mansion, but it was big and fancy and new, occupying a large footprint on a lot where a much smaller, more modest residence had once stood.

I knew the Reynoldses by reputation—he was a local boy made good at an industrial design firm in Appeldoorn, where he was now some kind of managerial bigwig, and she was his college sweetheart—but I'd never met either of them in person. They were a good fifteen years older than me, the sort of up-and-coming power couple that got invited to all the big fund-raisers and social events in town.

Me, not so much.

"You must be Daisy," Sonya greeted me at the door. She was a petite, pretty brunette whose conservative Talbots mom-on-the-go wardrobe made her look older than her years. Well, that and the haggard expression she wore today. "Come in. Can I get you a cup of coffee?"

"No thanks," I said. "Is there somewhere we can talk without disturbing your son?"

"I think Jennifer's finished in the kitchen," Sonya said. "We can talk there."

The Reynoldses' kitchen was one of those spacious affairs with big windows admitting lots of wintry November sunlight, sleek aluminum appliances, and granite countertops with inlaid mosaic backsplashes. We sat at a table in the breakfast nook.

"Okay," I said. "Tell me about Danny's nightmare."

She hesitated. "If you don't mind, I'm a little confused. What, exactly, is your role here?"

Not for the first time, I wished my job as Hel's liaison came with credentials other than a rune that mortal eyes couldn't see and a magic dagger that no one else could touch. Instead, I showed her my police ID card. "I work for the department on cases where eldritch involvement is suspected."

"And you think . . ." Sonya's voice trailed off.

"I think it's possible," I said gently. "How old is your son? Has he ever had this kind of nightmare before?"

It took some coaxing, but I got the details out of her. Danny was seven years old and in second grade at Pemkowet Elementary School. He was a sensitive boy with a vivid imagination. While he was prone to nightmares, he'd never had one of this bloodcurdling intensity. After telling her about the evil old lady sitting on his chest, he'd gone nearly catatonic for the better part of an hour, finally falling asleep between his parents in their king-size bed.

"May I talk to Danny?" I asked when she'd finished. "I'd just like to ask him a question or two about the old lady."

"I'm not so sure that's a good idea," Sonya demurred. "It could traumatize him all over again."

"What kind of questions?" a boy's voice piped up from the doorway.

"Danny!" His mother actually gasped and covered her mouth. "How long have you been standing there?"

"For one minute exactly," he said with childlike dignity, clad in a pair of pajamas with cartoon characters from the *Madagascar* movies. "I wanted a glass of chocolate milk."

"Why didn't you ask Jennifer to get it for you?" Sonya scolded him.

I would have high-fived the kid if he'd said, *Because you don't pay your cleaning lady enough to serve as my nanny*—I knew what Jen went through at some of these gigs—but his response was almost as good. "Because I can get it myself," he said, turning a haunted gaze toward me. "I know how to make it." Despite the bruised shadows under his eyes, he was a cute kid, with his mom's delicate features and a shock of dark brown hair. "What did you want to ask about the old lady?"

"I don't think—"

"It's not too scary to talk about her?" I asked him.

Danny shook his head, eyes grave. "Not in the daytime."

"Right." I nodded. "Because daytime's safe." He nodded in agreement. His mother's shoulders slumped in defeat. Glancing around, I lowered my voice to a conspiratorial whisper. "I'll let you in on a secret. That old lady can't actually hurt you, not even in the nighttime. All she can do is scare you. Can you tell me what she looked like?"

He considered. "Like a Halloween witch. Like this." He bared his teeth and clawed his hands.

"Did she have a hat like a witch?" I asked.

He shook his head again. "She had hair like a witch, and red eyes, like, like . . . a really *evil* witch."

"What did she do?"

"You don't have to talk about her, Danny," Sonya murmured. "Come here." He padded over to her on bare feet and she hoisted him onto her lap, holding him as though he were a much younger child. "It's okay. It was just a bad dream."

He regarded me from the security of his mother's embrace. "It wasn't, was it?"

"What do you think?" I asked carefully.

"She sat on me." Danny's eyelids fluttered involuntarily. "I was laid on my back and she sat on me and I couldn't move. Not one inch. And then . . ." Grimacing with all the ferocity a seven-year-old could muster, he made his hands into claws again and reached out in a throttling gesture. "I think it was a dream, but I think she's real, too." He lowered his hands, his gaze skittering around the room, his voice dropping to a frightened whisper. "And I think she's coming back."

His mother glowered at me. "See what you've done!"

I ignored her. "No way, Danny," I said firmly. "We're going to make sure she's not coming back here, ever."

"Yeah?" There was a faint spark of hope in his bruised gaze.

"Yeah." I unfastened the chain of dwarf-wrought silver around my neck and unthreaded the Seal of Solomon charm Casimir had given me a few months ago, tucking it into his small hand. "This will help protect you."

Danny examined it. "Don't you need it?"

"Not anymore." Strictly speaking, that might or might not be true, since Casimir had given it to me to ward off obeah magic that was no longer a threat. "You keep it as long as you need it. Then someday, you'll give it to someone who needs it more than you do, okay? That's how it works."

He nodded. "Like if that old lady comes after some other kid?"

God, I hoped not. "Exactly. Except I plan on catching her first, because that's what I do."

His hand closed over the charm. "Okay."

I refastened the chain around my neck, now strung with only the Oak King's silver acorn token. "Good job. Why don't you make yourself that glass of chocolate milk while I have a quick word with your mom?"

"Okay." Danny slithered down from her lap obediently and padded toward the refrigerator.

Sonya Reynolds escorted me to the front door. "I really don't appreciate you encouraging him," she said in a fretful tone. "Danny's a sensitive boy and he has *such* an active imagination."

"He didn't imagine this," I said quietly. "I wish he had."

She paled. "It's real? You're sure?"

"Unfortunately, yes." I handed her one of Casimir's business cards, having grabbed a few when I was in his store the other day. "The charm might help, but I wouldn't count on it. There are other precautions you should take. Tell Casimir that I sent you and that it's about warding off another Night Hag attack."

Sonya stared at the card.

Behind her, Jen descended the master staircase, a compartmentalized carryall of cleaning supplies in one hand, a dustrag in the other. We exchanged a wordless glance of understanding.

"You know, I didn't bargain for this when I agreed to raise our children—our *child*—in Pemkowet," Sonya said, her voice shaking. She raised her stricken gaze to mine. "Don said it was different, a special place, a magical place. A *safe* place. He didn't say anything about this."

I felt bad for her.

"Pemkowet *is* special," I said to her. "But there's no such thing on earth as a truly safe place. All we can do is try our best to make it safer, and here that sometimes means unusual measures. You'll take my advice?"

She nodded, squaring her shoulders. "You'll catch the bitch who terrorized my son?"

I nodded in reply. "You're damned right I will."

# Fifteen

Shortly after sunset, Cody swung by my apartment. Since he wasn't on patrol duty, he was driving his pickup truck and wearing his usual civilian gear of faded jeans and a worn flannel shirt, topped with a fleece-lined Carhartt jacket due to the cold weather. Like I've said before, he was one of the few guys who could pull off that look without it going redneck. Although it's also possible that I imprinted on jeans and flannel at a tender age thanks to countless episodes of *Gilmore Girls*. When it came to Lorelei Gilmore's love life, I was Team Luke all the way.

Now that I thought about it, I was probably lucky Cody didn't wear a backward baseball cap. Definitely not a look that ages well.

At any rate, I climbed into his truck and we headed out to the old Presbyterian camp. I filled him in on the latest during the drive, both the Night Hag attack and the Elysian Fields business.

He let out a low whistle at Daniel Dufreyne's born-of-an-innocent revelation. "That's pretty heavy, Daise. How do you feel about it?"

"I don't know," I admitted. "Right now, I just want to catch this freakin' Night Hag before she goes after someone else."

"Agreed." Cody turned onto a narrow road that wound up and

down through densely forested dunes toward the beach. "But if you want to talk about it, I'm here for you."

"Thanks."

That brought on a brief awkward silence. We passed the WATCH FOR PEDESTRIANS street sign over which someone with an irreverent sense of humor had plastered a sticker substituting the word *Presbyterians*, and turned onto the dirt two-track that led to the camp, which was nestled deep in the woods.

It was one of those places I'd known about all my life but had never visited, mostly because, well, I was neither a Presbyterian nor a camper. "Have you been out here before?" I asked Cody.

"Sure," he said. "Caleb and I used to ride our bikes out here and explore during the off-season when we were kids. Only during the day, though. You never did?"

"Nope," I said. "Guess I wasn't the adventurous type."

"It's a great piece of property." Cody concentrated on driving down the rutted path, which had steep drop-offs on either side. "It's been some kind of Presbyterian back-to-nature camp for over a hundred years. I hate to think of it being sold for development." He spared me a quick glance. "Your hell-spawn lawyer who may or may not work for Hades isn't nosing around it, is he?"

"No," I said. "As far as I can tell, it's just properties around Little Niflheim."

"Interesting."

"That's one way of putting it," I said. "I was thinking *disturbing*."

"That, too." Cody passed a couple of maintenance buildings and pulled into the first clearing of hard-packed dirt that served as a parking lot. Illuminated by the truck's headlights, various rustic signs indicated where additional tracks led deeper into the woods toward a dismaying number of cabins and lodges scattered throughout the grounds. "Any idea where to start?"

"You tell me," I said. "You're the nose."

"Just thought you might have some insider fey intel." He cut the engine and grabbed a flashlight. "Let's have a look and a sniff."

It was seriously dark out there, the kind of pitch-blackness that you forget exists away from the pervasive streetlights of civilization. I have great night vision—the one tangible bonus of my infernal heritage—but it takes a minute or so for my eyes to adjust, especially in darkness this impenetrable. Hel's sawmill had nothing on this. Cody swung the beam of his flashlight around, sniffing the night air.

"Do you actually know what a bogle smells like?" I asked, trying to avoid looking at the beam. The faster my eyes adjusted, the better. I felt like Jodie Foster fumbling around in Buffalo Bill's basement in *The Silence of the Lambs.*

"Not exactly," he admitted. "I never noticed any traces of eldritch presence when I was out here as a kid, but then, I wasn't old enough to hunt yet. I figure I'll recognize it when I smell it." He trained his beam on the nearest track. "Let's try down there."

We followed the track for a quarter of a mile or so, trees looming out of the darkness as my eyes slowly grew accustomed to the lack of light. Every few yards, Cody paused to inhale in short, sharp bursts.

"What did the, uh, hellebore fairy say again?" he asked me. "To be honest, I'm not entirely sure what a bogle *is*, let alone where to look for one."

"You know, neither am I. I'm embarrassed to admit it, but I always thought *bogle* was just another name for hobgoblins." I was beginning to shiver in the cold and wish I'd worn the Michelin Man down coat instead of my black leather motorcycle jacket. Served me right for succumbing to vanity, I guess. "All Ellie said was that the bogle's haunt was in the woods but it prowls the grounds here."

"Let's go back," Cody said decisively. "Try another trail."

"You're the tracker," I said.

We hiked back down the stretch of frozen, rutted mud to the clearing and struck out on a different track, trudging up an incline. I could hear the steady crash and hiss of waves breaking in the distance, and guessed we were heading west toward the lakeshore. Lake Michigan *sounded* cold.

Halfway up the incline, Cody held out one arm. "Hold on," he said, nostrils working. "I smell something."

"Bogle?" I asked.

He glanced at me, phosphorescent green flashing behind his eyes. "I'm guessing yes. Smells like moldy old leather and bracken."

"Sounds like a bogle to me," I said. "But what do I know?"

Cody grinned. "Let's check it out."

The wind picked up as we climbed higher, the sound of waves growing louder. All around us, trees creaked and groaned, branches scraping against one another. It was all very *Blair Witch Project*. I wrapped my arms around myself against the cold, trying not to think about the fact that that movie scared the crap out of me.

Atop the incline, the woods gave way to another clearing surrounded by outlying buildings. In the center was a jungle gym made of plastic timbers and wide tubes that looked surprisingly sinister in the darkness. Anything could be lurking in those seemingly innocuous tubes. With my right hand, I reassured myself that *dauda-dagr* was secure in the sheath I wore belted around my waist.

Standing in the clearing, Cody turned his head this way and that, testing the air. "It's been here," he said. "A lot. But I can't tell which scent trail is fresh." He gave me an apologetic look. "I'm going to have to shift to track it, Daisy."

"A wolf's gotta do what a wolf's gotta do," I said. "Just try to remember that if you plunge into the woods, I'm going to have a hard time following you."

"I'll try." He shrugged out of his jacket and handed it to me. "Here, put this on. You might as well stay warm. Be careful—the keys to the truck are in the right-hand pocket."

"Duly noted," I said. "And thanks."

Cody's jacket retained the warmth of his body and a trace of his scent, pine and musk and Polo. Engulfed in it, I watched him undress with unself-conscious efficiency, removing his off-duty shoulder holster and his Timberland boots, folding his clothing, and setting it alongside the flashlight on a rough-hewn wooden bench the Presbyterians had thoughtfully provided in the vicinity of the jungle gym.

For a moment, his naked human body was pale and luminous in my night vision, his skin stippled with gooseflesh.

Then he shifted.

It happened in the blink of an eye, one form flowing into another. Cody's wolf form was long-limbed and rangy, with tawny gray fur and alert amber eyes filled with inhuman intelligence. I'm not saying it was animal intelligence, not exactly, but it definitely wasn't human. Cody-the-human and Cody-the-wolf overlapped, but they weren't the same being.

"You know, you're the reason we can't be together," I said to the wolf. It cocked its head at me, ears pricked. "No offense. I know it's not your fault. I'm just saying."

The wolf merely continued to regard me.

I sighed. "Go on. Go hunt the bogle."

It turned and trotted into the darkness, muzzle low to the ground.

Let me tell you, it is *not* easy to follow a hunting wolf, night vision or not. I did my best, stumbling after the Cody-wolf on the frozen ground he seemed to glide over with effortless ease, trying to ignore the ominous creaking trees as the wolf made a circuit of this particular area of the camp.

I caught up with the wolf on the verge of a dense thicket where he'd paused to stare into the darkness. I was sure he was about to go where I'd have a hell of a time following, but to my surprise, he sniffed the ground, then turned and headed back toward the camp at that deceptively speedy trot.

The wolf made a beeline for a building with a wooden sign in the front reading MESS HALL, halting in front of the door.

"You're sure about that?" I said dubiously. "Ellie said the bogle's haunt was in the woods."

Raising one paw, the wolf scratched at the door.

"Okay, okay." I turned the doorknob and found it locked. "Looks like a pretty old door," I said to the wolf. "Let's try the credit card trick."

I didn't have a credit card on me, but I had my police ID card. The Cody-wolf obligingly got out of my way, sitting on its haunches on the cold ground behind me, panting softly and watching with its tongue lolling while I slid my ID card between the door and the frame and wiggled it in an effort to jimmy the lock. I was so focused on the task at hand, I forgot to be apprehensive about what I might find on the other side.

"I think I've almost—"

With a jerk, the door swung abruptly inward.

I let out a shriek as a tall black figure with eyes like molten lava, pointy, misshapen features, and bony hands the size of catcher's mitts lunged at me, teeth bared. I flung up a shield at the same time I hurled myself backward, tripping over the wolf and falling hard on my back on the frozen earth, knocking the wind out of me.

The Cody-wolf growled and launched itself at the figure, which staggered backward into the mess hall under the impact.

Oh, crap.

I got to my hands and knees, lungs working in a futile effort to draw breath. The sounds of battle inside the mess hall didn't bode well. Concentrating, I willed my diaphragm to unspasm.

It worked well enough that I was able to get to my feet and stumble into the mess hall after the wolf and the bogle. Sure enough, they were locked in combat. The bogle was on its back, long-fingered hands with too many knuckles and sharp black nails clamped around the wolf's throat. The wolf snarled and snapped, its muzzle inches from the bogle's face.

"Cody!" I wheezed. "Down, boy! We need to *question* him!"

The wolf ignored me, continuing its efforts to lunge forward and tear out the bogle's throat.

On the floor of the mess hall, the bogle rolled its molten-lava eyes at me. "You brought a werewolf?" he said. "Dude, that's a little extreme."

"Maybe you should have thought of that before you scared the ever-loving crap out of me," I retorted. "Cody, please! Back off!"

"Hey, you're the one trying to break into my crib." The bogle's long, sticklike arms were beginning to tremble. "A little help?"

Straddling them both, I wrapped my arms around the wolf's lean torso, planted my heels, and hauled with all my strength. The wolf squirmed out of my grip with terrifying strength and agility, turning on me with a savage growl as I fell backward.

"Cody," I whispered, grabbing two fistfuls of the thick, coarse pelt around his neck. "It's me. Daisy." The wolf didn't move, continuing to growl low and deep in its throat, lips drawn back from its teeth.

"Hang on." Behind us, the bogle clambered to its feet. "I'll get a chair and bash that bad boy over the head."

"Don't you dare!" I gazed into Cody-the-wolf's eyes, trying to find a trace of Cody-the-human in there. "Cody, come on. Please?" After a long hesitation, the wolf backed off. Heaving a sigh of relief, I clambered to my feet. The wolf angled itself into a position where it could keep watch over both me and the bogle, sitting on its haunches and looking alert. I waited a moment to see if Cody intended to shift back, but apparently not. Since shifting would have left him naked, shivering, and unarmed, staying in wolf form was probably the right choice.

"Hi," I said to the bogle, peeling off my glove to flash my rune-marked left palm at him. "Daisy Johanssen. I'm here on Hel's business."

"Aw, man!" The bogle looked disappointed, or at least I thought so. It was hard to tell on features that looked like they'd been hewn out of thorny black wood. "I totally took you for a human, dude."

"Yeah, well, you just attacked Hel's liaison," I said. "I'm afraid that's going to be a big black mark in the official ledger."

"Shit." The bogle scratched at its lank, mossy hair. "No fair! Any way you can let me off with a warning?"

"Maybe," I said. "What's your name?" It hesitated. I lowered my right hand to *dauda-dagr*'s hilt, drawing it to reveal a few inches of blade. "Come on, *dude*. Don't make me threaten you with cold steel."

The bogle's glowing orange eyes widened and it backed away. "Seriously? That's harsh."

"Yeah, yeah." I withdrew another inch of blade. "Your name?"

In a reluctant tone, the bogle said a word filled with consonants and crackling sounds that sounded like a bundle of sticks breaking. "Skrrzzzt."

"Okay, um, Skrrzzzt." I sheathed *dauda-dagr*. "If you can tell me what I want to know, I'll give you a clean record."

"Fire away." The bogle shrugged. "Hey, you want a beer? I've got beer. Scored it off some high school kids who thought they'd have themselves a little party out here." He grinned, baring sharp yellow teeth. "Man, were *they* scared!"

"No thanks," I said.

"Suit yourself," the bogle said. "Mind if I indulge? My nerves are shot to hell."

"Go right ahead." I watched the bogle pad over to fish a can of beer out of a case stashed on a trestle table. "So you're just lurking out here waiting to scare people?"

"Dude, I'm a bogle." Skrrzzzt pointed to himself with one over-articulated finger. "It's what we do."

"I thought your haunt was in the woods."

"It used to be." He cracked open the can and took a long swig. "Oh, man! That's better. Anyway, yeah. I've scared the shit out of at least four generations of campers."

"I'm surprised we never got any complaints," I said.

The bogle laughed. "Are you kidding? I'm an institution in this neck of the woods. The counselors *loved* me. I kept those kids in line, man. No one ever snuck out of their cabins twice on my watch." He shook his head. "So sad to see it go. What a shame. I figure hanging around here to scare off trespassers is the least I can do."

"What are you going to do if the property's developed?" I couldn't help being curious.

"Good question." With a wary glance at the wolf, Skrrzzzt pulled a couple of folding chairs around. "Have a seat," he offered, taking one himself and crossing the ankle of one long, bony leg over the opposite knee. "I don't know. If enough families with kids move in, maybe I can strike a deal with the homeowners' association." His orange eyes brightened like lava surging in a volcano. "Hey, would you be willing to negotiate it? First contact's always a little awkward, if you know what I mean."

"I bet," I said. "Sure, we can talk about it when the time comes."

"Awesome." He took another long pull on his beer. "So what can I help you with today?"

I sat opposite him. "Do you know anything about a Night Hag that's been preying on people?"

The bogle shook his head. "Not in Pemkowet. I knew a few in ye olde country back in the day."

"Well, there's one here now," I said. "And she's definitely *not* welcome. Can you tell me how to catch her?"

"Sure," he said obligingly. "Easy-peasy. You just have to bind her with a strand of her own hair. If you do, she has to obey you."

"Son of a bitch!" Call me gobsmacked. "Are you kidding me?" I said. "*Hair?* Stacey Brooks was *right?*"

"Huh?"

"Never mind." I waved one hand. "Just thinking out loud. So, um, how do I go about finding the Night Hag and getting a strand of her hair?"

"Yeah, that's the tricky part." Skrrzzzt grimaced and downed the last of his beer, crumpling the can in one bony hand. "See, you don't find a Night Hag. She finds you. I mean, the bit about the hair is pretty straightforward—all you have to do is pluck a strand and knot it around her neck. But she has to enter your nightmare in order for you to do it."

"There's no other way?" I asked.

"Nope."

Thinking, I touched the silver acorn whistle nestled beneath my two layers of coats. Maybe it was time to put the token to use. "But the Oak King could command her as a member of the fey, right?"

"Eh, not really." The bogle pursed his leathery black lips. "See, we're pretty informal in these parts, but technically speaking, we're members of different courts."

"Courts?" I echoed.

"I know! It sounds so archaic, right?" Skrrzzzt glanced around before leaning forward. "Truth be told, I consider myself a libertarian," he said in a confidential tone. "But when it comes down to brass tacks, bogles and Night Hags are members of the Unseelie Court and his majesty only presides over members of the Seelie Court."

I sighed. "So the Oak King is a no-go."

The bogle settled back in his chair, jiggling the long-toed, thorny foot crossed over his knee. "'Fraid so."

"Okay," I said. "So you're basically saying I have to lure the Night Hag into my dreams to catch her?"

He looked apologetic. "Pretty much."

"Any suggestions?" I asked.

"Well, they're summoned by nightmares, especially really intense ones. I could try scaring you again," he said helpfully. "Do you think it might do the trick?"

I smiled at him. "I'm sure it would, but not if I'm expecting it. Thanks, Skrrzzzt. You've been a big help."

The bogle shrugged. "No problem, mamacita. So we're cool? It's all good in the hood?"

"Yep." I stood. "We're cool." I glanced at the wolf. "Are you ready to go, partner?" The wolf stood. "I'll take that as a yes."

I have to admit, I was feeling very House Stark of Winterfell as I departed into the cold darkness, Cody trotting beside me like my own personal direwolf. At least until we got back to the bench beside the jungle gym where Cody had stashed his gear and he shifted back to human form and began scrambling into his clothes, his teeth chattering.

"So did you get all that?" I asked him. He grunted in response, fumbling with the buttons on his flannel shirt. I took off my gloves. "Here, let me help." I knew from personal experience that Cody's manual dexterity wasn't at its best when he was still a little wolfy.

"I can do it, Daise," Cody said in a rasping voice, turning away from me.

"Fine." I shoved my hands into the pockets of his Carhartt jacket. "Oops."

"What?" He gave me a sidelong glance.

"No car keys," I said. "They must have fallen out when I tripped over you. Or possibly when I was doing my damnedest to wrestle you off the bogle."

"Sorry." To his credit, Cody did look abashed. He sat down on the bench to put on his socks and boots. "Once instinct kicks in, it's almost impossible to turn it off. You took a big risk trying to pull me off that thing."

I shrugged. "You wouldn't hurt me. Not like that, anyway. I trust you. I even trust your wolf."

He laced his boots. "You shouldn't."

"Well, I do." I slid his jacket from my shoulders, laying it on the bench beside him. "Here. I'll go get the keys."

I backtracked to the mess hall, where Skrrzzzt was leaning against the doorjamb in a jaunty pose, the keys to Cody's truck dangling from one long, knobby finger. "Looking for these, mamacita?"

"Yeah." I took the keys. "Thanks."

"Sure." The bogle peered into the darkness, then lowered his voice. "Hey, so are you and the werewolf an item or what?"

I smiled wryly. "Unfortunately, or what."

"Yeah, I thought I picked up on a little somethin' somethin' there." Skrrzzzt nodded in sympathy. "You want me to jack his truck? Maybe a little alone time in the woods at night will get his romantic juices flowing. It always worked for the campers," he added. "Right up until the point where I scared the bejeezus out of them."

"I appreciate the offer," I said. "But his juices are fine. It's more of a noncompatible-species issue."

"Bummer."

"Yeah." There was something unexpectedly touching about being on the receiving end of his sympathy. Who knew a bogle would be so much easier to talk to than, say, a naiad or a hellebore fairy? Though I suppose it helped that his vocabulary appeared to come straight out of the mouths of the latest generation or two of campers rather than some Shakespearean Insult Generator. "Thanks again, Skrrzzzt."

He offered me a huge, gnarly-looking fist. "Gimme some dap."

"You got it, son." That was something I'd heard Jen's twelve-year-old kid brother and his friends say to each other. I bumped my fist against Skrrzzzt's. It felt like knocking on a knot of wood. "Take care."

The bogle flashed me a hideous grin. "I always do, mamacita."

# Sixteen

"So let me make sure I've got this straight." Behind the steering wheel, Cody glanced at me. "All you need is a strand of the Night Hag's hair to bind her."

"Right," I said.

"Except the only way to get it is to lure her into a nightmare."

"Yep."

Both of us thought about that in silence for a moment. "We might have to consider using someone she's already targeted as bait," Cody said reluctantly. "Get them to remove the protective charms."

"Not the Reynolds kid," I said. "He's only seven. Remember, the Night Hag is only corporeal to her victims. It's not like we can use one to summon her and then take charge. Even if his parents would go for it, which they wouldn't, you can't ask a seven-year-old to try to bind a fucking *nightmare.*"

"No." Cody drummed his fingers on the steering wheel. "But that only leaves Scott Evans."

"Scott Evans throttled his wife and nearly blew his brains out the last time the Night Hag attacked him," I pointed out. "Do we really want to take a chance on a repeat performance?"

Cody blew out his breath in a sigh. "We're screwed, aren't we?"

"Not necessarily," I said. "I mean, there are things you can do to induce nightmares, right? Watch scary movies before bedtime?"

He spared me another glance. "You want to take her down yourself, don't you?"

"Look, I'm not thrilled by the prospect, but I sure as hell don't want any innocent victims to suffer further damage," I said. "This damn Night Hag is here without permission and she's preying on fragile mortals in Hel's territory. That makes her *my* responsibility."

One corner of Cody's mouth quirked in a smile. "I kind of like it when you get all territorial, Pixy Stix."

"And I kind of like it when you tease me," I murmured. "Which is why I wish you wouldn't."

"Daise—"

I looked at him. "Don't."

"Okay." He was silent for a moment. "So what's your plan? Go home and watch a scary movie, eat a big sandwich before bed?"

"Basically, yeah," I admitted. "Only . . . crap, I forgot about Mrs. Browne."

"From the bakery?"

"She's a brownie," I reminded him. "Talk about territorial . . . I don't think a Night Hag would dare attack someone in a building that's been claimed and protected by a brownie. And Mrs. Browne comes in every night to bake."

"Can't you just ask her to take the night off?" Cody asked.

I shook my head. "You can't ask a brownie for anything. They bail if you do. And if Mrs. Browne's bakery shut down—"

"—Amanda Brooks would have a cow," he finished. "Hell, she wouldn't be the only one. You'd probably be run out of town if you were responsible for shutting down Mrs. Browne's Olde World Bakery, Daise."

"No kidding," I said. "I'd hate to lose her, too. Most of the time I'm grateful to know she's there in the wee hours."

"So do it at my place," Cody said without looking at me.

"Werewolves aren't territorial?" I said with a lightness I didn't feel. "I'm not buying it."

"Only when it comes to other clans." He gave me a quick glance. "Look, Daisy, I'd actually feel a lot better about it if you did. I'd do it myself if I could, but if something attacked me in my sleep . . ." He let the sentence trail off.

"You'd shift?" I asked.

Cody nodded.

"Yeah, it would be pretty hard to pluck a strand of someone's hair with paws," I agreed. "And I doubt a Night Hag would attack a werewolf in the first place. I'm guessing they just prey on humans."

"What makes you so sure she'd attack *you*?" he asked.

"I'm not," I said. "I'm just hoping I'm human enough to fool her, what with not having claimed my birthright and all."

Cody pulled into the alley alongside my apartment building and parked. "So are we going to do this or not?"

It felt awfully sudden, and the thought of spending the night at Cody's gave me butterflies in the pit of my stomach, and not in a good way. "I don't know," I said. "Do you have any scary movies on hand?"

"My cousin Joe's got the whole *Saw* franchise on DVD," he said. "I'm sure we can borrow it."

Oh, gah. "That would fit the bill."

"So?"

"Can we get hoagies from the Sidecar?" I asked.

Cody gave me a smile filled with rueful affection. "Yeah, Daise. We can get hoagies."

My tail twitched. "Okay, let's do it."

To make a long story short, it didn't work. It wasn't for lack of trying, that's for sure. After I grabbed an overnight bag from my apartment and filled Mogwai's bowl, we picked up a couple of hoagies from the Sidecar, then swung by Cody's cousin's place to borrow the first two *Saw* movies, which we watched in Cody's den, sitting a self-conscious distance apart on his couch. Let me say upfront that I'm not a fan, but if anything was going to give me nightmares, three solid hours of torture porn on top of a big, greasy hoagie ought to have done it.

It didn't.

Between the bogle hunt, the heavy food, the torture porn, and my conflicted emotions, I was so worn out that by the time I went to bed, I slept solidly through the night in sheets that smelled like laundry detergent and a lingering trace of Cody's scent. He'd insisted I take the bedroom while he crashed on the couch. It wasn't the soundest night's sleep I'd ever had—my dreams were restless and uneasy and filled with disturbing images, but I couldn't call them nightmares, and beneath them, I was aware of Cody's reassuring presence in the next room.

And once again, I awoke to a phone call.

Fumbling on Cody's nightstand, I found my phone and answered, croaking a sleepy "Hello" into my phone.

"Daisy?" It was Sandra Sweddon, who was a friend of my mom's, a volunteer in the community, and a member of the local coven. "Sorry to disturb you so early, honey, but I'm over at the Open Hearth Center." She lowered her voice. "Sinclair told us about the, um, situation. I'm afraid there may have another incident. A serious one."

A jolt of adrenaline brought me more fully awake. "Another Night Hag attack?"

"I can't be sure," she said. "Old Mrs. Claussen passed last night. Mind you, she was very sick. But I heard the nurse who was on duty last night telling another nurse about hearing Mrs. Claussen cry out in the middle of the night, before she passed. She was saying 'Get her off me, get her off me.'"

I swore. "Is the night nurse still there?"

"No, she's gone home."

"What about Mrs. Claussen's, um, remains?" I asked. "Did the M.E. take her?"

"No, she's here," Sandra said. "They're just waiting for Doc Howard to come by and sign the death certificate. She had advanced liver cancer, Daisy, so they're not considering it a suspicious death. But I thought you'd want to know."

"Thank you," I said. "I'll be there as soon as I can."

I wrapped myself in a big plaid bathrobe hanging from a hook on Cody's bedroom door and went into the living room to wake him. The call hadn't awakened him and he was still sprawled on the couch, sound asleep, a crocheted blanket tangled around his limbs. I allowed myself a wistful moment to gaze at him before calling his name.

He woke with a start, jerking upright and baring his teeth. His face softened at the sight of me. "Daise. No luck?"

"Bad luck," I said. "It sounds like she struck somewhere else last night. And this time it was fatal."

He ran his hands over his face and through his sleep-disheveled hair. "Tell me."

I filled him in on the details.

"Yeah, that doesn't sound good," he agreed. "I'll call the chief and ask him to meet us there. We'll see what the magic watch has to say."

Beneath Cody's plaid bathrobe, my tail lashed with pent-up fury. "Goddammit! I really wanted to catch her."

"I know." Standing, Cody laid his hands on my shoulders. "It's not your fault, Daisy. You did everything you could. But you can't force your subconscious to cooperate."

"I'm not going to stop trying," I informed him.

He gave me a faint, sleepy smile. "I never imagined you would. Nice bathrobe, by the way."

"Thanks." I fought the sudden urge to reach up one hand and caress the bronze stubble on his cheek. "Let's get moving."

I'd been to the Open Hearth assisted-living facility a few times as a teenager, tagging along when my mom helped Mrs. Sweddon out with her volunteer work, planning activities for the residents. One year Mom even sewed costumes for a pet parade that the seniors talked about for months. As Cody and I pulled into the parking lot, I felt ashamed that I hadn't been back since.

It was a nice enough facility as such things go—or at least as far as I knew, since it was the only one I'd ever visited. There were gardens surrounding it and a three-season room in the rear of the complex looked out into woodlands where the staff hung bird feeders. There were plenty of windows to admit a good amount of natural light, and all the residents had their own cozy little rooms, which were decorated with paintings donated by Pemkowet High's most promising art students.

Still, it was a place where people came to spend their final days, and there was no getting around that knowledge.

Sandra Sweddon greeted us at the door. "This is Nurse Luisa," she said, introducing us to a pleasant-looking woman in pink scrubs and a name tag that read LUISA MARTINEZ. "I'm sure she can answer any questions you have."

Nurse Luisa shook our hands, her expression slightly bewildered. "I'm afraid I don't quite understand."

"That's okay," I assured her. "We just have a few quick questions. Can we speak privately?"

"Of course."

"Do you want to take this, Daisy?" Cody asked me. "I'll stay here and wait for the chief."

"The chief of police?" Nurse Luisa paled a little. "Is that necessary? I'd really rather not alarm the residents."

"It's just a courtesy visit, ma'am," Cody said. "Chief Bryant likes to pay his respects to the deceased."

Nurse Luisa gave him a look that said *News to me*, but she escorted me to an office and closed the door behind us. "Can I ask what this is all about, Ms. Johanssen?"

"It may be nothing," I said. "If you don't mind, I'd like to wait until the chief arrives to discuss it. Can you tell me how Mrs. Claussen died?"

"Well, Dr. Howard will make the final call after he examines her, but she appears to have suffered an acute myocardial infarction," she said. "A heart attack."

I fished a notepad out of my messenger bag. "Is that unusual for someone in her condition?"

The nurse shook her head. "She had a mild coronary incident earlier in the year," she said. "Normally I'd say it was a blessing in disguise."

I jotted down "previous heart attack," mostly just because taking notes made me look more professional. "Why?"

"Because in Mrs. Claussen's case, the alternative was a slow, protracted death from liver failure," she said.

"So why is it that you're reluctant to say a sudden death was a blessing this time?" I inquired.

Nurse Luisa pressed her lips together. "The look on her face."

"Which was?"

"Terrified," she said briefly. "That and what Connie said."

"Connie's the nurse who was on duty last night?" I asked. She nodded. "What's her last name?"

"Adams."

I wrote that down. "And what did she say to you about Mrs. Claussen?"

"Connie said she was passing her room at around four o'clock in the morning, and she heard Mrs. Claussen saying, 'Get her off me, get her off me.'"

"Did she investigate at the time?" I asked.

"No," Nurse Luisa said. "Not until the morning. You must understand, it's not uncommon for residents to have nightmares or talk in their sleep. Unless there's a medical issue, we try to respect their privacy. Connie waited a moment, and when she heard nothing further, returned to the office."

"Was Mrs. Claussen prone to nightmares?"

She hesitated. "She'd had incidents in the past, yes. Lately it was hard to say. The medication she was on to manage her pain kept her fairly heavily sedated, but some patients do report nightmares as a side effect of opiate drugs."

"So she could have been having nightmares," I said. "But she was too sedated to complain about them?"

"Or possibly to remember them," Nurse Luisa agreed. "Or to distinguish between reality and a bad dream."

An assistant knocked on the door to let us know that Chief Bryant had arrived. I closed my notepad and put it away. "Thank you. If you don't mind, we'd like to take a look at the body."

In the foyer, the chief greeted me with a cordial nod. Nurse Luisa led us through the sunlit common room, where seniors looked up from their backgammon games and jigsaw puzzles—which, ew, reminded me of creepy Jigsaw from the movies last night—to speculate about our presence in loud whispers, to the residence halls, pausing outside room 14. It had a plastic nameplate with IRMA CLAUSSEN on it. The nurse swiped her keycard and opened the door.

Cody and I followed the chief inside. It was a modest room without a lot of personal effects—a few photographs atop a low dresser, a potted ficus tree in the corner. Mrs. Claussen's body lay atop the bed, loosely wrapped in a clean white sheet that had been placed beneath her. Striding over to the bed, Chief Bryant gently folded the sheet back from her face.

"We closed her eyes," Nurse Luisa said behind us, a slight tremor in her voice. "We did our best. We always do."

I made myself look.

Last night, I'd watched a number of actors and actresses meet their demise in a variety of sadistic and gory scenarios. Irma Claussen's death was infinitely more real and infinitely more affecting. She looked old and shrunken beneath the sheet, her fragile, liver-spotted skin tinged with yellow. At a glance, it wasn't obvious that she'd died in a state of terror. The Open Hearth nursing staff had done a good job of closing her eyes, of trying to coax the muscles of her face to soften from a rictus of terror.

Still, the impression lingered. It was there beneath her sunken eyelids, there in the rigid muscles that bracketed her mouth and corded her throat, there in the swollen, crabbed hands raised in a defensive posture.

She had died afraid. Very, very afraid.

Chief Bryant fished the dwarf-wrought watch out of his pocket and held it dangling over Irma Claussen's body. The watch began to rotate on the end of its chain, twirling like a gyroscope, the hands on its face spinning backward.

Night Hag.

The fucking *Night Hag* had scared this poor woman to death. A wave of helpless rage burst over me. Overhead, some old ducts creaked ominously in protest.

"Daisy," Cody said in quiet warning.

The nurse glanced back and forth among the three of us. "What is it?"

I gritted my teeth, trying unsuccessfully to wrestle my anger under control, to tie it up in a box to be opened later. "Cody, can you fill her in and tell her what she needs to do?" I said to him. "I think I need to step outside for a moment."

He nodded. "You've got it."

"I'll come with you," Chief Bryant said. "I want a quick update on where we are with this thing." He laid one meaty palm briefly on Irma Claussen's brow, murmuring, "Godspeed you, ma'am."

Outside in the parking lot, the cold air helped cool my temper. The chief listened impassively in his warm, fleece-lined uniform jacket while I told him the latest. "Why can't Hel just banish the bitch herself?" he asked when I'd finished. "She's a goddamn goddess, isn't she?"

"Yeah," I said. "But it doesn't work that way. See, Hel only has complete authority over her own subjects in Little Niflheim. Here, aboveground, she has to rely on an agent of her authority to maintain her order."

"You," he said.

"Me," I agreed. "I can banish the damn thing in her name, sir." Tears of frustration stung my eyes. "I just have to *catch* it!"

"All right, all right." The chief patted my arm in an awkward gesture of affection. "Keep it together, Daisy. This thing's turned serious, and it's going to be hard to keep a lid on it after this morning. I need you to find this Night Hag and fast. Do whatever you need to do. All right?"

I took a deep breath. "All right."

"Believe me, I don't like this any better than you do." In the wintry November light, Chief Bryant looked old and tired, deep lines etched into his heavy features. "As far as I'm concerned, we're talking about manslaughter here. A woman's been killed in *my* town, on *my* watch, and there's not a damn thing I can do about it. So I'm counting on you, Daisy."

"I understand."

"I know you do." The chief gave me one last pat. "Good girl. Keep me updated."

"Will do." I watched him lumber toward his squad car, wishing I had the faintest idea what to do next.

# Seventeen

I was still standing in the parking lot, watching the chief's taillights dwindle and trying to collect my thoughts, when a British motorcycle that looked like it belonged in a period piece about World War II sputtered into the entrance.

"Hey there, Miss Daisy." Pulling up to the curb outside the Open Hearth Center, Cooper knocked the kickstand into place with the heel of his boot and shoved a pair of vintage touring goggles onto his forehead. "Fancy meeting you here."

"No kidding," I said. "What are *you* doing here?"

"Lovely to see you, too," he said mildly, dismounting from the bike. "With the big man out of town, I'm filling in on Good Sam duty."

"Good Sam duty?" I echoed.

"Oh, aye, himself didn't tell you?" Cooper's angelic blue eyes were shrewd in his thin face. "Community outreach and the like." He nodded at the facility. "There's been a death here, don'tcha know? Got the call a little while ago. I'm here to console the bereaved and offer solace to those in need."

I eyed him uncertainly, trying to determine whether or not he was serious. "Someone from the center called you?"

"Your doubt wounds me, m'lady." Cooper rubbed his hands, clad in fingerless black leather gloves, together briskly. "It cuts me to the quick. Yes, someone did. But I confess, I can take no credit for the Good Sam program. That was the big man's doing." He assessed me, his pupils doing a quick wax-and-wane. "May I ask why anger hangs about you like a thundercloud?"

I told him.

"Ah." He nodded. "Nasty creatures, those."

"Any suggestions?" I inquired.

Considering my question, Cooper rubbed his hands together again and blew on his fingertips. "As I recall, you've been hexed before, Miss Daisy. If you're in need of a nightmare fit to make you soil your bedsheets and summon a Night Hag, why not ask that witchy lad with whom you were keeping company to oblige? Him and his coven?"

A spark of hope kindled inside me. "They can do that?"

He shrugged his narrow shoulders. "They ought do."

If he'd been anyone else, I would have hugged him. "Thanks, Cooper. That's a great idea."

"So it is." We gazed at each other across the gulf that divided us. Cooper cleared his throat. "I ought to be venturing within to offer my services. Are the residents greatly distraught at the loss of one of their own?"

"Honestly, I'm not sure," I said. "I think they may be more excited about the fact that Chief Bryant paid a call."

"It was ever thus," he said in a philosophical tone. "Let's go see if I can be of use, shall we?"

Inside the Open Hearth Center, Cooper was a big hit. The residents might not have been unduly grieved by the loss of Irma Claussen—I had the impression that most of them, being unaware that she died in fear, regarded her sudden passing as a blessing—but they had their share of pain and suffering, sorrow and regret.

And, too, there was the boredom of their circumscribed existence, dull routines alleviated by visits from friends and loved ones, visits that were always too short and too seldom. I'm not saying the staff and volunteers didn't do a great job of planning activities—from what I could see, they did—but those couldn't compete with a visit from a real live member of the Outcast, a youthful-looking lad who was willing to listen to the trials and tribulations of old age and illness, to flirt with the ladies and banter with the gentlemen, his eyes glittering in his too-pale face as he siphoned off a measure of whatever negative emotions afflicted them.

Cody, of course, didn't like it. "I wouldn't trust him with *my* grandparents," he grumbled.

"No one's asking you to," I observed.

"Mr. Ludovic expressed every confidence in Mr. Cooper." Nurse Luisa watched him interact with the residents. "I'd say it appears justified, wouldn't you?"

"Were you the one who called him?" I asked.

She nodded. "Under Mr. Ludovic's direction, the assistance of the Outcast has been invaluable here."

"He's feeding on mortals without their permission," Cody said quietly. "That's against the rules."

The nurse gave him a sharp look. "You used the Outcast for crowd control during the recent hauntings, didn't you, officer?"

"That was a matter of public safety," he said. "It was for the common good."

Nurse Luisa gestured at the residents. "And we make decisions regarding their care and the common good of the community here at Open Hearth on a daily basis. How many of them do you think are truly capable of giving informed consent? Half the time, someone else holds their power of attorney." She shook her head. "As far as I'm concerned, if one of the Outcast can give them a measure of comfort and gladness above and beyond what modern medicine allows, they're doing God's work whether the Lord acknowledges it or not." She crossed herself. "And if it brings those poor, doomed souls solace to know they're doing good work in this world, all the better."

"Amen," I said, ignoring Cody's arched eyebrow. "Ms. Martinez, did you send someone to the Sisters of Selene to pick up protective charms?"

"Yes, one of the nursing assistants." She shuddered. "Poor Mrs.

Claussen. Do you suppose there's anything Mr. Cooper could do for her departed soul?"

"You know, I have no idea." I called Cooper over to ask him.

Cooper heard me out, rocking back and forth on the heels of his boots, hands in the pockets of his jeans. "I'm afraid not," he said in a gentle voice, directing his comments to Nurse Luisa. "She's well beyond the likes of me. Gone off to meet Saint Peter at the pearly gates, I hope, or whatever fate she's earned in this life. I envy her the chance." His mask of boyish charm slipped, revealing something old and stark and weary beneath it. "Was she a good woman?"

She hesitated. "I can't really say. She was a lonely woman."

"Well, whatever she suffered in this mortal coil, it's all behind her," he said, his usual insouciance returning. "Including the Night Hag."

"Hey, Johnny boy!" one of the residents, a dashing older gentleman, called from the common room. "Don't forget, you promised us a rousing rendition of 'The Wild Rover' before you go!"

Cooper glanced over his shoulder. "So I did, Mr. Fergus. Never fear, I've not forgotten."

"Johnny boy?" I said.

"All these months and you've never asked after my Christian name?" Cooper teased me. "For shame, Daisy Johanssen."

"I guess I always thought of you as a one-name phenomenon," I said. "Like Bono or Sting."

"Ah, well, that's all right, then," he said.

"John Cooper," Cody said. "Funny, that sounds more English than Irish."

There are certain things you don't say to a two-hundred-year-old Irish ghoul who was hanged to death fighting in a rebellion. Cooper went very still, his pupils contracting to pinpoints. Cody faced him down, his upper lip curling. I reached for my mental shield, although I didn't kindle it.

"Cut it out, guys," I said. "Now's not the time."

"Well, and I'm sorry I'm not a MacGillicuddy or an O'Sullivan," Cooper said in a terse tone. "But I assure you, there've been Coopers in Ireland since the invention of the barrel, boyo."

"My apologies." Cody's apology sounded as sincere as . . . well, let's just say it totally didn't. "Just keep your cool."

"Oh, I will." Cooper cocked his head at me. "So I hear you and the big man are to have a proper date when he returns, Miss Daisy. I imagine he's looking forward to it."

I couldn't blame him for baiting Cody in turn, but I wasn't about to take part in it. "You'd better get back to the residents, Cooper," I said. "You don't want to leave Mr. Fergus hanging."

He gave me a little salute. "Good luck to you."

I'd planned to ask Sandra Sweddon about the possibilities of a nightmare hex, but she'd already left, probably on to her next volunteer gig. Cody and I took our own leave of the Open Hearth Center to the accompaniment of half a dozen residents clapping and stomping in enthusiastic counterpoint as Cooper sang in a surprisingly strong tenor that it was no, nay, never no more that he'd play the wild rover.

"Sorry about that." Cody's apology to me sounded marginally more sincere. "You're right. It was inappropriate."

"Cooper was a big help to us when we were questioning suspects about the Tall Man's remains," I reminded him.

The telltale muscle in his jaw twitched. "That was before he lost control and turned a couple of tourists into emotionless zombies."

"Stefan promised that they'd make a complete recovery," I said. "And we'll never know how much worse it would have been if the Outcast *hadn't* been there when the crowd panicked. You just said yourself that it was for the common good."

"Yeah, right up until the point where Cooper started ravening." He sighed. "I don't want to fight about this, Daise. I'm just frustrated. We're at a dead end here and I don't know what to do."

"Cooper—"

Cody raised his voice. "I don't want to talk about Cooper!"

"*Cooper* had a suggestion," I said, ignoring his objection. "He thought Sinclair and the coven ought to be able to create some sort of hex that would give me nightmares. I believe 'a nightmare fit to make me soil the bed and summon a Night Hag' was the way he put it," I added.

"Huh." He rubbed his chin. "Do you think they're capable of it?"

"I don't know," I said. "But Sinclair's sister, Emmy, put a hex on me that damn near made me think I was dying. It's worth a try."

Cody opened the passenger door of his pickup truck for me. "Ask him. We've got nothing else."

He drove me home and pulled into the alley. It seemed like a lot longer ago than just last night that I'd run upstairs to grab my overnight bag, hopeful that a few hours' worth of gruesome movies and a big hoagie would provoke a nightmare intense enough to bring the Night Hag to my bedside.

Now, it seemed more than a little naive. As grisly and sadistic as the *Saw* movies were, they were just movies. They weren't real. Watching a scary movie was nothing to facing down the prospect of a long, protracted death from liver failure like Irma Claussen, or reliving whatever trauma Scott Evans had experienced in combat in Iraq. I didn't know what haunted Danny Reynolds's dreams, but nighttime could be filled with outsize terrors for any child, real or imagined. In fact, I'd met one.

I found myself wishing I'd taken the bogle up on his offer of a beer. In the cold light of day, with a woman dead of terror, the memory of yesterday evening's bogle hunt seemed downright idyllic.

"You'll let me know about the hex?" Cody said.

I nodded. "Are you on duty tonight?"

"Yeah, but don't worry about it," he said. "I'll be available if you need me. As of today, the Night Hag's our top priority."

"Okay." I gathered my overnight bag and hesitated. "How are we full moon–wise?"

"Fine," Cody said. "We've got at least a week before I'm out of commission."

"Good." I reached for the car door handle.

"Daise?"

"Yeah?"

A hint of phosphorescent green shimmered behind Cody's eyes. "Did you really agree to a date with Ludovic?"

"Maybe." I met his gaze and held it. "How are plans for the great Pemkowet winter werewolf mixer coming along?"

"Oh, fuck the mixer!" he said. "It's just—"

"I know," I said. "Cody, we keep going around and around, but nothing changes, does it?"

"No," he murmured.

"Okay, well, yes, I agreed to . . . something . . . with Stefan," I said. "I don't even know what to call it, and frankly, I don't know what the hell he's doing in Poland or when he's coming back. But there *is* going to be a mixer, right?"

"Yeah." Cody looked away. "After the holidays. The second weekend in January." He looked back at me. "Actually, I'm supposed to invite you."

"To the *mixer*?"

"Just the initial meeting. Um, it's customary for a representative of the presiding deity of the demesne to make the acquaintance of potential new clan members." He read my expression. "Daisy, this was *not* my idea. The elders are insisting we need to follow the proper protocol."

"Did it occur to them that under the circumstances, that might be a wee bit insensitive?" I inquired.

"I raised that point," he said. "It didn't trump protocol."

"Great," I said. "Tell them I'll think about it. Right now, I've got bigger things on my mind. If we don't catch this Night Hag, I might not have to worry about carrying out any future responsibilities as Hel's liaison."

"It's not your fault, Daise," Cody said. "You're doing everything you possibly can."

I opened the car door. "Tell that to poor old Mrs. Claussen."

# Eighteen

After a quick shower and a bowl of cereal, I tried calling Sinclair. He didn't pick up, but I knew he was working at the nursery, which was a bonus since his boss, Warren Rodgers, was another member of the coven. I sent Sinclair a quick text to let him know I'd be stopping by before heading back out.

The Green Man Nursery was in the countryside a few miles north of town. It occupied a lot of acreage and there were several greenhouses. I wasn't sure where to start looking for Sinclair and Warren—you wouldn't think there was much to do in a plant nursery at this time of year, but according to Sinclair, there was a lot of prep work involved in getting the larger trees and shrubs ready to weather the long winter—but I checked my phone after pulling into the gravel drive and saw Sinclair had texted me back to say that he and Warren were working in the barn.

It was a picturesque old barn that had been lovingly restored and painted a bright fire-engine red, with a big sign advertising the nursery above the barn doors. As I crunched my way over the gravel, Sinclair slid the door open to greet me, a somber expression on his face. "Hey, Daise."

"I take it you heard," I said.

"Unfortunately, yeah." He opened the door wider. "Come on in. We're just getting ready for the farmers' market tomorrow."

Inside, it smelled like Christmas, the scent of freshly cut evergreen boughs hanging pungent in the air. Over on one worktable, Warren Rodgers was painstakingly pruning miniature potted firs into the shape of tabletop Christmas trees. Two additional tables were heaped high with boughs of white pine, juniper and fir, holly, pinecones, and spools of red and gold ribbon.

"Hey, Mr. Rodgers," I said. "It smells wonderful in here." He glanced up to give me a taciturn nod.

"Do you mind if I keep working while we talk?" Sinclair asked. "We've got a lot to do."

"Go right ahead." I took a seat on an available stool, watching as Sinclair selected pieces of evergreen, trimmed them deftly with a pair of shears, and affixed them to a circular form with florists' wire. As a Christmas wreath took shape beneath his hands, a look of serenity settled over his features. Working with plants, even cut plants, agreed with Sinclair. I almost hated to disturb him.

When I didn't say anything, Sinclair stole a quick glance at me. "So, no luck finding that bogle?"

"No," I said. "We found the bogle."

"And?"

"The bogle was a big help." I watched him wire a pinecone in place. "As a matter of fact, you can tell Stacey that she was right. She solved the Sphinx's riddle."

He looked up again in surprise. "No shit?"

"No shit," I said. "If I can bind the Night Hag with a strand of her own hair, she'll be compelled to obey me. The problem is, I need to lure her into a nightmare to do it, which is why I'm here to ask if you can hex me."

Sinclair's deft hands went still. "Daisy."

Over at the adjacent worktable, Warren Rodgers set down his pruning shears and straightened.

"I need a nightmare," I said to them. "Not just a bad dream, but a bona fide *nightmare*. I tried to do it myself with scary movies and greasy food, but I don't think that can compete with her victims' reality."

"I imagine you're right about that," Warren said.

I looked back and forth between them. Neither of them looked happy about my request. Not that I'd expected happy, but I'd expected a little more responsiveness. "So can you help?"

"I'm an herbalist." Warren's tone was brusque. "I don't know anything about that kind of magic."

Sinclair was silent.

"You do, don't you?" I said to him. "Sinclair, you know I wouldn't ask if it wasn't important."

"I know you wouldn't." He busied himself with a sprig of holly. "But that's dark obeah you're talking about, and I swore I'd never go down that path. Especially after what happened with my mother and sister."

"I'm asking for a good cause," I said. "Doesn't that count for something?"

"No one ever set out on the dark path thinking the end didn't justify the means, Daisy." Sinclair laced the holly in place, snipping the wire. "No one."

My tail stirred. "A woman died last night, Sinclair. She died alone in a state of stark terror. She cried out for help, but no one came, because they thought she was just having a bad dream. If I can't stop this Night Hag, there may be others. And as far as I can tell, if you won't help me, I *can't* stop her. Do you want that on your conscience?"

He shuddered, his beaded dreadlocks rattling softly. "That's not fair."

"You're right," I said. "It's not. But it's true."

Sinclair glanced at Warren Rodgers, who returned his gaze impassively and said, "It's your call, son."

"I'll need a few days," Sinclair said after another long pause. "It's not something I can prepare on short notice. And I need to consult with Casimir. I suspect he's walked down a gray path or two in his time."

"Thank you," I said to him. "Um . . . how many days are we talking about?"

"Three, more or less," he said. "If I push it, I can have it ready for you the night after tomorrow."

"I appreciate it," I said. "Truly."

Sinclair gave me a look that was hard to read. "I'll need something from you, too, Daisy. I'll need to know your deepest, darkest fear." He smiled without humor when I hesitated. "This kind of thing doesn't come without a price, you know. A *real* practitioner of the dark path would trick you into revealing it, or better yet, get one of your loved ones to inadvertently betray you."

"Okay." I squared my shoulders. "Here and now?"

He shook his head. "I've got to prepare the charm first. Can you be at my place around eleven o'clock tonight?"

"Of course," I said.

Warren made a shooing gesture at Sinclair. "Go on, get out of here. I can handle this on my own."

"You're sure?"

"I've done it before, haven't I?" he said wryly. "There's time yet. If we run short, folks will just have to wait until after Thanksgiving to buy their wreaths and swag. You need anything?"

"I could use some henbane," Sinclair said.

"You know where the herbiary is," Warren said. "Help yourself."

"Thanks, Mr. Warren," I said to him. "I appreciate your giving Sinclair the time off."

He considered me. "Well, I figure he owes you. We all do. Just you make sure the risk he's taking pays off."

"I will," I promised.

Outside, Sinclair took a deep breath. "There's really not much I can do to speed up the process," he said. "But it will be a blessing to have the extra time to concentrate on it. It's going to take a lot of focus."

"Is there anything I can do to help?" I asked. "Other than think about what my deepest, darkest fear is?"

"I may have been a *little* overdramatic," he admitted. "Phobias are good—phobias are rooted in our most primal instincts. Great stuff for invoking nightmares. Do you happen to have any phobias I don't know about? Snakes? Spiders? Heights? Rats gnawing on your entrails?"

"No," I said. "No, no, and ewww! Are you sure you're okay with this? I mean, I can keep trying the scary-movies-and-greasy-food approach."

Sinclair shrugged. "Honestly, I doubt it would do much good. Like you said, manufactured fear can't compete with the real thing. And since you brought it up," he added, "I'd really rather you didn't keep trying while I'm working on this. All you'd do is run the risk of numbing your psyche." His eyes were dark and grave. "Daisy, if I'm going to do this, I want to make sure it has every possible chance of succeeding."

I hesitated, then nodded. It would be hard to spend the next two nights idle, but my gut said he was right, and it was a fair request. "You didn't answer my question."

"Am I okay with this?" Sinclair said. I nodded again. "Not entirely, no. But what you said was true. A low blow, maybe, but true. And Warren's right, too. I owe you. I owe this entire town for what my mother unleashed on it. If I can help now . . ." He lifted his hands in a helpless gesture. "How can I say no? I just have to trust that I'm strong enough to handle it."

"You are." I caught one of his hands and squeezed it. "You're a good man, Sinclair. There's no one else I'd trust to hex me."

He squeezed my hand in response, summoning a faint smile. "Good to know. See you around eleven?"

"I'll be there," I said.

By the time I got home, all hell had broken loose.

"The cat's out of the bag, Miss Daisy," Casimir said briefly when I returned his call in response to the urgent voice mail he'd left me. "Someone at the nursing home talked. I suspect the fresh-faced young candy-striper you sent over this morning. I've had a run on supplies, and I am *fresh out*."

I winced. "Didn't you order more stock?"

"Yes, I ordered more stock!" There was an impatient edge to his voice. "These things aren't mass-produced, sweetheart. Do you know what the most effective charm against a predatory member of the fey is?"

"Iron?"

The Fabulous Casimir heaved a sigh. "Iron's fine as a general pre-caution. In fact, I've been sending customers to Drummond's Hard-ware to buy lengths of steel chain to lay around their beds. But as it so happens, the *most* effective charm under the circumstances is a genuine Saint Brigid's cross. *Mine* are hand-woven by an elderly hedge-witch in Ireland out of rushes that grow in a pond fed by a spring that's been sacred since pre-Christian times, sewn with red thread spun from the wool of sheep she raised herself, and dyed with rowan berries harvested on her property," he said grimly. "I've asked the dear old soul to put a rush on it, but I'm not holding my breath."

"I get it, I get it!" I said. "What do you want me to do about it?"

"For one thing, don't send anyone else my way," Casimir said. "I locked the door and put up the *Closed* sign, because all I've got to offer at this point is a set of instructions I printed off the Internet for weaving your own Saint Brigid's cross out of drinking straws."

I paused. "Will it work?"

"Probably not."

"I'm doing my best, Cas," I said. "Has Sinclair been in touch?"

"Not today. Why?"

"He will be," I said. "I've asked him to conjure a hex that will give me nightmares. Spine-tingling, bed-wetting nightmares. It's the only way I'm going to catch this Night Hag. Can you help?"

There was a silence on the other end. "Are you sure about that, Miss Daisy?" Casimir's voice had turned gentle.

"No," I said. "Have you got any better ideas?"

"No."

"Well, we're going forward with Plan Hex," I said. "The only down-side, other than the prospect of terrifying nightmares and the fact that I have to somehow manage to overcome the Night Hag, is that it's go-ing to take a few days. Sinclair thinks he can have the charm ready for me by the night after tomorrow—" I heard a muffled banging sound in the background. "What's going on?"

"Oh, just an angry villager pounding on my door," Casimir said dourly. "Demanding that I open for business."

"Cas, you're going to have to reopen," I said. "I need you to do whatever you can to reassure people and keep the peace, even if it's just handing out instructions for weaving a cross out of drinking straws. Keep sending them to the hardware store—that ought to help. The thing is, this Night Hag phenomenon is wired into the human subconscious. Lots of people have reported experiencing an attack when there's no possible way they could have. There's a whole syndrome named after it. If people start panicking—"

"It's going to be pandemonium," he finished. "All right, all right. I hate to stake my reputation on the placebo effect, but I'll do what I can."

"Thanks," I said. "You're the best."

"Damn straight," Casimir said. "Don't you forget it."

After calling Cody to give him a quick update on Plan Hex, I headed down to the police station. Pemkowet was a small town and the rumor mill worked fast. It had only been a couple of hours since the news of Mrs. Claussen's death got out, but the phone was ringing off the hook with people calling in to ask about the danger posed by the Night Hag, and Chief Bryant was seriously disgruntled.

"I've got half the town afraid they're going to be attacked in their sleep!" he thundered at me in the lobby. "And the other half will be by the end of the day! And I can't promise that they won't be. What, exactly, am I supposed to tell them, Daisy?"

The chief almost never yelled, but I hated it when he did. It made me feel about six years old.

"Tell them we're working on it," I said. "Tell them we expect to have the situation under control in the next seventy-two hours."

Chief Bryant fixed me with a long, hard stare. "Do we?"

"Absolutely," I said with a bravado I didn't feel. "In the meantime, the Sisters of Selene is back open for business, and people can buy steel chain to wrap around their beds down at Drummond's."

He looked dubious. "And that will do the trick?"

"It ought to," I said. "Anyone who's unsure or thinks they're at high risk can always leave town for a few days."

"I'd prefer not to tell anyone to leave town." Chief Bryant sighed and rumpled his graying hair. "You know, people wouldn't have gotten so worked up over this before the whole Halloween debacle. I'm not saying they shouldn't be concerned—a woman *is* dead, after all—but they wouldn't have panicked like this."

I didn't say anything.

"I know it's not your fault," he said to me. "So, seventy-two hours, eh?"

I nodded. "Yes, sir."

"Good." The chief returned my nod. "Then I'm going to put you on desk duty today, Daisy. You can give Patty a break, man the phones, and reassure folks that everything's under control."

My gut clenched a bit. I hoped like hell it was true. "Will do, sir."

"Oh, and the official word on Mrs. Claussen is that she died of natural causes," he added. "Right now, the less fuel we can add to the fire, the better. Doc Howard says that in her condition, she could have gone at any time, Night Hag or not. That's his verdict and we're sticking to it. Got it?"

"Got it."

I spent a long day fielding calls from the anxious citizens of Pemkowet, repeating the same advice and reassurances, praying that they didn't ring hollow. At least the chief spared me a confrontation with Amanda Brooks, who called to blister his ears with a rant about the fact that all the work she'd done promoting Pemkowet as a destination for the holidays was in jeopardy.

From what I could hear through the closed door of Chief Bryant's office, he gave as good as he got this time. Yay, chief.

Mercifully, the calls had begun to taper off by the time my shift finally ended, though that eleven o'clock meeting I'd agreed to with Sinclair was looking awfully far away. The last twenty-four hours had been kind of exhausting, and now that I'd accepted the fact that there wasn't anything I could do to catch the Night Hag tonight, all I wanted to do was order a pizza, open a bottle of wine, curl up on the couch with Mogwai and fall asleep watching some guilty-pleasure TV; something fluffy and girly to offset last night's *Saw* marathon.

Well, at least I could do the pizza, couch, and cat part, and I flipped around the TV channels until I found *Legally Blonde 2: Red, White & Blonde*, which, while not the girl-power tour de force of the original, was a good antidote to three hours of torture-porn. Instead of opening a bottle of cheap cabernet, I made a pot of strong coffee, which got me through the subsequent feature, *Failure to Launch*—the programming gods must have decreed tonight mediocre rom-com night, which was fine by me—and over to Sinclair's by eleven.

I wasn't exactly bright-eyed and bushy-tailed—no pun intended— but I was awake and coherent.

"Come on in." Sinclair ushered me into the living room, where his altar was located on a sideboard.

I glanced around. "No Jen?"

"Lee took her out to dinner and a movie," he said. "I asked them not to come back until eleven thirty or so. This won't take long."

Despite the fact that I'd set them up, I felt an irrational surge of jealousy. It was Friday night, after all, and tired or not, I'd rather be out on a date than getting hexed. "Okay, let's do it."

Sinclair sat cross-legged on the floor with his back to the altar. "Have a seat across from me."

I did as he said.

He opened one hand to reveal a small leather sack that looked a lot like the one his sister had used to place a hex on me a few months ago. Hell, for all I knew, it *was* the same bag. "All right. Tell me your deepest, darkest fear."

Steeling myself, I told him.

Sinclair's eyelids flickered. "Yeah, that's a pretty big one." Holding the bag cupped in both hands, he bent over and whispered into it, then tied it shut with a length of cord. Rising, he turned and placed it in an empty half of a coconut shell on his altar, which also held a handful of seashells, including a bead-encrusted conch, a dried starfish, and a framed print depicting Yemaya. There were three black taper candles surrounding the coconut shell, unlit, and a single blue pillar burning brightly.

The last time I'd seen Sinclair's altar, the candles had been white. It was an unpleasant reminder of the line I'd asked him to cross.

One by one, he lit the black tapers from the pillar, setting them carefully back in place. A faint acrid scent arose. "Okay."

"That's it?" I asked.

"More or less." Sinclair looked tired. "I need to let the candles burn down tonight, then another set tomorrow, and another the day after. Then it's all yours."

"You don't need a drop of blood or a lock of my hair or anything like that?"

He shook his head. "No. Put it under your pillow when it's ready. It's the same kind of charm Emmy used on you," he added. "A real practitioner would probably hide it under your mattress."

"Remind me to start checking under my mattress." I got to my feet. "Thanks. I owe you."

He gave me a tired smile. "Put it in your ledger."

"I know you're joking, but I will. I'm starting to take that thing seriously." A thought struck me. "Hey, Thanksgiving's next week, isn't it? Would you like to join Mom and me for dinner? I don't mean to brag, but we throw a mean feast."

Sinclair hesitated.

"That's okay." I backtracked. "You're probably going down to Kalamazoo to spend it with your dad."

"No, we never really celebrated Thanksgiving," he said. "It's not something my father grew up with. But, um, Stacey invited me to have Thanksgiving dinner with her family."

"Oh." I felt stupid. "Well, you should go, obviously."

"Look, it's not like this is some big introduce-the-new-boyfriend-to-the-family thing, Daisy," he said. "I mean, I already know her mother. It's just . . . Stacey knew I didn't have any relatives in town, and her brother's coming in for the holiday, and—"

"It's okay." I held up one hand. "Don't worry about it. It was just a thought."

"A nice thought." Sinclair smiled again, this time with genuine warmth. "Thanks, sistah."

"Anytime."

"Do you want to hang out until Jen gets back?" He nodded at the altar. "I've got to stay up until these burn down anyway."

"Thanks, but I think I'll pass." Even if I wasn't exhausted, the scenario had a definite third-wheel feel to it. It didn't help that Sinclair had used the words *new boyfriend* in reference to his relationship with Stacey freakin' Brooks. "I'm pretty beat. You'll let me know when the charm's ready?"

"Absolutely," he said. "I'll light the third set of candles as soon as my last tour ends on Sunday."

"Great."

On that note, I drove home alone to my couch and my cat, where I fell asleep watching Katherine Heigl agonize her way through *27 Dresses*.

At least the programming gods of mediocre romantic comedies were still with me.

# Nineteen

The good thing about the following two days was that there were no further Night Hag casualties.

The bad thing was . . . well, pretty much everything else. The chief was right; if it hadn't been for the Halloween debacle, the town wouldn't have gotten so riled up. Longtime residents of Pemkowet regarded the eldritch community with a complicated mixture of indulgence, pride, and tolerance. Everyone knew that if you didn't want to consort with ghouls, you avoided the Wheelhouse. If you didn't want to consort with vampires, you stayed the hell away from Twilight Manor and declined any offers from unnaturally pallid individuals hitting on you at last call.

By and large, there were places you didn't go and things you didn't do. As for the more malicious fey, the pranks they played on humans were considered the province of tourists, or foolish local kids who ignored their parents' warnings.

Now it was different.

It was different because the Night Hag was doing what the Tall Man had done: going after Pemkowet's own.

People were scared and angry, and they had a right to be. Even though Doc Howard had ruled that Mrs. Claussen's death was due to natural causes, which I guess was technically true, the rumor was out there.

Everyone knew.

Everyone was afraid.

And as a result, we got a steady stream of complaints regarding Night Hag attacks, with the majority of calls coming in from around three to six o'clock in the morning. With either me or Cody in tow, Chief Bryant followed up on each and every report personally, using the dwarf-wrought watch I'd given him to check for residual signs of eldritch presence.

Ironically, there weren't any.

Either the Night Hag was lying low or the precautions Casimir recommended had succeeded in protecting those at the highest risk of an attack. Or the bitch had left town altogether, which I almost hoped wasn't true, because I had plans for her.

Well, assuming Sinclair's hex worked, at any rate, and assuming I could manage to overcome the Night Hag. And yes, I know what they say about "assume." Call it wishful thinking; call it denial; but I figured I'd sweat the details when the time came.

Needless to say, no one in town took the chief's assurances that their perceived attacks were the products of an over-fevered imagination particularly well. It's just not a flattering thing to hear. Thank God for the Fabulous Casimir, because if it hadn't been for him, I suspect we would have had triple the number of complaints. As it was, Drummond's Hardware ran out of steel chain and Tafts Grocery sold out of boxes of drinking straws.

Anyway.

Suffice it to say that it was a grueling couple of days. By the time Sinclair called me at a little before nine o'clock on Sunday night to say that the hex charm was ready, my nerves were frazzled. I was on edge and ready to be done with it.

"Are you sure about this, Daisy?" Sinclair asked me, the leather pouch in his hand and worry in his eyes. "It's dangerous, you know."

Now that the moment was here, there was a part of me that wanted to say no. Hell, are any of us ever prepared to face our deepest, darkest fears? Not to mention the part where I had to subdue the Night Hag.

But there was the memory of Scott Evans, the muzzle of his pistol jammed under his chin; of seven-year-old Danny Reynolds afraid of the night and the terrors it held; of the lingering rictus of fear on Mrs. Claussen's face, her crabbed hands raised in a futile gesture of defense.

"Yeah." I held out my hand. "I'm sure."

Sinclair placed the charm into my palm. "Like I said, put it under your pillow. Make sure there's no cold iron around you, especially . . . what's it called? Your, um, magic dagger?"

"*Dauda-dagr?*"

"Right." He nodded. "It probably shouldn't even be under the same roof as you, okay?"

"Good point." I'd made sure *dauda-dagr* wasn't in the bedroom with me when we'd tried the other night, but maybe that wasn't enough.

"You're doing this out at Cody's?" Sinclair asked. I nodded. "Tell him . . . tell him to stay out of your way, to let the nightmare run its course. But to be careful." He sighed. "Shit, I don't know what to tell him, Daisy. Or you. Just . . . both of you be careful, okay?"

"Can you be more specific?" I asked him wryly.

He shook his head. "Not really. This is uncharted territory."

I tightened my fist on the hex charm in its leather pouch and kissed his cheek. "I'll do my best."

"Good luck," Sinclair said. "And when it's over, bring the charm back. I'll make sure it's undone."

"I will," I said to him. "Thanks, Sinclair. For everything."

Hex charm in hand, I drove out to Cody's place in the countryside.

If things had been a little awkward between us the last time, this time it was ten times worse. Somehow, the fact that working on the case had led directly to our initial attempt made it feel more like a professional undertaking. Even watching back-to-back *Saw* movies and downing hoagies was part of the job. This time, it was late enough that both of us had already eaten, but early enough that neither of us was ready for sleep, and there was nothing constructive and time-consuming to distract us from the fact that we were alone together in Cody's house.

"So, um, Sinclair suggested that *dauda-dagr* shouldn't be under the same roof," I said, casting around for a safe topic of conversation. "I thought maybe I could stash it in your workshop."

"Good idea," Cody said. "I'll store my duty belt and gear out there for the night." He frowned in thought. "What about silverware?"

"What about it?" I asked.

"It's stainless steel," he said. "It might have a high enough iron content to count."

"Well, I'm pretty sure none of the Night Hag's victims had emptied their kitchen drawers," I said. "On the other hand, it couldn't hurt."

"Right."

So in addition to stashing *dauda-dagr* and Cody's duty belt with his service pistol, flashlight, handcuffs, and other accoutrements in the outbuilding behind his house where he had his leatherworking studio, we hauled several drawers of silverware and kitchen utensils and a cupboard full of pots and pans out back, along with a toaster, a toolbox, his off-duty pistol, an ancient metal fan, a floor lamp, and a cast-iron poker.

At least it gave us something to do.

"What about the grate?" Cody eyed the fireplace. "That probably ought to go."

As far as fireplaces go, it was tidy and well swept, but that's not saying much. The grate was still encrusted with years' worth of soot and ash residue. "We might be overthinking this, Cody."

"Probably," he agreed. "Do you want to take that chance?"

I sighed. "I'll hold the door for you."

To call it a dirty job was an understatement. Wrestling the heavy cast-iron grate out of the fireplace and hauling it to the workshop out back was a *filthy* job. By the time it was done, Cody had sooty grime smeared all the way up to his elbows, and all over the front of his jeans and flannel shirt. Standing in the doorway of the workshop, surveying the array of household goods we'd dragged into it, both of us recognized the absurdity of what we'd done and burst into helpless peals of laughter.

"Oh, my God!" Cody rubbed tears of laughter from his eyes with the heel of one hand. "Okay, the grate was overkill."

"You just . . ." I pointed at him, laughing too hard to get the words out. At that moment in time, Cody's soot-smeared eye sockets were the funniest thing I'd ever seen. "Your face!" I finally managed to gasp. "You look like you lost a fight."

"What?" He glanced at his grime-blackened hands. "Oh, shit."

"Okay, let's go back to the house." I regained a measure of control. "Don't touch anything."

Cody fished the key for the padlock to his workshop out of the front pocket of his jeans, which I guess didn't matter since they were already filthy. Inside the house, he let me turn on the water in the bathroom sink so he could wash his hands without getting soot all over the faucet handles.

"I'm going to take a quick shower and throw these clothes in the washer," he said. "After that, I think I could sleep. You?"

"Yeah, me, too," I said. "I'll wash up when you're done."

In the aftermath of our shared bout of hilarity, apprehension set in. Before changing into a tank top and pajama bottoms, I did one last canvass of Cody's bedroom to make sure there was no cold iron we'd overlooked. Thank God his bed had a wooden frame. It was strange knowing that *dauda-dagr* was locked away in his workshop. Ever since Hel had given it to me, I'd kept it within easy reach—if not in my belt or my bag, then no more than a few steps away at most. Without access to it, I felt naked and vulnerable. Under the circumstances, I suppose that was a good thing.

Clad in his plaid bathrobe, Cody emerged from the shower as I was stowing the hex charm under my pillow. "Is that it?"

"Yep."

"What's in it?" he asked.

"Henbane," I said. "And my deepest, darkest fear. Other than that I don't know and I didn't ask."

"Here." Shrugging out of his bathrobe, Cody held it out to me. "Thought you might want to borrow it again."

"Thanks." I put it on over my pajamas, trying to ignore the fact that Cody was now bare-chested and in close proximity. "I'll just wash up and go to bed. Um, Sinclair said you should stay out of my way and let the nightmare run its course. So if you hear me screaming in my sleep or something, don't try to wake me."

Green flashed behind his eyes. "If I think you're in serious danger, I'm not making any promises, Daisy."

"If I'm screaming or thrashing, it means I'm alive," I said. "I think that's pretty much all we've got to go on."

"That and the possibility of permanent psychological trauma," he said. "Confronting your worst fear? You're swimming in some deep waters there."

"Yeah." I rummaged in my overnight bag for my toothbrush. "Right about now, I wish I had a bad case of arachnophobia. But it is what it is, Cody."

He nodded. "Good hunting."

"Thanks."

After washing my hands and face and brushing my teeth, I hung Cody's bathrobe on its hook and curled up in his bed, careful not to disturb the leather pouch under my pillow. The house was dark and quiet. I lay motionless, listening for any sound of Cody's presence in the other room, willing myself to sleep.

In time, I did.

I don't know how long I slept before the nightmare began. Hours, maybe. It's hard to say. Time is relative in dreams. I've had dreams that seemed to last for an entire day in the seven minutes it took for my alarm to go off after hitting the snooze button.

This one didn't *seem* like a nightmare at first. It was one of those dreams that started without a preamble. A mise-en-scène dream. I was standing in a hollow in the dunes, a long stick of driftwood in my hand, surrounded by a ring of people, mostly friends and family but a few others, too.

And I did something terrible.

Ever have a dream where you do something that would be unthinkable in real life in the most casual, nonchalant fashion? A dream where you kill someone, and your only concern is hiding the body so you don't get caught? It was like that. I didn't even have a *reason* for doing what I did. I just did it, like it was the most natural thing in the world.

With the stick of driftwood in my hand, I sketched the sigil to summon my father in the sand, called his name, and invoked my birthright.

For a moment, nothing happened, and I thought to myself, *Well, that's that. I guess it was a lie all along.*

And then the dune shuddered beneath my feet. The sigil turned into a funnel-shaped pit, sand draining from it like an hourglass. A bellow of laughter rumbled from somewhere deep beneath me.

The soles of my feet began to tingle. A sense of power rose through me like a steady tide, creeping from my ankles to my knees, to my thighs, rising in a rush when it reached my groin and belly. It filled my chest with brightness; it filled my mouth with words of power and persuasion; it filled my hands with lightning.

And it felt *good*, so good. I felt a hundred feet tall and crowned with fire, my tail lengthening and lashing like a deadly whip.

It was real.

I laughed aloud for the sheer joy of it.

And then, one by one, the people surrounding me averted their faces. Cody. Jen. Mr. Leary. Mrs. Browne. Sinclair. Casimir.

"It's all right," I said to them. "Look, it's okay!"

Only it wasn't. Now, only now, did the horrible magnitude of what I'd done strike me, and I desperately wanted to go back and undo it. But it was done. All my joy ebbed away, and I broke into a cold sweat, appalled beyond words by my own action. I'd done it. I'd done it without a thought, and no one would look at me.

Lee. Sandra Sweddon. Stefan. Dawn Evans. Lurine.

My mother was the last, and she *did* look at me before she turned her face away. She gave me a look of such profound horror and disappointment that it felt like my heart was shattering inside me.

There was even a sound of something vast breaking—but it wasn't my heart. With a clap of earsplitting thunder, a jagged crack tore open the sky above us. Golden brilliance spilled through it, accompanied by a celestial trumpet blast, a clarion call to arms that vibrated in the very marrow of my bones, announcing that the end of days was upon us.

It had happened.

I had broken the world.

I awoke with a gasp caught in my throat, trapped there by the gnarled, long-fingered hands that were strangling me. The Night Hag sat hunched on my chest like a spider, pinning me to the bed. In the dim recesses of my mind, it occurred to me that Danny Reynolds was right; she looked like a Halloween witch with sunken cheeks and a long, warty nose. The Night Hag's eyes glowed red as she leaned closer to me, her tangled gray hair falling around my face in a lank curtain.

I tried to move and couldn't. It wasn't just her weight on my chest; I was paralyzed. Utterly and completely paralyzed. A wave of sheer physical terror broke over me.

The Night Hag's face loomed in my vision as she licked her withered lips with a black tongue. "Oh, that was a good one, child," she whispered to me. "You can hear me, can't you?"

I couldn't even blink.

Her hands tightened around my throat. "You're not like the others, are you, half human? You wanted this. You *sought* this."

My lungs were burning for air, and I wasn't sure if I was actually awake anymore. I strained to lift a hand from the bed and snatch a lock of her hair, to move my fingers, to grit my teeth. Anything.

"Perhaps it would be for the best if you died in your sleep, child," the Night Hag mused. "After all, the world would be spared the terrible fate of your great and grievous folly. Don't you agree?"

I wanted to deny it, but I had no voice with which to speak. What was happening to me wasn't real. It couldn't be. None of her victims had had bruises on their throats. Scott Evans had broken the paralysis to throttle his wife. Poor old Mrs. Claussen had found the strength to cry out, to raise her hands in self-defense.

But then, none of them was a hell-spawn foolish enough to invoke her worst nightmare. I'd broken the world.

Oh, God, I'd done it.

Except I *hadn't* done it, not really. It was just a dream, a terrible, terrible dream, one I'd invoked into being. I needed to fight. I needed to find my anger, but all I could feel was terror—the terror that I was going to die like this, right here in Cody's bed, the terror that I was going to die knowing I was capable of doing the worst possible thing I could do, and that I'd lose my mother's love forever because of it.

I would have wept if I could have. Instead, all I could do was wonder whether if I passed out due to lack of oxygen, my heart would stop. I could almost hear my heartbeat faltering in my chest.

"Oh, this is truly delicious." The Night Hag's face was inches away, the tip of her long nose brushing mine. Sickened by the sensation, I strained every muscle in my paralyzed body in a futile effort to get away from her touch. Her eyes were like two pools of glowing blood, pupils like black stones in the center. She wriggled her bony buttocks on my chest and licked her withered lips again, deliberately and lasciviously. "You're the best ride I've had in a long time, child."

Okay, *ewww!*

Beneath me, my tail curled in revulsion, and all at once the anger I hadn't been able to access was there, molten and glorious. As my fear took a backseat to fury, the Night Hag's grip on my throat loosened, her strength waning.

I sucked a great, ragged breath of air into my lungs and found my voice. "I'm not your bitch, bitch!"

The Night Hag hissed at me, baring a mouthful of broken black teeth.

I felt her weight shift and grabbed two hanks of her greasy gray hair before she could pull away. "Oh, no, you don't!" I said grimly. Tangled in Cody's sheets, we grappled for purchase on the bed. The Night Hag might have been on top, but back when I was a kid, I'd been Mr. Rodriguez's star pupil in Li'l Dragonz Tae Kwon Do for four years running. All I needed was one opening to find the leverage to flip her onto her back—and she was careless enough to give it to me.

I pinned her arms with my knees and smushed her face with my left hand, using my right hand to yank a few strands of hair loose.

She let out an unearthly yowl and began to struggle with renewed vigor.

Let me tell you, it is *not* easy to tie a strand of hair around the neck of an eldritch crone fighting tooth and nail to prevent you from doing that very thing—and I'm not kidding about the tooth-and-nail part. I have the bite marks and scratches to prove it. The Night Hag shrieked and thrashed. I clamped down on her efforts with all the strength I could muster and swore, strands of hair slipping through my frantic fingers.

At some point, I was vaguely aware of Cody shouting at me to wake up, but it seemed to be coming from a great distance. Since I couldn't afford the distraction, I ignored him.

I don't know how many tries it took before I finally succeeded. Twenty? Thirty? It might even have been more. The first time I got a strand around her neck in a single knot, I thought I'd done it, but I was wrong. I should have known better. The fey tend to be literal. Anything easily undone can't be considered binding.

All I know is that I didn't give up. I just kept trying, over and over, with dogged determination.

At last I managed a double knot, drawing a single strand of greasy gray hair taut around the Night Hag's neck and tying two knots in quick succession without breaking the fragile strand.

Her body sagged beneath me, all the fight going out of her. Her red eyes glared up at me in sullen defeat.

I heaved a sigh of relief. "Gotcha."

# Twenty

"Daisy!" It sounded like Cody had been calling my name for a while. "Hey, are you okay?"

"I think so." I clambered off the Night Hag, who scuttled backward to crouch against the headboard of Cody's bed, scowling bloody murder at me. "You see her, right?"

"I sure do," he said. "Nice work."

Oh, good, apparently I really was awake this time and we were all on the same plane of corporeal reality. "Thanks. Will you do me a favor and fetch *dauda-dagr*?" I said to Cody, keeping my eye on the Night Hag. "Just grab the belt and be careful not to touch the dagger itself."

"You don't have to remind me," he said drily. "And by the way, it's considered impolite to ask a werewolf to fetch."

I gave him a tired smile. "I'll keep that in mind."

The Night Hag continued to glare at me in mute fury while Cody went out back to retrieve *dauda-dagr*, but when he returned and I buckled the leather belt around my waist and pulled the blade from its sheath, she let out a shriek and shrank farther back against the headboard. "You render me helpless and dare to draw cold iron on me?" she said in a querulous tone. "I have done nothing to warrant such a punishment!"

"I beg to differ." At some point during our struggle, Cody had turned on the overhead light in the bedroom. Let's just say artificial lighting wasn't kind to the Night Hag. She looked gray and shriveled, shrunken in on herself like the desiccated corpse of a spider. Only her crimson eyes were as malevolent as ever. "You killed an elderly woman."

"And nearly caused a man to kill himself," Cody added, leaning against the doorjamb, his arms folded.

The Night Hag sniffed. "I killed no one."

"Let's not split hairs." Standing beside the bed, I tilted *dauda-dagr* so the light made the runes etched on it flare to life. "What's your name?"

She bared the blackened stumps of her teeth at me. "You accuse me? *I* didn't destroy the world!"

"Neither did I," I said. "People do all kinds of things in nightmares that they'd never do in real life."

"Is that what mortals tell themselves in their waking hours that they may endure the fearsome truths of their dreams, half human?" the Night Hag asked me, a cunning expression on her face. "I always wondered."

"Ignore her, Daisy," Cody murmured. "She's just trying to get in your head."

The Night Hag glanced at him. "Wrong, wolf. I've *been* in her head and I know what's inside there."

I really, really didn't want to continue that particular line of conversation. "Did I or did I not just bind you to my will?" I inquired. "So I'm asking again, on pain of cold steel, what's your name?"

"Gruoch," she muttered.

"Gruoch," I repeated. "Okay, here's the thing. You're in Hel's territory without permission, preying on innocent victims. Whether you're willing to own it or not, you caused a woman's death. As Hel's liaison, as far as I'm concerned, that's a mortal offense."

Her crimson eyes widened. "I was invited!"

"Excuse me?" I said. "I don't think so. Hel herself told me you weren't welcome here."

"Not by Hel," Gruoch said in an aggrieved tone. "I never claimed it was Hel. But it's written plain and simple on the Pemkowet Visitors Bureau's website. It says Pemkowet is an inclusive community that welcomes all visitors."

I stared at her. "You've got to be kidding me. You're citing the PVB's website as justification?"

She sniffed again. "In accordance with eldritch protocol, that constitutes an invitation. This seemed like a nice place for a getaway," she added. "I'll be noting otherwise in my TripAdvisor review."

Oh, gah!

"No one invited you to *hunt* here," Cody reminded her in a low voice tinged with a hint of growl.

"It was not my fault that the old woman's heart stopped." Gruoch drew herself up with a semblance of dignity. "I did not cause the dreams that plagued her, no more than I did any of them. But she suffered. She suffered greatly. If I must be held responsible for her most timely death, I will claim it as an act of mercy."

"And the soldier?" I asked. "What about *him*?"

The Night Hag shrugged her bony shoulders. "He is a broken thing. It might have been better for him."

"He's a human being who served his country with valor and distinction," I said. "No matter how ill-conceived the cause. And broken things can be mended."

"Oh?" Her bloodred gaze fixed on me. "Will you be able to mend the vault of heaven after you've broken it, child?"

I hesitated, then shoved *dauda-dagr* back into its sheath. "Gruoch, in accordance with the binding I've laid upon you, I forbid you forevermore to prey upon innocents."

She let out an earsplitting screech. "You cannot deprive me of my very sustenance!"

"I can," I said. "Unless you'd care to try to convince me that the boy you attacked deserved it? Danny Reynolds?" I reminded her. "Seven years old? Afraid of the night? Is he somehow better off for having been terrorized by you?"

Gruoch glowered at me, but held her tongue.

"I'm sure there are plenty of mortals with guilty consciences out there for you to prey on," I said to her. "Mortals who actually *do* deserve nightmares. If you want to haunt the dreams of someone who committed murder and got away with it, fine. But not here. Not in Pemkowet, and not on *my* watch." I held up my rune-marked left palm. "Gruoch the Night Hag, in Hel's name, I banish you."

To be honest, I wasn't exactly sure what would happen. It was my first banishing. When Stefan banished members of the Outcast who rebelled against his leadership last summer, I'm pretty sure they just picked up and left town.

But then, they weren't fey dreamwalkers with a complicated relationship to corporeal reality. Well, actually that last part isn't exactly true, but they definitely functioned more like mortal humans than like fey. The Night Hag pulled a slow vanishing act, crumpling into an even tighter ball, the contours of her body fading. Her eyes were the last thing to go, crimson orbs filled with fury hanging in the air above Cody's pillows like the Cheshire cat's grin, only creepy as hell.

I was glad when they finally blinked out of existence. Now that it was over, the adrenaline rush that had sustained me drained away, leaving me wobbly and shaken. I sat down abruptly on the edge of Cody's bed.

"Good job, Daisy," Cody said quietly. "How are you, really?"

"I don't know." I glanced down at my trembling hands, gouged and scratched by the Night Hag's teeth and nails. "A little shaky."

"Damn, she really got you," he said. "Let me go get some disinfectant. God knows what you could catch from a Night Hag's bite."

I shuddered. "Good point."

Cody left and came back with a bottle of hydrogen peroxide, a bag of cotton balls and a tube of antibiotic ointment. I took off my belt, setting *dauda-dagr* safely aside while he administered a little basic first aid. "No offense, Daise, but from what I could make out of it, that must have been the least sexy girl-fight ever."

"No kidding." I watched hydrogen peroxide bubble and fizz in a long furrow on the underside of my right forearm, gritting my teeth against the sting of it. "You try tying a single strand of hair around a Night Hag's throat."

"Yeah, I think I'll leave that to you if it ever happens again." Cody rotated my left arm to examine it. "You're the seamstress's daughter."

"Do you think more are coming?" The prospect dismayed me. I could subdue another Night Hag if I had to, but I wasn't sure I could stand to revisit that nightmare.

He glanced up at me. "No, not really. There's no reason to think so. Especially not if they read Gruoch's TripAdvisor review." Despite the comment, his expression was serious. "Do you want to talk about it?"

I looked away, knowing full well he wasn't talking about eldritch tourism. "You heard what she said."

Cody smeared ointment on a bite mark. "Yes."

"I watched myself do it, Cody." Tears filled my eyes. "There wasn't even a *reason* for it! I just . . . did it."

His hands went still on mine. "You invoked your birthright?"

I nodded, unable to answer, my body jerking with the effort of holding back sobs.

"Daisy, it's okay." Setting down the antibiotic ointment, Cody slid onto the bed and put his arms around me. "It's okay. It wasn't real," he murmured against my hair. "It was just a dream. And you're right, people do terrible things in their dreams all the time. It doesn't mean anything."

"Cody, it felt so *good*," I whispered. "Before I realized what I'd done. That scares me. It scares the shit out of me."

"I know." Cody tightened his arms around me. I clutched his shoulder blades, yearning for even closer contact, my nails digging into his skin. "But I promise you, it wasn't real. You did what you had to do, Daisy. And it worked. It's over." Lifting his head, he gave me a fierce look, eyes shimmering green. "You did it. You caught the bitch, bound her, and banished her. It's done."

"It is, isn't it?"

He nodded. "Yeah."

There was a moment, maybe as long as it takes for a heart to beat four or five times, where one or the other of us could have withdrawn, could have disentangled ourselves. Neither of us did.

And then Cody kissed me savagely, his fingers sliding through my hair. I kissed him back with equal fervor, squirming to kneel astride his lap. He found the hem of my tank top and yanked it off. Placing my hands on his chest, I shoved him down onto the bed and straddled him.

"I need to be on top tonight," I informed him. The memory of waking with the Night Hag crouched on my chest was a little too fresh. "Understand?"

He flashed a wolfish grin. "Totally."

It was enough. I didn't think about my dream or the Night Hag. I didn't think about anything but this moment, here and now. About Cody's mouth on my breasts, suckling my nipples to aching points. About working my way down his lean, muscled torso, nuzzling the treasure trail of wiry bronze hair that led from just below his washboard abs to the waistband of his pajama bottoms. I untied the drawstring, easing them over his hips and freeing his erection—and no, for the record, neither boxers nor briefs. Cody watched with narrowed eyes while I took him into my mouth.

"Enough!" he growled after a minute. "Come here."

My tail twitching with anticipation, I wriggled out of my own pajama bottoms and crawled back up the length of his body, wrapping one hand around his throbbing cock and fitting it to me.

Cody let out a deep, guttural sound of satisfaction as I sank down onto him. I might have, too.

"Are you okay?" he asked me.

I leaned down to kiss him. "Uh-huh."

"Good." He ran a few strands of my blond hair through his fingers, his expression turning uncertain and vulnerable. "Because I hate to see you cry, Daisy. I *really* fucking hate to see you cry."

Since I didn't have a response, I kissed him again with lip-bruising savagery, then pulled myself upright to ride him for all it was worth, his hips thrusting upward to meet mine, my tail curling between us, shuddering my way to one minor and one fairly earth-shattering climax before Cody swore and arched his back in his own, his nails raking my thighs, his cock spurting inside me.

Okay, so that happened.

The thing I loved best about the aftermath with Cody was the sheer physical easiness of it. We were comfortable together. I lay with my cheek pressed to his chest, one leg thrown over him, while he stroked my spine from the nape of my neck to the tip of my tail, occasionally scratching the base of it with perfect and delicious unself-consciousness.

"We shouldn't have done this," I mumbled.

"Probably not," he agreed, his fingers working their magic on the base of my tail. "Are you sorry?"

I wriggled against him. "No. But I should go."

Cody looked at me. "Don't." Hoisting himself on one elbow, he fished the leather pouch of Sinclair's hex charm from beneath the pillows and threw it as far away as possible. "Stay." His topaz eyes were gentle, without a trace of green. "You shouldn't be alone, Daisy. Not tonight, not after what you went through. It's late—the sun's coming up in a few hours. Stay with me."

So I did.

# Twenty-one

I slept soundly in Cody's bed, with Cody wrapped around me. I'm not going to lie—it was nice. Very nice. It made me feel warm and safe and protected, which was exactly what I needed.

Of course, there was a certain irony to the fact that the thing I feared the most was the result of my own impulsive desires and struggles with temptation, but . . . never mind. I'd think about that later.

Thanks to daylight saving time, it was late when the dawn woke us, after seven thirty. I felt Cody stir, the bristles on his chin catching on my hair, and turned over beneath his arm. "Good morning."

"Morning, Pixy Stix." He smiled at me, eyes crinkled with sleep. "Did you sleep okay?"

"I did." I rubbed one hand over his raspy cheek. "You?"

Cody's smile deepened. "Mm-hmm."

I glanced at the clock. "You're not on duty this morning, are you?"

"No." He shook his head against the pillow. "I'm back on the night shift tonight. But one of us ought to call the chief ASAP and let him know the Night Hag's been bound and banished," he said in a more pragmatic tone. "He'll want to hold a press conference to announce it."

"Good point."

Cody levered himself upright, groping for his pajama bottoms. "You should have the honors, Daise. You're the one who got the job done." He yawned. "If you want to wash up first, go ahead. I'll put on coffee."

"Deal," I said.

Okay, so I felt a *little* self-conscious calling Chief Bryant while wrapped in Cody's plaid bathrobe, but the satisfaction I got from the chief's sincere praise more than made up for it. In the kitchen, Cody got a pot of coffee brewing.

"Help yourself when it's done," he said. "Let me brush my teeth. Then I'll see about breakfast."

I raised my eyebrows at him. "Let me guess. Venison sausage?"

Cody raised his eyebrows back at me. "For your information, Daisy Jo, there are bagels and cream cheese in the refrigerator. I just need to get the toaster out of my workshop. And, um, a butter knife."

"I'll get it," I offered.

"No, you sit tight." He pointed at the couch. "Relax. Turn on the TV, read the paper. You're my guest."

Thinking that I could at least tidy a bit and make room to sit, I hauled the ridiculously large—and frankly, quite hideous—brown-and-orange crocheted blanket off Cody's couch and folded it into an unwieldy parcel. Since I hadn't seen anything resembling a linen closet, I figured he stored the blanket in the battered steamer trunk that did double duty as a coffee table. At the moment, it had a couple of recent issues of the local newspaper and Cody's clunky old laptop sitting atop it.

I swear, I was *not* snooping. All I did was shift the laptop to the couch, but I must have hit a key or the touchpad. The screen was already up, and when the laptop emerged from sleep mode with a low, grinding whir, I couldn't help but see.

I froze.

Apparently, Cody had been carrying on an IM correspondence with a young woman named Stephanie. Based on her profile picture, she was lovely in a wholesome, sporty kind of way, with a frank, open face, blue-gray eyes, broad, high cheekbones, and glossy brown hair.

I closed the laptop softly, feeling like I'd been punched in the gut.

Cody emerged from the bathroom. "Daisy."

I turned to face him. "I'm sorry," I said dully. "I didn't mean to pry. It was an accident."

"Daise." He sighed and ran both hands through his hair. "I'm so sorry. We were chatting before you called last night. She's a member of one of the Seattle clans. They set up a private forum where we could look over each other's profiles before the mixer, maybe get to know each other in advance."

"Okay, well, I'm glad this is about the mixer and not some random online flirtation, but you don't owe me any explanations, Cody," I said in a clipped tone, trying not to betray the irrational extent of the hurt I felt. "You've been upfront with me the whole time. I'm a big girl. I knew what I was getting myself into. Last night . . . I needed that. I needed something to banish the nightmare; and you're right, I needed to not be alone. So thanks for that."

He closed his eyes in frustration. "I'm just trying to do what's right for my clan."

"I know." I shoved my hands into the pockets of his bathrobe, balling them into fists. "I get it—I do. I just wasn't expecting to be slapped in the face with it the first thing this morning. So if you'll excuse me, I think I'll skip breakfast. Just give me a minute to get my things and I'm out of here."

Without giving him a chance to respond, I turned and went into the bedroom, closing the door behind me. I changed into yesterday's clothes, belted *dauda-dagr* around my waist, and shoved my pajamas and toothbrush into my overnight bag. My dramatic exit was somewhat spoiled by the fact that I had to hunt around for the hex charm, but I finally found it under the couch in the living room where it had rolled after Cody had hurled it.

Cody stood before the front door; not exactly blocking it, but not making it easy to pass, either. "Daisy, look. We can talk about this."

"We *have* talked about it." I pushed past him, reaching for the doorknob. "There's nothing left to say."

Halfway down the walk to his driveway, I changed my mind. Cody looked at me in wary surprise as I reentered the house.

"Okay, here's the thing," I said to him. "Jen said something last week that made me think. Maybe you and I can't have kids, but it's not like there aren't thousands of couples struggling with the exact same problem. You don't just ditch someone because they might have fertility issues. And hell, we don't even know for sure, do we? Maybe there are medical solutions that didn't exist years ago. Outside of paranormal romance novels, I'm guessing there aren't any case studies on hell-spawn/werewolf cross-breeding. What if we *could* have kids, just not werewolf kids? I'm not even saying I want kids," I added. "I mean, at least not right now. But interracial couples deal with that kind of thing all the time. Do you think Sinclair would have broken things off with me because of the possibility that our babies might have looked more like their white mom than their black dad?"

Cody winced. "That's a low blow, Daise. Race in humans is mostly an artificial construct. Humans are all the same under their skin. We're *not*. And if we don't mate within our race, it *will* vanish."

"Tell me, is that a big problem in this day and age?" I gestured toward his laptop in the other room. "When you can use the lycanthropic version of Match.com to set up a transcontinental mixer?"

His jaw tightened. "It's a problem if we *don't*, Daisy."

"All of you, sure," I agreed. "But we're not talking about the entire werewolf community. We're just talking about you and me, Cody. Or is there an epidemic of werewolves developing feelings for someone their clan would consider an unsuitable mate? Because there aren't a lot of other hell-spawns running around and I seem to remember you telling me relationships with humans don't even count."

Cody drew a sharp breath, nostrils flaring. "It's not just the survival of the race! Do I have to say it? There's a huge part of my life, of who I *am*, that you could never, ever share. That's not fair to either of us."

"Yeah, Jen said something about that, too," I murmured. "What if you were a marathon runner and I was in a wheelchair? Would that be a deal breaker?"

He snarled, eyes flashing green. "It's not the same thing!" Cody thumped one fist on his bare chest, his upper lip curling back from his teeth. "I am me, and so is the wolf. The other day in the woods, you blamed the wolf for keeping us apart. You don't understand. The wolf *is* me. And no matter how well you think you know the man, you can never know the wolf."

I held my ground. "How can you be sure? Has your wolf-self ever tried to connect with a human? What about Kevin Costner in *Dances with Wolves*? What about that guy in the documentary who lived with grizzly bears?"

"Ah, God, Daisy!" Cody let out a ragged gasp of despairing laughter. "*Dances with Wolves* was a work of pure fiction. And that guy in the documentary? The grizzly bears *killed* him."

Crap. I hadn't actually watched the documentary; I just remembered seeing it on a shelf at the library.

"Okay," I said slowly. "Bad examples. My point is that it's possible that our problems aren't insurmountable. Maybe they are. Maybe your clan is right. But we'll never know, because we never tried."

Cody sighed. "Daisy, I don't pretend to have all the answers, but clan lore has the wisdom of centuries of experience on its side, passed down from generation to generation. I'm just trying to spare us both a world of hurt."

"Yeah?" I said. "And how's that working out for you so far?"

"Not so good," he admitted.

"Me either." I settled the strap of my overnight bag on my shoulder. "All right, I'm going. I've said my piece. At least the citizens of Pemkowet can sleep easier at night," I added. "Good work, partner."

Cody gazed at me with profound regret, but he didn't try to stop me from leaving. "You, too."

This time, I didn't turn back.

# Twenty-two

Things settled down in the aftermath of the Night Hag attacks. There were a few more false reports, but those tapered off quickly. People in Pemkowet placed a lot of trust in Chief Bryant. If he said the Night Hag was gone for good, that was a promise you could take to the bank.

Of course, there was no guarantee that another Night Hag might decide Pemkowet looked like a nice place for a getaway, but I was hoping that Gruoch's negative testimonial would help dissuade others. And I actually had a reasonably civilized meeting with Stacey Brooks in her capacity as the PVB's recently appointed head of online promotion regarding tweaking the wording on the website so it didn't constitute an open invitation to all and sundry, especially predatory members of the eldritch community.

I left Stacey mulling over new taglines like "There are no strangers in Pemkowet, only friends we haven't met yet." Cheesy, yes; safer, definitely.

Needless to say, I returned Sinclair's hex charm to him for disabling the same day I left Cody's place. Whatever he did to undo it worked. I didn't have the nightmare in all its immediate visceral sense of reality again.

But it hung over me.

Whatever I did, wherever I went, the memory of that nightmare hung over me like a dark cloud, casting a shadow over my thoughts.

Stefan called me from Poland the day after I dealt with the Night Hag, asking delicately if all was well. I should have known he'd have sensed my terror, though I hadn't been sure how well our one-way emotional bond held up with an ocean between us. Apparently, just fine. I gave him a brief rundown on the whole Night Hag affair without going into the particulars of my nightmare.

"You did well to bind her," Stefan said to me, his faint Eastern European accent more pronounced than usual. "I am glad the situation is resolved."

"Thanks," I said. "Me, too. How about you? How's your . . . situation?"

"I believe the matter is settled," he said. "I will remain a while longer to be certain." Stefan hesitated. "You may recall that I spoke of the possibility of asking a favor of you upon my return."

Actually, I'd totally forgotten. "Of course."

"I fear it will come to pass." He sounded somber. "And I wish you to know in advance that I do not ask it lightly."

"Stefan, I don't think you do *anything* lightly," I said. "You've done me plenty of favors. Of course I'd be happy to do you one in return."

"Do not be so swift to make assurances you may not wish to keep," he said. "Not until you know what I ask of you."

I sighed. "Oh, for God's sake! Enough with the cryptic eldritch crap. Can't you just tell me?"

"Forgive me." There was a hint of amusement in his tone. "It was not my intention to subject you to *cryptic eldritch crap*. But it is a grave thing I mean to ask of you in your role as Hel's liaison, Daisy." Any trace of levity vanished. "And it is a matter best discussed in person. I merely wished to forewarn you."

"Okay," I said, doing my best to conceal a rising sense of apprehension. "Consider me forewarned."

Stefan laughed softly; a tired laugh but a genuine one. "It's good to hear your voice."

I found myself flushing. "Yours, too. I miss you." Oh, crap. Had I really said that? Yes, I had. Did I mean it? Yeah, actually, I think I did. "Do you have any idea when you'll be back?"

"Next week, perhaps." He paused again. "May I ask if your circumstances have changed since we parted?"

"My circumstances . . . oh." Duh. If Stefan had felt my terror, he'd felt the rush of unbridled lust that followed it. My face got hotter. "No, that was just an, um, heat-of-battle kind of thing."

"Then I look forward to resuming our . . . conversation," he said. "Your existence in this world gladdens my heart, Daisy."

Whoa.

"Thanks," I said, feeling awkward, but sincere. "I really needed to hear something like that right about now. But you probably knew that, didn't you?"

He gave another soft laugh. "Perhaps. But that does not render the sentiment any less true. Take care."

"You, too."

So that was the situation with Stefan—infuriatingly cryptic, disturbingly intimate, distinctly apprehension-making, yet definitely intriguing.

Then there was the Cody situation, or the Cody nonsituation. I wasn't going out of my way to avoid him, but I was just as glad that our paths didn't cross in the days following the Night Hag incident. Maybe it wasn't fair of me to feel betrayed by his correspondence with Stephanie the werewolf in Seattle—if I had a Stefan in my life, he ought to be entitled to a Stephanie—but I couldn't help the way I felt. And somehow it was worse knowing Cody *did* have feelings for me—just not strong enough feelings to override his loyalty to his clan.

Maybe that was as it should be, but it didn't make it hurt any less.

I talked it out with Jen. It's not like there was anything she could do about it, but she gave me plenty of sympathy and a hearty "You go, girl," for having said my piece to Cody, which is all I wanted anyway. Well, that and the dish on her situation with Lee, about which she was a lot less forthcoming. The only reason I knew she was going to Thanksgiving dinner at his mother's house was because she turned down an invitation to join me at Mom's.

"It's not like it's a big deal," Jen said dismissively. "I'm just helping out because of his mom's arthritis."

"First Sinclair, now you," I said. "Okay, tell me this. Are you going as Lee's date or as his mom's helper?"

"I don't know." Jen made a face. "A little of both, maybe. His mom's weird about having people over, but she's comfortable with me since I helped take care of her when Lee's arm was broken. And it's a good excuse to get out of dinner with my family."

"Let me put it this way," I said. "Are you getting paid for being there?"

"No."

"Then it's a date." We were sprawled at opposite ends of the couch in Sinclair's living room while he was working at the nursery. I nudged her with one foot. "Talk about weird—why are *you* being so weird about this?"

"Oh, God." Heaving a sigh, Jen let her head flop back on the armrest. "Because it *is* weird, Daise. There's a part of me that thinks, am I really doing this? Am I really dating *Skeletor*?"

"You can't—"

"I know, I know." She propped herself on her elbows and lifted her head. "High school was a long time ago. But the thing is, there's another part of me that wonders if I'm good enough for Lee." Jen's gaze was uncertain and vulnerable. "I mean, Lee's a big deal in the gaming industry. He's a fucking *genius*, Daisy. And I clean houses for a living."

"Jen—"

"He's only here in Pemkowet to take care of his mom," she continued. "While I was living with my parents, he built a whole life out in Seattle. Hell, maybe he knows Cody's werewolf girlfriend! Lee's been to gaming expos all over the world. Do you know the farthest place I've ever been from home?"

"Chicago," I murmured.

"Chicago!" Jen echoed me. "I don't even have a passport. I don't even know how you *get* a passport. Do you know what I *do* know? How to get rid of stubborn toilet bowl stains! And I just—"

"Jennifer Mary Cassopolis!" I pointed at her. "Stop it. Stop it right now. Do you *like* Lee?"

"Yeah," she mumbled. "I think I do."

"Okay," I said. "Then that's really all that matters, isn't it?"

"Is it?" Jen asked.

I shrugged. "I'm not saying it's easy. But hell, at least you're both the same species." I softened my voice. "Lee likes you, Jen. He likes you a lot. And okay, maybe he's overcompensating a little with the gym and the protein shakes, but you know what? You guys have a lot in common. Whatever life he built for himself in Seattle, he gave it up to take care of his mom, just like you put your life on hold to stay at home and make sure Brandon was safe."

For the record, Brandon was Jen's little brother; only twelve years old, a change-of-life baby. Until recently, Jen had continued living at home to protect him from their abusive father. If you're wondering what changed, that would be the miraculous transformation of Bethany Cassopolis from a whiny, clingy blood-slut to a badass vampire bitch who threatened to drink her father dry if he ever laid a hand on his wife or children again. So far, it had proved an effective threat.

"That's true," Jen agreed.

"You're a good friend," I said firmly. "You're my *best* friend, Jen. You're smart, funny, gorgeous, and loyal as hell. I'm glad you like Lee. I like him, too. But do not for one instant even begin to think that you're not good enough for him. Okay?"

"Okay."

"Promise?"

"Promise."

"Good." I rearranged myself on my end of the couch. "So that's settled. Let's get to the juicy stuff. Any fooling around? Have you at least kissed?"

"We've only had one official date, Daise," Jen reminded me. "And that was to get me out of the house while Sinclair worked up his nightmare whammy for you."

I raised my eyebrows at her. "And?"

Jen sighed. "Okay, Lee kissed me good night at the front door. And, um, it may have turned into a minor make-out session. I'll say one thing—he knows what he's doing," she added. "Those girls out in Seattle must have taught him a thing or two."

I winced. "Not exactly what I needed to hear right now, girlfriend."

"Sorry!" Jen grimaced. "I wasn't thinking."

"Eh, it's not your fault." I waved one hand. "It's nobody's fault. It just sucks, that's all."

"Yeah, it does." She gave me a shrewd look. "Which is why I'm glad you're willing to give the hot ghoul a chance. You *are* going to see him when he gets back, right?"

"Right."

I hadn't told Jen about the part where Stefan forewarned me about asking for an ominously grave favor. I'm not sure why, other than the fact that since he'd made it clear he'd be asking me in my capacity as Hel's liaison, it probably wasn't appropriate fodder for girl talk, which meant . . . oh, gah.

I was totally complicit in this whole cryptic-eldritch-crap scenario.

I hadn't told her about the nightmare, either. It was inside me, eating at me like a cancer. For a moment, I thought about spilling my guts about the whole thing . . . but after our talk, Jen looked happier and more relaxed than I'd seen her in a long time.

I'd been able to reassure her. I'd been a good friend today.

I didn't want to burden her.

So instead, I kept my mouth shut, and spilled my guts to my mom instead.

# Twenty-three

Mom and I ended up celebrating Thanksgiving alone—which, I should add, was totally okay with both of us.

It felt like old times, just the two of us in her double-wide, cookbooks on loan from the library spread open all over the counters, Mom and I doing our best not to get greasy fingerprints on them while we pored over recipes in an effort to execute innovative variations on traditional holiday dishes.

Some dishes worked better than others, although the problem may have been too many disparate elements. For example, the whole turkey marinated in coconut milk and lemongrass was delicious; combining it with a chorizo-and-rice stuffing was probably overkill.

I didn't care. The main point was that we were together and having fun. The affectionate glances Mom sent my way as we put a feast together kept the memory of my nightmare at a distance. Plus, we finished with a triumph, a pumpkin crème brûlée that came close to pulling the whole meal together.

"That was awesome," I said, pushing my chair back a few inches from the dinette table. "Thanks, Mom."

She cast a critical eye over the remains of our repast. "I added too much chipotle to the whipped sweet potatoes. I'll have to remember that for next time. More coffee?"

"Sure. I'll get it." I cleared a few dishes from the table and fetched the carafe of her trusty old Sunbeam coffeemaker to refill our mugs. When I sat back down, she fixed me with one of those universal mom looks, the kind of look that says, "You're not fooling anyone, missy. I know you've been keeping something from me, and I mean to get it out of you, right here and now."

I squirmed on the vinyl-padded seat of my chair, my tail wriggling.

"All right," Mom said. "What's wrong?"

"It's . . . complicated."

She sipped her coffee and studied me. "Honey, if it's something you really, truly don't want to talk about, I won't pry. But I'm your mother. I'm here for you. I'm *always* here for you. And I promise you, there is absolutely nothing in the world you can't tell me."

I made a weak attempt at a joke. "So you're saying you'll help me bury the body?"

Her blue eyes, so unlike my own, were clear and steady. "Try me."

"Okay." I took a deep breath, steeling myself. "There's something I didn't tell you the other day about Dufreyne, that lawyer who's been making offers on plots of land around Pemkowet. He's a hell-spawn."

Mom's gaze didn't waver. "I heard a rumor to that effect. I wondered why you hadn't mentioned it."

"You heard a . . . Oh." That's right, I'd told Stacey Brooks. "Is it all over town?"

"Strangely, no," she said. "The whole thing seems to keep slipping people's minds. At least that's what Sandra said."

Huh. So Stacey must have mentioned something to Sinclair, and Sinclair must have alerted the coven, who were better protected from supernatural influence than ordinary humans were.

"Dufreyne's invoked his birthright," I said. "He's got powers of persuasion."

Mom inhaled sharply. "How—?"

"That's the part I wasn't sure how to tell you." I explained what Daniel Dufreyne had told me about his mother being complicit in his conception, and how only a hell-spawn born of an innocent had the power to breach the Inviolate Wall and unleash Armageddon by invoking his or her birthright.

She listened in a state of dazed disbelief. "So his birth was *planned?* Why would anyone—" Cutting herself short, she closed her eyes. "Oh, God. I'm so sorry. I didn't mean that."

A pang of pain squeezed my heart. "It's okay."

Mom opened her eyes, looking anguished. "No, it's not."

"Yeah, it is." I met her gaze steadily. "Mom, I'm not a kid. You don't have to protect me from the truth. I know getting knocked up by an incubus wasn't in your plan. I know I wasn't an easy kid to raise. And I know you've had to fight your whole life against the kind of assumptions people make about someone who would let that happen to them."

"You were probably too little to remember, but it was a lot worse when you were a baby and we lived up north with Grandma and Grandpa," she murmured. "They did their best, but it was hard on everyone. That's why I decided to move to Pemkowet. At least here there are people who understand."

"Some," I said. "Not all."

"Enough," Mom said firmly. "Enough to build a supportive, loving community, and that's all I wanted for both of us. When I said . . . what I said, I wasn't talking about *you*, Daisy. I meant the planning and begetting part. Not the having and loving part. Were you an easy kid? No. But you were a *wonderful* kid, and I wouldn't trade you for the world." Her expression turned stern, or at least as stern as it ever got, which wasn't very. "Are we clear?"

I swallowed hard against a lump in my throat. "Uh-huh."

"Good. I'm glad." Mom paused, searching for the right words. "So . . . is this lawyer the only one? Are there others?"

"You mean is there a whole hell-spawn breeding program?" I asked. "I don't know. He dropped his little bombshell and bailed, leaving me with a lot of unanswered questions. He said his mother was well compensated for the job, so whoever's behind it has a lot of money."

"And at least one attorney with demonic powers of persuasion," Mom observed. "Along with designs on Pemkowet."

"Right."

"Is that what's had you so worried?" she asked, a crease between her brows. "Because you're right—it *is* worrisome."

"It would be if I'd had time to worry about it," I said. "I've been busy with that whole Night Hag business. And there's something I didn't tell you about that, too."

I'd told her I managed to catch and bind the Night Hag. I hadn't told her *how* I'd done it.

Now I did.

She listened without comment as I described the nightmare that brought my deepest, darkest fear to life.

I was sort of hoping for a "That would never happen!" or a "You would never do such a thing!" at the end of my recitation.

Instead, my mom frowned in thought. "I'd like to read your cards tonight, Daisy. Would you be willing to let me?"

"Yeah. I would," I said. "But let's do the dishes first."

She nodded. "Good plan."

Half an hour later, the dishwasher was loaded to straining and the kitchen was spotless. I poured the final dregs of coffee into our mugs as Mom and I sat back down at the dinette table. She placed her worn old deck of *lotería* cards from a high school Spanish class on the table between us.

It wasn't the first time she'd read my cards, or the tenth or the twentieth. She'd practiced on me while I was growing up, working out her own complicated system of symbolism. Most of the time, the issues I'd concentrated on were the usual childhood or adolescent dramas, and if I really thought about it, her insightful readings probably owed as much to maternal instinct as they did to skill with the cards. But she'd done a reading for me last summer, when the Vanderhei kid drowned, that was incredibly accurate and literal.

It made me apprehensive. That had been a serious issue, but this was serious in a whole different way. This was terrifying and personal. I'd dreamed I'd broken the world, and I was afraid to find out what the cards said.

I pulled out my significator, *El Diablito*, the little devil, shuffled the deck, and cut it a few times before handing it to my mom.

"They're just cards, honey," Mom said gently. "They're not magic. They can't really tell us anything we don't already know somewhere deep inside."

"That would have been more convincing before the reading you did on Thad Vanderhei's death," I said. "Because I assure you, I did *not* know deep inside that a guy with a spider tattoo was involved."

Mom pushed the cards away. "Daisy, we don't have to do this."

"No," I said. "I want to. Whatever the cards say, I want to know. It can't be worse than my imagination."

"All right," she said. "Do you want to reshuffle?"

I shook my head. "Just do it. Maybe it will end up being about my love life," I added. "I could use some insight there, too."

"Let's see." With a deft hand, she dealt a seven-card spread in the shape of an inverted V. I never knew for sure what kind of spread Mom would use, or what significance she would ascribe to each position. Some of them were based on actual tarot spreads, but some of them she made up herself. According to her, it was an intuitive process. She turned over the first card at the apex of the V.

*El Mundo*, upside down. The World, reversed. All the breath left my lungs.

"It's not what it looks like, Daisy," Mom said quickly. "It's not literal. *El Mundo* represents attaining success in the material world. Just because it's reversed, all that means is you're dealing with a setback."

"Really?" I found my voice. "Because I haven't had any setbacks in my career lately, but I *have* had a dream that pretty much turned the world upside down. And the last reading you gave me was awfully fucking literal, Mom."

She gave me a look. "Language, honey."

"Sorry," I said. "Just don't soft-pedal it, okay? If it's bad, it's bad."

"Okay." Mom tapped the card. "Maybe it is literal. If it is, it's because that's what's on your mind. It's not a prediction of things to come. It's just the issue on the table for this reading. All right?"

"All right."

"Let's see what the past holds." She turned over the first card on the left arm of the V to reveal *El Arbol*, the Tree. "Ah. This represents your roots. Your history, your sense of place, your community."

"As in all the reasons I wouldn't want to destroy the world?" I said. "Why's it in my past?"

"Because it has bearing on the issue," Mom said patiently. "Possibly for the exact reason you just stated." She turned over the next card. "And this represents the future."

It was *La Corona*, the Crown. "Aristocracy?" I said, hazarding a guess. After all, Stefan was a count's son. A centuries-dead count from a nation that no longer existed, but still . . .

"Wealth," Mom said soberly.

Wealth, like the kind of wealth it took to bribe a woman into bearing a hell-spawn child, maybe.

"Lurine said Hades was the god of wealth," I said, remembering. "Although Lurine's pretty damn wealthy in her own right."

"Mm-hmm." She turned the next card: *La Bandera*, the Flag. "This represents a possible course of action."

"Well, it's a little late for me to join the color guard," I said. "So what does it mean?"

"Conflict."

"As in war?" I asked.

Mom gave a little shrug, her expression troubled. "As in conflict."

"With Hades, the god of wealth?"

She hesitated. "I don't know, honey. Maybe we shouldn't do this. I don't want you to take it too much to heart. Like I said, they're just cards."

"No," I said. "Let's finish it. What's next?"

"The major factor influencing the outcome." She turned over a card to reveal *El Corazón*, the Heart.

I laughed softly, the sound catching in my throat. "Funny, that's exactly what one of the Norns told me."

"One of the Norns?"

"Yeah." I rubbed my temples. "When Hel summoned me after Halloween. As I was leaving Little Niflheim, one of the Norns warned me that when the time came, the fate of the world might hinge on the choices I made." I glanced at Mom. "Guess I didn't mention that either, huh?"

"No." In the flickering light of the candles on the dinette table, her expression was unreadable.

"This whole deepest, darkest fear thing didn't come out of nowhere." I traced the outline of *El Corazón* with one fingertip. "When I asked her if she had any advice, she told me to trust my heart. The Sphinx said something similar," I added. "Something about learning to see with the eyes of my heart."

"Sounds like good advice," Mom said quietly. "You've got a good heart, Daisy, baby. *I* trust it."

My throat tightened again. "What's next?"

Her hand hovered over the penultimate card. "Your innermost desire and fear."

I pointed at the upside-down World. "I thought we already established that."

"That's an outcome you fear, not something you desire," she said. "This is both. It's a sword that cuts both ways." She turned it over: *El Mano*, the Hand. Unable to guess, I gave Mom an inquiring look.

"Power," she murmured.

The word fell into my thoughts like a stone into a pond, sinking deep and generating ripples. It was true. I hated the sense of impotence that plagued me. I was Hel's liaison, tasked with upholding her order, an honor I cherished; and yet I was forced to do it with threats and promises, operating within the tricky network of eldritch protocols, a weak mortal dependent on the tools that had been given me and the hard-won skills that had been taught me.

Did I want power, my *own* power? Power that I could claim through my birthright? Power that could make pissy back-talking fairies blanch in their tracks, power that could blow vampiric hypnosis out of the water, power that could trade stare for stare with a lamia, match an ogre's strength?

Hell yes, I did.

Did it scare the ever-loving shit out of me?

Hell, yes, it did.

My tail twitched restlessly.

"Do you think about it?" Mom asked softly.

I nodded. "Sometimes."

"That's okay, honey." Her gaze was steady and filled with trust, candle flames reflected in her pupils. "You wouldn't be human if you didn't. And whatever else you are, you *are* human."

I gazed at the spread laid out on our old Formica dinette table. A conflict was coming. An influx of wealth threatened to overwhelm the community where my roots lay. I had choices to make, and the world might hang in the balance.

My father's voice rumbled in the back of my mind, offering a promise of power. *You have but to ask, child.*

I shook my head to dispel it. "Why did you do it?" I asked my mother. "Choose to have me. You could have terminated the pregnancy. It's what everyone told you to do. Why didn't you?"

It wasn't the first time I'd asked, but it was the first time I'd asked her as an adult, woman to woman. In the past, she'd assured me that it was because I was *her* baby, and she'd been determined to love me no matter what. Even if I suspected that the truth was somewhat more complicated, that had always been enough for me.

Now I wanted to know the whole truth.

"You know, it's funny." Mom's gaze shifted onto the distance. "Growing up in a fairly conservative community, I wasn't expecting that kind of pressure. Everyone's pro-life until it happens to someone they know. An unplanned pregnancy, I mean," she added, looking back at me. "Not, um . . ."

"A demon seed?" I said wryly. "I thought a lot of people back home didn't believe that part."

She nodded. "Most assumed it was a fantasy I'd created to cope with the trauma of being sexually assaulted."

My tail twitched again, this time with anger. Mom had never actually used those words with me before. I might on occasion be tempted by the birthright my father offered me, but I would never, ever forgive him for what he did to her.

"So the ones who *did* believe thought you should get rid of the demon seed," I said. "And the ones who didn't thought that for the sake of your mental health, you shouldn't bear your rapist's child to term."

"You knew that, Daisy," she said, not flinching at the word *rapist*. "We've talked about this before."

"It's just that it's a pretty huge decision for a nineteen-year-old girl to make in the face of that much opposition," I said.

"Grandma and Grandpa stood by me," Mom reminded me. "It made a big difference."

"Yeah, but they weren't thrilled about it, were they?" I usually saw my grandparents a few times a year. We didn't have a bad relationship, but it wasn't exactly a warm one, either. They did their best, but it was obvious that they'd never been entirely comfortable having a granddaughter with an infernal temper and a tail.

"No," Mom admitted. She was silent for a moment. "Daisy, what I told you was always the truth. I *did* decide to love you no matter what. But teenaged girls have some grandiose fantasies, too. I thought . . . I thought maybe I'd been chosen by fate. That I could rise above what had happened to me, that if I raised you with love and kindness and taught you to avoid temptation, one day, if you were ever faced with the choice between good and evil, you'd choose *good*, and that somehow, it would make a tremendous difference in the world . . . And show your father he messed with the wrong girl," she added in a harder tone. "That was part of it, too."

I looked at the cards spread on the table, one left unturned. "Do you think that's what this is about?"

"Oh, honey!" She sighed, making the candle flames dance and sway. "I don't know that I'm any wiser than I was at nineteen, but I think the world's a more complicated place than I did then." She smiled a little. "For example, I never imagined you'd grow up to be the right-hand woman of the Norse goddess of the dead, protecting Pemkowet from things like the Night Hag."

I smiled, too. "Neither did I."

"Do I think this is about some epic showdown between good versus evil? No." Mom shook her head. "I don't believe in those kinds of absolutes anymore. Even your father must have *some* good in him to beget a child like you. But if it was just the cards . . . well, I'd say what I said before. They're just cards. But the Norns and the Sphinx, too?" She glanced reluctantly at the spread. "I think there's a serious conflict coming, and your choices will play a significant role in it."

My skin prickled and I shivered. "What about the outcome?" I asked. "What does the last card say?"

I think we were both a little bit afraid of what we might see, bracing ourselves as Mom turned over the final card in her spread: *La Estrella*, the Star.

I looked uncertainly at my mother.

"Hope," she said, her voice growing stronger. "It means *hope*."

# Twenty-four

I spent Thanksgiving night at my mom's place.

After a reading that intense, neither of us really wanted to be alone, so we blew out the candles, turned on the lights, curled up on the couch, and popped the first disk of season two of *Gilmore Girls* into the DVD player.

I fell asleep somewhere in the middle of the third episode, waking only briefly when Mom tucked a blanket over me.

"Sweet dreams, Daisy, baby," she whispered, kissing my forehead. "No nightmares."

It worked. Nothing like a mother's love to keep the nightmares at bay. Well, other than getting sexed up by a werewolf.

In the morning, the shadow of my nightmare returned to hover over me, anchored by the image of *El Mundo* reversed, the world turned upside down. I held the radiant image of *La Estrella* between me and my fear, kindling it like a mental shield.

Hope.

I could live with hope. Especially if it was all I had going for me.

Everything was still quiet in town, at least on the eldritch front. On the mundane front, things kicked into high holiday gear. By the time I wrapped up a plate of Thanksgiving leftovers and drove back to my own apartment, the decorative harvest-themed banners lining the bridge between East Pemkowet and Pemkowet proper had already been exchanged for banners depicting sprigs of holly and candy canes. I wouldn't have been surprised to hear that Amanda Brooks had workers out there at the stroke of midnight preparing to usher in a new holiday season. The official tree-lighting ceremony was scheduled to take place that evening in the park beside my apartment.

I didn't mind, not really. I know it's almost mandatory to complain about the crass commercialization of Christmas, but secretly, I kind of like all the pageantry; which is why, after I'd placated Mogwai with some leftover turkey in penance for abandoning him overnight, I called Jen to see if she wanted to come downtown for the tree-lighting ceremony.

Well, that and I wanted to find out how her Thanksgiving with Lee and his mother had gone.

"In a word?" Jen said. "Unpleasant. But then, that pretty much sums up Mrs. Hastings. How was yours?"

"Interesting," I said. "At least in terms of flavor profiles. For the record, lemongrass and chorizo? Not the best combination."

She laughed. "How many cookbooks were involved?"

"Four," I admitted. "So are you coming to the tree lighting?"

There was a sound of muffled conversation as she conferred with someone else. "Sure. Sinclair says if the weather holds, there might be a surprise. He'll finish his last tour of the day and meet us there."

"What kind of surprise?" I asked.

"I don't know." She sounded a little annoyed. "But he promised it would be a nice one. You know how it is with Sinclair and the nature fey. Right now, he's thick with that damned hellebore fairy in the backyard."

"Right," I said. "Ellie. Okay, bring a thermos. I'll make hot cocoa and peppermint schnapps. Lee can come, too, of course."

"I'll ask him," Jen said. "But you and me? We're on, Daise."

It made me glad, and that was enough. Friendship and community were another shield to raise against whatever darkness might come, whatever darkness lurked inside of me. *El Arbol*, the Tree.

These were my roots, and I needed to hold fast to them.

It was a gray, overcast day, the temperature hovering a bit below freezing. Nothing had changed by the time the sun began to sink in the west, so I guess whatever surprise Sinclair had hinted at remained within the realm of possibility. Inspired by yesterday's bout of extreme domesticity preparing dinner with my mom, I went to the trouble of making hot cocoa from scratch. I'd just finished whisking it to frothy perfection when Jen arrived with Lee in tow.

"Check you out!" Lee seemed impressed. "I never figured you for the Martha Stewart type, Daisy."

"Oh, I'm full of surprises." I took the cocoa off the heat and opened the bottle of schnapps. "Did you bring a thermos?"

Jen passed me hers. "We'll share."

Seeing them as a tentative couple made me happy for them both, but I'd be lying if I said it didn't make me a little jealous, too. Envy, one of the Seven Deadlies. Just the thought of it made the shadow of my nightmare loom larger. I pushed the emotion resolutely to one side, filling Jen's thermos with a generous pour of peppermint schnapps before ladling cocoa into it.

Outside in the park, the ceremony was beginning, the strains of "God Rest Ye Merry, Gentlemen" rising into the cold air. I filled my own thermos and put on my Michelin Man coat, and the three of us trooped down the stairs and into the park.

A good-size crowd had already gathered around the big spruce in the center of the park, tourists and locals alike. A dozen carolers bundled in layers of nineteenth-century costume attire launched into "Here We Come A-Wassailing" as we joined the throng. Stacey Brooks was there with a video camera, filming the picturesque scene.

"Daisy!" Mom called to me across the park, beckoning with one mittened hand. "Come on over." She was standing arm in arm with Lurine, who was looking fabulous in a full-length ermine coat. Damn, I really needed a new winter coat. Gus the ogre, my mom's neighbor, loomed behind them, imposing even to mundane eyes.

"You should have told me you were coming," I said to Mom. "I would have had you up for cocoa."

Mom waved a dismissive mitten. "Oh, we're just here for the lighting." She gave Jen a hug. "Good to see you, sweetheart."

"You, too, Mom Jo." Jen smiled. "I hear you put on quite the feast
yesterday. Hi, Lurine. Hi, Gus."

"Hey, pretty girl," Lurine said to her. "Nice to see you."

Gus ducked his boulder-size head, shuffled his feet, and rumbled
something inaudible. Have I mentioned that Gus has a crush on my
mom? Well, he does.

"You must be Lee," Mom said to Lee. "My, but you've turned into
quite the gentleman around town! I wouldn't have recognized you.
This is my neighbor Gus, and I think you know Lurine Hollister," she
said, squeezing Lurine's arm.

Lee's reaction also involved foot shuffling and mumbling, something about having had the pleasure. I couldn't tell if he was blushing
in this light, but I'm pretty sure he was. I may have rolled my eyes a
little, and Jen may have let out a faint sigh.

"Shhh!" Mom shushed us as the carolers finished a-wassailing and
the town crier stepped forward, ringing his bell. "They're about to
light the tree."

"Hey!" Sinclair squeezed through the crowd to join us, sounding a
little out of breath. "Glad I didn't miss it." I offered him my thermos
and he smiled at me before taking a swig. "Thanks, sistah. Don't mind
if I do." He handed it back to me, lowering his voice. "Are you doing
okay, Daisy?"

"More or less," I said. "Tonight, more than less. You?"

Sinclair hesitated a moment, then nodded. "Yeah. I think you were
right—the end justified the means. Just don't ask me to put a curse on
you again anytime soon, okay?" He shuddered. "I can't say I feel *good*
about having done it."

"No problem," I assured him. "I can't say I feel good about having
it done to me. So what's this big surprise you mentioned?"

He glanced up at the night sky and pursed his lips. "Wait and see."

I waited; we all waited, standing around the park, stamping our feet
on the frozen ground and blowing on our fingers while the town crier
announced Jason Hallifax, the mayor of the city of Pemkowet, who

made a long speech about the virtues of community and togetherness and the spirit of the holidays.

At last, the mayor gave the order.

The tall spruce came alive in a dazzling rush of light, a kaleidoscopic beacon against the darkness. The crowd applauded. Overhead, a generous handful of big, fluffy snowflakes drifted down from the hidden clouds—

No, wait. There were sparkling silver-white figures darting amid the snowflakes on gossamer wings.

"Frost fairies!" Jen exclaimed in delight.

There were oohs and aahs from the assembled watchers as the frost fairies spiraled around the tree, descending to hover just out of reach above our heads, their translucent wings making a faint, musical tinkling sound and refracting the Christmas tree lights in blurred glints of red, gold, blue, pink, white, and green. One alighted atop Sinclair's head and, with a smug look on her exquisite, minuscule features, gave his dreadlocks a fond tug that coated them with hoarfrost.

"Nice surprise," I murmured to him.

Sinclair gave a modest shrug. "After the Night Hag attacks, I figured we could use a little happy magic. We're lucky they cooperated."

I glanced around at the crowd, the upturned faces filled with wonder. "It's beautiful. Thank you."

The frost fairies' visit didn't last long, only a few minutes, but Sinclair was right—it was enough to make the night magical. At an unspoken signal, they vanished all at once, spiraling back upward into the clouds and darkness. Even though I knew what temperamental little bitches they were, my heart ached at the absence of their beauty.

A voice arose to fill the void with the opening lines of "O Holy Night"—a mortal, human voice, tremulous at first, but gaining confidence and settling into a soaring soprano.

It was the youngest of the carolers, a tall, awkward girl still in her teens, the too-short sleeves of her costume baring knobby wrists as she clasped her hands before her and sang, her eyes squeezed tightly shut.

I wanted to cry, or hug her. Maybe both.

It was a song of redemption and hope, and humility, too, something

I'd never been good at. But that night, I felt it. I gazed at the shining tree: *El Arbol*, my roots. All that I loved. A star shone atop it.

Hope.

I whispered the word to myself. *"Hope."*

All too soon, it was over, the last notes fading. The young woman singing blinked her eyes open, looking surprised at herself. Friends and strangers alike laughed self-consciously and hugged one another. Gus the ogre wiped away a surreptitious tear as the crowd began to disperse.

"Did you get footage of it?" Sinclair asked Stacey as she came over to join us, camera in hand.

Her face was still touched with wonder. It made her look younger, or like a softer version of her younger self. "Yeah, I did. That was pretty spectacular."

"And it's a safer bet than those ghostbusting videos you were posting earlier," I observed.

Stacey's expression hardened. "I was just doing my job."

Oops, that was on me. It was hard to lose the habit of a lifetime. I raised my hands. "I know, I know."

Sinclair cleared his throat. "So . . . anyone up for joining us for a drink at the Shoals?"

As much as I wanted to hold on to this feeling of transcendent humanity, I really didn't want to sit around in a bar trying to remember to be polite to Stacey Brooks while she fawned over my ex-boyfriend.

"No thanks," Jen said firmly, hooking her arm through mine. "We're going to hang out here for a while and watch the snow fall. Right, Daise?"

"Right." I snuck a guilty glance in Lee's direction. "Okay by you?"

He shrugged. "Sure."

After saying good night to my mom and Lurine and Gus as they made their way back to Lurine's Town Car, where her driver was patiently waiting, the three of us crossed the street to the playground across from the park, sitting on the swings and passing our thermoses of schnapps-laced cocoa back and forth, kicking our feet idly against the well-worn grooves in the gravel. The big spruce continued to blaze with Christmas lights. Slowly and steadily, big flakes of snow continued to fall, sparkling in the glow of the streetlights and accumulating on the frozen ground.

"We could make snow angels," Jen said in a speculative tone.

"We could," I agreed. "Or not."

"Do you think there really *are* angels?" Lee asked unexpectedly, taking a swig from Jen's thermos. "Thrones and powers and dominions and whatnot? The whole Judeo-Christian pantheon?"

Both of them looked at me.

I looked up. Snow fell from the night sky, dizzying from my narrow perspective. Or maybe it was the schnapps. "I guess there must be."

"Why?" Lee's voice held simple curiosity.

"Because I know my father is real," I murmured, taking a sip of cocoa. "Belphegor. So it only makes sense that his opposite must exist."

"You've *met* him?" Lee asked me.

I shook my head. "Not exactly. But we've . . . spoken. I know he exists. I know how to invoke him."

"Daise," Jen said quietly.

"It's okay." I wrapped my gloved hands around the thick chains of the swing, pushing off against the snow-covered gravel with my feet. "I wouldn't. You know I wouldn't." Once again, I set the memory of my nightmare aside, holding fast to the light. "It's just that . . . yes. I think there are all kinds of things that exist on the far side of the Inviolate Wall, angels and demons included."

"What about God?" Lee asked.

"Whose God?" I said. "Catholics? Lutherans? Baptists? Calvinists? What about the other apex faiths like Judaism and Islam and Buddhism and Hinduism?"

"I don't know," he admitted.

"Neither do I." Leaning backward, I pumped my legs, making the swing soar higher. "I mean, they can't *all* be right, can they?"

"Why not?" Jen asked reasonably. "There are different gods here on earth, aren't there?"

"Just the chthonic ones," Lee said. I raised my eyebrows at him in passing. "The ones with ties to the underworld," he clarified. "Those are the ones that have endured, right?"

I stilled my swing. "Yeah, but they're . . . diminished. Their de-mesnes are limited. They're not even doing battle with each other, let alone seeking dominion over the entire earth." At least I hoped not. I was still uneasy about that whole Hades business. "I don't think you can say the same thing for whatever God or gods are on the other side of the wall. So who's right?"

"Maybe it's like the many-worlds theory," Lee offered. Jen and I gave him blank looks. "In quantum mechanics. It postulates a reality in which every possible quantum outcome is realized. So in theory, there could be an infinite universe containing an infinite number of worlds in which every possible version of God exists."

Jen held out her hand for a thermos. "This conversation would be a lot better if we were stoned."

I was still trying to wrap my head around it. "Yeah, but what about *this* world, Lee?"

He shrugged. "Maybe the Inviolate Wall functions sort of like the box in Schrödinger's cat."

Okay, thanks to *The Big Bang Theory*—the TV show, not the actual scientific theory—at least I'd heard of that one, although I didn't en-tirely understand it. "That's the thing where there's a cat in a box and you don't know if it's alive or dead?"

"Sort of," Lee said. "Schrödinger conceived it as a thought experi-ment to illustrate the nature of quantum entanglement, which is a characteristic—" Noting our expressions, he caught himself. "Never mind. The point is that based on an unpredictable variable, the cat has either been poisoned or not. Until an observer opens the box to see if the cat is dead or alive, it exists simultaneously in both states."

"I bet the cat would beg to disagree," Jen observed.

"It's a thought experiment," Lee said patiently. "It's not an actual cat. It's meant to illustrate a theory."

She smiled at him. "I know. I'm just yanking your chain."

I gazed up at the night sky again, the snowflakes like stars drifting earthward. "So you're saying that there are infinite possibilities beyond the Inviolate Wall, but once it's broken, they collapse into one reality?"

"At least in this world." Lee shrugged again. "It's a theory."

I shivered, feeling the shadow of my nightmare returning to hover over me. Beneath my down coat, my tail gave a nervous twitch. "Let's not talk about this anymore."

Jen tilted her thermos to shake the last drops of cocoa into her mouth before hopping out of her swing. "C'mon," she said in a pragmatic tone. "All this stoner talk is making me hungry. Let's go get burgers at Bob's."

"It's not stoner talk," Lee protested. "It's—" He paused. "You're yanking my chain again, aren't you?"

She gave him another sidelong smile. "Maybe."

I didn't want to be alone right now, but I didn't want to intrude, either. "You guys go ahead. I'm fine."

"No, you're not." Jen stuck out one hand, waiting for me to take it. "You're in a weird mood, and that means you're not going home alone to put one of those old Billie freaking Holiday CDs on the stereo and mope around your apartment with your freakishly large cat. You're going to Bob's with me and Lee for a pitcher of beer and a nice, juicy burger, because we're your friends and we look out for each other. Okay?"

*El Arbol*, my roots.

"Okay." I grabbed Jen's hand and let her haul me out of the swing. "Thanks."

"Anytime."

# Twenty-five

That was the plan, anyway. Beer and a burger at Bob's Bar & Grill. We only got a few yards before a figure detached itself from the shadow of an oak tree and leaped to the top of the jungle gym in one inhuman bound, balancing in a crouch.

All three of us let out startled yelps. I kindled a shield without thinking, dropped my thermos, and yanked open my messenger bag, reaching for *dauda-dagr* in its hidden sheath. Or at least I tried to get a grip on it. Okay, so thick winter gloves, not such a good idea. Atop the jungle gym, the crouching figure grinned, revealing sharp fangs in a luminously pale face framed with glossy black hair.

Jen folded her arms over her chest. "Thanks, Beth. You nearly scared us half to death. What are you doing here?"

"Keeping an eye on my family, just like I promised." With another spectacular leap, Bethany Cassopolis descended from the jungle gym, the skirts of her Victorian frock coat flaring. "I remember you," she said to Lee. "You're the creep who tried to kill me with artificial sunlight."

"Do you mean the guy who kept you from choking Dad to death?" Jen asked. "Because that's the way I remember it."

"Whatever." Bethany grabbed the lapels of Lee's camel-hair coat—one of the purchases Jen had talked him into during their fashion makeover shopping spree—in one hand. Despite the fact that he had a good eight inches on her, she hoisted him effortlessly off the ground. At least Lee was tall enough that his toes still touched. "So are you dating my sister or what?"

"I don't know," Lee said in strangled voice. "Ask her!"

"Jen?" Bethany glanced at her.

She kept her arms folded. "None of your business."

"Oh, for God's sake!" Using my teeth, I stripped the glove off my right hand and got my fingers wrapped around *dauda-dagr*'s hilt. "Bethany, Jen, chill out. Let's not go through this all over again."

With a snarl, Bethany tossed Lee several yards through the air. He landed on his back in the new-fallen snow, the air leaving his lungs in a *woof*ing sound as she whirled on me. "*You* stay out of this! This is family business."

It's hard to pull off menacing in a coat that makes you look like you're wrapped in a sleeping bag, but I did my best, keeping a shield kindled between us and *dauda-dagr* held low and ready. "Actually, if you're threatening mortals without cause, it's *my* business," I said evenly, holding up my left hand palm outward. "Agent of Hel here, remember?"

"Um, yeah, you might want to take the glove off, Special Agent Johanssen," Bethany said. Oops. "And who says I don't have cause?"

"I do, you freak!" Jen retorted, kneeling beside Lee in the snow. "I wanted you to make sure Brandon was okay, not get all up in *my* business!"

Bethany cocked her head. "Um, I didn't hear you complaining when I took a bullet for you at the Halloween parade."

Jen shrugged. "Yeah, well, there's a big difference between saving me from a bona fide gun-wielding psycho and threatening my date."

"Does this mean we *are* dating?" Lee wheezed.

"Yeah, I guess it does," Jen said with reluctant affection. "I'd say being threatened by my sister makes it official."

"Oh, I haven't even begun to threaten," Bethany said. "Listen, Lee. If you even *think* of hurting my sister—"

"Hey!" I waved *dauda-dagr* in the air. "A little respect, here? Magic dagger? Capable of killing the immortal undead?"

Bethany shot me a dismissive look. "Oh, please. You wouldn't use that thing on your best friend's sister."

"Don't tempt me." I tightened my grip on the hilt. "I'm still curious about what would happen if I just injured someone with it, and I'm still betting on eternal never-healing wound. Shall we find out?"

"Oh, I don't think so." There was a shift in the tension between us as Bethany attempted to put a vampire whammy on me. Her tongue flicked out between her fangs to lick her lips, eyes gleaming.

Feeling the tug of her allure, I poured more energy into my shield, letting it blaze. "Nice try." Fledgling vampires have the full measure of preternatural speed and strength, but vampiric hypnosis takes years to master. I beckoned with *dauda-dagr*. "C'mon, what do you say? Just a scratch?"

With a catlike hiss, Bethany vaulted back atop the jungle gym in a swirl of frock coat. "You'd have to catch me first!"

Another figure emerged from the shadows of the oak. "I'd be willing to take that challenge," Cody Fairfax said in a silken growl. "And I suggest you don't try me." He put his hands on his duty belt and tilted his head to look up at her, phosphorescent green flashing behind his eyes. "I think you've had enough fun here tonight, Miss Cassopolis."

Oh, great.

"What are you doing here?" I asked Cody.

"Working," he said. "Trailing a suspicious vampire lurking in the playground. Are you okay, Mr. Hastings?"

Lee was back on his feet, brushing snow off his nice new camel-hair coat. "Yeah, I'm fine."

"Do you want to file a complaint?" Cody asked him. "I'd be happy to take your statement."

"Uh, no." He shot a nervous glance Bethany's way. "I'll pass."

That was probably a good thing, since the Pemkowet Police Department didn't really have the resources or the desire to take on the House of Shadows. It wasn't a confrontation that would end well for anyone, which is why Lady Eris, mistress of our local vampire brood, generally kept her people on the right side of the law.

"Okay." Turning back to Bethany, Cody addressed her in a gentler tone. "Look, I understand that you want to protect your family. Believe me, I do. You've been powerless for a long time, right? And now that's changed. You're the one with the power, more power than you've ever had in your life."

Atop her perch, Bethany sneered. "What, and with great power comes great responsibility? Spare me. I don't need a werewolf on the down low to spout dime-store philosophy straight out of a *Spider-Man* movie at me."

"Who said anything about responsibility?" Cody said mildly. "I was going to say something like, when you're a hammer, everything looks like a nail."

A look of confusion crossed Bethany's face. "What the fuck is that supposed to mean?"

"It means Lee's not a nail, so quit hammering him," I said. "No beating up innocents as a warning, okay? Because I *will* file a complaint, and I'll file it on Hel's behalf with Lady Eris or whatever the hell her real name is."

"Oh, fine." Bethany slumped in defeat. "I was just trying to look out for you," she said to her sister.

"I appreciate the sentiment." Jen's voice was softer than it had been. "But I promise you, Lee's *nothing* like Dad. He couldn't be less like him if he tried. Okay?"

"I really couldn't," Lee agreed.

"So are we good here?" Cody asked.

I glanced at Bethany. She returned my gaze with a stony one of her own, but she didn't say anything. "We're good," I said to Cody. "And thanks, but I could have handled this on my own."

He shrugged. "Just doing my job, Daise. I didn't know who Bethany was stalking when I spotted her."

"I wasn't *stalking*." Bethany came down from the jungle gym in another bounding leap. "I was observing." She came toward me, not halting until I could feel the undead aura that surrounded her—the absence of a heartbeat, of involuntary breathing, of human warmth. At close range, it was as creepy as all hell—and somehow even creepier with someone I'd known as a living, breathing mortal. "So you think you could have handled me, huh?"

Over her shoulder, I saw Cody raise his eyebrows in inquiry, and I gave my head a slight shake, standing my ground. I hadn't been truly angry before, just annoyed. After all, Bethany *had* taken a bullet for her sister at the Halloween parade earlier this year—literally, at point-blank range.

But I was getting angry now. I'd never had a lot of patience for the hierarchical bullshit that went on in the eldritch community, all the posturing and standoffs, and tonight, it was more than I could take. All I'd wanted to do was enjoy the lighting ceremony, have a nice time with my friends, and forget about the specter of Armageddon for one evening, not get into a virtual pissing contest with a vampire.

I let my anger slip its leash, feeling the atmosphere around us grow charged. My hair crackled with static electricity. My tail was lashing, and *dauda-dagr*'s hilt was solid and reassuring in my hand.

If Bethany made a move on me, I *would* cut her; and then we'd see what sort of lasting damage my magic dagger did to undead flesh.

Over at the swing set, the chains rattled uneasily. Bethany Cassopolis licked her lips, took a deliberate breath and a step backward. Score one for me—and without a single word spoken. With an effort, I reined in my temper. The atmosphere eased and the swings stilled.

Assuming an air of finality, I slipped *dauda-dagr* back into its hidden sheath. "So, how about that burger?"

"Yes, please," Lee murmured. "And beer. Lots of it."

Bethany pointed at him. "I stand by my warning. Don't you forget it."

Jen rolled her eyes. "I'm telling you, you've got nothing to worry about. And hey, it's not like your judgment is anything to brag about. Where's your snotty vampire boyfriend, anyway?"

Her sister shrugged. "Oh, didn't I tell you? I broke it off with him as soon as he turned me. You're right—he was totally passive-aggressive."

"Huh." Jen looked surprised. "Good for you."

"You can do that?" Lee asked, sounding equally surprised. "Isn't he, like, your maker or your sire or something?"

"Yeah, it doesn't work exactly like that," Bethany said. "I mean, we're *supposed* to be soul mates, blood-bonded for life and all that, but you know, once I wasn't a stupid, weak mortal under Geoffrey's thrall, I realized he was a controlling prick just like our father and I didn't really like him all that much." She shrugged again. "Lucky for me, in real life, vampire progeny can only be commanded by their brood-mistress or –master. I don't have to obey anyone but Lady Eris."

"Or whatever her real name is," I couldn't help adding under my breath. Opposite me, Cody suppressed a grin. Trust me when I say that Lady Eris of the House of Shadows embodied every vampire trope exploited by Elvira, Mistress of the Dark back in the day. Although it's also true that she works it pretty hard. In our last encounter, before I learned to shield, I was damn near ready to beg her to sink her fangs into my neck.

"Ha ha," Bethany retorted. "It's her real name, dummy. Her mother was the only daughter of a wealthy industrialist and her father was a classics scholar in Boston in the late eighteen hundreds. They fought a lot."

I didn't get it. "And?"

She raised one eyebrow. "Eris, as in the Greek goddess of strife? Which is also a pun on heiress, as in the heir to a fortune?"

Huh. Go figure.

"Hey, that's pretty good," Lee commented.

"I know, right?" Bethany agreed before jabbing her finger at him again. "Just remember what I said. I'll be watching." On that note, she made her exit, whirling away into the shadows along the edge of the playground.

"Ohh-kay," Jen said to no one in particular. "Sorry about that, guys. Let's go get those burgers, shall we?"

I paused to retrieve my thermos before following Jen and Lee.

"Daisy." Cody's voice halted me. "I lied before."

"Oh?" Thermos in hand, I straightened. "About what?"

"I knew you were here," he said quietly. "I caught your scent. And I know you could have handled Bethany on your own. I just wanted you to know I've got your back. I'll always have your back."

If my life were a movie, Cody would have gone on to say that he'd thought about what I'd said the other day and realized that I was right, that our problems weren't insurmountable, that he loved me, that we'd find a way to make it work no matter what, that all that mattered was that we were in this together. The sound track would have swelled and we would have clung to each other and kissed in the falling snow, while the Christmas lights sparkled in the background, and maybe a few townsfolk who'd been rooting for us all along would have cheered.

Also, I would have been wearing a much cuter coat.

Instead, Cody just stood there looking sexy and unavailable, snow-flakes dusting the fleece collar of his uniform jacket and melting in his hair.

"Thanks," I said to him. "Good to know."

So that's pretty much all there is to say about that, which is to say, nothing. Nothing had changed.

I caught up with Jen and Lee, and the three of us crossed the street and went around the corner to Bob's. It's one of those places that's swamped by tourists in the summer and reclaimed by locals in the off-season. Thanks to the lighting ceremony, it was crowded, but we managed to snag a table in the back.

"How very . . . quaint." Lee glanced around the room at the decor, which consisted of Christmas lights, vintage beer signs, and creative taxidermy that had seen better days. "What the hell is that supposed to be?"

"It's a jackalope," I actually have a soft spot in my heart for taxidermists; it happens to be my grandfather's trade, although he doesn't go in for that sort of novelty work. "Don't tell me you haven't been to Bob's before."

Lee shrugged. "What can I say? Until recently, my life in Pemkowet has been a sheltered one." He poured three glasses of beer from the pitcher the waitress had brought us and hoisted one. "Here's to it becoming a hell of a lot more interesting."

"You're in pretty good spirits for a guy who just got tossed around by a vampire," I observed.

He grinned. "I'm a guy who's dating a vampire's sister. That's pretty badass, don't you think?"

Jen muttered something incoherent into her beer glass, but on the whole, she didn't look displeased.

We rehashed the Bethany incident while we waited for our food. When our burgers arrived, the waitress set a fresh pitcher of beer that none of us had ordered on the table along with our plates. "Courtesy of your friends at the bar."

"What friends?" Lee's voice took on a suspicious edge. "Is this a joke?"

Oh, gah. I'd sort of hoped that paranoid streak of his had become a thing of the past, but high school damage runs deep.

Jen gave him a mild look. "Let's not jump to conclusions, okay?"

Scanning the bar, I caught sight of Dawn Evans swiveling on her stool. With a shy smile, she raised a beer bottle in our direction. "It's okay. I know who it's from," I said, extricating myself from the table. "Be right back."

I squeezed through the milling throng to where Dawn and Scott were sitting side by side at the bar. Although I'd touched base with Dawn to make sure the charms Casimir had provided to ward off the Night Hag had worked, I hadn't seen either of them since the morning of Scott's attack.

They looked good, both of them; calmer and clear-eyed. "Thanks." I clinked my glass against Dawn's bottle. "You didn't need to do that."

"Oh, ah know," she said in her Alabama drawl, stroking Scott's arm. "We just wanted to thank yuh."

"We heard Chief Bryant announced that you caught the bitch." Scott's left eyelid twitched at the mention of the Night Hag, but his gaze was steady. Still haunted, but steady. "She *was* real, wasn't she?"

I nodded. "Too damn real by half."

"Yeah." Scott nodded, too. "I've seen some bad shit in my day, but I don't ever remember feeling so goddamn helpless. It's good to know that there's someone out there fighting the good fight and holding the line against things that go bump in the night. Because that shit? That shit's uncanny. That shit can make you crazy. That shit can kill you." He took a swig of beer, eyeing me. "I don't know what you had to do to put an end to it, Ms. Johanssen, but I know there was a price. There's *always* a price."

"It was worth it." At least I hoped it was.

"Well, we sure do 'preciate it," Dawn murmured. "And it ain't all bad, is it?" Her face brightened, touched with lingering wonder. "Were yuh at the tree-lightin' ceremony tonight? Did yuh see them frost fairies?"

"Yeah, I did." I smiled. "Beautiful, weren't they?"

She smiled back at me. "Sure were. Yuh won't see *that* anywhere else in the world, will yuh? And that little girl singin' a solo sure was somethin'." Dawn gave her husband's arm another affectionate squeeze. "Scott thinks she should try out for *The Voice*, but ah still lahk *American Idol*."

"Nah." Scott took a pull on his beer bottle. "*Idol*'s played out."

"You seem like you're doing a lot better," I said to him in a low voice. "Are you, um, still sleeping okay?"

"Yeah." Scott nodded. "I have good days and bad. But it's better." He shuddered. "That bitch caught me hitting rock bottom. I don't ever want to go back there." Turning on his barstool, he stuck out his hand. "Put 'er there, soldier. You saved my life."

I shook his hand, feeling self-conscious. "Oh, God, it's nothing. I mean, it doesn't compare to what you've been through. Thank you for the beer. Speaking of which, I should get back to my friends. I think their burgers are getting cold waiting for me."

Dawn Evans caught my shoulder as I turned to go. "It weren't nuthin', honey," she said softly. "Don't yuh ever think that. Yer fightin' a different kind of battle, that's all."

I shrugged. "Just trying to keep the peace."

She gave me a sweet, weary smile. "Aren't we all?"

I made my way back to the table and explained the situation to Jen and Lee, or at least as much of the situation as discretion permitted, while we dug into our burgers. His paranoia allayed, Lee was surprisingly understanding. I'd forgotten that Ben Lewis, one of his two close friends from Pemkowet High's nerd posse, was serving in Afghanistan. Ben had been a short, stocky, quiet little guy, the Hobbit to Lee's Skeletor. It was hard to imagine him in combat, but then, it was hard to imagine Dawn Evans driving a Humvee, too.

Later that night, walking back to my apartment after Jen and Lee and I had said our good-byes, I thought about what Dawn had said to me. I'd never thought of myself as a soldier—rather more of a diplomatic liaison—but Hel had given me a dagger, not a talking-stick to pass around the speaking circle. She hadn't given it to me for the purpose of threatening Bethany Cassopolis. I'd used it before to end lives, twice.

I didn't relish the thought of using it again, but if I had to, I would.

And my mom's reading had indicated there was a conflict coming. There was a hell-spawn lawyer out there who might or might not work for Hades, Greek god of the underworld and wealth.

There was my nightmare.

But there was also a blanket of new-fallen snow on the world, Christmas lights, and a star sparkling atop the tree. There was the memory of frost fairies glittering amidst the snowflakes, and of a young woman lifting up her voice in song to fill the aching void of their absence with a different kind of wonder.

There was Scott Evans's firm handshake and the clarity in his eyes, the knowledge that I'd done good in the world.

Those were the thoughts I chose to hold close as I climbed the stairs and let myself into my apartment. Mogwai greeted me with yowls, protesting his confinement, but he let himself be assuaged with a full bowl of kibble. After a hearty meal, Mog deigned to plunk himself on my lap, flex his claws in and out, and purr with satisfaction while I sat at my desk and entered Bethany's transgression into the Pemkowet Ledger database, because hell, yes, that was going on her record.

In the park outside my window, the Christmas lights on the big spruce continued to sparkle through the falling snow. I gazed at them for a while, absently petting Mogwai, before turning out my own lights and going to bed.

I slept well. Tonight, the shadow of my nightmare kept its distance, and I was at peace with the world.

And then in the morning, Stefan called, shattering that peace.

# Twenty-six

I was making coffee when the call came.

"Daisy." Stefan's voice sounded grave when I answered, and I got a sinking sensation in the pit of my stomach. Whatever dire favor he'd been hinting at, it was going to be asked of me.

"Hey," I said with a lightness I didn't feel, trying to fend off the inevitable. "Are you back in Pemkowet?"

"Yes," he said.

"Is everything okay in, um . . . ?" I couldn't for the life of me remember the name of the town in Poland where he'd been for the past weeks.

"Wieliczka," Stefan supplied. "Yes, thank you. Would you happen to be free anytime today? There's someone I'd like you to meet."

I poured a carafe of water into the coffeemaker. "Does this have to do with that favor you mentioned?"

"Yes," he said. "I'm afraid it does."

Great. I switched on the coffeemaker. "I don't suppose you'd care to cut the cryptic eldritch crap and enlighten me, would you?"

"No." There was a trace of humor in his voice, but it didn't alleviate the gravity. "As I have said, this is something that must be done in person, Daisy."

I sighed. "Yeah, I figured. I have to go into the station for a few hours this morning, but I'm free in the afternoon. Will that work?"

"Yes," Stefan said. "Would you be able to come to my condominium at two o'clock?"

The word *condominium* sounded funny in his Eastern European accent; or maybe it was just the idea of a ghoul—my bad, one of the Outcast—living in a condominium. Immortality and homeowner's leases didn't seem like two things that went hand in hand. "Sure," I said. "I'll be there."

"Thank you."

So much for peace.

All morning long, a fog of apprehension clung to me. What, exactly, constituted a dire favor for one of the Outcast? Maybe Stefan had suffered some kind of injury doing whatever the hell he was doing in Poland and wanted to feed on my super-size emotions to restore his strength. That would explain why he had to make the request in person . . . sort of. But I'd seen Stefan's method of dealing with a serious injury last summer. When that psychopath Jerry Dunham had shot out his knees, Stefan had freaking *impaled* himself on his sword, dying and reincarnating in a heartbeat, as good as new.

Besides, Stefan had mentioned the possibility of a favor before he even left for Poland . . . right before he kissed me.

Oh, I hadn't forgotten about that kiss. As far as kisses went, it was fair to say that one had rocked my world.

By noon, I gave up trying to guess. I logged my hours on my time card, went home and made myself a tuna salad sandwich, watched an old *Law & Order* episode—ever notice that there's always a *Law & Order* episode on somewhere?—and spent the remaining time practicing my psychic shield drill, just in case Stefan tested me to make sure I'd been diligent. Last night's encounter with Bethany was a good reminder that I needed to keep my skills honed.

At two o'clock, I presented myself at Stefan's condominium.

"Daisy." Stefan greeted me at the door. He gave me one of his courtly little bows and smiled at me, and my heart lurched absurdly in my chest. "It is good to see you. Please, come in."

"It's good to see you, too," I said in the small foyer. It was, although he looked tired. I wondered if it was due to jet lag, the draining effect of being away from a functioning underworld while traveling, or the ominous favor.

"Let me take your coat," he said, helping me out of my leather jacket. Yes, it was freezing outside, and no, I hadn't worn the Michelin Man coat. "Come inside. I'd like to introduce you to a dear friend."

Aside from an impressive array of edged weapons hung on one wall and a museum-quality fourteenth-century Bohemian parade shield on display in a Plexiglas case, Stefan's condo featured sleek, minimalist furnishings, high ceilings, polished wood floors, and a big picture window with a great view of the river.

Today, there was a wheelchair parked in front of the window. The man sitting in it gazed at me with dark, luminous eyes, an indecipherable yearning in his expression.

"Daisy, this is Janek Król," Stefan said. "Janek, this is Daisy Johanssen, who serves as liaison to the goddess Hel in Pemkowet."

"It is a pleasure," Janek Król said in slurred, softly accented English. Reaching for a pair of forearm crutches, he began struggling to rise.

"Oh, please!" I said quickly. "There's no need to get up!"

"Please." He gave his head a dismissive shake. "Sometimes manners are all that stand between us and the end of civilization."

So I waited while Janek Król completed the arduous task of levering himself upright and taking a step away from his wheelchair, his feet dragging reluctantly. At least it gave me time to study him. He had a thick crop of bushy gray hair and a gaunt, lined face, those dark, expressive eyes set in deep sockets. It was hard to place his age; he looked to be in his mid-sixties, but I had a feeling he was younger. I realized with a shock that he was one of the Outcast. It shouldn't have been a shock—after all, he was a friend of Stefan's—but I'd never considered the fact that an Outcast could be disabled.

"There." With a lopsided smile, Janek extended one hand. His ring and pinky fingers remained folded back against his palm, unable to straighten. "It is not a *good* handshake, but it is a handshake. A proper greeting for a beautiful American girl."

I shook his hand. "It's a pleasure to meet you, Mr. Król."

"And you, Miss Johanssen." His pupils waxed briefly as he drew a sharp breath, but they steadied just as fast. His body might have been compromised, but it was obvious that his willpower and discipline were strong—as strong as Stefan's or maybe even stronger. "Please, call me Janek."

"Daisy," I said in turn. "How can I, um, help you?"

Janek glanced at Stefan, who gestured to a table in the dining space. A tray sitting on it contained a clear glass bottle of amber liqueur and three shot glasses. "I procured a bottle of *nalewka* for the occasion," Stefan said. "Traditional Polish spirits. Let us sit together and drink while Janek tells you his story."

Janek nodded in agreement. "Then you may decide if you are willing to help me, young Daisy."

My tail twitched reflexively. "Okay."

With another prodigious effort, Janek returned to his wheelchair. He set the forearm crutches aside and allowed Stefan to maneuver him to a seat at the head of the table where a chair had been cleared. I took the chair to his left, and Stefan sat opposite me. It all felt very formal, which didn't help settle my nerves. My thoughts skittered all over the place. I found myself wondering if it was a regular thing for Stefan to hold councils at his dinner table. Somehow, I didn't think so. Hell, I didn't even know if he ever used his dinner table—the Outcast can eat and drink, but a lot of them don't bother, since they can't take any sustenance from it.

Then I tried to recall if I'd ever seen Stefan eat or drink anything other than a parsimonious sip of water, and finally remembered that yes, we'd had coffee together at Callahan's after Thad Vanderhei's funeral, which didn't seem like a particularly good omen. Stefan had commented that it was dreadful—the coffee, that is, which was true, but it was cheap and refills were free. Although Thad Vanderhei's funeral was pretty dreadful, too. That was where I'd been on the verge of *totally* losing my temper and causing a major scene—as well as possible structural damage—and had voluntarily consented to let Stefan drain my fury, which had averted the crisis but forged the bond between us.

And thinking about *that* made me wonder how many other people Stefan was bonded to—if the bond was as powerful, or if that was a dubious side effect of my super-size emotions—and why I hadn't seriously wondered about it before.

Yeah, those are the thoughts that flashed through my mind in the time it took Stefan to fill three shot glasses with traditional Polish spirits and distribute them. Did I mention that I was nervous?

Janek Król raised his glass, holding it carefully in his crabbed hand. "*Na zdrowie!*" he said. "To your health."

Unsure whether to sip it or slam it, I watched and waited. Sip, apparently. It tasted sweet and faintly herbaceous, a bit like cough syrup. Not that I'd ever had a cough—I never got sick—but Jen and I had dared each other to drink a bottle when we were teenagers in search of a legal buzz.

"You will be wondering about my condition." Janek set the glass down. "In English it is called amyotrophic lateral sclerosis." He pronounced the foreign words with care, struggling not to slur. "I believe in America you call it after a famous player of baseball, Lou Gehrig."

I nodded. "Lou Gehrig's disease."

"It is a *bitch* of a disease." He spat the word. "And I have endured it for almost three-quarters of a century."

"I'm sorry," I murmured. Stefan sipped his liqueur without comment.

"It is not your fault." Janek waved his hand. "It is no one's fault. But it is a bitch of a disease."

He told me his story.

Before that afternoon, I hadn't known much about Lou Gehrig's disease. I hadn't known much about the history of Poland under German occupation during World War II, either. I mean, I knew about the Holocaust and the concentration camps and the general course of events, but it had all seemed very distant. Well, except for that time I watched *Saving Private Ryan*, which obviously doesn't count.

Listening to Janek Król tell his story, it felt very immediate, very real, and very, very horrifying.

He told it in a matter-of-fact manner without belaboring the details.

He had been a teacher, a man of profound Christian faith, and a child-less widower. He had been diagnosed with Lou Gehrig's disease after experiencing symptoms far milder than he did today shortly before the Nazi German invasion in 1939.

Oh, and for the record, the disease is incurable, inexorably debilitat-ing, and inevitably fatal. It really is a bitch.

I hadn't known about the Nazis' efforts to eradicate ethnic Poles, the thousands sent to the concentration camps or killed outright, and I hadn't known there was a Polish government in exile, coordinating re-sistance efforts including an organization dedicated to providing shel-ter, food, and false documents to Jews across the country.

"Oh, yes," Janek said in a dry voice. "It is estimated that it took ten Poles to save the life of one Jew."

In the ongoing cultural genocide during the occupation, in which a lot of academic institutions were destroyed, surviving Polish children were forbidden to receive an education beyond the elementary level, the theory being that it would prevent a new generation of leaders from arising. Even as his condition continued to deteriorate, Janek's role in the resistance had been as a teacher, part of an underground campaign to educate those very children.

"An important role," he acknowledged. "Not a *vital* role. But I knew people who performed such roles, providing military intelligence to the government in exile. In 1941, the Gestapo began to suspect such a man of my acquaintance, an asset of great value." He shrugged. "I took his place."

"How?" I asked softly.

Stefan refilled our shot glasses with liqueur. Janek took an effortful sip and coughed. "How is not important," he said. "Nowadays, such details do not matter, only to historians. It is enough to say it was done. The suspicions of the Gestapo were diverted, and they took me instead of him." A spasm convulsed his right shoulder and ran down his arm, and the shot glass slipped from his hand, falling onto the table. Janek swore in Polish.

"It's okay," I said while Stefan rose to fetch a dishcloth. "You really don't have to tell me this."

Janek fixed me with his intense gaze. The hunger in his eyes was palpable, and I fought the urge to kindle a shield. "Yes," he said. "I do." He waited until Stefan had mopped up the spill and refilled his glass before continuing. "I knew I would never return from this mission and I was at peace with it. Already, I was a dead man walking. I told myself it was not a form of suicide, that there was no sin intended, and that God would forgive me for the sacrifice I made. But I lied to myself. I knew what I was doing and why. And so did God."

There wasn't a whole lot one could say in response to that, so I didn't say anything.

Wrapping his two fingers and thumb around the shot glass, Janek lifted it to his lips, sipped and grimaced. "The Gestapo questioned me for many days. You will have read about such techniques, for your own government used them not so very long ago. It was only the knowledge that I was giving my life to save another's, to serve my country, that gave me the strength to endure." He stared into the distance. "To this day, I do not know how it is that I failed."

An involuntary sound escaped me.

"Oh, yes." Janek's gaze shifted back to me. "Just before he killed me, my tormentor made certain I knew. *You let a few things slip, Mr. Król*, he said to me. *You're not who you're pretending to be. But that's all right. We've got the right fellow now.*" His crippled hand tightened around the glass. "To prove it, he recited my acquaintance's name and address, the names of his wife and children. I was filled with a rage and despair such as I have never known. Seeing this, my tormentor laughed. And then he said they had no further use for me, and shot me."

Across the table, Stefan's pupils waxed in silent fury.

"So." Janek relinquished his grip on the shot glass. "I died; and I returned. The first of many times. That is how I discovered that God did not forgive my sin." His mouth tightened. "Of what happened next, I will not speak to such a beautiful young woman."

"Daisy should know," Stefan murmured. "Janek was in captivity when he became Outcast. Had he been physically hale, it is likely that he would have been able to orchestrate an escape once he gained sufficient mastery of his new ability."

"Even without an underworld present?" I asked. "Or did this take place in, um . . . ?"

"Wieliczka?" Stefan shook his head. "No. But the ground was soaked with sufficient blood for necromancy to function."

"I thought that only worked on islands," I said. "Because they're circumscribed by salt water."

"There are places in this world that have seen sufficient horror to fuel death magic for centuries," Stefan said. "Janek was sent to Dachau." With an abrupt motion, he downed the contents of his shot glass at a gulp. Apparently, there were times when that was called for, and this was one of them. "The Nazis conducted medical experiments at Dachau," he said in a dispassionate voice. "They were excited by the possibilities presented by a man who could not die. Until the encampment was liberated in 1945, the Nazis tried many experiments to see if Janek's ability could be transferred to another subject. Many, many experiments. Blood transfusions, organ transplants, limb grafting—"

"Stop!" I felt sick. "I'm sorry," I said to Janek Król. "Oh, God! I don't mean to be rude. I mean, your story *should* be told. The world should bear witness to it or something, but . . . why me? Why here and now?"

Janek gazed at me without blinking, his pupils wide and fixed in his dark eyes. "So that you will understand what I have suffered when I ask you to put an end to this immortal existence of mine."

"When you—" I swallowed hard. "You're asking me to kill you?"

"Yes, young Daisy." Janek Król inclined his head to me. "I am asking you to kill me."

# Twenty-seven

I found myself on my feet with no memory of having risen from my chair, pacing back and forth in Stefan's condo, my tail lashing while the two Outcast at the table watched me without speaking.

"I don't get it." I stopped pacing and flung my arms out. "How is asking *me* to kill you any less suicidal than sacrificing yourself to the Gestapo?"

Janek Król sat upright and dignified in his wheelchair. "It is not."

"So . . . *why*?"

He folded his hands in his lap. "I have prayed on this for many days, since first my good friend Stefan told me of your existence, and the great and terrible weapon you possess. I believe it is a sign from God that He has forgiven me. I believe He is calling me home."

I stared at him. It was hard to believe that after all Janek had been through, his faith remained so strong; and even harder to believe the logic behind his conclusion. "By means of a hell-spawn with a dagger given to her by the Norse goddess of the dead? *That's* God's way of telling you it's okay to commit assisted suicide?"

"Yes." Janek's eyes glittered fervently. "Beyond the Inviolate Wall, God cannot intervene directly on the mortal plane, but He can use any tools that come to hand. Including a pagan goddess, and yes, the off-spring of a fallen angel."

I plopped back into my chair, poured myself a shot of liqueur without asking and downed it. "What about you?" I asked Stefan. "Do *you* think my existence is a sign of God's forgiveness?"

Stefan hesitated. "I think it is possible," he said at length.

I eyed him. "Tell me you're not planning on asking me to kill you."

He gave me a faint smile. "No."

"Good." I looked back at Janek. "Why does it have to be me? I mean, there *is* another way, right?" I felt guilty even suggesting it—the only other way for one of the Outcast to die was to starve to death, deprived of all emotional sustenance until they lost their wits, devoured their own essence and ceased to exist. Stefan had told me once that it would require many months of solitary confinement.

And yes, I'd just suggested that prospect to a Holocaust survivor who'd spent years in a concentration camp being subjected to medical experiments too gruesome to contemplate.

On the other hand, he *was* asking me to kill him.

"It is true," Janek said. "But that way leads only to nonexistence and the eternal void, not the possibility of heaven or hell."

"I don't mean to question the tenets of Outcast lore," I said. "But, um . . . how do you *know*? I mean, presumably no one's come back from the eternal void to report on their dissolution and nonexistence, right?"

By the way, yes, I'm aware that I hadn't questioned that particular tenet when I'd been called upon to dispatch two ghouls last summer; maybe because Hel herself had sentenced them to death and ordered me to ensure that it was done, maybe because they were guilty of a heinous crime. Or maybe because if I'd looked too closely at what I was doing, I'd have lost my nerve.

Across from me, Stefan shifted. The two men exchanged a glance.

"I have seen the void," Janek said quietly. "And it terrified me."

"Oh."

"At some point in our long existence, most of us have made the attempt," Stefan murmured. "Many have seen the void. Few have continued willingly."

I swallowed. "I see."

Janek gave Stefan an inquiring look. "Have you spoken to Daisy of your first death?"

"No." He shook his head. "I have spoken to her of how I died and was made Outcast. Not the death itself."

"It is a painful subject." Janek drew a slow, deep breath. "At the moment of passing . . . for some, it is the white light, or so they say. I think it is because there are no true words to describe it. For me, it was like a sound, like the sweetest chord ever struck; only it was not music or even truly a sound, but a sense of homecoming, as though I had been lost in the wilderness for the longest time, wandering lonely and afraid, only to hear my mother call my name, her voice filled with love, and the promise of rest and comfort—" He halted and clenched his teeth, a tremor running through his body. "Forgive me."

I nodded.

"It was a fleeting glimpse of glory," Janek continued with an effort. "And then it was gone, as though a door had been shut with great violence. And I was Outcast, filled with all the rage and despair with which I died, and a hunger, a terrible hunger, ravaging my soul. But I have never forgotten that glimpse." His voice grew stronger. "And I will not sacrifice its promise to the eternal void."

Well, it was kind of hard to argue with that. "Is that how it was for you, too?" I asked Stefan.

"Yes," he said quietly. "I would use different words, but the sense that Janek describes . . . yes."

"Does it happen every time you, um, die?"

"No." Stefan shook his head again. "I think we would go mad if it did. To be offered such a glimpse and denied it, over and over."

"Some of us do go mad, old friend," Janek said quietly. "Some of us embrace the ravening."

"Yes," Stefan said. "And some of us fight it."

"Yes."

They sat together in silence, two veterans of battles I couldn't begin to imagine sharing memories I couldn't begin to fathom. It felt unseemly to disturb their reverie, but again . . . hello? I'd just been asked to kill one of them.

"How can you be sure it would be different this way?" I asked Janek. "What if I, um, do what you ask"—I couldn't bring myself to say *kill you*—"and there's nothing there but the void?"

It was Stefan who answered. *"Dauda-dagr* is a charmed weapon given to you by a goddess of the dead, Daisy. It is my belief that it will dispatch its victims to the afterlife, not the void of nonexistence."

I raised my eyebrows at him. "You seem awfully certain about something that can't be proved."

"I am," he said mildly. "Perhaps you have forgotten that I told you that when I was a Knight of the Cross with the Red Star, I was a member of a branch of the order that studied occult afflictions."

"At a hospital in Prague," I said. "Oh, I haven't forgotten. I may forget how to pronounce Wie . . . Wiel . . ."

"Wieliczka," Stefan said. "And since my days with the order, I have had six centuries to study eldritch phenomena. You witnessed two members of the Outcast meeting their final deaths at your hand some months ago," he reminded me. "Tell me, did it seem to you that it was the void they faced?"

"Wieliczka," I repeated. "Okay, fine. No. It seemed to me that they faced a second chance at redemption or damnation—most likely the latter, given the whole business of engaging in rape and torture. Which leads me to my next point." I turned toward Janek. "It's not that I'm not flattered to be considered a sign of divine grace and all, but what if you're wrong? What if God *hasn't* forgiven you, and it's damnation and hell that you face? It could be worse than Dachau."

"I am willing to take that chance," Janek said.

"I'm not sure I am," I said.

"Daisy." His dark eyes blazed in his gaunt face. "This I believe to be true. It is as I have said; when I faced death the first time, I lied to myself. I told myself it was not a true form of self-murder, that it was only for the greater good. That was the lie. Yes, I wished to spend my death for a purpose, but it is also true that I wished to hasten the process of dying."

I raised my voice. "And you revere a God who *blamed* you for it?"

"I revere a God who abhors lies," Janek said firmly. "Now, I no longer lie to myself. I think perhaps there is no sin greater than losing faith in God's infinite forgiveness. That is where I failed before. Now, I am ready to make an end to my long suffering, and God in His mercy has restored my faith and shown me the way. You."

Tears stung my eyes. "I don't want that responsibility!"

Across the table, Stefan stirred. "*Dauda-dagr* is a weapon of great power, Daisy," he said softly. "When you accepted it from Hel's hand, you accepted the mantle of responsibility that came with it."

Oh, for God's sake. "I'm not fucking Spider-Man!" I shouted at him.

Stefan's pupils waxed abruptly as my temper ratcheted up, his irises shrinking to frosty rims. "Excuse me?"

I stood up and walked away from the table. At the big picture window, I leaned my forehead against the cool glass, probably leaving a smudge. Outside, it was a gray November day. The river reflected the overcast sky, its gray surface ruffled by the cold breeze. Bit by bit, my anger drained away.

Stefan approached me from behind, standing close enough that I could feel the warmth of his body. Part of me wished he'd put his arms around me. Part of me was afraid I might slug him if he did. Okay, maybe I was holding on to some residual anger after all. But Stefan didn't do anything. He just stood there, offering his presence.

"I don't want to do this," I whispered without turning around.

"I know."

"You could take it away from me, couldn't you?" I said. "The fear, the uncertainty, the doubt?"

"Most of it," Stefan said. "The intellectual questions you are wrestling with would remain. But without the underlying emotions, they will no longer seem to matter." He paused. "Is that what you want?"

"No," I murmured. "If I do this, I need to own it. I just . . ." I shrugged. There were no words.

"I know," Stefan said again. He was quiet for a long moment. I didn't expect him to speak again until I succumbed to the inevitable and gave in to their request, but he surprised me. "Daisy, what does all this have to do with Spider-Man?"

It caught me off guard. I let loose an involuntary gasp of laughter that turned into a ragged sob, and Stefan did put his arms around me then. I leaned back into his embrace, letting the tears streak my cheeks. "This isn't how I imagined our reunion."

"I know," he said for a third time, his breath stirring my hair. "I'm sorry."

"I know." I freed one hand to wipe at my tears. "It's because what you said reminded me of a line from the movie. *Spider-Man*," I added, realizing my explanation was a total non sequitur. "The one with Tobey Maguire, I mean, not the new one. It just came up the other night. With great power comes great responsibility."

"I see." Stefan took a deep breath, possibly trying not to laugh. "Actually, I believe the quote may first be attributed to Voltaire."

"Oh." I didn't want to admit I wasn't entirely sure who Voltaire was. I thought he might be the guy who said, *I think, therefore I am*, but I wasn't positive. Actually, that's not true. The part about not wanting to admit it, I mean. I'd rather stay here, gazing out the window with Stefan's arms wrapped around me while he allayed my ignorance regarding French philosophers, than face what would follow, but delaying wouldn't make it go away. No matter how long I stood here, Janek Król would be awaiting my answer with terrible patience.

I didn't want to do what he asked. I really, really didn't. But there was no one else in the world who could grant Janek the release he yearned for, and if I tried to walk away from this responsibility, his story and the sight of his tortured body that had endured so much for so long would haunt me for the rest of my days.

"All right," I said. "I'll do it."

Stefan's arms tightened briefly around me. "I am in your debt, Hel's liaison," he murmured against my hair. "I am grateful."

We returned to the table. I nodded at Janek Król and forced myself to say the words again. "I'll do as you ask."

"Thank you!" His voice was thick with emotion. He took my hands in his and kissed them, his eyes bright with tears. "You are my angel."

I wanted to laugh at the absurdity and cry at the awfulness of it all over again. "Wrong team, I'm afraid."

Janek shook his finger at me. "Do not say such things about yourself," he said in a stern voice. "I have seen more than I hope you will ever witness of the good and bad in human nature. The Jews have a phrase, *tikkun olam*. Perhaps you have heard it?" I shook my head. "In the camp, there was an old man, a scholar, who spoke to me of such things. It means to repair the world."

The reference was a little too close to my nightmare for my liking. "Jews believe the world is broken?"

"For some, *tikkun olam* means only a commitment to social justice and the common welfare," he said. "But according to the old scholar, in kabbalah it is believed that when God created the world, He placed a part of Himself in vessels of divine light. These vessels shattered in the act of creation, and their shards became sparks of light trapped in the material world, unable to pass through the Inviolate Wall and return to God. That is the cause of much evil in the world. But through prayer and *mitzvot*, the sparks may be released."

"I'm not sure I follow," I admitted.

"The divine sparks are like the souls of the Outcast." Janek tapped his chest with one finger. "Trapped on the mortal plane. In freeing mine, you are performing a *mitzvah*, an act of kindness. You are engaged in *tikkun olam*, repairing the world. It is the great work of humanity. So, please." His voice took on a dismissive edge. "Do not tell me you are on the wrong team, Daisy Johanssen."

I wished I had his certainty. It would be nice to think I was repairing the world instead of posing the threat of destroying it.

But then, it would be nice if I didn't have to kill him, too.

Stefan cleared his throat. "How do you wish to proceed, Janek?" he asked quietly. "Do you desire time to prepare?"

Janek Król shook his head. "I am ready," he said. "I have been ready for a long time. And once upon a time, you were a member of a religious order, old friend. Will you hear my final confession?"

Stefan inclined his head. "I will." He glanced at me. "Daisy, will you procure *dauda-dagr*?"

I went to fetch the dagger from the hidden sheath in my messenger bag while Stefan helped Janek rise from his wheelchair and kneel on the hardwood floor. I hung back discreetly in the foyer while Janek made his confession. I suppose it wouldn't have mattered, since he did it in Polish, but it seemed like the right thing to do.

My hands were sweating and the worn leather wrapped around *dauda-dagr*'s hilt felt cold and slick against my palm.

Oh, God, I really, *really* didn't want to do this.

In the main room, Janek's voice fell silent. I watched Stefan sketch the sign of the cross in the air.

"*Ego te absolvo a peccatis tuis in nomine Patris, et Filii, et Spiritus Sancti,*" he said in a firm tone, going to one knee. Taking Janek's face in his hands, he planted a kiss on his brow. "Amen."

"Amen," Janek whispered in response. "Thank you, old friend. If I achieve heaven, I promise, I will petition God on your behalf. I will petition Him on behalf of all of those who are Outcast."

Stefan smiled with affection and sorrow. "I know you will." Rising, he beckoned to me. "Daisy?"

I wanted to drag my feet like a little kid, but Janek deserved better, so I did my best to approach him with dignity, *dauda-dagr* in hand.

On his knees, Janek smiled up at me. "Be at peace, child. I tell you, it is an act of great mercy you perform." With difficulty, he unbuttoned his shirt, baring a pale, sunken chest laced with scar tissue. "Here."

Like Stefan, I dropped to one knee before Janek. Unlike Stefan, I did it because I figured I'd need the leverage.

Janek circled my wrist with two fingers and a thumb, guiding my hand to place *dauda-dagr*'s tip beneath his breastbone. A thin wisp of frost rose as it burned his skin with cold. He let out a sigh.

I met his gaze. "Is this truly what you want?"

"Yes." Janek's dark eyes were luminous, his pupils dilated not with hunger, but ecstasy. "Please. Send me home."

Stefan moved to support him from behind, strong hands grasping Janek's shoulders. I was grateful for it. Blue light glinted along *dauda-dagr*'s keen edges, shimmered in the runes etched on its length.

Gathering my strength, I shoved it hilt-deep into Janek Król's chest, upward and under his breastbone. For an instant, his eyes widened and his mouth shaped an ecstatic O. *Dauda-dagr*'s hilt tingled against my palm as it drank in Janek's death, his final death.

And then Janek's long-suffering body vanished in the blink of an eye, departing the mortal plane.

That's what happens when you end the existence of one of the Outcast, and it's every bit as disconcerting as it sounds. Even though I'd known what was coming, it took me unprepared. I was still braced for the thrust. Unable to halt my momentum, I overbalanced and fell forward into the space where Janek had been.

Stooping swiftly, Stefan caught me, the hands that had supported Janek's shoulders grasping mine and steadying me. *Dauda-dagr* fell from my grip to clatter on the floor between us, its blade dark with blood, smearing the polished hardwood.

"Are you all right, Daisy?" Stefan asked me.

"Yes." I sat back on my heels, burying my face in my hands. It felt as though I'd taken an immense weight on my soul. "No."

Stefan's hands flexed on my shoulders, firm and reassuring. "It was an act of mercy," he said. "An act of grace."

I lifted my face to peer up at him, hoping to hell or God or whoever would listen that he was right. "Sorry about your floor."

"Daisy . . ." The expression on Stefan's face was a complicated mix of grief and exasperated fondness. He released me and pulled a bandanna from a pocket. One thing about Stefan, he always seemed to have a clean bandanna on him. I think it's some kind of biker etiquette. "Here."

I wiped *dauda-dagr* clean, then wiped up the bloody smear it had left on the floor. "I don't think it will stain."

Taking my arm gently, Stefan eased me to my feet and relieved me of the bandanna, balling it up in his other fist. He held my gaze, his own intent. "Can you at least try to believe me?"

"I do believe you," I said. "I would never have done it if I didn't. It's just . . . hard." I reached up to touch his cheek. "I'm sorry. This must be much harder for you. Janek was your friend."

"Yes," Stefan said simply. "Thank you."

For the space of a few more heartbeats, we continued to gaze at each other. There was a lot of heavy emotion in the room. Like, seriously heavy. Intense, fraught emotion, laced with underlying tension between us. I could see the strain it was putting on Stefan's control in his glittering pupils, his quickened breathing.

I lowered my hand. "This would be a good time for me to leave, wouldn't it?"

Stefan inclined his head. "I am sorry."

I took a deep breath. "Crap, our timing really sucks, doesn't it?"

He gave me a faint, dimpled smile filled with profound regret. "Yes, Daisy Johanssen. Our timing . . . sucks. But if you are willing, I would like to see you under better circumstances."

I nodded. "I'd like that. But, um, I think I need a little time and space to process what happened here today."

"Would a week's time suffice?" Stefan inquired.

It was an impossible question to answer. How the hell was I supposed to know if a week was enough time? That wasn't the kind of thing you could anticipate. Or maybe you could, if you'd lived as long as Stefan had. Maybe someone should write an eldritch dating handbook. I could see the chapter heading now: "How Long Should You Wait to Go on a First Date After Mercy-Killing Your Immortal Suitor's Friend?"

Then again, even among the eldritch, I was an unusual case. *Daudadagr* made me different. All things considered, I should probably reconcile myself to the fact that I didn't lead an ordinary mundane life and never would, and stop looking for ways to make my life fit within some imaginary framework of cultural normalcy.

Meanwhile, Stefan was still waiting for an answer. "Honestly?" I said. "I have no idea. Let's try it and find out."

He inclined his head again. "Next Saturday, then."

"Okay."

Stefan escorted me to the door and helped me into my jacket. "Until then," he murmured. "Be well."

Outside, the cold air made my eyes water. I slung my messenger bag over my shoulder and walked slowly to my car. I couldn't think about what had transpired today, not yet. Hell, maybe never.

And yet, despite everything, I'd just agreed to go out on a date with Stefan next Saturday.

My life definitely wasn't normal.

# Twenty-eight

I might have avoided thinking about Janek Król during daylight hours, but my dreams that night were haunted and fragmented.

No surprise, I guess.

It wasn't a reprise of my nightmare, not quite, but there were elements of it. I dreamed of vessels of blazing light bursting into shards; and I dreamed of the dome of heaven cracking asunder with a thunderclap.

I dreamed of the faces of my loved ones turning away from me in disappointment.

*It's* tikkun olam, I protested in my dream, *dauda-dagr*'s hilt clenched in one fist. *I'm repairing the world!*

My mother shook her head at me, and I realized blood was dripping from the dagger's blade, falling silently in the dune hollow in which I stood, drops of blood making dark pits in the sand.

I dropped the dagger in horror. In his wheelchair, Janek Król stared at me with his hollow, haggard gaze and pointed a stern finger at me, then turned his hand palm outward, transforming it to a symbol from my mother's reading: *El Mano*, power, the thing I yearned for and feared. In my dream, his hand was hale and unravaged.

Heavyhearted, I knelt to retrieve *dauda-dagr*.

*With great power comes great responsibility*, Bethany Cassopolis whispered in my ear from behind. *Right, devil-girl?*

Still on my knees, I whirled on her, but no one was there. I fell, catching myself on my free hand.

*Dauda-dagr's* tip scored the sand.

*Daughter*, my father's voice rumbled from beyond, *you have but to ask.*

Absently, as though I stood outside my own body, I watched myself inscribe a sigil in the loose sand, stand, and call my father's name.

Overhead, the sky cracked open all over again and the trumpets of Armageddon sounded with a clarion blast.

"No!"

My cry of denial jolted me awake, a whimpering sound stuck in my throat. I was tangled in my sheets, my heart was racing, and my skin was damp with sweat. On the bed beside me, Mogwai let out a low, purposeful yowl. Reaching out with one forepaw, he extended and retracted his claws to prick and knead my sheet-shrouded arm.

It was strangely reassuring. My racing heart slowed. Mogwai withdrew his paw and began purring deep in his chest, regarding me with slitted green eyes.

"Thanks, Mog." I disentangled my arm and stroked him. "As kind-of, sort-of familiars go, you're not half bad." Mogwai flicked one notched ear in acknowledgment and continued purring contentedly.

Once I'd gotten out of bed, washed, and dressed to face the day, I didn't know what to do with myself. I wasn't scheduled to work until tomorrow, but between Janek Król's death and my disquieting dreams, I was filled with restless energy and a sense of foreboding. I wanted to *do* something, but I didn't know what. I wanted to talk to someone, but I didn't know who.

My mother always said that when you didn't know what else to do, you might as well clean house, so I put my restless energy to good use and gave the apartment the kind of top-to-bottom thorough scouring it only got . . . well, that it pretty much never got. I even pulled out the refrigerator so I could vacuum and scrub the floor behind it, which, by the way, was pretty gross.

At least it was productive, and it freed my mind enough so I could think about who I might talk to.

The only person who could really, truly understand the decision I'd made yesterday was Stefan, but he was the one person I *didn't* want to see today. It sure as hell wasn't something I wanted to discuss with my mom. I mean, yes, I can talk about almost anything with her, but somehow I couldn't see myself telling her I'd mercy-killed a hundred-and-some-year-old Dachau survivor.

Or Jen, or Sinclair, or . . . anyone fully human, really.

I could have talked to Cody about it, I thought wistfully. The wolf in him would have understood. But I was too hurt and, frankly, too pissed off at Cody for that to be an option.

Lurine was the logical choice, but she was also a good friend of my mother's. I didn't have any problem asking her to keep minor confidences—after all, she was my friend, too—but this was major. And there was the fact that when it came to me, Lurine didn't trust Stefan any further than she could throw him. Actually, scratch that; Lurine in her true form could probably heave Stefan a considerable distance. Let's just say she didn't trust him and I didn't particularly feel like defending him to her.

Cooper was a possibility. I'd come to consider him a friend, and there was no doubt in my mind that he would understand. Then again, that was the problem. Cooper might understand *too* well. He'd been Outcast at seventeen, and while the body he was trapped in might be strong and healthy, more than two hundred years as a never-aging seventeen-year-old boy had given him a nihilistic streak. When he'd been ravening, he'd practically dared me to use *dauda-dagr* to take him out. I didn't want to give him any ideas.

So no, not Cooper.

By the end of the day, my apartment was spotless, and I was no closer to a resolution than I'd been when I started. All I knew was that I didn't want to be alone—no offense to Mogwai—in my apartment for another minute.

On a total impulse, I drove to the grocery store, bought a case of beer, and headed out to the abandoned Presbyterian camp to pay a visit to Skrrzzzt the bogle.

Honestly, I have no idea what made me think of the bogle, except that he'd been strangely easy to talk to and I was pretty sure I could count on him to be nonjudgmental about the whole mercy-killing thing. Not that I planned on bringing it up or anything. At this point, I just didn't want to be alone with my thoughts anymore, and the idea of kicking back with Skrrzzzt and cracking open a couple of beers was oddly appealing.

Of course, what had seemed like a good idea in the warmth and comfort of my living room seemed decidedly less so in the dark woods with a cold wind blowing off Lake Michigan. I parked in the lot near the mess hall and left the beer on the hood of my Honda. Snow crunched underfoot as I made my way to the porch and knocked on the door.

"Hey, um . . . Skrrzzzt?" I called. "Are you in there?"

There was no answer. I tried the handle and found it unlocked, so I pushed the door open and jumped back, bracing myself in case Skrrzzzt was on the other side, waiting to pounce at me again.

Nope, no bogle.

I waited a moment for my eyes to fully adjust to the darkness before entering the mess hall. The folding chairs were stacked and the dining tables stood empty. No beer cans, no evidence that a bogle had been there. I took a quick peek in the deserted kitchen and found that was empty, too.

This had been a dumb idea. No way was I going to search the entire camp on my own for one elusive bogle. I backtracked to my car.

"Hey, Skrrzzzt!" I said aloud. "I don't know if you can hear me, but it's Daisy Johanssen. I just wanted to say thanks for helping me out with the Night Hag. I brought some beer. I'll just, um, leave it on the porch for you."

There was no response, unless you count tree branches creaking eerily in the cold darkness. Feeling more than a little foolish, I hoisted the case of beer and hauled it over to the porch of the mess hall.

"*Boo!*" a familiar voice said inches from my ear.

I let out a shriek and dropped the beer, whirling around and tripping over the porch steps in the process.

Skrrzzzt doubled over laughing as I landed hard on my butt on the steps. "Oh, man!" Orange flames of mirth danced in his eyes. He held up two immense, knobby hands in apology. "I'm sorry, mamacita. My bad. I couldn't resist. Oh, but if you could have seen the look on your face!"

Gathering what was left of my dignity, I stood. "Yeah, well, I'm glad it amused you. I'll see you around, okay?"

The bogle sobered. "Oh, hey! Don't go away mad. I didn't mean anything by it." He grimaced. "Shit! Is this going on my record?"

"Let's say we're even and call it a day," I said, reaching in my coat pocket for my car keys.

"Aw, man!" Skrrzzzt spread his long-fingered hands in a pleading gesture. "Come on, cut a brother some slack." I hesitated. He contorted his grotesque features into a winning smile. "C'mon! You brought beer and everything. Join me for a cold one?"

Feeling somewhat mollified, I shrugged. "I guess it couldn't hurt."

"Great!" The bogle scooped up the fallen case of beer and perched it on one gnarled shoulder. "Let's head over to the rec room," he said. "After that spill you took, I bet your badonkadonk could use a comfy chair—am I right?"

My bruised tail twitched in agreement. "Don't remind me."

The rec room was a cabin with a handful of overstuffed chairs that smelled faintly of mildew. The walls were lined with bookshelves filled with battered paperbacks and stacks of board games. It would have been cozy in a dilapidated sort of way if there had been a fire in the fireplace, but at least it was warmer inside away from the wind than it was outdoors.

"How's about a little mood lighting?" Skrrzzzt suggested, setting down the case of beer and reaching for a battery-operated camping lantern on a high shelf. "Let's see if there's any juice left in this bad boy." He switched on the lantern, which emitted a dim glow. "Perfecto! Beer me?"

I opened the case and handed him a beer. "So is the camp just leaving all this stuff here?"

"Yeah." He glanced around. "They've salvaged anything worth saving. Pity. Lot of love in these old walls."

I fished out a beer for myself and took a seat on one of the big chairs. "I bet. I'll be sorry to see it go."

"You and me both, mamacita." Skrrzzzt set the lantern on the floor between us and sat in a chair opposite me, slinging one arm along the headrest. "So what's on your mind?"

I shrugged. "Nothing special."

"Now, now!" The bogle wagged a long, black-clawed finger at me. "You didn't come all the way out here all by yourself just to say thanks. Is it man trouble?" His orange eyes glowed with avid curiosity. "A certain werewolf, perchance? You can tell old Skrrzzzt," he said in a wheedling tone. "I've got the experience of listening to four generations' worth of camp counselors under my belt."

"Okay." I cracked open my beer and took a gulp. "I killed a man yesterday."

Skrrzzzt let out a low whistle and opened his own can. "You got me there, mamacita. Not what I expected." He took a long pull on his beer, then wiped his leathery lips. "He deserve it?"

"You tell me." Despite the fact that I'd had no intention of doing so, I found myself giving the bogle an abbreviated account of what had happened yesterday. What can I say? He really was easy to talk to.

"Sounds to me like you did the man a kindness," Skrrzzzt said when I'd finished. "You losing sleep over it?"

"You could say so," I said.

"Figures." He drained his beer. "You mortals have soft hearts to go along with your soft little bodies. Beer me?"

I tossed him a fresh one. "So what advice do four generations' worth of camp counselors have for me?"

"Are you kidding?" The bogle chuckled, a sound like dry branches snapping underfoot. "This is way out of their league. I was hoping you were here to talk about your love life. You want *my* advice?"

"Sure."

"Get over it," Skrrzzzt said simply. "Like it or not, it's part of your job."

"That's it?" I asked him. "That's your sage advice?"

The bogle shrugged. "It is what it is, mamacita. Did you think it was all gonna be beer and skittles when you accepted that nasty-ass magic dagger you've got hidden under your coat from a goddess of the freakin' dead?"

"No, but . . ." I couldn't think of a way to finish my protest. "No."

"Well, there you go, then." Skrrzzzt hoisted his beer in my direction. "Feel better?"

Oddly, I did. Skrrzzzt's advice notwithstanding, I wasn't about to "get over it" now or ever—I don't think killing someone, even if for the best possible reasons, is something anyone should "get over"—but I felt calmer.

"Yeah," I said. "Actually, I do. Thanks."

"No problemo," the bogle said. "Sometimes it just helps to talk things out, and sometimes it's easier with someone you've only just met. Fresh perspective, no emotional baggage, yadda, yadda, yadda." He swigged his beer. "And that, little lady, *is* wisdom gleaned from eavesdropping on four generations of camp counselors."

"Well, I appreciate it." I set down my empty beer can. "Consider yourself off the hook for scaring me. You're still up a favor in my ledger."

"Cool." Skrrzzzt looked relieved, then dismayed as I rummaged for my keys. "Hey, you're not taking off already, are you?"

"I don't mean to confess and run, but it's getting late," I said. "And I have to work tomorrow."

"Pffft!" He waved a dismissive hand. "It gets dark so early this time of year. It's barely past six o'clock. C'mon, keep me company for a while longer. We can play a board game." Rising, he padded on backward-bending legs over to the bookshelves and perused them. "What have we got here? *Risk, Monopoly* . . . eh, not really my bag . . . *Scrabble* . . . you like *Scrabble*?"

"It's okay," I said. "Do you?"

Skrrzzzt scratched his lank, mossy hair. "You know, I can't say I've actually played any of these—I've just watched humans do it. Seems like a decent way to pass the time."

"Well, maybe we should pick an easy one." I got up to look. "One where I can remember the rules."

We settled on *Battleship* and played three rounds. I won the first two and Skrrzzzt won the last, after which I left over his protests, promising I'd come back some other time.

"You'd best mean what you say, mamacita," the bogle said to me. "Because I'm gonna hold you to it."

"I know." I smiled at him. "Don't worry. I know better than to make false promises in the eldritch community."

"Right on." Skrrzzzt nodded and held out one fist. "Respect."

I bumped his fist with my own. "Respect."

It's funny, but Skrrzzzt was right. I did feel better after talking to him, and part of it was because he wasn't involved in any of my drama. Feeling generous, I drove home, fed Mogwai, and logged in to the Pemkowet Ledger to record an additional favor owed in the bogle's record. I figured lending a sympathetic listening ear to Hel's liaison counted. If and when the old campsite sold and was developed as residential housing, I'd definitely put in a word with the homeowners' association on Skrrzzzt's behalf.

After all, if the bogle had managed to maintain a good working relationship with the Presbyterian camp for four generations, there was no reason to think he couldn't do the same with new owners.

If I had dreams that night, I didn't remember them. I awoke feeling well rested—and, as a bonus, in an immaculately clean apartment, thanks to yesterday's flurry of housekeeping. I celebrated by making a big breakfast of scrambled eggs, toast, and bacon before heading down to the police station on foot.

About twenty yards before I reached the station, an inexplicable tingle ran the length of my spine.

Something felt *wrong*.

I glanced around, my tail twitching. Nothing seemed amiss. There were a few cars parked along the street, but most of the shops weren't open for business yet. On the opposite side, a couple of women carrying yoga mats were chatting in an animated fashion on their way to the studio at the end of a picturesque little alley.

Shrugging, I continued onward.

Inside the station, it was pandemonium. Chief Bryant, Bart Mallick,

Ken Levitt, and Patty Rogan were all crowded in the foyer around the reception desk, all of them talking at once, trying to talk over one another.

My bad feeling intensified.

"Hey!" I called. "What's up? What's going on?"

Glancing over at me, the chief held up one hand for silence and the conversation came to a halt. "Daisy." The expression on his heavy face was grim. "We're being sued."

# Twenty-nine

I stared at Chief Bryant. "What do you mean we're being sued? All of us? The Pemkowet PD?"

He shook his head. "Not the department."

"It's the PVB." Behind the desk, Patty was unable to contain the news. "*And* the city *and* East Pemkowet *and* the township. They're all named as codefendants."

I shifted my blank gaze to her. "Who? How? Why?"

"It's a class-action lawsuit to the tune of forty-five million dollars." The chief's mouth twisted in distaste. "The plaintiffs are suing for damages for physical, emotional, and psychological injuries sustained during the events of last October."

I blinked. "Can they even *do* that?"

"Apparently so," he said. "As far as I know, there's no precedent, but a judge has certified the claim. That means that one way or another, it's moving forward." He drummed his thick fingers on the desk, scowling at me. "Guess which particular attorney filed the suit and has been appointed representative counsel for the plaintiffs?"

I drew in a sharp breath. "Son of a bitch!" It hit me then. One of the cars parked on the street where I'd felt the first tingle of wrongness had been a sleek silver Jaguar, a car I'd last seen hell-spawn lawyer Daniel Dufreyne getting into and driving away in, leaving me with unanswered questions.

"Excuse me," I said, turning on my heel and heading for the door.

Outside, Daniel Dufreyne had emerged from his car in anticipation of my return. It looked like he was posing for a photo shoot for *GQ*. He wore a long, expensive-looking charcoal wool coat with a burgundy cashmere scarf around his neck, and he was leaning back against the hood of the Jaguar, feet propped on the curb clad in highly polished black oxfords, hands laced before him in black leather gloves that fit like, well, really expensive gloves.

He was smiling, his unnaturally white teeth gleaming. I struggled with the urge to punch him in those white, white teeth.

"Daisy Johanssen." His voice turned my name into an unwelcome caress. "I was hoping to see you this morning."

I gritted my teeth. "Why?"

Dufreyne's smile widened like a shark's. "Schadenfreude," he said. "It means—"

"I know what it means!" I shouted. "It means you came here to gloat. What the hell do you have against Pemkowet? What the hell do you have against *me*?"

His smile vanished. "Why, I've got nothing whatsoever in the world against Pemkowet," he said in a disingenuous tone. "It's a charming little community. It's not *your* fault that the conjoined local governments and the visitors bureau made bad decisions that led to a lot of innocent tourists suffering harm. All I want to do is ensure that redress is made, so it never happens again."

"Bullshit," I said bluntly. "You were here trying to buy property on behalf of some developer—Amanda Brooks's property in particular. You can't tell me that's not a conflict of interest."

"A point of correction." Dufreyne held up one gloved finger. "I *did* facilitate the purchase of several parcels of land on behalf of Elysian Fields. Naturally, that party is concerned about property values declining based on governmental malfeasance." He shrugged. "However, they have no stake in the outcome of this lawsuit beyond the general well-being of the community."

"And bankrupting Amanda Brooks in the process, forcing her to sell her property, too?" I said.

A gleam of unholy amusement lit his black eyes. "The lawsuit doesn't target Ms. Brooks as an individual. The fact that she happens to own a parcel of interest is entirely coincidental."

Something about Dufreyne's barely suppressed glee made me believe he was telling the truth. I remembered the map that Lee had shown me—God, it felt like months ago—with the red blotch of lots that Elysian Fields had purchased encroaching on Hel's territory. The old Cavannaugh property that belonged to Amanda Brooks had been a decent-size wedge of unsold green, but it was dwarfed by Hel's territory.

And *that* was owned by the City of Pemkowet.

My skin prickled under my old down coat. The reek of the hell-spawn lawyer's wrongness filled my sinuses. "You don't give a damn about the Cavannaugh property," I whispered. "You're going after Hel's territory."

Dufreyne widened his eyes in mock innocence. "Now, why in the world would I do that?"

"I don't know." My initial shock was giving way to a rising vortex of anger. "But if this lawsuit bankrupts Pemkowet's tri-community governments, something's going to have to be sold, isn't it? Something big?"

"In the event of a decision in favor of the plaintiffs, the terms of the settlement would be determined by the presiding judge, Ms. Johanssen," he said primly.

I ignored the comment. "Why? Who's behind Elysian Fields? Is it Hades?" I asked. Dufreyne's eyelids flickered. "I saw his mark on your palm."

"Ah, is that what you think you saw?" His voice turned smooth and velvety. "You were mistaken."

Now that he was trying to use powers of persuasion on me, the theory seemed a lot more convincing. "Yeah, I don't think so."

"Yes, you were." Dufreyne's voice took on a new, weird resonance, like his voice was an electric guitar and he'd just stepped on an invisible reverb pedal. It washed over me like a vibrating wave of sound, broke, and receded, leaving me unaffected. He raised one manscaped eyebrow. "Hmm."

I folded my arms over my chest. "It doesn't work on me, does it?"

Dufreyne was unperturbed. "Apparently not."

"Is that how you're planning to convince the judge to settle in your favor?" I inquired. "Because I'm pretty sure there's no legal precedent for holding mundane authorities responsible for eldritch transgressions. And you should have done your homework, because unfortunately for you, the nearest courthouse is in Allegan." I pointed south. "Miles outside of Hel's sphere of influence. It won't work there."

Daniel Dufreyne burst into laughter—laughter filled with cruelty and genuine unfettered mirth. "Is that what you think?" Reaching into his coat, he drew out a silk pocket square and wiped his eyes. "Ah, Daisy! You poor, provincial little thing." He replaced the pocket square. "You've lived your whole life in this town, haven't you?"

"Not my *whole* life," I said defensively.

Abandoning his insouciant pose, Dufreyne drew himself upright to his full height. "I'm a demon's son," he hissed in my face, his breath filled with that awful stench of wrongness. "Offspring of a genuine apex faith, not some pathetic remnant of a dwindling pagan god's twilight years. Do you really think *my* power is dependent on having a functioning underworld beneath my feet?" He touched his chest. "I carry the underworld inside me, just like you do, cousin."

I held my ground, trembling with fury. "Does your master Hades know you talk about him that way?"

His nostrils flared. "Hades is not—"

"Hey, there!" Chief Bryant's gruff voice interrupted. "Dufreyne, is it?" He settled his meaty hands on his duty belt. "Step away from her."

Dufreyne paused, then took a deliberate step backward. His eyes were black and icy. "We were just talking, officer."

"Well, keep moving." The chief jerked his chin at the lawyer. "Or I'll write you up for disturbing the peace."

"Oh, but you wouldn't do that, officer." Dufreyne skipped the dulcet tone and went straight for reverb. "Would you?"

Chief Bryant frowned. "No. No, I guess I wouldn't."

Dufreyne nodded. "Leave us."

And just like that, Pemkowet's chief of police, a stalwart, strong-willed man who'd been a father figure to me for almost as long as I could remember, turned and walked back into the station, meek as a lamb.

I felt sick with rage and helplessness. "*Why*? Why are you doing this? What does Hades want with Pemkowet? Is he declaring war on Hel? And why the fuck are you hell-bent on tormenting me?"

"So many questions!" Daniel Dufreyne steepled his gloved fingers, tapping his lips. "Oh, my. Why do you think you deserve answers?"

"Because this is *my town*!" I shouted at him, unable to contain my fury. Overhead, a power line whined and a streetlight burst into shards, littering the pavement below.

"Ah, see!" Dufreyne said with satisfaction. "There you go. It's not that I want to torment you, per se, but there's just something unspeakably delicious about your impotent rage. And let's face it," he added. "The last time we met, you must admit, you were unbearably smug about your innocent and oh-so-loving mother."

I hadn't been smug. I'd committed the crime of feeling sorry for him and letting it show. It punctured my anger like a balloon.

"I'm sorry," I murmured. "Please, don't punish Pemkowet for my offense."

Dufreyne shrugged and shoved his hands into his coat pockets. "Look, I don't mean to burst your bubble, but this isn't about you. As far as I'm concerned, the schadenfreude's a bonus. Everything else is just business. You can't take it personally."

I rolled my eyes in exasperation. "Yeah, it's kind of hard not to when you show up on my doorstep to revel in my impotent rage, *cousin*."

His black eyes gleamed. "Of course, it doesn't have to be that way. But you'll never take that risk, will you?"

*Daughter . . .*

I shuddered, remembering my nightmare, the vault of heaven cracking open above me. "No."

"Pity."

"Does your master Hades know you feel that way?" I asked. "Hankering for Armageddon and all?"

Dufreyne didn't rise to the bait this time. "I represent an investment on the part of my sponsor," he said. "Any investment carries a certain amount of risk." He showed his white teeth in a grin. "So far, I've proved worthwhile."

"Good for you," I said. "But I'm still wondering what in the hell Hades wants with Pemkowet, because I have it on pretty good authority that no god can maintain two demesnes. Am I wrong?"

"Do you expect me to answer that?" Dufreyne inquired.

"It would be nice," I said.

He considered it. "All right. I'll give you one for free. No, Hades isn't declaring war on Hel. Hades has no interest in Pemkowet."

I searched Dufreyne's blandly handsome face, trying to determine if he was telling the truth. I thought he might be—he had that same barely hidden smirk, hinting at the delightful irony that the truth was as bitter as a lie. You'd think a hell-spawn would have a better poker face, but then again, if his emotions ran as high as mine did, I guess it made sense.

"So who does?" I asked him. "Whose behalf are you acting on?"

Removing his hands from his pockets, he spread them in a gesture of wounded innocence. "Why, the plaintiffs, of course."

"Yeah, right," I said. "Do the plaintiffs have a stake in Elysian Fields?"

"Of course not," Dufreyne said in a virtuous tone. "As I told you, beyond a general interest in the well-being of the community, Elysian Fields has nothing whatsoever to do with the lawsuit."

"I don't believe you," I said flatly.

"I don't care." His tone shifted again, this time taking on a genuine intonation of boredom. Daniel Dufreyne, hell-spawn lawyer, was finished with this conversation. Of course it didn't matter what I believed. What mattered was what the judge believed, and the judge would believe whatever Daniel Dufreyne told him. He turned to open the door of his Jaguar and eased into the driver's seat. "I'll see you in court, Daisy."

Wait a minute.

I caught the door before he could close it. "What do you mean, you'll see *me* in court? Am I named as a defendant?"

"You?" His sharklike smile returned, filled with gloating and schadenfreude. "Of course not. You're a witness for the prosecution."

With that, he yanked the car door closed, started the Jaguar's motor and backed into the street. Shards of broken glass from the streetlight crunched under the Jag's tires as he put the car in drive and roared away, crushing the symbol of my impotent rage into dust.

Oh, crap.

This was bad.

# Thirty

Needless to say, the lawsuit was all anyone in Pemkowet could talk about. The town was buzzing like a hornet's nest, the tone a mixture of outrage and salacious curiosity as details emerged and rumors circulated.

I found myself in the unlikely position of feeling sorry for Stacey Brooks. Apparently, the ghostbusting footage that she'd shot and uploaded, the footage that had gone viral, received national attention and brought a thousand or so thrill-seeking tourists to Pemkowet last fall, provided the impetus for Dufreyne's case.

After all, it wasn't like he could sue the ghosts of Pemkowet's dead that had risen last fall or the no-longer-reanimated remains of Talman Brannigan or the duppy of Sinclair's dead Grandpa Morgan's spirit. Aside from the Tall Man's moldering bones, they couldn't even be proved to exist at this point, let alone summoned to appear in a court of law.

But what could be proved was that the Pemkowet Visitors Bureau, with the blessing of the tri-community governing authorities representing Pemkowet, East Pemkowet, and Pemkowet Township—and members of all three sat on the PVB's board—had deliberately and willfully used Stacey's videos to entice tourists to visit.

Hell, she'd just gotten a *promotion* for it.

And no, nowhere had there been any disclaimer, any mention that there was the possibility it could be dangerous.

It was stupid and shortsighted. I'd thought so for a long time, even before the events of last fall. Even under the best of circumstances, the eldritch community wasn't *safe*. A simple will-o'-the-wisp could lead tourists astray for days out in the dunes. Fairies could abduct children and replace them with changelings. Hobgoblins mostly confined their antics to relatively harmless pranks and scams, but it's not like being bilked on vacation is exactly a selling point.

And that was just the nature fey. God knows there was nothing safe about Lady Eris's vampire brood. Since Stefan's arrival, the Outcast had become a far more benevolent force in the community . . . but that didn't make them safe. Hell, Cooper had practically zombified that tourist and his teenaged daughter.

Based on the fact that the plaintiffs were suing for emotional and psychological damages, I had an uneasy feeling that Dufreyne might have tracked down that particular family, along with other bystanders who'd sustained physical injuries. There was a part of me that felt vindicated by the repercussions of the PVB's careless promotion, but I didn't have it in my heart to blame Stacey the way others were. She'd just been trying to please her mother—and right up to the point where it looked like Amanda Brooks's strategy to make Pemkowet a destination for paranormal tourism was about to blow up in our faces, pretty much everyone in town had thought it was brilliant.

Now . . . not so much.

I'd fully intended to use one of my remaining bark chips to request an audience with Hel that evening, but it was already dark when I left the station, and halfway down the block, Mikill the frost giant pulled up alongside me in his dune buggy.

"Daisy Johanssen!" He hailed me in a booming voice, holding up his rune-marked left hand. "I am bidden—"

"Yeah, yeah." I tugged my Pemkowet High School ski cap down further over my ears and climbed into the buggy. "Hi, Mikill. I take it Hel's heard the news?"

Mikill nodded gravely, his beard crackling with ice. "Her harbingers brought word today."

I scrunched down in the buggy's passenger seat, bracing myself for the arctic blast of wind. "Let's go."

Twenty minutes later, we'd successfully navigated our way across the dunes, appeased Garm—another distinctly *not* safe eldritch entity—and spiraled down the vast interior of Yggdrasil II's trunk.

I knelt before Hel's throne, feeling the weight of her displeasure. It wasn't directed at me personally, but oh, I could still feel it. The air in the abandoned sawmill was almost humming with tension.

"Rise, my young liaison," she said to me. I got to my feet and met her gaze with an effort. Both eyes were blazing; the left with malevolence, the right with stern disapproval. "It has come to my attention that this infernally begotten lawyer has shown his hand. Tell me what this *lawsuit* betokens."

"Nothing good," I said. "I can't be sure, my lady, but I think that this lawyer Dufreyne means to bankrupt the city of Pemkowet and force us to sell a large, valuable piece of land."

Hel's voice dropped to a subterranean register that echoed in the marrow of my bones. "*My territory.*"

"Yes."

"To whom? For what purpose?" Her ember eye flared. "Is it the Greek Hades? Does he declare war after all?"

I shook my head. "Dufreyne didn't deny that he worked for Hades, but he said Hades isn't declaring war on you and isn't interested in Pemkowet."

Hel's gaze sharpened. "And you believed this to be true?"

"Yes," I said. "Again, I can't be sure. But to the best of my ability, I believe he spoke the truth. Not the *whole* truth, but a part of it. Beyond that . . ." I turned up my hands in a helpless gesture. "I'm sorry, my lady. I don't know. I just don't know."

Hel did that immortal deity thing where she sat motionless on her throne and stared into the unknowable distance for a seemingly endless period of time, thinking unknowable thoughts. Mikill and the other frost giants attending her did the same, standing like ice sculptures.

I did that chilled-to-the-bone mortal thing where I shifted from foot to foot in the biting cold of Little Niflheim in an effort to keep my blood circulating, periodically removing my gloves to blow on my fingers.

Right about the time I was beginning to worry in earnest about frostbite, Hel's gaze returned from the distance. "In the days of old, I would have heaped great wealth upon my champion without a thought," she mused. "I would have sent the *duegar* forth to delve beneath the mountains for the precious stones and metals that all humans prize beyond reason, and bidden them wreak their craft to create treasures of such cunning and magic and beauty that mortals would fight and die to possess them. But now I preside over an empire of sand, and I have hoarded no treasure against this day. I have already bestowed the greatest gift in my possession upon you, Daisy Johanssen." She paused, letting that sink in. "I trust *dauda-dagr* continues to serve you well?"

I pushed aside an unbidden memory of Janek Król's face as he died. "Yes, my lady."

"That is well." Hel closed both eyes briefly, then opened them again. "I have no weapons to fight this battle of words and mortal laws," she said grimly. "But if there is merit to your fears, I would have this unknown adversary know that I will defend my territory with every weapon at my disposal."

There was a low rumble as the frost giants murmured in agreement. I inclined my head. "Duly noted, my lady."

"Convey my warning to this *hell-spawn* who has claimed his birthright in service of the Greek Hades," Hel said in distaste. "It is in my thoughts that he parses the truth to a fine edge in denying his master's role."

It took me a moment to translate that into twenty-first-century lingo. "You think Hades is involved?"

Hel's stare shifted back onto the distance. Damn. At least this time it returned before I lost feeling in my fingertips. "You speak of one who is well acquainted with matters of judgment," she said. "The Greek Hades appointed not one, but three former mortals to judge the dead and determine which were worthy of the Elysian Fields, and which were condemned to Tartarus."

I shrugged. "So maybe Dufreyne lied."

"Perhaps," Hel said. "Or perhaps the Greek Hades acts in the interests of another."

"Who?" I asked her.

Hel shook her head slowly and deliberately, giving me a disconcerting twofold glimpse of her fair, unspoiled profile and her blackened, ruined one. "To name a god in a place of power is to draw their attention, my young liaison. We have spoken enough of the Greek Hades. I will not speculate further."

Well, okay then.

I rubbed my hands together, the padded nylon of my gloves rasping. "As you will, my lady. Do you have counsel for me?"

"Watch," Hel said. "Listen. Convey my warning as I have bidden you. Perhaps the matter will come to naught."

Yeah, I wasn't buying it, either. "And if it doesn't?"

The oppressive atmosphere in the old sawmill intensified, the air thickening until I had to fight to draw breath. Somehow it brought to mind my vision of the dome of heaven cracking open above me.

"For the sake of all involved, let us hope that it does," Hel said in a low, ominous tone that made the rafters tremble, the blackened claw of her left hand curling on the arm of her throne. She raised two fingers of her fair right hand in dismissal. "Although your report is unwelcome, it is appreciated, my young liaison. You have my leave to depart."

I took it, hieing myself out of the sawmill and waiting beside the dune buggy for Mikill to catch up to me. Scores of *duegar* clustered at a respectful distance on the main street of the buried lumber town, watching me with a mixture of hope and apprehension, but none of them spoke.

Neither did the Norns when Mikill drove past their well at the base of Yggdrasil II's roots, although they watched me with grave eyes, and one tapped her chest with one long silver fingernail, reminding me of prior soothsaying.

Right. Trust my heart—*El Corazón* in my mom's reading.

Like I could forget.

Mikill drove me home in silence, pulling into the alley beside my apartment. To my surprise, he laid one massive hand on my shoulder before I could get out of the dune buggy, chilling me through my down coat. "Whatever comes, remember that one battle does not a war make, Daisy Johanssen," he said to me. "Do not be quick to lose heart."

My teeth began to chatter. "I'll try."

The frost giant gave me one last solemn nod, regarding me with his slush-colored eyes. "That is well."

Once safely back inside my apartment, I took a long, hot shower, standing under the spray and letting the warm water sluice over my skin and chase away the bone-deep chill of Little Niflheim.

I hoped it would ease the chill in my heart, too.

It didn't.

# Thirty-one

On the day after the news broke, Chief Bryant issued a statement on behalf of the joint codefendants that they would be pooling their resources and their respective legal counsel to review the situation and determine how to proceed, calling for cooler heads to prevail in the interim. He noted that there was a sixty-day opt-out period before the case could go to trial, which meant it probably wouldn't be scheduled until early February.

Apparently, once a judge has certified the plaintiffs as a class—in this case, any visitors to Pemkowet who sustained injuries or damage due to supernatural causes during the time the PVB was actively promoting the ghost uprisings—all potential plaintiffs have to be notified of the class action by mail or advertisements.

Funny, I'd seen those kinds of ads plenty of times on TV—the ones that promise if you suffer from, say, mesothelioma, you might be eligible for compensation and should contact Dewey, Cheatham & Howe, etc. I'd never really thought about it.

I'd never given any thought to why someone would opt out of a class-action law, either—which, in a nutshell, was because they thought they might get a better settlement suing as an individual.

Yeah, somehow I was pretty sure *that* wasn't going to happen. Any potential plaintiffs that came forward during the opt-out period were going to do exactly what Daniel Dufreyne suggested to them.

At any rate, the fact that there wouldn't be any trial for at least two months gave us breathing room.

What, exactly, we could do with that time was another matter.

At least one person took a pragmatic approach: Lurine, who offered the services of Robert Diaz, an attorney at a high-powered Los Angeles law firm she had on retainer. Robert Diaz was famous for, among other things, successfully defeating the attempt of Lurine's late husband's family to overturn his will.

"I tried to be diplomatic about it," Lurine told me confidentially when I stopped by her place to discuss it. "But this is a huge case, cupcake. Anything over five mill, and it's got to be decided in a federal court. Pemkowet's not going to stand a chance with any of these small-town yokels who've never settled anything bigger than a sexual harassment claim at the local high school."

"You do know it's not going to matter how good the defense attorney is, right?" I said to her. "Dufreyne's a goddamn hell-spawn with powers of goddamn persuasion. He doesn't *need* to be good."

Lurine shrugged. "You've got to take the long view, baby girl. The more holes Diaz can poke in the case, the more grounds for appeal."

"Which we're also likely to lose against Dufreyne's powers of persuasion," I pointed out.

"Maybe," she said. "I suspect he'll have to be judicious about how he uses them, no pun intended. If he's *too* obvious, at some point it's going to raise more suspicion than he can control. He doesn't want to risk being the first lawyer in history to get disbarred for supernatural coercion. Anyway, Robert Diaz has a high profile, and a little extra media scrutiny can't hurt."

"Did you warn him about Dufreyne being a hell-spawn?" I asked.

"No." Lurine pursed her lips. "If the city and township boards vote to take me up on my offer—which they'd be idiots not to do, but stranger things have happened—I thought I'd wait until Robert's gotten a feel for the eldritch community before I broke the news to him."

"Does he know about you?" I asked her.

"That's privileged information, cupcake." Her tone was light, but the warning in it was clear. "I can't divulge it."

"Sorry." I spread my hands. "I didn't mean to pry."

Lurine studied me. We were sitting in her living room, wintry light pouring through the big glass windows that looked onto the landscaped yard and woods surrounding her private mansion. "You seem a little out of sorts, honey. Is it just this lawsuit or is there something else going on?"

"Isn't the lawsuit enough?" I said drily.

"Your mom told me about your nightmare," Lurine said. "And the reading she did for you at Thanksgiving. She just needed to talk," she added when I didn't respond right away. "You can't blame her for worrying."

"I'm not mad that she told you," I said. "I just . . . It's like this shadow hanging over me that never goes away. And now there's this lawsuit, and Dufreyne smirking at me with his birthright and his goddamn schadenfreude, and I'm just so sick of feeling *helpless*!"

The atmosphere in the room tightened as I lost control of my emotions, a hot, acid-tinged wash of pent fury spilling over me. A flawless crystal vase on an end table vibrated with a high-pitched sound in protest. Lurine reached out to lay one hand atop the rim, stilling it. "I know."

Closing my eyes, I struggled to control my anger, putting it in a box. No, a trunk. A trunk reinforced with steel bands. "I had so much power in my dream, Lurine," I whispered. "And it felt *so good*."

"I bet it did."

It wasn't exactly the response I'd expected. I opened my eyes to find Lurine watching me, a neutral expression on her beautiful face. "Shouldn't you remind me that it was all just an illusion or something?" I said to her. "Or maybe just reassure me that I'm not capable of it?"

"You know perfectly well that it was just a dream," Lurine said. "Daisy, you invoked your worst nightmare. On purpose. And you set your friend Sinclair on a dark path he didn't want to walk to do it."

"The Night Hag—"

She raised one hand. "Baby girl, I'm not saying it wasn't worth it. You did what you had to do, and now you're paying a price for it. That's all."

"So you *don't* think I'm capable of it?" There was a part of me that really, really wanted to hear those words spoken out loud by someone who knew and loved me.

Lurine didn't oblige me. "Would you believe me if I said I didn't?" she asked with genuine curiosity in her voice.

I thought about it.

No. No, I wouldn't. Because it wouldn't scare me so much if I didn't believe in my heart of hearts that I *was* capable of invoking my birthright, of risking destroying the entire freaking world because I'd been pushed to the point where I couldn't stand my own powerlessness another second longer.

Strangely enough, the realization was bracing, maybe because it also made me realize that I was a long, long way from that point. "No."

Lurine smiled a little. "Good. Look, I know you're upset and frustrated, but there's nothing you can do about it right now, Daisy. Like it or not, sometimes you just have to accept it."

"Just like that?" I asked ruefully.

"Ah, well." Lurine's expression of deliberate neutrality shifted to something more complicated, a hint of the millennia-old monster surfacing behind the gorgeous mask of a B-movie starlet. "I didn't say it would be *easy*. But patience is a virtue worth practicing, especially in the face of the unknown." She paused. "Did Hel offer any insight as to who might be behind this?"

I shook my head. "Hel suspects that Hades, or the Greek Hades, as she likes to call him, is acting on behalf of another's interests. Beyond that, she refused to speculate. Any thoughts?"

"When it comes to the Olympians, none worth voicing," Lurine said with disdain. "The mere thought of them makes me restless." She shivered, then wriggled herself upright with serpentine grace, her entire body undulating. "In fact, I think I'd like to go down to the lake for a swim." She winked at me. "Want to come watch?"

Um, yeah. Totally.

I flushed. "I'll pass."

Extending one hand, Lurine tugged me off her couch. "Your loss. How *is* your love life these days, cupcake?"

I thought about my upcoming date with Stefan. "Interesting."

"Interesting," she echoed. "Care to clarify?"

"No."

"Hmm." Lurine cocked her head slightly, contemplating me, then flicked her tongue like a snake, leaned forward, and kissed me.

I was too startled to react. It wasn't much more than a light, friendly peck on the lips, and coming from anyone else, it would have been almost innocuous. Coming from anyone else, it wouldn't have resulted in my lips getting numb and tingly in a not-unpleasant way, followed by a rush of euphoria that warmed my skin all over and set the blood to singing in my veins. All I could do was blink at her in a stupefied manner.

"That's better," Lurine said with satisfaction, as though she'd just fixed my lipstick or wiped a smudge off my cheek. "You need to get out of your head, cupcake. Stop worrying so much."

I blinked a few more times.

"It'll wear off in a minute or two." She gave me an affectionate pat on the head. "Don't feel you need to mention this to your mother, okay?"

I ran my tongue around the inside of my tingling lips and tested my voice. "Um . . . okay."

"Good girl." Lurine patted my head again. "Oh, and tell that tall hunk of a ghoul that if he hurts you in any way, I'll crush him to pieces. Slowly. All right?"

"Uh-huh." Apparently she'd figured out what *interesting* meant, or at least I assumed that's what she meant. It was hard to think clearly. It still felt like there were firecrackers going off inside me, in a good way, if that makes any sense.

"Okeydokey." Taking my arm, Lurine steered me toward the foyer. "Edgerton, will you bring Miss Johanssen's coat?" she called down the hallway. "I'll be out at the lake for a while."

By the time Lurine had escorted me to my Honda, the blissful fizzing in my blood had subsided and I felt more or less normal, though I couldn't help but regard her with a new wariness.

Standing in the driveway, Lurine rolled her eyes. "Oh, don't give me that look. You needed a jolt, baby girl. You'll make yourself crazy obsessing over things that are beyond your control."

"You could have just slapped me and told me to snap out of it," I said mildly. "It would have been less disconcerting."

She gave me a wicked smile. "Yeah, but where's the fun in that?"

I couldn't help but smile back at her. Lurine was what she was, which wasn't human and definitely wasn't safe. "Oh, fine. Do you want a ride to the end of the driveway?" It was, by the way, a long driveway.

"No, I'll walk." Lurine gave me a gentle shove. "Go home. Call your friends, go out for pizza and a movie or something. Do something fun."

Driving home, I had to admit, Lurine had a point. For the first time in days, I wasn't thinking about killing Janek Król, or that damn class-action lawsuit, or who was behind Elysian Fields, or the fear that I was capable of destroying the world.

No, I was thinking about the faint tingling sensation that lingered on my lips and that vivid rush of ecstasy.

Gah! It must be something like the way certain snakes' venom paralyzed their victims, or maybe more like those hallucinogenic toads that people licked—which, okay, wasn't exactly a flattering comparison.

Whatever it was, I was pretty sure that all of Lurine's victims over the millennia had died happy.

Hell, no wonder her dead octogenarian millionaire husband had left her his entire fortune! He'd probably considered it a fair exchange for the occasional peck on the lips. It was a good thing she'd just wanted to give me a jolt. If there'd been actual tongue involved, I'd have been on the floor.

Yep, I was definitely distracted.

Score one for Lurine.

And I *definitely* wasn't mentioning this to Mom.

# Thirty-two

I ended up taking Lurine's advice, sort of. When I got home and checked my phone, I found a text from Sinclair, which led to an impromptu meeting of the Scooby Gang out at his place.

And yes, that included our new unlikely mean-girl ally, Stacey, who looked like she'd been crying for days, all red-nosed and puffy-eyed. Like I said, I couldn't help but feel sorry for her.

It turns out that Sinclair had called his twin sister, Emmeline, for insight on using obeah magic to influence the outcome of a lawsuit, a development that made me profoundly uncomfortable. The fact that Sinclair was consulting her on dark magic was . . . worrisome. I was surprised they were even on speaking terms, but apparently they'd reached some sort of understanding when Sinclair went to Jamaica to lay his grandfather's spirit to rest.

At any rate, it was a moot point since dear Emmy didn't think there was a damned thing we could do on the magic front, as the trial would take place in a distinctly mundane setting. The nearest federal court was the U.S. District Court in Grand Rapids, some forty miles away. No offense to Grand Rapids, which is a perfectly charming place in its own right, but a city whose chief claims to fame were that it was the office-furniture-manufacturing capital of the United States and the hometown of President Gerald R. Ford was definitely not conducive to magic.

"According to Emmy, Pemkowet should have spent years building an intimidating reputation," Sinclair reported in a wry tone, "so that a judge would be afraid to rule against us. But even if we had time . . ." He shook his head, his beads rattling faintly. "I don't see how we could pull it off outside Hel's sphere."

"If we could find out where the judge assigned to the case lives, I could send Bethany to pay him a visit," Jen suggested, only half joking.

"I can find out," Lee volunteered.

"Hello?" I stared incredulously at my friends. "In the first place, vampires need to be on underworld territory to feed. As below, so above, and all that. Vampiric hypnosis won't work in Grand Rapids any more than obeah will. In the second place, shouldn't we be finding a way to *protect* the judge? I kind of feel like you're going all Dark Willow on me," I added to Sinclair.

He frowned. "Say what?"

"Never mind." I waved a hand. Now was not the time to enlighten Sinclair on the finer points of *Buffy the Vampire Slayer* references. "But seriously, what about trying to protect the judge from Dufreyne's powers of persuasion?"

"Same problem," Sinclair said. "Any spell we cast wouldn't be effective outside of Hel's turf."

"It's not *fair*!" Stacey burst out. "I was just doing my job! And *I'm* the one the Tall Man tried to chop into pieces!" She blew her nose into a ratty piece of tissue. "Stupid curse of the Cavannaughs! If anyone should be suing, it should be me."

Okay, that didn't entirely make sense, but since she was right about the attempted chopping, I let it slide. "What about a protection charm?" I asked Sinclair. "Stefan has a pendant that casts a glamour, and it works for a day or so away from an underworld before the magic fades. I know—he let me borrow it last summer."

Sinclair looked intrigued, but skeptical. "This trial's likely to last a lot longer than a day, Daisy."

"At least it would be worth a try," I said. "Dufreyne said I'd be called as a witness. I'm sure he'll call Stacey, too. If one of us could slip a charm into the judge's briefcase or something, maybe it would help."

"Or you could get caught, arrested, and held in contempt of court," Lee pointed out. "As long as they're setting legal precedents, why not charge you with attempted supernatural tampering?"

"You're not helping," I informed him.

He shrugged. "I'm just being realistic. We don't even know if it's going to be a jury trial or not. If it is, that's twelve more people you have to worry about, right?"

"Yeah, but it's the judge who has the final say on the terms of the settlement," Jen observed. Over the course of days, everyone in Pemkowet had become an armchair expert in class-action lawsuits, mostly based on gossip, anecdotes, and something someone thought they remembered hearing Nancy Grace say on television. "Even if the jury voted to award the plaintiffs the full forty-five million bucks, the judge has to approve it. Or he could decide we've got ten years to pay it."

Stacey sniffled. "If you think anyone in Pemkowet's going to vote to approve a ten-year millage for this, you're delusional."

Jen shot her a look a lot like the one she'd given Stacey back in high school when she'd threatened to cut all her hair off. I didn't blame her, although Stacey was probably right.

"It would be a risk," Sinclair mused, still thinking about the charm. "A big risk for something that might only work for a day, and probably wouldn't make a difference in the long run."

"Is there any way one could create some sort of magical battery or generator?" Lee inquired. "Something that would allow magic to function in a limited way in a mundane environment?"

Sinclair shook his head again. "Not that I've ever heard."

I had, though. A faint spark of hope kindled inside me. "Dufreyne," I said. "When he told me his powers of persuasion worked everywhere, he said he carried the underworld inside him."

Everyone stared at me.

"So it *might* work," Sinclair said slowly, a grin spreading across his face. "A hell-spawn's presence in the courtroom might be enough."

I smiled back at him. "Wouldn't that be ironic?"

"Yeah." He nodded. "It would. At least it's worth a try. I'll call Casimir and the coven so we can strategize."

"Is that our cue to leave?" Stacey asked him, a slight edge to her tone. "I'm not sure about the others, but I know *I'm* not coven-approved."

Sinclair hesitated, his brow creasing.

Okay, I'll admit it, there was a part of me that wasn't sorry to see that there was trouble in paradise; but there was another part that was all too aware that Stacey's habitual bitchiness was a defense against her insecurity, which was at an all-time high right about now.

"It can wait until tomorrow," I said to Sinclair. "There's time. I think we all need to take a step back and calm down, maybe do something normal for a change. Order some pizza, watch a movie."

His expression eased. "You've got a point. I don't know what I was thinking, turning to Emmy for advice. You're right—we should be focusing on protection rather than influence; the right-hand path, not the left."

I knew exactly what Sinclair was doing. He was continuing on the path I'd set him on when I'd asked him to curse me, but that's not what I said. "Is that like the path of light versus the path of darkness?" I asked him instead.

"Yeah, that's the terminology the coven uses," Sinclair said. "Same idea, fewer racial overtones."

"It's an old term in the craft," Lee offered. "Its usage in Western culture dates back to the nineteenth-century occultist Madame Blavatsky, who founded the Theosophical Society." He shrugged at the startled glance Sinclair gave him. "What? Lots of us in the gaming industry are knowledgeable in all sorts of arcana."

Jen raised her hand. "As a left-handed person, I'd like to lodge a protest against the whole right-equals-good, left-equals-bad analogy. Why not say that up equals good and down equals bad?"

"As the representative of an underworld deity, I take offense," I said to Jen with a straight face. "That's so . . . directionist of you."

"How about four legs good, two legs bad?" Stacey suggested. It drew blank looks. "Um . . . *Animal Farm*, remember? We read it in ninth-grade English?" She flushed. "I know, it's stupid. I'm sorry. Sometimes I don't quite get your jokes."

"Sometimes our jokes aren't funny," Lee assured her. "If you ask me, if we don't want to offend anyone, we'd have to use nonsense words, like zig equals bad, zag equals good."

"Really?" Jen nudged him. "Zig equals bad? Now you're discriminating against the Spice Girls?"

He blinked at her. "Huh?"

All three of us girls, including Stacey, sang the chorus of "Wannabe" in unison. *"I wanna really really really wanna zigazig ha!"* We burst into laughter; probably more laughter than the situation warranted, but it felt good.

"Oh, God!" Jen wiped her eyes. "I remember Bethany and me dancing around her bedroom, singing into our hairbrushes. I must have been all of seven years old."

"Me, too," Stacey admitted.

Sinclair let out a groan. "Enough with the Spice Girls. Didn't someone mention pizza?"

I got up to fetch the menu from the pizza place. It was tacked to the refrigerator with a magnetic clip, just like it had been when Sinclair and I were dating, which gave me a bit of a pang . . . but that was my own fault.

Half an hour later, the women voting in favor of *The Princess Bride*, the five of us were lounging around the living room eating pizza and watching Buttercup's heart break at the news of Westley's death at the hands of the Dread Pirate Roberts. Given that our group contained a pair of exes, an uneasy triad of former high school nemeses, and one slightly paranoid genius, it was surprisingly companionable.

I tried to picture Stefan in our midst, and couldn't do it. I wondered what, exactly, it was that Stefan saw in me. I really didn't know if there was room in Stefan Ludovic's centuries-old reality for an impromptu Spice Girls sing-along.

Maybe I'd feel differently after our big date on Saturday, but honestly, I couldn't picture that either. It sounded like a setup for an eldritch joke: A ghoul and a hell-spawn are on their first date . . .

Where would we go and what would we do? I didn't know if Stefan even had a car. I'd never seen him on anything but a motorcycle.

One way or another, I guess I'd find out.

God, and I'd have to figure out what to wear, too.

# Thirty-three

Sinclair called me with an update on the protection charm idea the following morning. "Casimir thinks it's a long shot, but it's worth a try if you're willing to take the risk of planting it on the judge." He paused. "Are you sure about that, Daise? Stacey won't risk it. She's under enough pressure as it is."

I swallowed, my stomach lurching at the prospect. "Yeah. I don't know how, but . . . yeah."

"Okay," he said. "The coven will meet tonight to discuss it. It will have to be something small and easily concealed, like the Seal of Solomon charm that Casimir gave you last fall."

"No offense, but that thing didn't actually prevent your mom from putting the obeah whammy on me in the cemetery," I reminded him. "Do you really think it will be effective against Dufreyne?"

"It's just the vessel," Sinclair said. "We'll take advantage of the fact that we've got a whole moon cycle to, um, amplify its power."

"Pimp my charm?" I suggested.

He gave a low chuckle. "Something like that, yeah. Rituals, spells, herbs, white-light casting, maybe some of Mrs. Meyers's knotwork . . . I don't know. Casimir's already doing research. Do you need the details?"

"No," I said. "I just need it to work."

"That depends on whether or not you're right about Dufreyne's personal underworld providing enough juice for magic to function in his vicinity," Sinclair said. "That, and you not getting caught."

My stomach lurched again. "Right. Keep me updated."

"Will do."

It might be a long shot—okay, it was definitely a long shot—but at least it was *something*. Better a half-baked plan than nothing at all. Well, except for the nauseating fear of getting caught—but I'd worry about that later. At the moment, I had far more mundane things to worry about, like the fact that I didn't have a decent winter coat, which came home to me when Stefan called on Saturday morning to confirm our date and suggested that we attend the East Pemkowet Holiday Stroll that evening, followed by dinner at the Market Bistro.

Whatever I'd expected, it wasn't anything quite so . . . quaint. It left me slightly dumbstruck.

"You want to do the Holiday Stroll?" I said dubiously.

"Why not?" Stefan asked in an equable tone. "Is that not the sort of thing you enjoy, Daisy?"

"Well . . . yeah." That was an understatement. I loved the Holiday Stroll as much, if not more, than the tree-lighting ceremony. I couldn't believe I'd forgotten it was this Saturday.

"So?"

"It's totally corny," I warned him. "I mean, it's totally Stars Hollow." Oh, for crying out loud! Stefan wasn't going to get a *Gilmore Girls* reference. "I'm just saying I don't think you'd be into it."

There was a brief silence on the other end. "I am not entirely sure I follow your meaning," Stefan said carefully. "But this Holiday Stroll appears to be a charming local custom."

"Oh, it is," I assured him.

"Are you reluctant to be seen with me?" He sounded curious, not angry.

"No!" I took a deep breath. "Okay, fine. You know what? That sounds perfect. Delightful, even."

"Then I will call for you at your apartment at six o'clock," Stefan said. "Is that agreeable?"

"I don't know," I said. "Do you have a car?"

"Yes, Daisy." Amusement laced his voice. "I have a car. I will see you this evening."

Okay, so that whole what-to-wear issue? No longer a joke. Oh, I had a decent wardrobe, thanks to the fact that I finally let my mom contribute to it. In fact, I'd been meaning to ask her if the cocktail dress she was making me out of that midnight blue silk shantung that Lurine had purchased was anywhere near finished. But Mom didn't have the sewing equipment to handle heavy-duty outerwear, and the one thing I *didn't* have was a winter coat that was both warm and attractive.

I'd been planning to wear my leather jacket, figuring that whatever a date with Stefan entailed, we wouldn't be outside long. Sure, it wasn't exactly evening wear, but if a twenty-four-year-old hell-spawn can't rock an edgy look, who can? Besides, Stefan was a member of a biker gang.

Although as I recalled from the Vanderhei funeral, he cleaned up nicely. God, what was Stefan wearing?

Okay, I couldn't worry about that. But the Holiday Stroll meant ambling down two blocks of East Pemkowet, admiring the window displays, popping in and out of stores, chatting with friends. And the cold snap had held. There was no way I could wear my leather jacket without freezing, and there was *no way* I was wearing the Michelin Man down coat on a first date with Stefan.

I called my mom to see if she wanted to hit the thrift stores and help me find a decent winter coat. She's got a great eye for that sort of thing.

"Funny you should ask, sweetheart," Mom said in pleased surprise. "I was planning on getting you a coat for Christmas. I, um, noticed at the tree lighting that you needed one."

No kidding. I grimaced. "You don't have to do that."

"But I was planning on it!" she protested. "And Macy's is having a sale on outerwear this weekend."

*"Macy's?"* We never shopped at expensive department stores. "Mom,

no! I'm sure we can find something at Goodwill or one of the consignment shops in Appeldoorn."

"No, I'm buying you a *new* coat." Mom's voice had that firm tone that meant her mind was made up. "It just means Christmas will come a little early this year." She paused. "Is it for a special occasion?"

"I have a date for the Holiday Stroll tonight," I admitted.

"Anyone I know?" she asked in a light trying-not-to-pry tone. "Cody hasn't come to his senses, has he?"

"No." I hadn't told her *everything* about Cody and me, but enough. "It's, um, Stefan Ludovic."

"Oh!" Mom sounded surprised again, but not in a pleased way. "Is that . . . safe, honey?" she asked cautiously.

"I trust Stefan," I said, hoping she didn't notice it wasn't a direct answer. No, the combination of Stefan and me together wasn't *safe*. But apparently, I'd become someone with an appetite for risk, at least where my love life was concerned. Or maybe I always had been, and I was only just realizing it.

At any rate, Mom accepted the answer. "Well, you know I trust your judgment," she said. "Pick you up in half an hour?"

"Sounds great," I said with relief.

There was a light snow falling, just enough to make the drive picturesque, not enough to make the roads slippery. We headed north on the highway, and I felt a familiar intangible sense of loss as we passed beyond the range of Hel's sphere of influence, the world becoming a little more drab, a little more gray, as magic leached out of it.

I thought about what Dufreyne had said about me carrying the underworld within myself, too. It didn't feel like it, or at least I didn't think so. But then again, maybe it wasn't something you could feel. Maybe it just was. I remembered bad things happening when I had temper tantrums as a toddler.

It was one of the reasons Mom had decided to move to Pemkowet, where the community was considerably more understanding.

Anyway.

Unsurprisingly, Macy's was crowded. Mom made a beeline for the outerwear section, slipping deftly through the throng and flipping through the racks. I checked out the price tags. Even at forty percent off, these were expensive coats. Maybe not to everyone, but they were to me, and I felt guilty.

"Mom, you *really* don't have to do this," I said in a stage whisper, pointing at a tag. "Come on, let's go!"

She gave me an absent look, pulling a beautifully tailored red wool coat with a luxuriant fur collar from the rack. "What do you think of this one?"

"I think it's gorgeous," I said. "And too expensive."

Mom held it up in front of me and squinted. "Oh, don't worry. It's not *that* bad. The trim's fake. They're doing amazing things with faux fur these days. Try it on."

I hesitated.

She gave me a non-absent look. "Just indulge me. Okay?"

"Okay, okay!"

I tried the coat on. It looked fantastic. *I* looked fantastic. I looked sultry and grown-up and polished. Somehow the vibrant red hue worked with my black, black eyes, while tendrils of my white-blond hair escaping to spill over the glossy dark-brown fur collar made for the perfect contrast. All I needed was a fur hat and a slash of crimson lipstick to go the full *Dr. Zhivago.* Oh, and maybe a muff and a troika.

Behind me, Mom regarded me with a complicated mixture of pride and rue. Catching me looking, she raised her eyebrows. "Well?"

I sighed.

Sensing a sale in the offing, one of the clerks on the floor swooped down on us. "Isn't that coat to die for?" she gushed. "And darling, let me tell you, it looks fabulous on you!"

"We'll take it," Mom said firmly.

We took our purchase and departed. The snow was coming down a bit heavier on the drive home.

"So when do I get to meet this Stefan Ludovic?" Mom asked, concentrating on the road. "He sounds . . . interesting."

That was putting it mildly. Of course, she knew who Stefan was. After Stefan and his broadsword did battle against the axe-wielding specter of Talman Brannigan's reanimated corpse last Halloween, *ev-*

*eryone* in Pemkowet knew who he was. But at Mom's gentle prodding, I'd filled her in on a little of Stefan's backstory on our outbound journey. Not the whole thing, but just enough to reassure her that I knew what I was dealing with.

"I don't know," I said. "Are you going to the Holiday Stroll this year?"

"Lurine and I promised to take Gus," Mom admitted. "But I can get out of it if you think it's too soon."

I thought about Stefan asking if I was reluctant to be seen with him. "No, you know what? That's fine. Let's not make a plan to meet up or anything, but if our paths cross, so be it. Just make sure Lurine agrees to play nice," I added.

"Oh, she's just looking out for you, honey," Mom said in a dismissive tone. "You know she's fond of you."

"Oh, I know." I cleared my throat. "It's just that Lurine's idea of looking out for me can be, um, unconventional."

We passed the threshold of Hel's territory and I felt a profound sense of relief as the world brightened, coming alive and vital, filled with the promise of wonder and the potential for magic. I let out a sigh and wriggled in my seat, a knot of tension I hadn't been aware of easing inside me.

"It's always good to be home," Mom said softly.

I glanced at her. "You feel it, too?"

She nodded. "Probably not as strongly as you, but yes."

Fifteen minutes later, Mom pulled into the alley alongside my apartment building.

"Thank you." I leaned over to kiss her cheek. "You really, really didn't have to do this. But I love it."

"Good." She smiled at me. "You've had a lot on your mind, and I just thought you deserved something nice for a change. Just promise me . . ." She stopped and gave her head a little shake. "Have a nice time tonight."

"I'll do my best."

True to his word, Stefan arrived promptly at six o'clock to pick me up, disembarking from his car, which turned out to be a silver Lexus sedan, and waiting in the alley to hold the passenger door for me when I emerged. It was the first time we'd seen each other since Janek Król's death, a fact I tried to ignore.

Stefan gave me an appraising look, his pupils dilating. "Good evening, Daisy. You look lovely."

"Thanks." I patted the messenger bag hanging from my shoulder. "The accessories don't exactly match, but it was either this or the sword belt. I don't like to leave *dauda-dagr* unattended."

"Nor should you." Stefan ushered me into the front seat. "Such a weapon is a grave trust." Shutting my door, he went around the car and slid into the driver's seat. "Are you ready?"

I found myself acutely aware of his proximity and the fact that we were in close quarters. It gave me butterflies in the pit of my stomach. "Let's do it."

We drove across the bridge and parked in downtown East Pemkowet, the site of the infamous Halloween parade. Tonight it was aglow with cheer, all the trees and shrubs bedecked with old-fashioned Christmas lights with the oversized bulbs in primary colors. The same carolers who had graced the tree-lighting ceremony were strolling the streets, competing with the music that spilled out of the storefronts every time a door was opened, which was frequently. There were a few tourists, but it was mostly townsfolk who streamed in and out of the stores, blocking one another's passage as they paused to exchange pleasantries or gathered in groups on the sidewalk.

"Shall we?" Stefan offered me his arm. He'd eschewed his motorcycle leathers for a navy blue peacoat, and his longish black hair brushed the collar.

I took his arm, feeling a little self-conscious. It was a crisp, cold night, feathery snowflakes falling, but I was warm and toasty in my new coat. Scents of mulled cider and gingerbread wafted from the doors as we promenaded past them, pausing to admire the window displays.

"Are you shopping for anything in particular?" Stefan inquired in front of a boutique featuring expensive home furnishings.

"Are you kidding?" I laughed. "I can't afford to shop here. I just like to look. And all the stores have free holiday goodies," I added. "When I was a kid, I'd gorge on punch and Christmas cookies."

"Ah." Stefan smiled. "Hence the appeal." He opened the door to the boutique. "Allow me to indulge your fond memories?"

I have to admit, the whole chivalry thing was new to me and I kind of liked it. After escorting me into the store, Stefan proceeded to the refreshments table and procured a cup of mulled cider and a couple of gingersnap cookies. He cut quite a swath, shoppers moving instinctively out of his way as they took in his unnatural pallor and sensed themselves in the presence of an unknown danger.

Okay, I kind of liked that, too.

"Here you are, my lady." Stefan returned to offer me the cider and cookies with a courtly little bow.

I eyed him suspiciously. "Are you making fun of me?"

"Not at all." He smiled again, this time with dimples. "I'm enjoying myself, Daisy. It's been a long time."

I wanted to ask him exactly how long it had been, but I didn't want to spoil the mood, so I took a bite of gingersnap before responding. "Sorry, I didn't mean to be ungracious. As long as we're here, let's check out those throw pillows," I suggested. "No offense, but your condo could use a touch of color."

"Thus has it ever been with women and decorative cushions," Stefan commented. I shot him another glance and determined that this time he *was* teasing me. And this time, I didn't mind it.

"Do you blame us for wanting things to be nice?" I asked lightly. "At least consider the maroon ones with the gray stripe."

Not only did Stefan consider them, but he bought a pair. The clerk trembled a bit as he rang up the purchase, whether out of fear or excitement at waiting on a member of the eldritch community, I couldn't say.

Outside, we ran into Sandra Sweddon engaged in conversation with a city council member dressed in a larger-than-life-size snowman's costume, who was handing out candy canes.

"Oh, my!" Sandra took in the sight of the two of us together. "Well, aren't you an attractive pair?" She extended a gloved hand to Stefan. "Mr. Ludovic, I want to thank you for your work with the Open Hearth facility. It's been a godsend."

Stefan shook her hand. "It's been my pleasure. I trust my lieutenant Cooper proved an able replacement in my absence?"

"Oh, yes. The residents adore him." Sandra turned her gaze on me. "And Daisy, I haven't had the chance to thank you for banishing the Night Hag. Everyone's sleeping better for it."

"I'm glad to hear it," I said sincerely, my hand nestled in the crook of Stefan's arm. Holy crap, Stefan and I had the makings of an eldritch power couple. Now *that* was a surprising notion.

Not a bad one, just . . . strange.

After a few more pleasantries, Stefan and I continued down the block. When I caught sight of Gus the ogre hulking outside Once a Notion, his massive hands braced on the window and his broad nose practically pressed against the glass as he watched a miniature choo-choo train make its way through the toy store's elaborate display, I'm ashamed to say that I thought about crossing the street. Somehow I hadn't expected our first outing to be quite such a public occasion.

Instead, I squeezed Stefan's arm. "Ah, unless I'm mistaken, you're about to meet my mother," I murmured. "Also, Lurine wanted me to let you know that if you hurt me, she'll crush you to pieces. Slowly."

Stefan's pupils waxed and waned as he drew a long, slow breath. "I have no intention of hurting you, Daisy."

"I know," I said. "But you and I both know that's no guarantee."

He didn't deny it, which I appreciated.

It wasn't as awkward as it might have been. Having made her point the other day, Lurine was content to be polite. Gus was happily transfixed by the train—don't ask me why, but toy trains had always held a special fascination for him. Maybe when you have fingers the size of kielbasas, miniatures are particularly compelling.

When I introduced Stefan to my mom, he laid on the Ye Olde World charm without overdoing it. Her eyes sparkled as he complimented her, telling her he could see where her daughter got her looks.

Actually, the whole thing was kind of surreal. I felt like the Mary Sue in a lousy piece of fan fiction, taming the big bad monster with my oh-so-winsome ways. I mean, cookies and cider? Throw pillows? Come on.

Beneath my coat, my tail twitched restlessly. "We should probably keep going," I said to Stefan. "Dinner reservations and all."

He gave me an amused sidelong glance. "Of course. It was a pleasure to meet you, Ms. Johanssen."

"You, too, Mr. Ludovic," Mom said in a bright tone. "Oh, and please call me Marja."

Stefan inclined his head to her. "Enjoy your evening."

As much as I loved the Holiday Stroll, it was a relief to complete the circuit in time for our reservation at the Market Bistro, where Stefan and I were seated at a table in a secluded corner of the restaurant. Even at that, we got a lot of covert stares from the other diners, not to mention the waitstaff.

"I apologize, Daisy," Stefan said. "I thought this excursion would be a pleasurable one for you, but I fear it's made you uncomfortable."

"No, I'm sorry," I said. "It was a great idea, totally thoughtful. It's just . . . you brought me cookies and cider. You met my *mom*. You bought *throw pillows*."

He gave me a perplexed look. "Forgive me, but I fail to comprehend the significance. The pillows were your suggestion."

"I know." I fell silent as our waiter came over to take our drink orders and inform us of the specials. After he'd left the table, I said, "I'm not even sure what I'm trying to say, Stefan. It's all just a little too perfect. Especially given the circumstances of our last encounter."

"Ah."

I waited to see if he would elaborate. He didn't. "I guess . . . I don't know exactly what we're doing here," I said. "You and me."

He raised his eyebrows. "Need it be more than enjoying each other's company and exploring an attraction?"

"No, but . . ." I couldn't find the words to explain how bringing throw pillows into it changed things.

The waiter came to deliver two glasses of wine, promising to return shortly. Stefan took a sip, fixing his gaze on me. "How old do you imagine I was when I was Outcast?"

I hazarded a guess. "Thirty-two?"

Stefan shook his head. "Twenty-nine. Daisy, there are days when I feel the weight of every century of my life. There are days when I despair of this immortal existence, this endless hunger that must be fed. But there are days when I feel like the young man that I was before I became Outcast and I desire nothing more than life's simple pleasures, including the companionship of a beautiful woman."

"Cooper said something like that to me once," I murmured.

He nodded. "Yes. Cooper feels it more acutely than most, being Outcast at such a young age."

I swirled the wine in my glass. "So you're saying that life's simple pleasures also include buying throw pillows?"

"Yes," Stefan said after a moment's thought. "If buying pillows means taking part in the ordinary rituals of human life, yes."

"You're not an ordinary human, though," I said quietly.

"No." Stefan's pupils surged, dilating in his ice-blue eyes. "I know what I am, Daisy. And I know what *you* are. What we might be together, I do not know."

My pulse quickened. "Volatile?" I suggested.

"To be sure." There was a predatory edge to the smile Stefan flashed me. "All I know is that your existence gladdens me."

"Why?"

"A fair question." He inclined his head to me. "I take delight in the vibrancy of your youth and your tempestuous nature. I admire your sense of responsibility, compassion, and justice. I had never thought to find such a thing in a demon's spawn, and it intrigues me."

I paused. "You've known others?"

"Yes." Stefan's voice went flat. "But I would prefer not to have that discussion tonight."

Ohh-kay. I guess my oh-so-winsome ways hadn't entirely tamed the big bad monster. I filed that topic away for another day.

"I might ask you the same question," Stefan added in a lighter tone. "Why are *you* here with me tonight, Daisy?"

"Because you scare me in a way that excites me," I said honestly. "You're right—you and me together is an unknown. But it's one I can't help being curious about."

He raised one eyebrow. "So it's not because I'm . . . *hawt*?"

Oh, God. I'd forgotten about Jen's damned text. Feeling my face flush, I held my ground. "Okay, fine. Yeah, that, too."

Stefan hoisted his wineglass and smiled at me. "To the unknown."

"To the unknown," I echoed, touching the rim of my glass to his.

# Thirty-four

Despite an uneven start, dinner was a reasonable success.

I'll say one thing—you'll never run out of topics of conversation with someone who's lived the equivalent of seven or eight mortal life spans. There were tons of questions I was dying to ask Stefan, but for the most part I managed to restrain myself and let him steer the conversation.

The one exception was the topic of Janek Król. I couldn't help it—I wanted to know more about the man whose existence I'd ended, and the role he'd played in Stefan's life. To his credit, Stefan didn't balk at discussing him. I heard the story of their friendship from start to . . . well, I knew how it finished.

One of the more intriguing things I learned was that Janek's abiding interest in the Jewish notion of *tikkun olam*, repairing the world, had set Stefan on his current course.

"Why not try it in Wieliczka?" At that point, we were lingering over after-dinner drinks—port for Stefan, single malt for me—and the name of the Polish town fell trippingly from my tongue.

"I wished to start anew," Stefan said. "Somewhere I was not known, somewhere I had no history."

"And Pemkowet seemed small enough to be manageable," I said. "That's what you told me last summer."

"Yes."

I took a sip of scotch, letting it linger on my palate. "So that's what this whole business of banishing the meth trade in favor of alleviating grief at the old folks' home is about. *Tikkun olam*?"

Stefan cupped his snifter of port in his hands. "It is about seeking to find meaning in the existence of the Outcast."

"Have you?" I asked.

He gave me a half smile. "I am striving, Daisy. It has been a long time since I made such an effort."

How long? I wondered. As long as it had been since the last time he'd dated a woman? Longer? I decided not to ask, taking a different tack instead. "Do you believe Janek was right about God's forgiveness?"

"Yes," Stefan said. "In Janek's case, I do." A distant look touched his features. "I believe that my old friend Janek is in heaven bargaining with God and His angels on behalf of the Outcast."

"I hope so," I said. "Although I don't think you can bargain with God. I mean . . . that's sort of the point of God, isn't it?"

"Abraham bargains with God in the Old Testament," Stefan said. "He begs the Lord not to destroy Sodom and Gomorrah, and the Lord agrees to spare the cities if fifty righteous people can be found there. Abraham bargained him down to ten."

"And look how well that turned out," I observed. "Why did God agree to bargain with him in the first place?"

"Ah, well, the Lord had great plans for Abraham," Stefan admitted. "He was to become the father of many nations." He sipped his port. "And it has come to pass, as the faith of Abraham and his descendants has risen to prominence."

"So in other words, Abraham had leverage," I said, finishing my scotch.

Stefan laughed softly. "I would not have thought to phrase it thusly, but yes, I suppose you're right. Perhaps I should not have used the word *bargain*. Perhaps it is enough that Janek reminds God of our existence and pleads on our behalf."

"Do you think God has forgotten about the Outcast?" I asked with genuine curiosity.

"I do not know." He drained the last of his port. "It may be that a thousand years may pass in the blink of an eye for the divine. It may be that each of us has a lesson yet to learn. Or it may simply be that God can no longer intervene from beyond the Inviolate Wall, and must use other hands as His tools."

I looked at my hands. "You know, I'm really not comfortable with that whole idea."

"I know." Stefan's voice was surprisingly gentle. "Forgive me. I did not intend to trouble you."

"No, it's my fault," I said. "I brought it up. Will you excuse me for a minute?"

"Of course."

I didn't really need to visit the restroom, but I wanted to collect my thoughts. And I don't know how the evening would have ended if I hadn't encountered Daniel freakin' Dufreyne on my way.

The reek of wrongness hit me as I was passing the bar, where Dufreyne was paying his tab. I stopped dead in my tracks. "What the hell are you doing here?"

"Hello, cousin." Dufreyne bared his white teeth in his sharklike grin, winding his cashmere scarf around his throat. "What a happy coincidence. I was just passing through and taking in a bit of local color. That's an interesting date you've got there."

My skin crawled. "What's it to you?"

"Nothing." Dufreyne shrugged into his expensive coat. "But if I were you, I'd want to know a lot more about his history with our kind before I sealed the deal." He fished his gloves from his coat pocket. "Take care."

Son of a bitch.

I stared after Dufreyne as he made his exit, then ducked into the ladies' room to wash my hands and splash water on my face before returning to the table. "We should probably be going," I said to Stefan.

He rose to retrieve my coat. "As you will."

Based on what I knew of Daniel Dufreyne, I was ninety-nine percent sure he was just seizing the opportunity to mess with me, which really sucked, because it had been a relief to spend a whole evening not worrying about that damned lawsuit or my nightmares about destroying the world. I did my best to put his words out of my head and enjoy the chivalry thing. Back at my apartment building, Stefan got out of the Lexus to walk me to the door. On the doorstep, chivalry gave way to something else, something filled with sexual tension and unspoken possibilities. That fluttery feeling was back in my stomach, along with the molten stirrings of desire.

I wanted him.

I wanted to do this, to embrace the danger. I wanted to lose myself in simple lust, in the deadly knife-edge play of emotion between us. And thanks to the bond between us, Stefan knew it. I could see it in the swift dilation of his pupils, in the quickening of his breath in the cold night air.

"Daisy." Stefan said my name in a husky whisper, drew me against him and kissed me. It wasn't as explosive as the last time he'd kissed me, before he'd left for Poland, but it was a kiss that meant business. It was a kiss that was the start of something serious, intense enough to weaken my knees and leave me no doubt of his intentions.

And yet, this time I was the one to end it. Ninety-nine percent wasn't a hundred. I needed to know more before this went further.

I didn't pull away or raise my shield, but I broke off the kiss. "Thank you." My voice sounded as unsteady as I felt. "It was a lovely evening."

Lifting one hand, Stefan brushed my lower lip with his thumb. "You're not going to invite me inside?"

"No." With an effort, I let go of the lapels of his coat. Huh. I didn't remember clutching them. "Not tonight. It's too easy for me to abandon myself with you, Stefan. I need to take this slowly. I need to know I've got *some* measure of self-control. And I want to get past the cryptic eldritch crap," I added. "I don't want to wake up tomorrow morning wondering why I went to bed with you after you shut down any conversation about your history with hell-spawns."

"I see." Stefan's pupils glittered at me. "Then I will court you, Daisy. Slowly and deliberately, until you beg me for release."

A shiver ran down the length of my spine, and my tail twitched reflexively. "And the cryptic eldritch crap?" I challenged him.

Stefan dialed it down a notch, his expression easing into a wry smile. "I will endeavor to answer your questions with candor. Perhaps our next outing should be dedicated to such a conversation."

"I'd like that," I said. "Very much."

He inclined his head. "Next Saturday, then. I'll call for you at eleven o'clock in the morning and take you to brunch."

Like *condominium*, *brunch* was one of those words that sounded incongruous coming from Stefan, and it made me smile. "It's a plan. And, um, thank you for understanding."

"Anything worth pursuing is worth waiting for." Stefan dusted a few snowflakes from the collar of my new coat, then leaned over to kiss me again, his lips lingering on mine. "You looked very beautiful tonight."

Okay, I had to make my escape before I changed my mind. "I'll see you then," I promised, backing away from him and fishing my keys out of my messenger bag. With that, I turned tail—no pun intended—and fled into the stairwell and the subsequent safety of my apartment.

All in all, Dufreyne's insidious insinuation notwithstanding, I thought that had gone well.

Unsurprisingly, the news of my date with Stefan traveled fast. On Sunday morning, I got a phone call from an indignant Jen demanding to know why I hadn't told her about it, and insisting on details.

"I can't believe I had to hear about this secondhand," she said. "I'm the one who set this thing in motion, girlfriend!"

I winced. "I know, I know!"

"So?"

"It was nice," I said. "But it was weird, too. He bought throw pillows, Jen. Ninety-dollar ones."

"Why is that weird?" she asked. "Do you think it means he's gay or something?"

"No, definitely not." Apparently, I couldn't communicate why I found the notion of Stefan purchasing throw pillows so disconcerting. I didn't tell her about Dufreyne's warning. That could wait until I knew more.

"Did you hook up?" Jen asked.

"No," I said. "We're taking things slowly."

"That's probably a good idea," she said. "Are you going to see him again?"

"Yeah." I nodded. "We're having brunch next Saturday."

*"Brunch?"*

"Yep."

"Something about the idea of Stefan the hot ghoul doing brunch just seems . . . wrong," Jen commented.

"I know, right?" I said. "That's what I'm trying to say about the throw pillows."

"Okay, well, I want a full report next Sunday," she said. "Sinclair said to let you know that the coven's working on the charm. He has something else he wants to talk to you about, but they need to do more research."

"Okay."

On Monday, I was called in to the station to cover the front desk for Patty Rogan, who was out with the flu. Chief Bryant gave me a long, appraising look, the expression on his face unreadable.

"I hope you know what you're doing, Daisy," he said to me.

Most of the time I appreciated the paternal interest the chief took in me, but today it rubbed me the wrong way. "Duly noted, sir."

He gave me a slow nod of acknowledgment and didn't push the issue, for which I was grateful.

Other than my debut with Stefan as Pemkowet's premier eldritch power couple, the pending lawsuit was still the main topic of conversation in town. The big news was that the tri-community boards had voted to accept Lurine's offer, and her high-priced celebrity lawyer, Robert Diaz, was coming to town to consult with the defendants and their lawyers. Since Diaz wasn't licensed to practice in Michigan, he couldn't actually represent us, but he would be providing counsel every step of the way, starting with a formal request that the judge replace Dufreyne due to conflict of interest.

Under normal circumstances, I thought, that seemed like a no-brainer. But these weren't normal circumstances.

I had an hour to go on my shift when Cody entered the station, bringing the scent of snow and pine trees with him. Without a word, he tossed a folded sheet of thick stationery, battered and dirt-smudged and sealed with a blot of red wax, on the desk in front of me.

"What's this?" I asked.

"I was supposed to give this to you a week ago." Cody's tone was flat. "Open it."

I broke the seal and opened the paper to find an official invitation to attend a gathering of the Fairfax clan on Sunday, January 19, in my capacity as Hel's liaison. It was signed by Cody's uncle Elijah, who was officially the head of the clan.

It wasn't quite a punch to the gut, but it hurt. "I see." I folded the invitation. "Why did you wait so long?"

Cody shrugged. "Guess I had mixed feelings about the whole thing. But now I hear you've moved on."

Okay, that was a low blow. "Not by choice," I reminded him.

His upper lip curled, revealing eyeteeth that were a bit too long. "You could have chosen anyone but Ludovic!"

My temper stirred. "Don't go there," I said to Cody. "Just . . . don't. You have *no* right."

"I can't help—" He cut off his sentence as Chief Bryant poked his head out from his office.

"Everything all right?" the chief asked, glancing back and forth between us.

"Fine, sir," Cody said stiffly. "My apologies. I didn't mean to raise my voice."

"I see." The chief's gaze was shrewd. I had a feeling Cody and I had just blown our cover, but the chief didn't pursue it. "Don't forget to swing by the Chandlers' place," he said to Cody. "They're in the Bahamas this week and I promised we'd keep an eye on it. They had a break-in when they were on vacation last year."

"Right." Cody nodded. "Will do."

Chief Bryant waited for Cody to leave, then ambled over to my desk. "This business with you and Ludovic," he said, without looking directly at me. "Does it have anything to do with Officer Fairfax?"

"No."

"Good." He rapped his knuckles on the desk. "These are difficult times. Try not to make them harder, all right? We really can't afford distractions that affect morale in the department."

I wanted to say that it wasn't my fault; that Cody had made his choice and he had to live with it. But I figured it probably wasn't a good idea to openly admit that we'd had a relationship, sort of. "Understood, sir."

The chief clapped a hand on my shoulder. "Glad to hear it."

# Thirty-five

The following Saturday, Stefan and I had our second date.

As promised, he took me to brunch—a fancy, upscale buffet brunch at the Brookdale Country Club.

I'd only ever driven past the place. If the weather had held, the snow-covered grounds would have been picturesque, but the cold snap had broken, and the golf course was a vast expanse of sodden, patchy turf.

As before, our appearance was greeted with excitement and consternation, gray-haired patrons whispering as Stefan and I were seated. The Brookdale Country Club definitely catered to an older demographic.

At least they put on a good spread. And yes, the sight of Stefan standing in line at the buffet and meticulously placing smoked salmon, paper-thin slices of red onion, and capers on blini with a schmeer of herbed cream cheese was . . . bizarre.

"You know, you don't have to do this," I said to him when we returned to our table.

He raised his eyebrows at me. "I gave you my word, Daisy."

"I mean the food thing." I gestured at his plate. "You don't actually derive pleasure from it, do you?"

Stefan paused. "Not exactly, no. But I enjoy the ritual of dining and the sense of communion it evokes." Wielding his utensils European-style, he cut his blini in quarters. "So." He speared a piece with his upside-down fork. "I promised you candor. You wish to know my history with others of your kind. Is there more?"

I sliced into my own first course, a thick slab of prime rib that was just shy of medium rare. And yes, I realize it wasn't even noon yet, but, hey, it was offered at the carving station. "Well, that's the big one. But of course, there's more."

"Such as?" he inquired politely.

Chewing a succulent bite of prime rib, I studied Stefan. The overcast daylight filtering through the windows alleviated the impact of his unnatural pallor, making him look almost mortal. Twenty-nine. I'd been sure he was older; but then, I suppose twenty-nine in the fifteenth century was a more mature age than it was in the twenty-first. Still, I could see it now that I was looking.

"The thing is, I'm not sure where to draw the line between getting to know you and prying into painful topics," I said. "I mean, there are the obvious questions."

"Of course." He gave a faint, wistful smile. "You wonder if I had a wife and children."

Actually, I wondered if there had been multiple wives and children over the centuries. "Did you?"

"A wife, yes." Stefan reached for the bottle of champagne in the free-standing ice bucket beside the table and topped off our glasses. "No children. She miscarried twice, and the third was stillborn."

"I'm sorry."

"At the time, it was cause for great sorrow. Since then . . ." Stefan shrugged. "I do not know. It may have been worse to become anathema to my own flesh and blood, to watch them age and die at a distance, while I endured."

I took another bite. "Did you ever marry again?"

"No," he said. "Never. There have been women, women I have loved. But it seemed unfair to wed them, when I could give them neither children nor the comfort and solace of growing old together."

"So the Outcast can't have children?" I murmured. That was something I'd wondered about. Not that I was considering it or anything, but I'd wondered.

Stefan shook his head. "Those of us who have been touched by death can bring no new life into the world."

"I'm sorry," I said again.

"Forgive me," he said gravely. "I did not know you were unaware. I did not mean to mislead you, Daisy."

"You didn't." I fiddled with my fork. "I wasn't sure. I mean, obviously, I was aware that there were, um, drawbacks to any relationship we might have, what with the fact that you're immortal and I'm not."

"Does it frighten you?" Stefan asked.

"Of course it frightens me!" I said. "I'd be crazy if it didn't. But honestly, right now, it doesn't frighten me as much as what I *don't* know, like why you were so reluctant to talk about your past with hell-spawns."

"Why does it concern you so?" He sounded genuinely interested. "It was a very long time ago."

"Because you're avoiding the issue!" I said. "And, um, someone implied that I ought to know."

Stefan frowned. "Someone?"

I sighed. "Daniel Dufreyne, okay? I saw him at the Market Bistro the other night. And no, I don't trust him, but frankly, I don't know what to think. So just tell me, all right?"

"Very well." Bracing himself, Stefan took a deep breath. "When I was mortal, we hunted and dispatched hell-spawns."

Yikes. Okay, not what I expected. "We?" I asked in a small voice.

"The Knights of the Cross with the Red Star," he replied in a quiet tone. "It was part of our mission. There were more of them in those days, when faith was a simpler matter."

I didn't say anything.

"It was a different time, Daisy," Stefan said. "And I was a different man. And they . . . they were unlike you. Creatures of chaos and destruction, bent on bringing about the end of the world."

A resounding crash made me jump in my seat and glance involuntarily upward, half expecting to see the dome of heaven cracking, but it was only a busboy dropping a tray full of dishes.

Even so, it made my skin prickle. "How many did you kill?" I whispered.

Stefan's gaze didn't waver. "Three."

"Were any of them born of innocents?" I asked him. "You said they weren't like me, but . . . were they?"

He hesitated. "Two were part of an intricate occult conspiracy, conceived under circumstances rather, I suspect, like this lawyer Dufreyne. Perhaps its legacy is where his knowledge of our history comes from. And one . . . one was not."

"Tell me about him," I said. "Or was it a her?"

"It was a boy," Stefan said. "*He* was a boy."

"You killed a *child*?" I pushed my plate away, my appetite gone. "Jesus, Stefan!"

"We followed the report of rumors in the countryside," he said. "We found a simple unwed peasant woman, her mind shattered beyond repair. We brought the woman and her ten-year-old son to the hospital in Prague. We gave her the best care possible and took in her son as a ward of the order. We watched and observed as he grew toward maturity."

"Oh, so you didn't slaughter him outright?" I said with bitter sarcasm. "Bravo. That could have been my mom, you know. That could have been *me*."

"Your mother's mind is very much intact, Daisy," Stefan murmured. "This woman taught her son to believe he was the new Messiah and that he must claim his heritage and his birthright when he came of age."

"So you killed him?"

"We watched him," Stefan repeated. "We attempted to educate and guide him. And we failed."

"Did he claim his birthright?" I asked, gesturing around me. "Because as far as I can tell, the world's still standing."

Stefan looked away. "When he was thirteen years of age, he slaughtered every horse in the hospital's stables in a fit of rage, with a cleaver he'd stolen from the kitchen. I was the one who found him. I heard the horses screaming in panic, but I arrived too late. Outside of a battlefield, it was the worst scene of carnage I had ever witnessed. The boy was covered in blood, laughing. He told me that now that he'd been baptized, he meant to claim his birthright, and that we would all be sorry for it. And then he began the invocation." He looked back at me, his pupils steady in his ice-blue eyes. "So yes, I killed him."

I swallowed hard. The sight of my prime rib swimming in red meat juices had gone from unappetizing to sickening. "I don't know what to say, Stefan. I don't even know where to begin."

"I told you it was not a fit topic for dinner conversation," he said.

"What made you think it would be better suited to *brunch*?" I'd raised my voice, turning heads.

"I thought it would be better suited to daylight," Stefan said quietly. "It is not a memory I care to revisit."

"Okay." I grabbed my champagne glass and downed half its contents. "So what happened to make you go from executing hell-spawns to dating one?"

"There were great scholars in the Church in those days," he said. "Great thinkers, great humanitarians. But in certain matters, their doctrine was rigid. When I became Outcast, I became anathema, shunned and reviled. And I began to perceive that God's plan for humankind may be more vast and complex than we can comprehend. Perhaps one of the Outcast could have helped that boy."

"Like you offered to help me the first time we met?" I asked him. "Jesus! Is that what you think I need?"

"No." Stefan's expression was grave. "I offered my services unknowing. I have encountered few of your kind since I was Outcast, and none like you. Until I made inquiries, I was uncertain of your nature."

"And now?"

"Daisy . . ." He sighed. "No, I do not think you *need* my help. You are a grown woman capable of managing your emotions. But I think that the methods you have learned so well prevent you from being your truest self."

"Yeah, well, maybe that's a good thing," I said. "What with the existential threat I represent and all."

"Do you believe that?" Stefan asked.

"I'm not sure what I believe." I raked a hand through my hair.

"Okay, here's a question for you. Would you be interested in me if I *wasn't* a demon's daughter?"

"We cannot separate who we are from what we are, Daisy," Stefan said. "I suspect the hell-spawn Dufreyne has his own reasons for wishing to sow doubt in your mind. Perhaps in becoming your truest version of yourself, you pose a threat to his goals. You have powerful emotions that you yearn to express." His pupils flared. "And I have powerful needs. What we can offer each other is . . . unique."

Stefan and I regarded each other in silence for a moment. The background murmur of voices in the restaurant increased in volume. The clumsy busboy made a careful exit with his reloaded tray of dirty dishes.

I had a feeling we'd just provided the patrons of the Brookdale Country Club with a month's worth of gossip.

I cleared my throat. "Would you be offended if I asked you to take me home?"

"Of course not."

It was a silent drive through the gray drizzle back to my apartment. I didn't quite know what to think about Stefan's past. I felt like a vampire who'd just learned she was dating Van Helsing, although that wasn't entirely fair. As he'd said, it had been a different time and he'd been a different man—a mortal man.

A mortal man who'd executed a thirteen-year-old boy. A sociopathic hell-spawn of a boy bent on bringing about Armageddon.

"What was his name?" I asked Stefan as he pulled into the alley. "The boy."

He parked the Lexus. "Tomik."

"Why did he kill the horses?" I asked. "Why was he angry at the *horses*?"

"He wasn't." Stefan came around to open my door. "He was angry because one of the brothers had refused to allow him a horse to ride to market that day."

"That's all?"

Stefan nodded. "That's all."

I shuddered.

"Daisy." He reached out and touched my hair lightly, running a few strands through his fingers. "You asked for candor and I have given it to you. I do not think you have extended me the same courtesy."

I gave him a puzzled look. "What do you mean?"

"I knew that this matter would be disturbing, but I did not expect you to take it so closely to heart," Stefan said. "It is more than this infernal lawyer. Something has been troubling you since you dispatched the Night Hag. There is a fear that preys on your mind, something of which you are reluctant to speak."

I didn't deny it. "You know, it's not fair that this bond only works one way. I don't know what *you're* feeling."

"Yes." Stefan inclined his head to me. "Which is why I have respected your privacy, and have made no inquiries. Which is why I recant the words I spoke on our last meeting. I will not press my suit, Daisy. I am willing to wait." Leaning over, he brushed my lips in a fleeting kiss, one that left me yearning for more. "You know where to find me when you are ready."

Standing on the doorstep, I watched him get into his Lexus and drive away.

Well, damn.

# Thirty-six

I did a lot of thinking.

Stefan was right—I *hadn't* been candid with him, but it's not like I wasn't planning to be . . . eventually. We were still in the getting-to-know-you phase, and revealing my deepest, darkest fear seemed a little heavy for a second date, especially since that fear was that I would be responsible for the world's destruction.

Then again, one could say the same of Stefan's revelation, although to be fair, I was the one who had pushed for it. Oh, I could blame it on the lawyer, but it was Stefan who brought it up in the first place and then went all cryptic on me. And Dufreyne was right; there was history there that I needed to know. On the other hand, Stefan was probably right about him, too. Odds were, Dufreyne had his own nefarious reasons for wanting me to doubt Stefan.

Or maybe he just saw a chance to mess with my head and took it.

I could drive myself crazy thinking about it. I was willing to set aside my doubts and give it a try, I really was, but I didn't know if I could handle another devastating favor or horrific revelation.

In the end, I waited three days before calling him. "Okay, here's the thing," I said. "Is there anything else in your past that's likely to freak me out?"

There was a brief pause on the other end. "I have lived a long life, Daisy," Stefan said carefully. "There have been times when I was filled with anger and despair. I do not doubt that I have done things that you would find . . . troubling. But I do not believe that there is anything else in my past that would strike such a personal chord with you."

"How about your present?" I asked him. "Can you tell me there won't be another Janek Król?"

"I cannot promise you that no other Outcast will ask you to end his or her existence," he said. "I can promise you that I will never ask again on another's behalf."

"Good," I said. "Let's take this slow. Do you like jazz?"

"Yes." Stefan sounded mildly bemused. "Are you inviting me on a date?"

"Yeah, but not right away," I said. "You're right. I've been holding back, but I need more time to figure out how I feel about Stefan Ludovic, Hell-spawn Hunter. Next Saturday? I heard there's going to be a fantastic harmonica player sitting in with the house band at the Bide-a-Wee Tavern."

"I look forward to it," Stefan said.

I felt good about the decision. I wished I could say the same about the latest idea Sinclair and the coven laid on me.

While I'd been absorbed in my fraught pas de deux with Stefan, not only had the coven been working on developing the mother of all protection charms, but they'd been wrestling with the issue of how to get it onto the judge's person or hidden in his briefcase.

"There's one major problem with that plan," the Fabulous Casimir said after convening a meeting at his house. "Metal detectors. It's a federal courthouse. Everyone, lawyers and judges included, entering the building gets scanned. The minute they find a strange metal object in the judge's briefcase . . ." He fanned his hands. "The jig's up."

Oh, crap. I hadn't thought of that. "Does the charm *have* to be metal?"

The eight members of the coven looked at me with varying degrees of pity. Apparently that was a stupid question. "It does in this case, Daisy," Sinclair said. "Pure silver, consecrated with holy water."

"So we're screwed?" I asked.

"Perhaps not." Casimir steepled his fingertips. "You shouldn't have any difficulty conveying the charm into the courthouse. Jewelry is permitted, and the charm will appear to be nothing more than a simple silver cross on a chain." He peered at me from beneath his luxuriant false eyelashes. "You can wear a cross without harm, can't you?"

"Of course." Actually, the only reason I knew it to be true was because back in high school, I'd gone to an eighties-themed dance as vintage Madonna, including dangly cross-shaped earrings I'd found at the flea market, but I figured it counted. "But if we can't risk slipping it in the judge's briefcase, what's the alternative?"

"You're gonna stick it to the underside of his chair," said Kim McKinney, who worked at the deli counter at Tafts Grocery. "That way it never leaves the courthouse, but it'll always be in virtual contact with him. I got the idea from my brother," she added. "He used to punk us with a remote-controlled fart machine."

I stared at assembled members of the coven. "Look, no offense, but I was already pretty wigged out about trying to sneak it into a coat pocket or a briefcase. How, exactly, am I supposed to get past the bailiff, crawl behind the desk, and stick something under the judge's freakin' *chair*?"

"Two words, *dahling*." Casimir smiled at me. "Invisibility spell."

"Is that a real thing?" I asked.

"It's a real thing," Sinclair assured me. "Well . . . sort of. It's really more of an unobtrusiveness spell than full-on invisibility. You'd have to practice. Sandra's offered to help teach you. It's mostly about aura manipulation, and she's got mad skills."

Sandra Sweddon gave me a little wave. "At your service, honey."

"Thanks, Mrs. Sweddon," I said automatically. "Sinclair, what do you mean by *mostly*?"

He glanced at Warren Rodgers, who owned the nursery. "We're

looking into old recipes based on wolfsbane and working on an amulet for you. It should intensify the effect."

"Already got the wolfsbane," Warren added in his laconic way. "Just need a chameleon skin to wrap it in."

"I can get you a chameleon skin," Casimir said to him. "Miss Daisy, we just need to know if you're still on board with this."

"Tell her about the distraction, dear," Mrs. Meyers said, not looking up from her knitting.

"Right." The Fabulous Casimir raised his artfully plucked brows. "We thought it would be ideal if we could arrange some sort of distraction on the day that you testify. Something to clear the courtroom, and give you a chance to do your thing in the ensuing confusion."

I sighed. "Please don't tell me you want me to pull the fire alarm."

Casimir pursed his lips. "Don't be absurd. You can't take *that* many chances, *dahling*. No, no. We're thinking a bomb scare."

"Are you out of your mind?" I demanded. "Do you know how easily that could be traced these days?"

"No, but Lee does," Sinclair said. "Or at least he knows people who do. He's sure he can make it happen without being traced, and you know how paranoid he is. Lee's really thought this through," he added. "If we call in a highly detailed threat regarding a bomb releasing nerve gas into the ventilation system, they'll *have* to evacuate. And the bomb squad can rule out the threat without conducting an in-depth room by room search that might turn up the charm."

I looked blankly at him. "Nerve gas."

Sinclair shrugged. "Hey, apparently Lee did a lot of research into it for one of the video games he worked on. Some *Splinter Cell* knockoff. All I know is that he sounds awfully convincing."

I fought the urge to yank my hair out. "Okay, so assuming that works, how am I supposed to stick a silver cross to the bottom of the judge's chair? Chewing gum?"

"We've got industrial-strength mounting tape we use to hang artwork at the tattoo parlor," Mark Reston said. "Sheila and I are testing it with a pendant that's about the same weight. Once you get inside the courthouse, you'll need to wrap the cross in a piece of duct tape for a more adhesive surface, but so far, so good."

"Crap." That sinking feeling in the pit of my stomach had returned. "You're serious about this, aren't you?"

"Did you hear the latest, Miss Daisy?" Casimir inquired.

"Yeah. I did." The judge had dismissed the request to assign a different lawyer to the case, citing the fact that Dufreyne had voluntarily recused himself from representing Elysian Fields's interests in Pemkowet for the duration of the case. I steeled my resolve. "Do you really think you can teach me to turn invisible?" I asked Sandra Sweddon.

"Unobtrusive," Sandra corrected me. "I don't see why not. After all, you've been working on visualization exercises since you were a little girl. Would you feel better if I demonstrated it?"

"Yes, please."

The Fabulous Casimir clapped his hands. "Break time! Daisy, you try to keep your eye on Sandra as everyone else mills around the house," he added. "Oh, and people! Help yourself to the lovely cheese tray Kim brought from the deli."

Clearly, this little exercise had been planned in advance.

I stayed seated while everyone else rose, watching intently as Sandra Sweddon's lips moved in an invocation.

"Excuse me, dear," Mrs. Meyers apologized, passing between us en route to the cheese tray.

That was all it took. One moment of lost visual contact, and I had a hard time locating Sandra. It's not that she wasn't *there*—she couldn't have made it out of the living room in the time it took Mrs. Meyers to place a slice of cheddar cheese on a Ritz cracker—but my gaze skated over and past her.

I got up and paced the room, counting the members of the coven as they moved to and fro. Sandra moved unobtrusively with the flow, drifting from one place to another, periodically obscured by others. I kept losing sight of her, and if I hadn't known she was there, I'm not sure I would have seen her at all. My mind simply refused to register her presence. No matter how many times I counted the people in the room, I kept coming up short.

"Pretty cool, huh?" Sinclair said behind me.

It was.

"Okay," I said to the room at large. "I'm in. Sign me up for invisibility lessons."

Sandra Sweddon appeared as a solid presence in Casimir's living room, standing next to a sleek Art Deco–looking bronze sculpture and beaming in my direction. "Wonderful! We'll start tomorrow afternoon."

So *that* was decided.

The following afternoon, I reported to Sandra's house for my first invisibility—unobtrusibility?—lesson.

The Sweddon place was a big old farmhouse on the outskirts of East Pemkowet. We sat in the breakfast nook in the sunlit kitchen. Outside the windows, chickadees, juncos, goldfinches, and cardinals vied for birdseed at a welcoming array of feeders while Sandra taught me the basics of invisibility.

In theory, it shouldn't have been that difficult. The visualization exercises I'd done since I was a kid provided me with a solid grounding in the concept. The problem was that for the past several months, I'd been assiduously applying those methods to the shielding technique Stefan had taught me, which was essentially the exact opposite of what you needed to do to make yourself unobtrusive.

"You need to let go, Daisy," Sandra explained patiently for the umpteenth time. "Allow your aura to disperse."

"I'm trying!" I protested.

"You're trying too hard," she said. "Every time you do, you gather energy. Let it go. Imagine that you're insubstantial, inhabiting only your etheric body. Envision particles of light passing through your physical being." She extended one hand into a sunbeam, offering an invocation. "Light pass through me, gaze pass over me."

At point-blank range, the effect was subtle. Sandra didn't vanish before my eyes or anything, she just turned . . . vague. When I tried to look directly at her, my eyes prickled and my brain felt skittery.

"Light pass through me, gaze pass over me," I echoed, willing myself to relinquish the energy Stefan called pneuma.

It didn't work.

The harder I tried, the more present, immediate, and solid I felt, aware of my heart beating steadily in my chest, the air moving in and out of my lungs, my pulse sounding in my ears, the hard surface of the kitchen chair beneath my butt and my neatly tucked tail. I stared at dust motes swirling in the wintry sun until my eyes dazzled, and didn't feel one iota less substantial.

"Let *go*, Daisy," Sandra repeated. "Let go of the notion of self. Let yourself be of the world and in it. Let yourself be everywhere and no-where."

"I'm not sure I can," I said apologetically. "I'm sorry. Maybe I don't have an, um, etheric body."

"Of course you do." She gave me a thoughtful look. "You've got the skill to do it, honey. It's taking the leap of faith that's hard. To achieve invisibility—pure unobtrusiveness—is a trade-off. There's a consider-able measure of protection in it, but you have to lower your guard en-tirely in order to attain it."

Okay, that might be the problem.

I made a face. "Is the lowering-your-guard part a deal breaker on the whole invisibility thing?"

"I'm afraid so," Sandra said. "But if you can find a way to give it a chance, you might be surprised. There are strengths you can only find by embracing vulnerability." Rising, she went to peruse a shelf on the wall opposite the breakfast nook, which held a handful of books and bric-a-brac including decorative antique butter molds and an oven mitt in the form of a gingham-covered chicken. She selected a slender, dog-eared paperback and handed it to me. "Try this. It might help."

I glanced at it, expecting something Wiccan and New Age-y, maybe with a feminist slant. Maybe *Our Etheric Bodies, Ourselves.* Instead, I found that what I held was a reprint of the original 1855 edition of Walt Whitman's *Leaves of Grass.*

"Poetry?" I asked. "No offense, Mrs. Sweddon, but do you think that's going to help?"

Sandra smiled at me. "It worked for Susan Sarandon in *Bull Durham*, didn't it?"

*Bull Durham* was one of Mom's favorite movies, and I knew exactly what Sandra meant. In an ongoing effort to get her seasonal hookup and protégé, rookie pitcher Ebby Calvin "Nuke" LaLoosh, to stop psyching himself out, Susan Sarandon ties him to her bed and reads Walt Whitman to him.

Well, among other things, like convincing him to wear one of her garter belts under his uniform and to breathe through his eyelids like a Galapagos Islands lava lizard. Anyway, that's how it worked in the movie. I wasn't exactly optimistic that a dose of poetry would have the same effect in real life.

Sandra saw the doubt in my expression. "Oh, give it a try, Daisy. It can't hurt. Spend tomorrow with Whitman, and we'll try again the day after."

I slid the book into my messenger bag. "I'll do my best."

To say that Walt Whitman's poetry was over my head was an understatement.

It's not that I don't like poetry; I just don't entirely get it. Not this kind, anyway. Lacking any kind of discernible rhyme or structure, it assailed me like a verbal deluge.

I tried reading aloud at home and quickly discovered that I was drowning in a sea of words while Mogwai stared at me with profound disinterest. And somehow it didn't seem like the kind of poetry that should be read in the comfort of a living room. A grassy hillock above a babbling brook probably would have been ideal, someplace where I could meditate on what Whitman meant when he said grass was the handkerchief of the Lord, or a uniform hieroglyphic, or the uncut hair of graves . . . okay, actually, I got that last one. But it was too damn cold to sit outside and read poetry.

Instead, I went to the Daily Grind, treated myself to a mocha latte, and plowed doggedly onward.

At least for the first couple of hours, I was able to enjoy relative peace and quiet while I wrestled with Whitman's endless observations of the world and its glorious multitude of inhabitants, interspersed with ruminations on the nature of self and existence, trying to figure out how on earth this was supposed to help me learn to become invisible. After a while, I gave up and just started skimming the pages, letting the words wash over me.

I was beginning to think it might be easier to start trying to breathe through my eyelids like a Galapagos Islands lava lizard.

Shortly after three o'clock, the coffee shop was hit with an influx of high school students released for the day, bringing the scent of cold air and the sound of myriad competing voices with them.

So much for concentrating. And yet I found myself looking at the scene through different eyes, wondering how good old Walt Whitman would have viewed it. He certainly described the world like an unseen observer, filled with immense tenderness. And words. Lots and lots of words. I thought Whitman would have loved the lanky, broad-shouldered boys in varsity jackets jostling for position at the counter, strong-boned wrists protruding from leather cuffs; the pretty girls snapping chewing gum and flipping their glossy hair; the stoic barista with the tattoos and the pierced nose taking their orders, drawing hissing spouts of espresso into a cup, foaming steamed milk in a pitcher . . .

. . . and something clicked.

*Let yourself be of the world and in it*, Sandra had said to me. *Let yourself be everywhere and nowhere.*

"Light pass through me," I whispered beneath the exuberant jumble of chatter. "Gaze pass over me."

Taking a deep breath, I let go.

It was a strange sensation, at once exhilarating and unnerving. I felt porous, there and not-there at the same time, the essence of myself diffusing like mist to fill the space contained within the coffee shop.

Everywhere.

Nowhere.

With a solid thump, a heavily laden backpack landed on my table. I startled in my seat, coming back to myself.

"Whoa!" A teenaged boy with floppy bangs and a smattering of acne on his chin blinked at me. "Sorry," he apologized, sweeping his bangs to one side with a toss of his head. "I didn't see you sitting there."

"That's okay." I smiled up at him. "More than okay, actually. You can have the table. I was just leaving."

It's amazing how one simple breakthrough changes everything. Poetry—who would have thunk it? Well, Sandra Sweddon, I guess. Plus the screenwriter of *Bull Durham*, and probably every literature professor everywhere, not to mention poets themselves since the dawn of time. And it probably didn't have to be poetry. It could be anything: a garter, a song, a lamia's kiss.

Outside, I murmured the invocation again, willing my aura to disperse in the crisp winter air. I circled the block, flowing down the sidewalk. Pedestrians passed by me without seeing me, their absent gazes skating past me. I felt immensely powerful and extremely vulnerable, invisible yet exposed.

Casimir's shop, the Sisters of Selene, was adjacent to the Daily Grind. Upon completing my circuit of the block, I pushed the door open, closing it gently behind me, letting the chimes sound with a faint tinkle.

Behind the counter, the Fabulous Casimir looked up, an uncertain expression on his face. His gaze hovered over me, then sharpened. He muttered something under his breath and made a banishing gesture with one hand, and I felt myself solidifying beneath his gaze, coming into focus.

"Well, well!" He arched his eyebrows. "Not bad, Miss Daisy."

I was a little deflated that Casimir had banished my unobtrusibility spell that quickly. "Really?"

"For a neophyte who doesn't even practice the craft?" he said. "It's an impressive start."

"I owe it to Walt Whitman," I informed him.

The Fabulous Casimir shrugged his shoulders, which were clad in a replica of a quilted Chanel jacket today. "Whatever it takes, *dahling*."

# Thirty-seven

Despite my abiding love of the holiday season, even I had to admit that this was a particularly unfestive December in Pemkowet.

The prospect of that damned lawsuit hung over the town like a massive gray cloud, dampening everyone's spirits. A date—February 10—had been set for the beginning of the trial. In the meantime, there was nothing anyone could do about it, but it was still all anyone could talk about.

Well, there was *almost* nothing. The lawyers were preparing their case, advised by Lurine's celebrity hotshot attorney, Robert Diaz. Lurine admitted in private that his confidence had been shaken by the whole hell-spawn angle and the judge's refusal to replace Dufreyne, but her outlook remained sanguine.

"Even if we're talking about a worst-case scenario, forty-five million dollars isn't *that* much money, cupcake," she said to me.

"Yeah, well, it's a lot more money than all three communities have in their rainy-day funds. Like, thirty-eight million dollars more, I hear." I gave Lurine a speculative look, trying to remember how much her octogenarian husband's estate was rumored to have been worth. "Are you offering to make up the difference to cover the damages?"

"Well, not the *whole* amount," Lurine said. "Do you have any idea what the property taxes are on my place? But I'd be happy to spearhead a fund-raising effort." She cocked her head thoughtfully. "You know, that would make for great PR if I planned on a third act in the public eye." She struck a pose and read an imaginary headline. "Can't you just see it? 'Gold-Digging, Trailer-Trash, D-List Celebrity Uses Ill-Gotten Fame and Fortune to Save Her Hometown!'"

I couldn't help but smile. "Let's hope it doesn't come to that."

"Let's," Lurine agreed. Then she added, "But I'll update my contact list just in case."

If it hadn't been for the shadow cast by my mom's reading, I might have found Lurine's assurances more, well, reassuring. After all, Lurine *was* hella wealthy, at least by ordinary mortal standards. But Mom's reading had indicated that wealth was part of the problem in the brewing war, not the solution.

I was not reassured.

All things considered, a worst-case scenario was best avoided, and so I practiced the art of unobtrusibility, scheduling regular sessions with Sandra Sweddon, slowly mastering the craft of diffusing and gathering my aura at will, trying not to think about the day when I'd face the ultimate test of putting it into practice in a courtroom in Grand Rapids, because it still made me feel sick to my stomach. Sinclair promised me that the wolfsbane charm he and Warren were assembling would augment the effect, though they didn't want me sapping its power by testing it beforehand.

I did attempt the unobtrusibility spell outside the boundaries of Hel's territory, though. That was something I needed to know. Did I carry enough of the underworld inside myself to make magic function in the mundane world?

As it happens, I did.

I drove twenty minutes north and spent a day in downtown Appeldoorn, wandering up and down the sidewalks, my aura as vague and insubstantial as a winter breeze. I browsed my way around various boutiques and department stores, slipping through the crowds of holiday shoppers, overlooked and unseen deep in the heart of the mundane world.

I owed that revelation to Daniel Dufreyne, which was an uncomfortable thought. I still didn't know what his ultimate angle in this whole business was.

And I still didn't know who was behind Elysian Fields.

Since that was beyond my control, I concentrated on things that weren't. That pointedly did *not* include Cody Fairfax and his clan's upcoming werewolf mixer, a prospect that still made my heart feel bruised.

However, it did include dating Stefan.

It was probably a gross exaggeration to suggest that I was in control where anything involving Stefan Ludovic was concerned, but at least for the moment, he seemed content to let me establish the pace of our evolving relationship.

As far as dates went, our outing to the Bide-a-Wee Tavern was the most successful one, well, to date.

It was one of my favorite places in town, and I hadn't been there since I'd taken Sinclair and his sister there on Labor Day. To be honest, the Bide-a-Wee with its cheap wood paneling, worn carpets, and outdated decor had seemed a little shabby to me when I looked at it from the perspective of the very composed and Oxford-educated Emmeline Palmer, and I was a little bit worried that seeing it through Stefan's eyes would have the same effect, but I didn't have any cause for concern. Stefan saw what I saw in it, a place where an unlikely assortment of professional, semiprofessional, and flat-out amateur musicians and singers gathered to share their love of jazz and blues.

Okay, the quality varied, but the house band was always solid, and the harmonica player I'd heard about was outstanding.

I watched Stefan as I listened. He lounged in his chair, jeans-clad legs stretched out before him, motorcycle boots crossed at the ankle, longish black hair brushing the collar of his leather vest. In the dim light, there was no mistaking his ghoul's unnatural pallor. Stefan's eyes were at half-mast, pupils gleaming beneath his lids. I had the feeling he was surfing the wave of complex emotion coming from the bar's patrons, and maybe siphoning off just a hint in the process. Strictly speaking, that was against the unwritten code of the Outcast, but I trusted Stefan.

I also had the feeling that the band was playing *to* Stefan, sensing in him an audience that appreciated the emotions they evoked on the deepest possible level.

"They're good," Stefan said when the band took a break. He smiled at me, flashing those unexpected dimples. "Thank you. I'm enjoying this."

I smiled back at him. "I'm glad."

There were things I wanted to ask him. I wanted to know if I was right about his siphoning emotion from the audience. I wanted to know what that felt like. I wanted to know if something Cooper had told me was true for Stefan, too: that it was more painful to devour positive emotions than negative ones.

But instead, I kept my mouth shut for once. Right now, it was enough that we were actually enjoying ourselves together.

Afterward, I drove Stefan home to his condo. Since this excursion was my idea, I'd offered to drive and he'd taken me up on it with only the slightest hesitation, allowing me to maintain my illusion of control.

"Would you like to come inside for a drink?" Stefan asked when I pulled into his parking space, his voice courteous and neutral.

There was a part of me that did, a reckless part that wanted to throw caution to the wind, stop being careful and controlled, and dive into this dangerous affair that we both knew we wanted. Despite Stefan's courtesy, the amused glint in his eyes gave away the fact that he knew what I was feeling. Hell, of course he did. Stefan *always* knew what I was feeling.

Well, unless I raised a shield against him, which wasn't exactly a polite way to end a date. And the truth was, there was another part of me that was enjoying the prolonged suspense and the sense of being in control.

It might be an illusion, but it was an illusion I liked. Probably in the same way a lion tamer enjoys the illusion of control right up to the point that a big cat goes all Siegfried-and-Roy on his ass.

I shook my head. "Not yet."

"As you will." Stefan didn't make a move to get out of my Honda, but he didn't make a move to kiss me, either; he just sat there with that infernal look of amusement on his face.

Okay, fine. Against the restraint of my seat belt, I leaned over and kissed him, sliding one hand into his black hair. I felt a faint shudder run through him. So, this *wasn't* easy for him. Good.

Settling back into my seat, I took a deep breath. "Good night, then."

"Good night, Daisy." Stefan's pupils were dilated and glittering, but he opened the car door. "Shall we do this again next week? You may choose the time and place."

"Mom and I are driving up north to spend Christmas with my grandparents," I said. "How about the following week?"

"Christmas," Stefan murmured, half to himself. "Yes, of course. Do you have plans for New Year's Eve?"

"No."

He smiled, and got out of the Honda. "You do now. And *I'll* make them."

It sounded like a promise, or maybe a warning. Probably both. I didn't think this particular tiger was content to stay on a leash for long.

Between the general malaise that gripped the town and my complicated love life, it seemed like it might be a relief to get away for a few days—*might* being the operative word. Visiting the grandparents wasn't exactly a chore, but there was always a certain awkwardness. I know they couldn't help but feel guilty that they hadn't been able to give Mom unqualified support and reconcile themselves to having a half-demon grandchild. I couldn't find it in my heart to blame them. My grandparents were salt-of-the-earth types, hardworking descendants of Scandinavian immigrants. Growing up in hunting and fishing country, Grandpa had learned his trade from an early age. He was considered one of the best taxidermists in the state, and his business was his pride and joy. Up until his semiretirement a few years ago, Grandma helped run it and kept the books.

My mom was supposed to be the first one in the family to earn a college degree, not drop out to raise her hell-spawn daughter. And to say that I was a challenging child is a massive understatement. Lots of things spontaneously broke or blew their circuits when I had temper tantrums. I'm pretty sure that Grandma went through seven or eight toasters during my terrible twos.

It's odd, but it never occurred to me to wonder about why that happened in a perfectly ordinary mundane setting. Conventional eldritch wisdom held that magic only worked in the presence of a functioning underworld occupied by a deity; as below, so above. I hadn't thought of the supernatural side effects of my childhood tantrums as *magic*.

I guess they were, though.

All things considered, it was a nice visit. My grandparents were solicitous hosts in their own taciturn way. On Christmas Eve, we went to a candlelit service at the Lutheran church where they were members. It was a service I'd attended plenty of times before, but it was always reassuring to know that lightning didn't strike me down when I crossed the threshold of God's house, my tail curled discreetly between my legs. I'm pretty sure Grandma and Grandpa found it reassuring, too.

Afterward was my favorite part, when we drove around town in Grandpa's SUV to look at the Christmas lights on our way back to their ranch house. It had been a family tradition since before I was born.

This year, it felt different.

Oh, the Christmas lights were the same. If anything, they were more spectacular than ever. Now that anyone could buy giant inflatable snowmen or pre-strung illuminated Santa's sleighs complete with eight reindeer at their local Lowe's or Menards, the ante on holiday displays had been upped.

And yet it felt hollow. No, that wasn't quite right. *I* felt hollow, disconnected. This wasn't *my* town, *my* place. I hadn't fought for it, put myself on the line to defend it. I may have carried my own underworld inside me, but it made me feel alone and lonely, and longing for home.

In the morning, we celebrated Christmas and exchanged gifts. I already had the coat that Mom had bought me, but I'd purchased perfume for her, and fancy knitting yarn that Mrs. Meyers had recommended for

Grandma, and a pair of shearling-lined leather slippers for Grandpa, who beamed when he opened the package.

"Well, won't *these* just keep my old dogs cozy in the winter!" Grandpa declared, donning them right away. He smiled at me. "Thank you, Daisy."

I smiled back at him. "I'm glad you like them."

It felt like a genuine family moment. I wanted it to be real. No, that's not fair, either. It was real. Of course it was real. I wanted it to be *enough*.

It wasn't.

It's not that I didn't care for my grandparents. I did. Seeing them age between visits filled me with a sense of terrible tenderness. Somehow that made it seem even more bizarre that I was dating someone whose life span eclipsed theirs six or seven times over. Which, by the way, came up at Christmas dinner. Apparently Mom had mentioned something to Grandma in the kitchen.

"So I hear you've got a young man, Daisy," Grandma said in a chipper tone as she passed me the cabbage. "What's he like?"

I choked on a bite of ham and shot my mom a look.

She gave me a helpless shrug in reply. "Your grandmother asked if there was anyone special in your life."

Oh, Stefan was special, all right. "It's nothing serious," I said. "Not yet, anyway. We've just been on a few dates."

"Is he a local fellow?" Grandpa asked.

"No," I said. "He's not originally from the area."

"Oh." He seemed disappointed. "One of those transplants from the east side? Or is he from the Chicago area?"

It made me want to laugh and cry at the same time. Sitting in my grandparents' dining room over Christmas ham, potatoes, and boiled cabbage, I really, really couldn't imagine myself explaining that I was involved with a six-hundred-year-old immortal Bohemian knight and former hell-spawn hunter who'd been cast out of heaven and hell for murdering his uncle.

"No," I murmured. "No, he's, um, European."

That didn't sit well with the grandparents, who expressed immediate concern that Stefan was after a green card, but my mom managed to play the diplomat and reassure them before changing the topic.

By the time Mom and I headed back home the following afternoon, I was more than ready to return to Pemkowet. It had been good to spend a few days away, but a few days was enough to remind me that even with the specter of a lawsuit hanging over the town, Pemkowet was where I belonged.

This was my home, and whatever was coming, I meant to defend it.

Assuming I survived my New Year's Eve date with Stefan, anyway.

# Thirty-eight

On New Year's Eve, I had no idea what to expect.

All I had to go on was a cryptic message from Stefan saying that I should come to his condo at nine thirty and plan on a late dinner. So I did, wearing the midnight blue shantung silk cocktail dress that Mom had finally finished for me.

"Daisy." Stefan greeted me at the door. I was glad I'd gone semiformal. He was wearing a dark suit with an immaculate white dress shirt beneath it, no tie, collar unbuttoned, but crisp French cuffs fastened with ornate cuff links. He helped me out of my coat. "It's good to see you."

"You, too." Hearing music, I peered around him. His condominium was strung with a tasteful array of white Christmas lights and there was a young man playing a cello in the living room. "You decorated. And hired a musician to serenade us?"

"I did," he confirmed. "And a caterer."

I caught my breath in a half laugh. "Stefan, you really didn't need to go to this much trouble."

His eyes gleamed. "Oh, but I wanted to. Is that not my proper role in such a scenario? To dazzle a young ingénue such as yourself with an ostentatious display of wealth and sophistication?"

I eyed him dubiously. "Oh, my God, what have you been reading?"

Stefan laughed and led me over to the dinner table, where a bottle of champagne was chilling in an ice bucket. "Don't worry. You make a rather uncooperative ingénue, and I do not think you will be overly dazzled by the lengths to which I have gone." He poured a glass of champagne and handed it to me. "The young cellist is Dylan Martinez. I made his acquaintance through his mother, Luisa, who is a nurse at Open Hearth."

"I remember," I said. "I met her on the Night Hag case."

"Yes, of course. Dylan is saving money to attend college in the fall on a musical scholarship. I promised to pay him handsomely for to-night's entertainment and release him in time to attend a party with his friends." Stefan nodded toward the kitchen, where two women in aprons were working quietly and efficiently. "That's Maureen Capaldi, and her sister, Meghan, assisting her. Maureen was a regular at the Wheelhouse."

"I'd heard," I said, which was basically a polite way of saying I'd heard Maureen Capaldi was a total meth-head, at least before Stefan banished the drug trade among the Outcast.

"Maureen is attempting to start a new business after taking part in a rehabilitation program," Stefan murmured discreetly. "I'm told she was once a rather promising young chef. I offered her a chance to demonstrate it." I contemplated Stefan for a moment. "What is it?" He looked uncertainly at me. "Forgive me, but have I somehow offended you with these arrangements?"

"No." I was touched by his uncertainty. "Quite the opposite. You're trying to help people whose paths have crossed yours. *Tikkun olam*, right? Believe me, I like it a lot more than if you'd flown in Yo-Yo Ma and some private chef to impress me."

"Yo-Yo Ma?" Stefan raised his eyebrows. "I fear you vastly overestimate my resources."

"It's possible." I had no idea what the extent of Stefan's resources were. "Can we apply your resources to dinner?"

"Of course." He smiled. "Let us see what Ms. Capaldi is capable of."

It was a beautiful meal served by candlelight on bone-white china that I suspected Stefan had purchased for the occasion. Young Dylan Martinez played classical music I didn't recognize on his cello in the background, his eyes closed in a private reverie as his bow danced over the strings. For a recovering meth addict, Maureen Capaldi had put together an ambitious menu: oysters on the half shell, vichyssoise, endive salad with blue cheese, a roasted rack of lamb, and a panna cotta infused with cardamom for dessert.

It was a far cry from the homely comfort of Christmas dinner at my grandparents' house, and I couldn't help but compare the two. Not the meals themselves so much as the atmosphere. I wondered what meals had been like in Stefan's ancestral home, and felt the centuries stretch between us.

I wasn't the only one aware of the strangeness of it. The Capaldi sisters served every course with a nervous attempt at formality that I was pretty sure they'd learned from watching *Downton Abbey.*

And okay, fair enough. Cooking for and waiting on a six-hundred-year-old ghoul had to be approximately as intimidating as serving the Dowager Countess. Stefan ate sparingly, but it was clear that as he'd said, even if he couldn't enjoy food and drink like a mortal, he took a great deal of pleasure in the ritual. At his request, I described each dish as I found it, drawing on a vocabulary honed by hours of watching the Food Network, and causing him to laugh softly when my descriptions got a bit florid.

"Is the texture truly . . . silken?" he asked in a low, teasing voice as I dug into the panna cotta.

My blood rose, my cheeks flushing with heat. "Hey, your palate may be cursed, but your sense of touch works, doesn't it?" I challenged him. "How would *you* describe it?"

Stefan took a lingering bite. "Silken."

It's funny how laden one word can be. With that one word, the mood shifted from Stefan and me enjoying an elegant private dinner to Stefan and me playing a dangerous private game.

Stefan felt it, too. "Ah," he said, glancing at his watch. "The hour grows late. Allow me to thank our guests for their service, and then you and I may finish our desserts in time for the fireworks display. The view from the balcony should be very good."

What came after that was the unspoken part.

I waved my spoon at him with a jaunty insouciance I didn't feel. "Please, go right ahead."

Ten minutes later, we were alone together.

I've never gone skydiving, but I imagine this was what it would feel like the first time you go up in that plane and the door opens. I hadn't jumped yet, but I was staring at the prospect of free fall, and the window of opportunity to change my mind was narrowing. Once I'd finished my panna cotta, I couldn't think of anything to say, and Stefan didn't offer any conversational gambits. We gazed at each other across the dinner table. The candle flames were reflected in his pupils, flickering in time with my pulse.

The thunderclap of the first fireworks made me jump. "It must be midnight," I said, stating the obvious.

"Yes." Stefan rose gracefully. "Shall we venture onto the balcony or would you rather stay inside?"

"Outside, please." The thought of cold air on my skin was appealing.

Stefan fetched my coat and opened the sliding door onto his balcony, following me. He was right, the view was excellent. Across the harbor, mortars thumped, launching their contents to burst in the night sky above the water.

Usually, I love fireworks, but tonight the sight of a great golden chrysanthemum blossoming above me made me shiver.

"Are you cold?" Stefan said behind me, close enough that I could feel the warmth of his body. It was tempting to lean back against him, but I didn't. Not yet.

"No." I watched trails of sparks fall from the sky. "Stefan . . . do you remember how I told you I caught the Night Hag?"

"Of course," he said. "You summoned her with a nightmare and bound her with a strand of her own hair."

"It wasn't just any nightmare," I said. "It was my *worst* nightmare.

That was the nature of the hex Sinclair created for me." Two more star-bursts exploded overhead. "In the dream, I invoked my birthright." I wrapped my arms around myself. "For a minute, it felt good. It felt *great*. And then the sky cracked open above me, and I knew I'd broken the world."

"I see." Behind me, Stefan's chest rose and fell in a long, slow breath. "No wonder the revelation regarding my past troubled you so."

"Yeah."

"You're not that boy, Daisy," he said. "You're nothing like him."

"But I am," I said. "I'm capable of it."

Stefan slid his arms around me, and now I did let myself lean backward into his strength. "I won't allow it to happen," he murmured against my hair. "I suspect *that* is what the hell-spawn Dufreyne dislikes about our union. If I had been Outcast, I could have helped the boy. I could help you. Perhaps that necessity is what brought us together."

"Maybe." Despite his warmth, I shivered again. "Because I can't shake the feeling that something's coming, Stefan. Something bad. Worse than what happened at Halloween. Way worse."

"Is it this business of the lawsuit that disturbs you?" he asked.

"Not exactly," I said. "It's whoever's behind it, whatever's behind it. Not just Dufreyne. It's Elysian Fields. It's Hades, or whoever's behalf he's acting on." I was starting to get worked up, my tail lashing as my sense of furious helplessness rose. "It's the reading my mom did for me. It's the fact that one of the goddamned *Norns* told me that the fate of the world might hinge on the choices I make."

"Daisy." Stefan turned me around to face him, putting his hands on my shoulders. "I'm here for you. As the leader of the Outcast. As your friend. As your lover, if you'll allow it. Let me help."

"How?" I whispered.

His eyes were filled with reflected fireworks. "Whatever battle is coming, it lies in the future. For tonight, just one night, let me take your fear and anger away."

I hesitated, then nodded. "Do it."

Stefan drew on the connection between us. I felt the unnerving intimacy of my jagged emotions spilling out of me, spilling into him—into the cool, still place of discipline within him, into the endless yearning and hunger that lay beneath it. I felt the terrible pleasure that he took in it, how it sated and stoked his hunger at the same time. For the Outcast, this desire was one that could never be truly slaked.

It worked for me, though.

I felt cleansed—purged of anger, of fear, of worry. All that was left was a tug of powerful attraction and a sense of reckless abandon.

And of course, Stefan knew it.

He smiled at me, and it was a predator's smile. "Happy New Year, Daisy."

Reaching out, I grabbed his belt buckle and yanked him closer. "Happy New Year to *you*."

Wrapping one arm around my waist, Stefan pulled me tight against him. His other hand rose to cup the back of my head and hold me in place as he kissed me, his tongue exploring my mouth with six hundred years' worth of accumulated skill as a final barrage of fireworks burst in the sky behind us.

Yep, I was definitely in free fall now.

"Inside." Stefan's voice was rough with desire as he reached behind us to wrench the sliding door open, propelling me through it.

"Bedroom?" I asked breathlessly, shrugging out of my coat and tossing it on the nearest piece of furniture.

"Yes." Placing a hand between my shoulder blades, Stefan shoved me in the right direction. It should have been off-putting, but it wasn't. The master bedroom was up a flight of stairs. Halfway up, Stefan pinned me against the wall and kissed me some more. I kissed him back, biting his lower lip until he made an inarticulate sound, pried himself off me, and pulled me up the stairs after him.

There were white Christmas lights strung in the bedroom, too; just enough to illuminate it. There were unlit candles. And there was a bed, a big one, with a pewter-gray duvet cover that had a faint satin sheen.

"Daisy." Stefan whispered my name like a prayer. Positioning himself behind me, he kissed the nape of my neck before undoing the hook-and-eye fastener at the top of my dress, his breath warm against my skin. "Enough haste. I want to take this slowly. Very slowly."

This time I shivered in a good way, a tingle of pleasure running the length of my spine, making my tail wriggle.

Oh, crap.

I swallowed. "Stefan? There's, um, one minor detail I don't think I mentioned to you."

His fingers toyed with my zipper. "You bear a mark?"

"A mark?"

"Of your infernal heritage." He unzipped a few inches, tracing the course with his lips. "Somewhere on your person."

"Um . . . yeah." I whipped my tail between my legs out of reflex. "It's kind of more than a *mark*."

The zipper descended another six inches, the dress hanging loose on my frame, baring my upper back. "Well, it's not vestigial wings."

Momentarily distracted, I craned my head around. "You've seen a hell-spawn with vestigial wings?"

"Yes. Horns, too. Fleshy little nubbins." The zipper continued its descent and stopped. Stefan's hand kept going, sliding over the curve of my buttocks, reaching beneath the hem of my dress and between my thighs. I felt him stiffen slightly at the shock of finding a firm, well-tucked appendage instead of yielding flesh with nothing but a pair of silk panties between us. "Oh."

Turned on and mortified at the same time, I closed my eyes. "I should have told you."

Instead of withdrawing, Stefan bent his head to kiss a sensitive spot on my throat beneath my earlobe. "A warning would not have gone amiss. But I was prepared to find . . . something." He took his hand away and turned me around to face him again, easing the dress from my shoulders to fall in a puddle of midnight blue shantung around my feet. "You are who you are, Daisy," he said softly. His dilated pupils eclipsed his irises like black moons. "You are *what* you are. And I find that to be beautiful. All of it."

I felt naked beneath his gaze. Well, I was naked. But I felt extra-naked, vulnerable, and exposed.

And really, really turned on.

All of which Stefan knew, which only made me feel *more* naked and *more* turned on. Without asking permission, he tasted my desire, drawing on it. Just a little. Just a taste.

And I let him.

Stefan shuddered with pleasure. "You don't make it easy for one of the Outcast to maintain control, Daisy Johanssen. Even one such as me."

"Am I supposed to?" I asked in a small voice. "Because I *could* raise a shield . . ."

"No." Eyes glittering, he stripped off his dinner jacket and unfastened his cuff links with deliberate slowness. "Don't."

Making love with Stefan Ludovic wasn't like skydiving; it was like walking a tightrope across the Grand Canyon. Well, if walking a tightrope included having mind-blowing sex at the same time. Six hundred years' worth of practice included acquiring six hundred years' worth of patience and self-restraint. After taking off his shirt, Stefan scooped me up in his arms and laid me on his bed, straddled my body and proceeded to spend the next hour or so thoroughly undoing me with his hands and mouth, until I was babbling with mindless ecstasy.

Seriously, I have *no* idea what I said.

And yet I was conscious all the while of that connection between us, drawn dangerously taut.

I was aware that there was an edge beyond which he would be sent ravening. And I became aware, too, that I had to maintain some measure of control, however faint and incoherent. Lust was one of the Seven Deadlies, and apparently the well of my desire was bottomless. I couldn't afford to lose myself entirely. I never raised a shield against Stefan, but there were times when I had the presence of mind to hold back, allowing my aura to diffuse and dissipate while I caught my breath.

As I said, it was like walking a tightrope. A sexy, sexy tightrope. Also, it was probably a good thing that we hadn't gone to bed before I'd gotten skilled at manipulating my aura.

Everything slowed and intensified when Stefan finally shed the last of his clothes, settled between my thighs, and entered me, inch by deliberate inch. He braced himself above me on strong arms, his broad chest hovering above mine as he rocked his hips, his long, firm cock plowing my depths with sure, steady strokes.

Who was it that said something about being careful about gazing into the abyss, and the abyss gazing back? Nietzsche, I think. I don't know; I'm pretty sure I heard it in a Lifetime movie.

Well, with Stefan inside me and the connection between us open, I gazed into *his* abyss. I saw the centuries' worth of pride and anger and loss, half a millennium and more of hurt and loneliness, of endless hunger and abiding patience, and what it meant to be Outcast.

And I wrapped my arms and legs around him, embracing it all. Oh, and I came again, too. There's a lot to be said for the rhythm and timing of a partner who can sense exactly what you're feeling and when you're on the verge.

With a shudder, Stefan let himself find his own release. Breaking the connection between us, at least on my end, he collapsed against me, his body heavy atop mine.

"Well, *that* was intense," I murmured.

After a pause, he laughed deep in his chest and rolled off me. "Yes."

Propping myself on one elbow, I gazed at Stefan. His eyes were closed, giving me no clue regarding the current extent of his inner turmoil. His unnaturally pale skin was faintly luminous in the glow of the white Christmas lights, in stark contrast to his slightly-too-long black hair fanned across the pillow. He had a lean, muscular warrior's body, trained for battle rather than sport in an era long before gym memberships or CrossFit workouts. I flattened one hand on his chest, feeling the living warmth of his skin and the steady throb of his heartbeat.

I remembered watching him impale himself on his sword, the blade piercing his chest and emerging from his back. There was no scar, not from that injury. Stefan had died and come back in the flicker of an eye. But there were other scars that his mortal body had sustained before his first death.

I traced one, a lumpy ridge that slanted from his left clavicle across his pectoral muscle. "Are these battle scars?"

"Yes," Stefan said without opening his eyes. "But most of them were old before I was made Outcast and no longer pain me."

"What about this one?" I circled an angry pink pucker of scar tissue on his side a few inches above his right hipbone.

He exhaled softly. "That was more recent. I caught an arrow in ambush. I was fortunate that nothing vital was pierced."

"It looks like it still hurts," I said.

Stefan opened his eyes to reveal still-enormous pupils, irises like frosty rims around them. The hunger in them made my heart skip a beat. "Sometimes, yes." He caught my hand, drawing it to his lips to kiss my fingertips one by one. "Daisy, I would like to ask you to stay the night with me, to drift gently into sleep as I tell you the story of each and every scar, if that is what you wish. But I fear that making love to you has taxed my control to a greater degree than I anticipated, and I am finding it difficult to retreat from the precipice."

"Oh," I whispered.

"Forgive me." He gave me a rueful smile at odds with that avid black gaze. "But it is best if I leave."

"Leave?" I felt slow-witted. "But this is your place."

"I cannot be so ungentlemanly as to turn you out of my bed and send you out into the cold, Daisy," Stefan said. "I'm sorry. This is not the way I would have wished our first night together to end."

I laid my hand against his cheek. I didn't want Stefan to leave. I wanted him to stay. I wanted both of us to stay. I wanted him to hold me and tell me again that I was beautiful. I wanted to fall asleep with him holding me, feeling safe and protected. But that wasn't going to happen, at least not right now. Maybe never. "I know," I said. "It's all right. I'll go. I'd rather."

He searched my face. "Are you certain?"

Leaning over, I brushed his lips with a kiss. "Yes."

So instead of lying in Stefan's embrace and reveling in the languorous aftermath, I climbed out of bed and put on my clothes.

Downstairs, clad in trousers and an unbuttoned dress shirt, Stefan found my discarded coat and helped me into it. "Good night, Daisy," he murmured in the foyer as he reached for the doorknob. His black hair swung forward to touch the collar of his white shirt and his dilated pupils gleamed in the darkness. "I hope I have given you no cause for regret."

I thought about it and shook my head. "You know what? All things considered, I think this went well."

It was a hell of a way to start the New Year, at any rate.

# Thirty-nine

In the morning, I awoke to the sound of someone pounding furiously on the downstairs door to the building, periodically pausing to shout my name in an annoyed Irish accent.

Looking out my bedroom window, I saw Cooper in the alley below holding a large bunch of shiny, helium-filled Mylar balloons.

I raised the window, letting a blast of wintry air into the apartment. "Cooper! What the hell are you doing?"

He squinted up at me. "Well, I'm supposed to be deliverin' flowers on behalf of the big man himself, but there's no feckin' flower shops open on New Year's Day, so I'm doing my best, aren't I?"

"You can come up," I said. "The door's not locked."

"I'd rather you came down," Cooper said. "Don't reckon himself would like me intruding on you en déshabillé, as it were. In your nightie," he added, seeing my lack of comprehension.

"Oh, fine. I'll be right down." Closing the window, I wrapped myself in my Michelin Man coat, shoved a pair of boots on my feet, and descended the stairs, pausing at the top of the landing to apologize to the disgruntled neighbor poking his head out the door of the apartment opposite mine.

In the alley, Cooper looked me up and down. "Nice coat." He thrust the ribbons anchoring the balloons at me. "Here. The finest the dollar store had to offer. It was meant to be a dozen red roses, but it comes with the big man's apologies."

I gazed in bemusement at the assortment, which included a number of birthday wishes, Spider-Man, a football, various Disney princesses, and a bright yellow SpongeBob SquarePants. "Um . . . thank you."

Cooper shrugged. "Don't mention it."

"Just out of curiosity, did Stefan approve the substitution?" I asked him. "I don't want to say the wrong thing and get you in trouble."

Cooper flashed a quick, feral grin at me. "Oh, that he did. I think the notion quite tickled him." He touched two fingers to his brow in a mocking salute. "Happy New Year to you, m'lady."

"You, too, Cooper." After he left, I tugged the unwieldy bunch of balloons up the narrow stairwell and into my apartment, where I set them free to roam at will. A dozen Mylar balloons drifted and bumped gently against the ceiling while Mogwai stalked their trailing ribbons.

I was making coffee when Jen called.

"Okay, girlfriend," she said without preamble when I picked up. "What's the scoop on your New Year's Eve date with the hot ghoul? And don't hold out on me. I know it was a big romantic shindig."

I poured another scoop of coffee into the filter. "Oh, yeah?"

"I ran into Greta Hasselmeyer at the grocery store the other day," Jen said. "Her niece Michelle is a junior in high school. Michelle's dating a senior named Dylan Martinez who's some kind of musical prodigy, and she told her mom that some spooky-hot ghoul hired Dylan to play his cello at a private party on New Year's Eve. Which, I'm thinking, was for you. So yeah."

"Touché."

"Daise!" Jen sounded aggrieved. "C'mon."

Once upon a time, not very long ago, it would have been hard to imagine that I might be involved in a relationship that I wouldn't want to hash over in detail with my BFF, but for the first time, I found myself hesitating.

There was just so much that Jen wouldn't understand. Then again, there was a lot I wasn't sure I understood myself. The desire to dish won out. "Can you come over?"

"On my way." She hung up.

Ten minutes later, Jen was batting her way through the hanging forest of balloon ribbons in my apartment. "What the hell, Daise?" she asked me, eyeballing SpongeBob SquarePants. "Are you having a kids' party I don't know about?"

I handed her a cup of coffee. "It's an apology."

"For what?"

I gave Jen an abridged version of my night with Stefan, glossing over the actual sex and skipping to the part where I had to make an unplanned early exit. "Hence the balloons," I explained.

"At least he's got a sense of humor," Jen commented. "So . . . how are you with all of this? Are you okay?"

"I don't know." I sipped my coffee. "It was . . . intense."

Jen gave me a shrewd look. "Funny, that's exactly what you said about hooking up with Cody."

I'd managed to avoid thinking about Cody, because thinking about Cody included thinking about how easy and comfortable we'd been together in the aftermath of lovemaking and how nice it had been waking up in his bed that last time, all of which made my heart hurt. "Yeah, well, it's a different kind of intense."

"Where do you see yourself going in this relationship with Stefan?" Jen asked. "I mean, do you have a future together? Do you *want* a future together?"

"I don't know! Do I have to figure it out at this stage?" I asked. "Can't I just enjoy the good parts?"

"If you were dating an ordinary human being, I'd say yes," Jen said. "But under the circumstances, you might want to put some forethought into it."

"Oh, believe me, I'm well aware of the whole immortal vs. mortal issue," I said. "It's not something you lose sight of."

"It's not just that." Jen's voice was gentle. "Hot supernatural sex is all well and good, Daise, but at some point, you just want to be with someone who you can fall asleep with on the couch watching TV together."

"We'll see." I changed the subject. "What did you and Lee do for New Year's Eve?"

She smiled. "Drank too much champagne and fell asleep on the couch watching TV together."

Okay, I'll admit it. I was a little jealous.

But things with Stefan *were* good, and continued to be good in the weeks that followed. By mutual accord, we backed away from the intensity of that first encounter and kept things light for a while before scheduling an official date to attend a performance by a visiting bossa nova band at the Pemkowet Center for the Arts.

When we went back to Stefan's place afterward, I was hoping that it would be different this time. Not the mind-blowing sex part, obviously, or the profound connection that took place during it, but the aftermath.

It wasn't.

At least this time I was prepared for it. "Does being with a woman always drive you to the edge of ravening?" I asked Stefan as I put my clothes back on.

"No." He smiled, but it was strained. "Only with you, Daisy. You and your outsize emotions."

"Could you, um, refrain from sampling them?" I inquired. "At least during the deed itself?"

Stefan's eyes glittered. "Then? No. At other times, yes. But then, no."

He didn't explain, but he didn't need to. I understood. It was part of what I saw in him when he was inside me and the connection between us worked both ways. Stefan was Outcast, and that was what it meant to make love with one of the Outcast.

"Okay," I said. "You don't need to send Cooper over with balloons this time."

Stefan laughed, his swimmingly huge pupils dwindling a bit. "Very well, then. I won't."

The fact that he could laugh about it was an encouraging sign. We could work on this, Stefan and I. I could continue to work on controlling my aura. Stefan could continue to hone the self-control and discipline he'd developed over the course of centuries. I didn't envision us dozing off on the couch together anytime soon, but I thought a little postcoital cuddling and conversation was a realistic expectation.

And if it hadn't been for the goddamned werewolf mixer, maybe it would have been.

Oh, yes, I'd agreed to go.

I didn't want to be there any more than Cody wanted me there, but it was a matter of status. If I hadn't accepted the invitation, I would have insulted the Fairfax clan and lost face in the bargain. I was Hel's liaison. I couldn't let my love life compromise that authority.

The weekend got off to a bad start before it had even begun. On Friday afternoon, a process server visited the police station and presented both me and Chief Bryant with subpoenas to testify in the upcoming trial. Dufreyne had warned me I'd be called as a witness, but receiving the actual document brought it home. It was a jarring reminder that the trial date was approaching all too soon. I'd been practicing my unobtrusibility skills diligently, but the thought of putting them to the test in the courtroom still made me want to throw up.

On Saturday evening, there was an unexpected fracas at the Wheelhouse, and Stefan had to cancel our plans when Cooper called him for backup in sorting it out. Not a big deal in the grand scheme of things, but it left me in a more disgruntled frame of mind on Sunday afternoon when I drove out to Cody's uncle's place to attend the mixer.

The Fairfax clan owned a big tract of land out in the countryside adjacent to the county game preserve. It was secluded and heavily wooded, perfect werewolf territory. I pulled into the long driveway and had gotten about halfway to the house when Cody's cousin Joe, a tall figure clad in a bulky tan Carhartt jacket and pants, a shotgun held casually in one hand, stepped out from behind a pine tree to bar my way, pointing at me and mouthing something I couldn't hear.

I rolled down the window. "What?"

"I said roll down the window!" Joe came over and stuck his head in the window, nostrils flaring as he sniffed me. "Daisy, right? You were with Cody the night he borrowed my *Saw* videos."

"Right," I said. "I'm here representing Hel, who probably wouldn't appreciate your detaining me at gunpoint."

Joe looked apologetic. "We're just being careful. This isn't the kind of gathering you want curious neighbors to drop by, you know?" He waved me on. "Go ahead, everyone's out back."

"As in . . . the backyard?" Foolishly, it hadn't occurred to me that the event would be held outside in the dead of winter. Of course it would. It was a freaking werewolf mixer. "Never mind."

I parked on an expanse of hard-packed snow beside someone's rental car and followed a well-trodden path around the ranch house to the backyard, where twenty or so young men and women ranging in age from teens to early thirties were having . . . well, a mixer.

At a glance, aside from the fact that it was the middle of winter, it looked like any ordinary backyard bash. There were picnic tables. On the deck, there was a keg with a half-empty plastic bag of red Solo cups beside it, as well as a charcoal grill with a variety of meat products sizzling away. Some of the younger teens were racing back and forth and hurling snowballs at one another in a complicated game of tag, and members of the older cohort were playing volleyball on either side of a sagging net that had probably been erected in the summer, laughing and lunging and diving for the ball.

The bearded older gentleman manning the grill caught my eye and set down his tongs. "Daisy Johanssen?"

"Yes."

Approaching me, he held out his hand. "Elijah Fairfax, clan patriarch." His tone was reserved. "Thank you for coming."

I shook his hand. "Of course."

There was a glint in Uncle Elijah's eyes that suggested he knew it wasn't that simple. Well, he should know, since he'd called for this mixer to set Cody on the path toward finding a suitable mate. But he didn't say anything, just released my hand, stuck two fingers in his mouth, and uttered a short, shrill whistle.

And . . . it was at that point that it ceased to resemble an ordinary, mundane gathering.

All across the backyard, heads turned attentively, phosphorescent green flashing behind myriad eyes. Conversations were put on hold, games of tag and volleyball were abandoned. The out-of-town visitors converged on me with careless athletic grace, forming a greeting line of sorts, nudging and elbowing, snarling and snapping their strong white teeth playfully at one another in a bid to gain position.

In the woods on the far verge of the yard, a pair of young wolves broke cover, racing to join us. One wolf planted a stiff foreleg and shoulder-checked the other, sending it tumbling.

From the cloud of snow and fur that ensued, a naked young woman arose. Shaking out her hair, she laughed and called, "No fair!" before trotting over to one of the picnic tables to retrieve her clothing.

Yep, definitely not a mundane keg party.

One by one, the dozen visiting werewolves introduced themselves to me by first name, clan name, and city. They'd come in groups or pairs—four from Seattle, two from Denver, four from Montreal, and two from New York. Although I hadn't actually met all the members of the Fairfax clan, especially the younger ones, they hung back. Apparently this formality was for the benefit of the visitors, each of whom shook my hand with a solemn politeness that was somewhat undermined by the way each one leaned in to get a good whiff of my scent. Werewolf etiquette—go figure.

Out of the corner of my eye, I could see Cody in the background, his hands shoved into the pockets of a heavy, shearling-lined suede jacket that hung open to the cold, a studiedly neutral expression on his face.

I recognized Stephanie from Seattle—Clan Hawthorne, by the way—in the greeting line. She looked just like she did in the profile picture I'd seen on Cody's laptop, only prettier—tall and sporty-slim, blue-gray eyes sparkling in the cold air, a healthy pink flush on her cheeks. I bet she was a great volleyball player.

"Thank you for inviting us to visit," Stephanie said cheerfully after leaning over to sniff my hair.

"You're very welcome," I said as though I'd had any choice in the matter, suppressing a violent surge of jealousy. After all, it wasn't her fault that my relationship with Cody was a nonstarter. "I hope you enjoy it here."

Her eyes widened. "Oh, it's *wonderful*!" She made an expansive gesture. "So much territory to roam! Just to see it is worth the hours spent confined in mundane airspace."

"Isn't Seattle, like, the hiking capital of the United States?" I asked.

"Outside of the Yama King's territory, it is," Stephanie said, looking wistful. "Oh, there are miles and miles of wilderness! But we can't shift there. Only in the city, above the underworld."

"That must be frustrating," I said.

Stephanie's upper lip curled in an unself-conscious half snarl. Oddly enough, she still looked wholesome doing it. "It is."

Once I'd met the whole visiting contingent, it appeared that my official duties were done. I wasn't sure if Cody was going to ignore me, but he manned up and came over to greet me as the receiving line dissolved and hungry and thirsty young werewolves headed for the keg and the platters of rare steak, underdone burgers, and half-cooked sausages stacked around the charcoal grill.

"Hey, Daise," Cody said quietly. "Thank you for doing this."

"I didn't do it for you."

"I know."

It was awkward. I didn't know what to say, what to do with my feelings. By the look on his face, neither did Cody. "So how long am I expected to stay at this thing?" I asked him.

He glanced at the horizon. "Not long. Until the sun sinks below the tree line. Come dusk, there will be a hunt."

"I bet these city-slicker werewolves are looking forward to *that*," I said. "So much territory to roam!"

"Daisy." Cody squared his shoulders. "Don't."

I sighed. "She seems very nice, Cody. They all do. It's just—"

"I know!" He raised his voice, then lowered it. "I know. Sorry. I'm in a shitty mood. On top of everything else, I got a subpoena Friday night. I heard you and the chief got served earlier. Any idea why?"

"Nope." I watched the mingling tribes fill their plates. Stephanie headed over toward us, a plate in either hand.

"I brought you a steak," she said to Cody, setting the plates down on a picnic table beside us. "Liaison, can I get you anything? A beer?"

"I'll get it," Cody said before I could answer. "I'll get beer for all of us. I'm supposed to be one of the hosts here. Daisy, can I bring you a plate?"

"No, thanks." Even if I'd had an appetite, which I didn't, I wasn't a big fan of werewolf grilling techniques. "Beer's fine." I didn't really want a beer, either, but I didn't want to be rude.

Actually, that wasn't true. I was in a shitty mood, too. Right now, I was angry at the world. But it wasn't the fault of our visitors, including the fresh-faced werewolf Stephanie taking a seat at the picnic table, so I shoved my anger into a padlocked trunk and sealed it away.

"You work with Cody, right?" Stephanie said when I sat opposite her.

"Sometimes," I said. "Just on cases with an eldritch angle."

She glanced toward the keg, where he was filling a cup. "He's different than I expected from chatting online."

"Oh?"

Stephanie sawed off a big chunk of exceedingly rare steak. "Moodier, I guess."

"He's got a lot on his mind," I said. "Everyone does. The town's facing a big lawsuit."

"I heard." She paused, fork in hand. "Are you worried about the outcome?"

I wanted to say hell yes, I was worried about the outcome—and worse, I was worried about what happened if we lost. I was scared and worried and pissed off and jealous, and I didn't want to be sitting at a picnic table in Cody's uncle's backyard in the middle of January, feeling like a visiting diplomat in my red wool coat with the faux-fur collar while a bunch of werewolves in casual sportswear gorged on half-cooked meat and got to know one another.

The padlocked trunk in my mind rattled with the force of my suppressed emotions. I reinforced it with a couple of steel bands.

"I'm concerned," I said in a level tone. "But we can always appeal it."

Cody returned, carefully carrying three red Solo cups full of beer. "All right, here we are."

Stephanie took one and hoisted it with a cheerful smile. "To new friends!"

Great. Now I felt guilty, too.

Over the course of the next half hour, I learned what Stephanie did for a living—for the record, she was a phlebotomy technician and worked at a hospital in Seattle. I learned that *phlebotomy technician* was the official medical term for the person who draws your blood. I learned that the Yama King who presided over Seattle's underworld was one of eight, or possibly ten, infernal Chinese deities, several of whom had emigrated to the United States. I learned that most of the older, married, or mated members of the Fairfax clan weren't at the mixer today because they were on sentry duty in the woods, making sure the gathering was undisturbed and scouting for signs of game. I learned that yes, it was customary to gorge before a hunt, especially at a mingling of the clans, since there was no guarantee that a kill would be made, and if it was, it would be shared by everyone, even if it was just a rabbit.

Throughout it all, I managed to keep a pleasant smile on my face, tending to the rattling trunk in my mind.

As the sun sank toward the tree line, the mood of the gathering began to change. Playful banter gave way to a charged excitement. All those gleaming white teeth took on a menacing edge.

The hunt was nigh and there was bloodlust in the air, and it affected all of them. I saw Cody and Stephanie exchange fierce grins. Oh, Cody might not be entirely happy about this whole mixer, but right now he was filled with heady exhilaration, looking forward to shedding his cares, shedding his clothes, shedding his humanity, and plunging into the snowy woods, where he and oh-so-suitable mate Stephanie from Seattle, Clan Hawthorne, would roam the territory side by side in the hope of bringing down a deer, or at least a rabbit.

God, I envied them. If I could turn into a wolf, forget everything, and just hunt beneath the moon for the night, I would.

Over by the grill, Elijah Fairfax, clan patriarch, gave me a grim smile and a faint nod, as if to say, *Now you understand. Now you see why you and my nephew could never be together.*

I fought the urge to flip him off.

Tree shadows stretched long and stark across the trampled snow.

Here and there, the younger werewolves began to strip off their clothes and shift in preparation for the hunt, milling eagerly.

"I should go." I extricated myself from the picnic table. "Good night and . . . good hunting."

Cody rose. "I'll walk you to your car."

I shook my head at him. "No, be a good host and stay. I'll see myself out." I raised one gloved hand to Stephanie. "It was nice to meet all of you."

She smiled brightly at me with too many teeth, her eyes flashing that eerie hue of green. "Give our thanks to Hel for her hospitality."

"I will."

I should have gone home, or to my mom's, or to Jen and Sinclair's place. Hell, I should have grabbed a six-pack and headed out to the abandoned Presbyterian camp to play another game of *Battleship* with Skrrzzzt the bogle, listening for the faint sound of wolves howling in the distance.

What I *shouldn't* have done was go to the Wheelhouse to see Stefan, which is exactly what I did.

# Forty

It's not like I had a plan. I didn't. I parked in the Wheelhouse's lot without thinking and entered the place, my pent-up emotions ticking inside me like a time bomb.

Bad idea.

The atmosphere took on an immediate charge, the Outcast clientele responding to my presence faster than werewolves anticipating a hunt. And why not? After all, their prey had come to them. At least I had the presence of mind to kindle a shield as I made my way across the bar.

"Daisy." Stefan abandoned the conversation he was having with his lieutenants Cooper and Rafe, grabbed me by the arm and steered me into his office, closing the door behind us. "What is it? Did something happen at the clan gathering to upset you?"

"No, nothing *happened*." On impulse, I dropped my shield. "I want you to take it away."

He blinked at me. "I beg your pardon?"

"These feelings." I gestured at myself. "These fucking feelings! I don't want them! It's too much."

Stefan's expression changed. "Ah. Your feelings for Officer Fairfax."

"It's what you wanted, isn't it?" I asked him. "You said you could help me. Well, I'm coming to you for help, Stefan."

"No." He shook his head. "Not this way."

"Why not?" It fueled the anger I was barely keeping in check. "Hell, you don't have any problems doing it on *your* terms! There's too much at stake. I can't afford to be knotted up with jealousy over some stupid school-girl crush right now, so I'm asking you to *take it away!*"

The overhead lights in Stefan's office flickered. "No," he said in a steely tone. "Even if it could be done in a lasting manner, if you and I are going to be together, it will be because you chose me over the wolf, Daisy. Not because I tampered with your emotions."

*Daughter*—my father's voice rumbled in my mind—*there is another way. All that you desire could be yours. You have but to ask.*

Oh, God, not this, not now. A rill of fury ran through me. I pressed my knuckles against my temples. "Shut up! Go away! This isn't fair!"

"Daisy, you're being unreasonable," Stefan said in a calmer tone. "You can't ask me—"

The padlocked trunk I'd envisioned was straining at the seams, ready to burst. I hurled it at Stefan like a soldier lobbing a live grenade, shouting at him. "In that case, I'm not asking!"

His pupils snapped open. *Fully* open.

It happened so fast, there should have been a sound—an explosion, a thunderclap. Instead there was only silence as Stefan went from controlled to ravening in the space of a single heartbeat. For a split second, I wasn't afraid. Purged of the roiling emotions I'd locked away, for a split second I felt peaceful and empty.

It didn't last.

Stefan's eyes were like black holes, all trace of iris swallowed by his immense pupils. I thought I'd looked into the abyss before, but I was wrong. Dead wrong. *This* was the abyss. This was Stefan with all his humanity stripped away, until nothing was left but the endless hunger.

"Oh, you stupid, stupid girl," he said in a soft, terrifying voice, slamming me bodily against the door to his office. "Look at what you've done."

And then the fear came: great, crashing waves of fear rushing in to fill the emptiness. Holding me in place, Stefan drank it in with parted lips, wave upon wave. The earth tilted on its axis and I was falling into him, falling into the blackness of that bottomless void. Deeper and deeper, with every pulse of fear, every surge of helpless rage, feeling myself emptied into him, an awful hollowness blossoming inside of me. The vacant faces of the father and daughter that Cooper had drained on Halloween flashed before my eyes, creating a fresh wave of terror.

It didn't matter. Whatever I felt, it only fed Stefan. The more I struggled, the blood pounding in my ears, the stronger he grew. Belatedly, I tried to raise a shield, but I'd waited too long. I was weak and couldn't focus. My fingers scrabbled ineffectually at my messenger bag, trying in vain to unbuckle it and reach for *dauda-dagr*, but I might as well have been reaching for the moon.

Stefan was right. I was a stupid, stupid girl.

And he was going to drain me. The thought made me feel sick with fear . . . and then that passed, too.

"Stop it," I whispered. "Stefan, please!"

He pressed closer against me, his face looming above mine, and smiled a terrible smile. "I can't."

I closed my eyes. I couldn't bear to watch him do it. And then that emotion vanished like the others, the hollowness inside me growing.

If Cooper hadn't yanked open Stefan's office door, uttering a steady stream of Irish-accented invective, I don't know what would have happened. A pair of wiry arms grabbed me from behind as I fell, hauling me backward. Opening my eyes, I saw Stefan's gaze shift off me. It felt like I'd been released from the gravitational pull of a black hole seconds before crossing the point of no return.

"Cooper." Stefan's eyes glittered ominously. "Get out."

"You'll thank me for this in the morning, big man," Cooper retorted. "At least I sure as feckin' hell hope so. Rafe!"

I didn't actually see what happened when Stefan's second lieutenant pushed past Cooper and me, but I heard the distinctive crackling sound of a Taser, accompanied by a furious bellow of pain, more crackling, a thud, and then the sound of a door being slammed shut and a chair wedged under the doorknob.

"Get her the fuck out of here!" Rafe shouted.

"Go." Cooper spun me around and shoved me in the direction of the exit. "Move it, Daisy! Before you set the whole lot of us off!"

If any of the Outcast in the Wheelhouse had attacked me, I would have been easy prey. It took all my concentration to move my feet, putting one in front of the other, stumbling toward the far door. I might as well have been a hamstrung deer, leaving a trail of blood spoor behind me. Beside me, Cooper exhorted me with curses, his voice filled with fear.

The other ghouls watched with avid eyes, but no one attacked. Maybe due to fear of Stefan's wrath, or maybe I'd gone past the point of being easy prey. Maybe I was little more than a picked-over carcass by now.

Outside, I slumped against the hood of my Honda and gazed up at the sky. Nightfall came quickly in winter. It was almost fully dark and the stars were beginning to emerge between a scattering of clouds.

Closing the door to the bar behind him, Cooper shuddered with relief. "What the fuck was that all about, Miss Daisy?"

"I was angry," I murmured. "And I did something stupid."

"Do you reckon?" Cooper regarded me with dilated pupils, his breath frosting in the cold air. "You were lucky. *Damned* lucky. Rafe only brought that stun gun in today after last night's fracas. If we hadn't had it . . ." He let his words trail off. "Well, you were lucky. Don't you ever try anything like it again, hear me? The big man won't let us get the jump on him twice."

There were words I should say, but I couldn't think of what they were. I clutched my battered leather messenger bag to my chest. Cody had made it for me. Cody. I'd been angry at Cody.

Why? It didn't seem important now.

I tried to string the evening's events together in my mind. Yes, I'd been mad at Cody. I'd provoked Stefan, and Stefan had attacked me. Stefan had attacked me, and Cooper had rescued me.

Oh, and there had been Rafe with the Taser, too. I hoped Stefan was okay. It hadn't been his fault.

"I'm sorry," I said carefully, thinking, yes, those were the right words. "Thank you?"

Cooper sighed. "Can you drive?"

Drive? I looked around for my car.

"Never mind." He jerked open the passenger door. "Get inside." Oh, right. I was leaning on my car. I got in obediently, looking up at Cooper. "I'll call someone," he said. "I'd drive you myself, but . . ." He glanced toward the bar. "It's going to take some doing to restrain himself in a fit of ravening. Can you wait here like a good girl?"

I could do that. "Yes."

"All right, then." Cooper paused, his eyes gleaming in the light of the beer signs that adorned the Wheelhouse's windows, filled with neon and regret. He looked older, much older, than the seventeen years he'd been when he was made Outcast. "And here I thought you and the big man would be good for each other."

"I'm sorry," I repeated.

"Stay here." He closed the passenger door. "Wait."

Staring straight ahead, I waited.

It was probably ten minutes later that Lurine's sleek black Town Car glided into the parking lot and pulled into a space beside my Honda, though it could have been longer. It could have been an hour or hours. I wouldn't have known the difference or cared. The here and now was all that mattered. There was some kind of ruckus going on inside the bar, but I didn't care about that, either. Cooper had told me to wait, so I waited, clutching my bag in my lap.

Lurine emerged from the back of the Town Car, opened the door opposite me, and slid into the driver's seat, regarding me with a stony look. "I warned you about this, baby girl."

The hollowness inside me cracked open to admit a tendril of fear. Lurine *had* warned me about dating Stefan, and said . . . what? Oh, yes. She'd threatened to crush him to pieces if he hurt me in any way. She was capable of it, too.

The tendril of fear put down roots. "Lurine." I searched for words. "It's not his fault. I provoked him."

She raised her brows at me. "Do you have any idea how many abused women have said those exact same words?"

"I did, though." It was important that I make Lurine understand. If I didn't, she would hurt Stefan very, very badly. "I really did. Please. Don't hurt him." The words were coming better now. I managed to put a few more together. "Stefan doesn't deserve to be punished for this," I said. "*I* do."

Lurine drummed her fingernails on the steering wheel. "Stefan Ludovic is a six-hundred-year-old ghoul, Daisy," she said in a cold voice. "I hold him responsible for his conduct. He ought to know the risks of messing with someone as young and volatile as you."

"He does." I leaned back against the headrest. "Stefan's been careful, very careful. What I did . . . it came out of nowhere. He was unprepared."

She hesitated. "You threw a tantrum at him?"

"Yes." I couldn't remember why I'd done it—oh, wait, there had been Belphegor's ill-timed outreach, too—but that was exactly what I'd done. I'd thrown a grown-up temper tantrum.

One of the Wheelhouse's windows shattered as a body was hurled through it. Lurine pursed her lips. "Looks like Mr. Ludovic is putting up a fight. All right, fine. I'll lend them a hand with him and then drive you home."

"You won't . . . squish him?" I asked in a faint voice. I'd seen her handiwork before.

"No." Lurine reached into her purse and donned a pair of oversize sunglasses, turning her darkened gaze my way. "For your sake, I'll be gentle. Just this once."

The snaking tendril of fear growing inside me faded and gave way to a vague sense of relief. "Thank you."

As I watched from the relative safety of the car, Lurine proceeded to the porch of the Wheelhouse, where the ghoul who'd been flung through the window was just staggering upright. Shoving him before her, she entered the bar, the doorway offering a brief glimpse of a full-blown brawl.

It got quiet fast.

A few minutes later, Lurine exited alone. She had a word with her driver, then got back into my car, stowing her sunglasses. "Keys?"

I managed to find them and hand them over. "Is everything . . . okay?"

"It will be." Lurine started the Honda. "There's a panic room in the back for restraining ravening ghouls. Stefan will be fine once it passes."

"And you didn't, um, have to hurt him?" I asked her. "You got him to enter it of his own will?"

She pulled out of the parking lot. "Mm-hmm."

"How?"

Lurine gave me a pointed look. "I told you I'd be gentle."

Oh, right. The lamia's kiss. Yeah, if Lurine had given Stefan the full business, that would have been enough to render even a ravening ghoul docile with ecstasy long enough to persuade him to enter a panic room.

Somewhere in the dim recesses of my mind, I was aware that I should have strong feelings about this whole situation—horror at Stefan's attack; mortification that I'd provoked it; a complex mixture of gratitude and jealousy that my immortal former babysitter had subdued my immortal ravening lover with a kiss.

Somewhere, anyway, but right now, all I felt was empty. And it wasn't a good feeling.

But I had no one to blame but myself.

# Forty-one

Bit by bit, my emotional state returned to normal. Well, normal for me, anyway.

It took days, though, and while the effects lasted, I definitely wasn't myself. For better or worse, my emotions defined me. They were what made me *me*, and with a core part of myself missing, I was hollow and vague. I lost time, finding myself staring into space only to realize that the better part of an hour had passed. I couldn't focus long enough to kindle a shield, let alone invoke an unobtrusibility spell, and I had to cancel a couple of practice sessions with the coven—not a good thing with the court date bearing down on us.

At least the rumor mill hadn't gotten hold of the incident. In a small town, that was almost a miracle, but the Outcast had their own reasons for not wanting anyone to know that their leader was out of commission, and apparently Lurine had decided to be discreet.

It was actually a relief when my emotions began to trickle back to normal levels, including all the violent guilt and shame I deserved to feel.

I rehearsed my apology to Stefan a hundred times, and picked up the phone more than once to leave a message on his voice mail. I didn't, though. It seemed like the sort of thing that really had to be done in person.

Instead, I called Cooper and asked him to let me know when Stefan was no longer ravening. He agreed to, although he didn't sound pleased about it.

I didn't blame him. I mean, I'd seen Cooper ravening, but that had been because of an error in judgment on his part, not because some idiotic hell-spawn had pitched a temper tantrum.

During my recovery, I thought a lot about that father and daughter that Cooper had drained, though. At least I'd walked into this with my eyes open. I'd known I was playing with fire. They hadn't had a clue. And Cooper had drained them *dry*. He'd done it in the blink of an eye, and when it was done, neither one of them looked like they knew who or where they were.

God, what was it like for them? I'd looked into the void, and I never, ever wanted to get that close again. Stefan had said they'd be fine in time, but Stefan had never been drained by a ravening ghoul. Maybe he didn't understand that the void inside him was every bit as terrifying as the eternal void of nonbeing that the Outcast faced.

Come to think of it, maybe those voids were one and the same. Either way, once seen, it couldn't be unseen.

Oh, I'd be okay . . . eventually. Wiser and warier, but I understood what had happened to me and I knew full well that I'd brought it on myself. Cooper's victims had been innocent and ignorant. They'd had no idea what had happened to them or why, and there wasn't any counseling out there in the mundane world for victims of an eldritch attack suffering from a supernatural form of post–traumatic stress disorder.

No, just a smooth-tongued hell-spawn lawyer with an offer to join a class-action lawsuit.

Too bad there was no way to prove how much worse things would have been that night if Cooper and the other Outcast hadn't been there to help disperse the panic and control the crowd. As it was, there had been a number of fairly serious injuries and a couple of nonfatal cardiac incidents.

By the time Cooper left me a voice mail saying that Stefan's ravening had passed, it was a full two weeks later. And in case you're wondering, yes, two weeks was a long time for that sort of thing.

With profoundly mixed emotions, I went to see Stefan.

I probably should have called or texted him in advance, but to be honest, I wasn't sure he would *want* to see me. And to be equally honest, I wasn't sure how I felt about him after his attack. Wary enough that I didn't want to meet him alone just yet, anyway. But the one thing I was sure of was that I owed him a huge apology for acting like . . . well, a stupid, stupid girl, which is why I screwed up my courage and paid a visit to the Wheelhouse.

It felt like I was returning to the scene of a crime. Hedging my bets, I paused on the front porch, murmured the unobtrusibility invocation and willed my aura to disperse before slipping into the bar.

It was the first real test of my hard-won ability since my emotional strength and focus had returned. Entering into a nest of ghouls may have been a little ambitious for my first outing, but the truth was, I didn't feel like dealing with Cooper's disapproval, and I needed to know I could do this. A courthouse in the heart of mundane territory was going to be a lot riskier.

Oddly enough, the fact that it worked settled my nerves, at least for a moment. Seeing Cooper's disinterested gaze pass over me without recognition gave me the last ounce of courage I needed to drift unnoticed to the back of the bar.

The door to Stefan's office was open. He was seated behind his desk, head bent over some paperwork, looking surprisingly . . . well, not ordinary, but more like a hard-core bar owner who would threaten a beer distributor for ripping him off than a terrifying immortal predator intent on draining my emotions to the last drop.

Then Stefan lifted his head, sensing my presence. His ice-blue eyes narrowed and my heart felt like it skipped a beat. Apparently, an unobtrusibility spell couldn't mask the bond between us.

I let it go, regrouping my energies in case I needed to kindle a shield and dropping one hand to *dauda-dagr*'s hilt. "I'm sorry," I said in a rush, needing to get the words out before he spoke. "Stefan, I'm so fucking sorry."

For a long moment, he didn't say anything. The hollows of his eyes looked bruised, but his gaze was steady as he regarded me inexpressively. My heart thudded hard in my chest, and I wondered if we'd gone past a point of no return, and what that made us now. Enemies? Adversaries?

And then, against all odds, Stefan laughed, pushing his chair back from his desk. "Daisy Johanssen," he said, his voice husky. "You have . . . what is it they say in the Westerns? One hell of a wallop."

I stared at him. "You're not mad? You can *laugh* about it?"

He shrugged. "What would you have me do?" One corner of his mouth lifted in a half smile, a dimple forming there. "We've done our worst to each other, Daisy, and we are still standing."

A vast sense of relief filled me, my heart soaring. I gave a breathless laugh at the sheer unexpectedness of it, and realized in that instant that I was at least a little bit in love with Stefan Ludovic.

"Close the door and come here," he ordered me, and I did. Stefan pulled me onto his lap. "You were not the only one at fault. I pushed you. I lectured instead of listening. I knew what you were feeling. I should have known better."

"I shouldn't have come in the first place," I said. "Not in that state."

"True." His lips brushed my shoulder. "I believe it is fair to say that we have both learned a lesson."

"It wasn't just you that pushed me," I said. "It was my father, too. That last thing I said . . . it was to him."

Stefan's body tensed beneath me. "He . . . spoke to you?"

"Um, yeah," I said apologetically. This wasn't a conversation we'd had yet, not after the whole hell-spawn hunter revelation. "It happens sometimes, mostly when I'm on the verge of losing my temper."

"I see." Stefan cocked his head at me. "What does your father say to you at such times?"

"Oh, you know." I didn't feel entirely comfortable talking about it. Not sitting on Stefan's lap, anyway. "Just the usual temptation scenario. All that you desire could be yours, you have but to ask, yadda, yadda, yadda. I said no," I added with a touch of indignation. "I will *always* say no."

"And your father's offer is what prompted you to hurl your emotions at me?" he inquired.

I squirmed on his lap, my tail wriggling. "Pretty much. Well, that and a stupid fit of pique."

Stefan slid one hand over my lower back, stilling me. "Next time, I will listen to you."

"Next time, I won't ask you to," I said. "I'll handle it on my own. I was just . . ." I didn't finish the thought. "It was stupid."

"You were upset, Daisy. You should be able to come to me at such times. And if you hadn't caught me unprepared, I would not have been sent ravening." He stroked my hair. "Do you wish to discuss *why* you were upset?"

I shook my head. No, I didn't want to discuss my feelings for Cody with Stefan. "Isn't it enough that I'm here?"

"One day you may have to make a more . . . definitive . . . choice," Stefan said. "But for now, yes." His hands rested on my waist, careful not to touch *dauda-dagr*'s hilt, and there was a rare hint of vulnerability in his expression. "I was not sure you would ever wish to see me again, having seen me in that state."

I slid my arms around his neck and kissed him. "I don't scare away that easily," I whispered against his lips. "Although you came close. I think we both owe Cooper a big debt."

Holding me firmly in place, Stefan returned my kiss. "Perhaps you'll find a way to give him his heart's desire someday," he murmured. "To be free from the shackles of immortality and grow to full adulthood."

I pulled back a little. "Do you believe it's possible?"

"No," Stefan said with regret. "It was a wishful thought. I would that it were so, but I have been Outcast for many centuries. Over the course of ages, I have come to believe that there is no force on this side of the Inviolate Wall capable of freeing us. Until such time as God in his heaven takes notice of us and relents, the Outcast are bound to our fates."

"Maybe Janek Król is persuading him as we speak," I suggested.

It won a faint smile from him. "I hope so. I would like it to be true, not least of all because it would give meaning to my friend Janek's long suffering."

"I hope so, too." I contemplated Stefan. "You said it was Cooper's heart's desire. Is it yours, too?"

His pupils dilated, then steadied. "Yes."

There was a lot unsaid in that simple "yes." I sighed, leaning my forehead against his and closing my eyes.

It would be nice to have a lover I didn't have to worry about turning into a ravening monster, a lover in whose arms I could safely sleep, a lover with whom I could contemplate a future.

But we were what we were, Stefan and I.

"I should go," I murmured. "You probably have a lot of work to do."

"Yes."

He didn't move, though, and neither did I, not for a long moment. "We're okay?" I asked at length. "You and me?"

"Yes, Daisy." Stefan shifted me off his lap, and both of us stood. "Somewhat to my surprise, you and I are okay." *Okay* was another one of those words that sounded incongruous coming from his mouth, making me smile. He raised an eyebrow at me. "What is it?"

"Nothing." I shook my head. "Oh, and by the way? It's *pack* a wallop. Not have a wallop."

Stefan laughed softly, tossing back his hair. His eyes gleamed. Leaning over, he kissed me, his lips lingering on mine. "Well, then, you pack a very large wallop."

Yep, still hot.

And still dangerous.

# Forty-two

The trial date arrived with unnerving speed. It seemed as though the New Year had barely started when the lawsuit was upon us.

Local media had picked up on the precedent-setting case, thanks in part to the involvement of Lurine's celebrity lawyer, Robert Diaz, and there was nightly coverage on all the networks.

Unfortunately, that gave Daniel Dufreyne a chance to make his case in the court of public opinion, as well as to the jury, and oh, did he. The sole piece of good news was that his powers of persuasion only worked in person. Dufreyne's televised sound bites reviling Pemkowet's tri-community governments for the decision to knowingly lure unsuspecting tourists into a deadly situation didn't translate into infernal influence in living rooms across west Michigan.

It worked on the reporters, though. Coverage turned hostile right out of the gate. I felt sorry for Robert Diaz. In addition to providing counsel to the Pemkowet legal defense team, he'd appointed himself their spokesperson, assuming that his media savvy would prove an invaluable asset.

Wrong.

Dufreyne turned it against him with sly digs about how the powers that be in Pemkowet thought they could buy their way out of trouble using a slick Los Angeles attorney. And that *did* play well in living rooms across west Michigan. It was a conservative area and there had always been a strain of fear and resentment toward Pemkowet with its under-world and eldritch community. Hell, just last summer, we'd had protes-tors picketing the town hall, chanting, "No sanctuary for Satanism."

Ironic, given the fact that a hell-spawn was prosecuting the case, but it meant that the seeds of resentment Dufreyne planted fell on fertile ground. Sensing a rising tide of bloodlust in their audience, reporters took savage glee in describing the cavalcade of eyewitness testimony for the prosecution in the days following the opening arguments.

It was an impressive array. I was right—it included the victims of Cooper's ravening, but there were dozens of others, too, and those dozens represented more than five hundred additional claimants.

The majority of them had been present at the fateful Halloween pa-rade, but some claimed to have been scarred by gruesome hauntings that they witnessed after Stacey Brooks's footage went viral. With the exception of two nonfatal heart attacks and one case of broken ribs and a punctured lung, most had suffered only minor injuries—scrapes and bruises, a few sprained ankles. But each and every one of them was claiming severe emotional and psychological trauma, and court report-ers described the witnesses as "haunted," "fearful," and "hollow-eyed."

No cameras were allowed in the courtroom, but that's pretty much what the sketch artists' work reflected. Then again, the sketch artists were vulnerable to Dufreyne's powers of persuasion. All he had to do was plant the suggestion during the course of his questioning.

It pissed me off. I may have had sympathy for Cooper's victims, but those idiots who flocked to town, bought copies of *Bloody Pemkowet* from the historical society, and staked out likely sites for grisly ghost uprisings didn't have the right to blame us when their macabre curios-ity was rewarded.

It wasn't fair.

But all I could do was pray that the judge would realize it. And that was only going to happen if our plan to offset Dufreyne's influence with the coven's charm was implemented.

To the naked eye, the charm wasn't much to look at—just a plain silver cross pendant. But it had been consecrated in holy water, dedicated on an altar beneath an entire moon cycle, and imbued with the combined magic of the entire coven. When Casimir strung it on the chain I wore around my neck, I could feel the subtle vibration of power in it.

Lee, who had been granted coven privileges, promised us that the mechanism was in place to deliver a highly credible nerve gas bomb-scare warning via an untraceable phone call, although he wouldn't provide any details, saying that the less we knew, the better.

"All I need to know is exactly when you'll be on the witness stand, Daisy," he said to me. "It's going to take some time for the, um, relays to function."

"I don't know *exactly*," I said. "I have to be there by eight thirty, but when I actually testify depends on how the trial progresses. Hell, I could end up having to go back the next day."

Lee frowned in thought. "Right. Okay, text me as soon as you're called to the stand . . . oh, shit. It's a federal courthouse."

I followed his train of thought, my heart sinking. "Which means I won't be allowed to bring in a cell phone."

All of us sat in glum silence, realizing our already harebrained scheme had a fatal flaw.

"What about Cody Fairfax?" Kim McKinney ventured. "Aren't you both scheduled to testify on Wednesday?" she said.

"Yeah," I said. "Along with Chief Bryant and Amanda and Stacey Brooks. All five of us. Why?"

"Because Cody's a police officer and he's sort of your partner, right?" Kim said. "At least on eldritch cases. I'm pretty sure cops are allowed to have cell phones in the courthouse. My brother's gotten in a lot of legal trouble," she added. "I've spent a fair amount of time in courthouses because of it."

The Fabulous Casimir raised his eyebrows at me. "Yes, but would he be willing to do it? Or perhaps Chief Bryant?"

"Not the chief, no. But Cody might. Not if he knew why," I said slowly. "But if I asked him as a favor, asked him to trust me . . . maybe."

Casimir looked around the room. "Do we have any other options?" No one answered. "Then I think you're going to have to try it, Daisy."

I sighed. "Great."

As if that wasn't enough of a curveball, before the coven's meeting disbanded, Sinclair presented me with the wolfsbane amulet that he and Warren Rodgers had developed to enhance the unobtrusibility spell. It was another small leather pouch filled with herbs, a dried chameleon skin, and God knows what else.

"No dry runs with this one," Sinclair warned me. "It'll lose potency every time you use it."

"How can you be sure it will work?" I asked him.

"Sandra helped us test and refine the recipe," he said. "It'll work. But, um, don't get caught with it. Wolfsbane's not illegal, but . . . well, it's extremely poisonous. Not the kind of thing you want to get caught carrying in a federal courthouse. If I were you, I'd hide it in my underwear."

I sighed again. "Good to know."

Later that evening, I tracked Cody down on a coffee break at Callahan's Café. His expression brightened as I slid into the empty seat across from him, then settled into something more complicated. "Hey there, Pixy Stix," he said quietly. "Everything okay? You've been keeping a low profile."

"Yeah, I know." I'd managed to avoid him since the afternoon of the werewolf mixer. "Cody, I have a favor to ask you."

"What is it?"

I took a deep breath. "When we're at the courthouse on Wednesday, I need you to text Lee Hastings when I get called to the witness stand."

Cody tilted his head and narrowed his eyes at me. "Why?"

"I can't tell you," I said. "I just really need you to trust me on this one. Please?"

For a long moment, he didn't answer, and I felt sure he was going to refuse. Cody wasn't stupid. He knew I wouldn't ask this way if there wasn't something illegal involved. But he also knew I wouldn't ask if I didn't think it was important. After a small eternity, he gave me a brief nod and pulled out his cell phone. "What's Lee's number?"

I gave it to him. "Thank you."

Cody pocketed his phone. "I don't know what you and your friends are up to and I don't want to know, but if there's a chance that it might help level the playing field, I'm for it. This trial's as crooked as hell." He gazed steadily at me. "And when I told you I'd always have your back, I meant it."

My eyes stung. "Thanks," I whispered again, hoping I hadn't just gotten Cody involved in something that would end with Homeland Security on his doorstep. "It means a lot." I coughed and wiped my eyes surreptitiously. "So, um . . . everything all right with you?"

"Fine." He hesitated. "Fine."

We shared a moment of awkward silence before I exited the booth. "Okay, well, I'll see you in court."

# Forty-three

On Wednesday, I presented myself at the federal courthouse in Grand Rapids with a protective charm in the form of a silver cross strung around my neck beside the Oak King's token, a leather pouch full of poisonous wolfsbane tucked into my brassiere, a small roll of electrical tape—at the last minute, it had occurred to Mark Reston that duct tape might set off the metal detector—and a rigid square of double-sided industrial-strength mounting tape in my purse.

I felt sick. I passed through the security checkpoint with my heart in my throat and my tail clamped between my thighs, terrified that a cursory pat-down would give me away.

It didn't, though.

After being directed to the witness waiting room, I ducked into the adjacent bathroom. Sitting atop the toilet, I unclasped my necklace and slid the silver cross charm free. I wrapped it in electrical tape and stowed it in my right front pocket, transferring the square of mounting tape to my other pocket. That part went smoothly enough, but my hands were trembling and slick with sweat, and it took me multiple tries to refasten the clasp of my necklace.

By the time I reemerged, Cody and Chief Bryant had arrived. The latter greeted me with a nod and wished me a good morning before settling in a chair with a fly-fishing magazine.

Cody took a seat, too, but he was restless, slouching in his chair with one ankle crossed over the opposite knee, his foot jiggling. I wondered briefly if I should have tried the chief instead, then dismissed the thought. I'd been right to go with my gut on this one. Chief Bryant was a by-the-book kind of guy. There's no way he would have agreed to my request without knowing why, and no way he would have allowed us to go through with it once he'd heard it.

No, Lee's involvement notwithstanding—and the hacktivists of Anonymous, for all I knew—this was eldritch business.

We waited.

There was a clock mounted on one of the walls, and I swear it seemed like its hands moved backward. Time would have passed slowly anyway, but the dread I felt at the prospect of pulling off my stunt in the courtroom made it positively crawl.

At an hour and a half into our wait, Amanda and Stacey Brooks arrived. "Do we know anything?" Amanda asked tersely.

"Nope." Chief Bryant turned a page in his magazine. "Still waiting."

Stacey caught my eye and made a series of exaggerated facial contortions meant to ask if everything was in place for the plan—to which she'd obviously been privy as a new member of the gang, a development about which I had mixed emotions—to take effect. I put on a stoic look and gave my head a slight shake, willing her to back off. I had a feeling her mother would do everything she could to throw Stacey under the bus in the courtroom, and I felt bad about it, but I really, really didn't need her drawing attention to our little conspiracy. I'd never thought I'd miss the old days, but it would have been a lot safer if she'd just stuck out her tongue and flashed devil horns at me.

A little over two hours had passed when Cody heaved himself out of his chair and began pacing the waiting room. When he paused at the water cooler, I went over to talk to him.

"You okay?" I asked.

"Yeah." He poured himself a cup of water and downed it with a shudder. "Just feeling trapped in my skin."

"Oh." Of course, I hadn't thought about how uncomfortable it would be for a werewolf to be stuck in mundane territory for a prolonged period of time. I'd never spent more than an hour with Cody outside of Hel's demesne. "I'm sorry."

"No big deal." Cody gave me an unconvincing smile. "It's not like I've never had to testify in court before. Comes with the job."

"It sucks, though," I said.

"Yeah." He took a deep breath, let it out slowly. "Funny, I feel better with you beside me." Realizing what he'd said, his expression changed. "Sorry, Daise. I didn't mean—" He paused. "It's just that . . . well, it's true, but I didn't mean to be thoughtless."

"It's okay." I shoved my hands into my pockets, fingering the wrapped charm and the square of mounting tape. "It makes sense. Apparently, I carry my own personal underworld inside me."

"Huh." Cody glanced toward the courtroom. "So that's what enables Dufreyne's powers to function?"

"Mm-hmm. His, um, infernal battery's probably stronger than mine, since he's claimed his birthright and all," I said in a light tone. "Care to put it to the test when you take the stand?"

Cody grinned at the thought of shifting in the middle of the courtroom—a real grin, fierce and wolfish, one that made my pulse quicken. "It's an incredibly bad idea, but it would be a hell of a way to come out, wouldn't it?"

I smiled ruefully. "Yeah, it would."

The damned thing was, *I* felt better, too. I missed the partnership and genuine rapport that Cody and I had. This was the most civilized conversation we'd had in a long time, and it helped to ground me, helped settle my nerves.

That lasted all of another ten seconds, before the bailiff came and called me to the stand. "Daisy Johanssen?"

The courtroom was smaller than I'd expected and the atmosphere more ordinary. Given the scope of what was at stake, it should have felt . . . I don't know. Bigger? But I could smell that not-actual-smell reek of wrongness that announced hell-spawn lawyer Daniel Dufreyne's presence, and it took an effort not to lash my tail in response.

Dufreyne was glancing over some papers and didn't bother to look up as I was sworn in and stated my name for the court. Neither did members of the Pemkowet legal defense team, conferring in quiet murmurs. Judge Martingale, an innocuous-looking man in his late fifties or early sixties, gave me an absentminded nod as I took my seat on the witness stand, then adjusted his glasses and stroked his thinning gray comb-over. In the jury box, members eyed me with mild interest, hoping my testimony would alleviate their tedium.

Then Dufreyne lifted his head, meeting my gaze with his own too-black eyes and a bland smile.

I stared daggers back at him, wishing I had *dauda-dagr* on my belt, not safely stashed at home. I felt unprotected without it.

"Miss Johanssen." He rose. "You're a part-time file clerk for the Pemkowet Police Department—is that correct?"

"Yes."

He arched one manscaped eyebrow. "But you have another title and a greater role in the community, don't you?"

I shrugged. "Not on paper."

The other brow rose to join its fellow. "Please state your unofficial title for the court."

"Hel's liaison," I said.

Dufreyne consulted his notes. "To clarify, that would refer to Hel, Norse goddess of the dead, yes?"

Members of the jury perked up. Yep, they were curious now. "Yes."

"And Hel presides over the underworld known as . . . Little Niflheim?"

"Yes."

He checked his notes again. "And what do you do in your capacity as Hel's liaison?"

"I'm, um, a diplomatic liaison between Little Niflheim and the Pemkowet Police Department," I said. "I work to ensure that the eldritch and mundane communities coexist in peace."

Dufreyne gave me a significant look. "And do they?"

"Most of the time, yes."

"What happens when they don't?" he inquired.

"I do my best to deal with it," I said. "That's my job."

Daniel Dufreyne turned to the judge. "Your Honor, I'd like to re-visit the video footage previously introduced into evidence." The monitor displayed footage of Cody's and my ghostbusting forays from last autumn. "Miss Johanssen, can you describe in your own words what we're seeing here?"

"Officer Fairfax and I are in the process of laying a ghost to rest," I said.

"Can you explain this process for the court?" he asked. "Exactly how does one lay a ghost to rest?"

I wondered where Dufreyne was going with this and how long it would take for Lee's untraceable call to go through. "You cast a ghost's shadow using a spirit lantern, then drive a nail into it." I pointed at the screen, where Cody was executing a knee slide on the parquet dance floor of the S.S. *Osikayas*, hammer in hand. "Like that."

"And where does one obtain a spirit lantern?" Dufreyne inquired.

"Hel provided it."

"Ah." He nodded. "So Hel herself, the Norse goddess of the dead, was concerned about this ghost uprising and took measures to quell it?"

"Yes," I said. "As did the Pemkowet Police Department."

Dufreyne glanced at Judge Martingale, who gave his gavel an officious little tap. "The witness will confine her responses to the question."

"Thank you, Your Honor." Dufreyne turned back to me. "Miss Johanssen, can you explain the cause of the ghost uprising to the court?" I gave a brief account of Sinclair's mother setting her father's spirit loose on the town and stirring up the restless dead. "I see. And this . . . duppy . . . resulted in the monstrosity that terrorized East Pemkowet at the Halloween parade?" Dufreyne asked, clicking the remote to show footage of the Tall Man's axe-wielding skeleton rampaging down Main Street, spectators shrieking, shoving, and attempting to flee.

"Yes." I wished Lee's call would come through. I was beginning to sweat and I could smell a faint odor of acrid herbs and warm leather rising from my cleavage.

Dufreyne consulted his notes again. "Miss Johanssen, isn't it true that on October twenty-ninth, you and Officer Fairfax met with Police Chief Bryant and Amanda Brooks of the Pemkowet Visitors Bureau and asked them to cancel the Halloween parade?"

Oh, crap. So *that's* where he was going with this. I wondered how he'd found out about it. "Yes," I murmured.

His gaze bored into mine. "What were your reasons for the request?"

I wiped my sweating palms on my pants. "We were concerned."

"Can you be more specific?" he asked. "What, exactly, were your concerns?"

"Well, Officer Fairfax and I were concerned because we hadn't managed to catch the duppy," I hedged.

"You were concerned for the public safety?" Dufreyne pressed me. "Is that fair to say?"

I gestured at the screen, where the image of the Tall Man was frozen in midrampage. "Look, we didn't expect *that!*"

Judge Martingale gave his gavel another tap. "The witness will answer the question."

Dufreyne raised his eyebrows at me.

"Yes," I said reluctantly. "We were concerned for the public safety."

"So." Daniel Dufreyne smiled his bland smile, but his voice took on that weird note of reverberation as he exercised his powers of persuasion for the first time since I'd entered the courtroom. "In your authority as Hel's liaison, you asked the chief of police and the director of the visitors bureau to cancel this event in the interest of public safety, and they refused?"

I gritted my teeth. "Yes."

"So you're saying that knowing that this . . . duppy . . . was still at large," he continued at full reverb with an added blast of thunderous indignation thrown in for good measure, "and with the complete support of the Pemkowet, East Pemkowet, and Pemkowet Township boards and city councils, Chief Bryant and Amanda Brooks refused to consider a direct request from Hel herself and continued to promote this parade as a fun, safe activity, encouraging visitors to attend?"

In the jury box, heads were nodding. So was the judge's.

"I didn't say that!" I protested. "Asking to cancel the parade was Cody's and my call, not Hel's. And none of the members of tri-community government even *heard* about our request! You can't just lie about it!"

That earned me another gavel tap, this one a bit sterner.

"Withdrawn," Dufreyne said smoothly, his voice back to normal. "No further questions, Your Honor."

Double crap.

Of course, it was at that moment that the alarm sounded, and not a minute before, when it would have done the most good. A security officer entered the courtroom and spoke to the bailiff, who announced in a reassuring voice that everyone should gather their personal belongings and proceed to evacuate the building in an orderly fashion, using the staircases instead of the elevators.

"Light pass through me," I whispered under my breath, uttering the words like a desperate prayer as I willed my aura to disperse to the four corners of the courtroom. "Gaze pass over me."

The evacuation was quicker and more orderly than I'd expected. Judge Martingale exited through the door behind him into his chamber; everyone else filed toward the main exit. I held my breath and slouched low in my seat on the witness stand as Daniel Dufreyne cast a curious glance around the room, but his gaze didn't linger on me, and he didn't seem overly suspicious.

I didn't want to take any chances, though. I waited until everyone's back was turned before sliding out of my seat and squeezing through the narrow aperture between the box that housed the judge's bench and the wall, fishing in my pockets for the wrapped charm and the square of mounting tape. With shaking hands, I peeled the backing off the double-sided tape, stuck the charm to the tape, and affixed it to the underside of Judge Martingale's oversize leather desk chair.

Done.

I scrambled out from behind the judge's bench and squeezed myself back through the gap so fast that I overbalanced and nearly took a header. The pouch of wolfsbane fell out of my bra in the process, causing me to lose my focus.

"Ma'am?" The security officer at the door beckoned politely. Forget invisibility; even unobtrusibility is impossible when you're the only person left in the room and you've dropped your wolfsbane. "Everyone out, please."

"Sorry, just dropped my coin purse." Stooping, I grabbed the pouch and shoved it in my pocket, hoping like hell that the security officer hadn't noticed me until it fell out of my bra.

Apparently, she hadn't.

"This way," she said. "Down the hall and to your left."

Breathing a sigh of relief, I followed her instructions.

# Forty-four

Outside, we gathered in a parking lot across the street. Having left my coat in the witness waiting room, I wrapped my arms around myself in the cold, dank February air, shivering in nothing but trousers and a thin silk blouse.

Cody found me with my nice new red wool coat over one arm and fire in his eyes. "Here!" he hissed, shoving my coat at me. "Put it on. You're freezing." I didn't argue. He waited until I'd buttoned the coat to grab me by the shoulders and shake me hard. "Are you out of your mind?" Even through the thick wool, Cody's fingers dug into my flesh. "Tell me I did *not* just send a text message to trigger a bomb scare," he said in a tone low enough that only I could hear him.

I winced. "Well . . ."

"Daisy!"

"I'm sorry!" I hissed back at him. "I needed a distraction. Anyway, what makes you think it was a bomb scare?"

"I'm a cop," he said grimly. "Security guards tell cops things they don't tell civilians, because we're useful people to have on the scene." He let go of me. "Did you at least accomplish . . . whatever you were trying to accomplish?"

"Yes."

"Will it help?"

"I sure as hell hope so," I said. "Because it's not going well in there. Cody, Dufreyne knows that you and I tried to have the parade canceled. He's claiming that the request came directly from Hel and that the board and council members backed the chief's refusal. That's how he's putting blame on the local governments."

"What?" Cody frowned. "None of them had any idea."

"That's what I said," I said. "And he withdrew the question, but the damage was already done."

"Well, I'll just have to push back against it as hard as I can," he said.

"Push back against what, son?" Chief Bryant inquired, approaching us with Stacey and Amanda trailing behind him. I explained. The chief shook his head. "That's one decision I'd like to take back," he said. "But you're right—the blame for it rests squarely on our shoulders. I'll do my damnedest to make it clear." He glanced at Amanda Brooks. "And I hope you'll do the same."

She looked around nervously. "I don't want to be accused of witness collaboration."

The chief sighed. "Just tell the truth, Amanda. No one's suggesting you perjure yourself. Word is we're dismissed for the day," he added. "Report back tomorrow at the same time unless you get a call instructing you otherwise."

"Did they tell you why we were evacuated?" Amanda asked with a shiver.

"Bomb threat," Chief Bryant said soberly, rubbing the pouchy skin beneath his left eye. "Apparently, the call originated in Abu Dhabi, and they're taking it seriously. So go home and kiss your loved ones." He clapped a hand on my shoulder. "See you here tomorrow."

Abu Dhabi? Holy crap. I wasn't sure whether to be impressed with Lee's hacker connections or vaguely terrified. Both, maybe.

I drove home and spent the remainder of the day half expecting a knock on my door from Homeland Security. Cody was right. I was out of my mind to take part in such a dangerous, illegal scheme. And I shouldn't have dragged him into it. I'd betrayed his trust.

I just hoped it worked.

The next morning it was business as usual at the courthouse, the bomb squad having combed the ventilation system and found nothing. At least I didn't have to wait before being called back to the witness stand, since proceedings picked up where they'd left off the previous day.

Pemkowet's legal defense team was headed up by Cheryl Munz, Lurine's celebrity lawyer having determined she was the shrewdest of the local lot. "I just have a few questions for you, Miss Johanssen." She pulled a photograph from a file and showed it to me. "Do you recognize the people in this photograph?"

It was a family portrait of Cooper's victims. "Yes. That's Doug and Lois Blumenthal, and their daughter Emily. I didn't know their names until the trial, though," I added.

"That's all right." Cheryl Munz gave me a smile that was meant to be encouraging, but came off as exhausted. This trial had to have been a nightmare for her. "When did you first encounter the Blumenthals?"

"At the Halloween parade," I said.

"Where they were victims of a ravenous ghoul," she said. "Is that correct?"

"Ravening," I said, wondering exactly how this line of questioning was supposed to help the defense's case. "And they prefer the term *Outcast*. But yes."

"And why were there ghouls—excuse me, Outcast—present at the parade?" Cheryl inquired.

"Objection, Your Honor," Daniel Dufreyne said without looking up from his notes. "I fail to see the relevance."

"Overruled," Judge Martingale said.

Dufreyne's head snapped up and he put on the reverb, his voice deepening. "I said I *object*, Your Honor."

Light flashed off the judge's glasses as he gave the prosecuting hellspawn attorney a stern look. "And I said *overruled*, Mr. Dufreyne." He gestured at me. "The witness may answer the question."

I suppressed a gleeful smile. It looked like the charm was working. "The Outcast were there to provide crowd control."

"Crowd control?" Cheryl echoed.

I nodded. "To prevent widespread panic in the event of a supernatural manifestation, yes."

"And did they achieve that goal?" she asked me.

"Yes."

"Objection!" Dufreyne said curtly. "The witness is being asked to speculate on an outcome that can't possibly be known."

The judge hesitated, then nodded. "Sustained."

"Withdrawn," Cheryl said. "Miss Johanssen, please clarify something for the court. Who authorized the presence of the, um, Outcast at the parade?"

Okay, I saw where this was going now. Cheryl Munz was attempting to throw *me* under the bus. Under the circumstances, that was just fine with me. I might have cause to regret it later, but right now, I'd gladly take a dive under those wheels. "I did."

"And did you consult with anyone regarding this decision?" she asked. "The chief of police, the director of the visitors bureau?"

"No," I said.

"Did you consult with any members of the township board or either of the city councils?" Cheryl asked.

"No."

"So you made the decision to have ghouls—excuse me, Outcast— present entirely on your own?" she pressed me.

"*Objection!*" Dufreyne thundered, his voice making the rafters tremble. "Leading the witness!"

Judge Martingale scowled at him. "Overruled!"

"Yes," I said. "I did."

Cheryl Munz looked slightly delirious at the prospect of actually being allowed to continue this line of questioning. "And again, just to be perfectly clear, that includes the, um, member of the Outcast who attacked the Blumenthals?"

"Yes," I said. "Absolutely. All of the Outcast, including Cooper, were there at my request."

She conferred briefly with her colleagues, then asked to revisit the video footage of the parade, fast-forwarding to a sequence of Stefan and his broadsword battling the Tall Man. "In fact, as we see in this footage, it was one of those very Outcast who engaged the, um, revenant, and prevented it from harming spectators, wasn't it?"

Oh, that was a good angle. The jury murmured with interest.

"Yes," I said. "It was." I made deliberate eye contact with each member of the jury. "I'm very sorry for the unpleasantness that the Blumenthals endured, but if it wasn't for the presence of the Outcast that night, in particular the man you see defending innocent bystanders there, there would have been near-certain fatalities." I expected Dufreyne to object or the judge to rebuke me, but neither did. Emboldened, I continued. "I take full responsibility for that decision."

"Thank you, Miss Johanssen." It sounded like Cheryl Munz was ready to cry with relief. This had probably been the first break the defense team had gotten during the entire trial to date. "No further questions, Your Honor."

"Mr. Dufreyne?" Judge Martingale inquired.

Narrowing his eyes, Dufreyne fixed me with a long, speculative look. He knew something had happened to nullify his powers of persuasion, but he didn't know what or how. Taking a page from his book, I returned his gaze as blandly as possible. "I have no additional questions, Your Honor."

The judge dismissed me. I exited the courtroom with my head held high, feeling Daniel Dufreyne's gaze boring into my back the whole way.

Granted, it was a limited victory. Dufreyne's infernal influence over the jury and members of the media was still in full effect. But any settlement would have to be approved by the court, and Judge Martingale was now a neutral party. By the time the local news aired that evening, it was obvious that while the media remained biased in favor of the plaintiffs, the tone of the proceedings had shifted.

Oh, and it appeared that Lee's untraceable bomb threat was proving to be well and truly untraceable.

I was willing to call that a win.

So was the coven. The Fabulous Casimir hosted an impromptu victory celebration at his place.

"It's far too soon to break out the champagne, *dahlings*," he announced to us. "But I think the occasion deserves at least a passable merlot." Casimir hoisted his wineglass. "To a job well done."

"And to never having to do anything like it again," I added fervently before drinking.

On my way home, I noticed Cody's cruiser parked in front of Callahan's again, and stopped to tender a more formal apology.

"That thing I asked you to do yesterday?" I said. The waitress was nowhere near us, but I figured it was best to be oblique. "I just wanted to say that I'm really, truly sorry, Cody."

He sipped his coffee and eyed me. "You should be."

"I am," I promised him. "I wouldn't blame you if you never trusted me again."

"Ah, well." Cody's mouth quirked. "I thought Judge Martingale was evenhanded while I was on the stand. I did my best to push back against Dufreyne's narrative. Whatever you did, it sounds like things went better in court today for our side."

"Yes," I said. "They did. And anyway . . . thank you."

Cody took a breath as if to speak, then let it out in a long sigh. "It's okay, Daise. I've still got your back." He slid out of the booth and shrugged into his uniform coat. "Look, my break's over. I've got to get back on patrol. I'll see you later."

I watched him go, feeling like I'd missed something. Or maybe that was just the way it would always be with Cody and me.

It was the one detail I didn't tell Stefan when I reported on the success of our venture to him. It's funny, but since his ravening, we were both more relaxed and more careful with each other. He was right; the worst had happened, and we were both still standing.

We were also both very, very aware that we didn't want it to happen again.

"Are you feeling better about the business of this lawsuit?" Stefan inquired, stroking my back as I lay against him in bed that night, cautiously testing the limits of postcoital cuddling.

"A little," I said. "It felt good to *do* something, anyway. Terrifying, but good."

Stefan smiled at me, eyes glittering. "I'm glad."

"Me, too." Stretching, I leaned up to kiss him. "I should go, shouldn't I?"

"Probably," he said with regret.

Including the weekend, the celebratory phase of our victory lasted approximately four days.

It ended at around a quarter past five on Monday. I was passing Mrs. Browne's Olde World Bakery on my way home when the warm aromas of bread and cinnamon wafting through the door as a patron exited mingled with something foul and rank, a smell that wasn't a smell. Reaching into my messenger bag, I eased *dauda-dagr* from its sheath before I rounded the corner and entered the alley, where a sleek silver Jaguar was idling.

And there was Daniel Dufreyne, leaning against it, his hands in the pockets of his long charcoal-colored wool coat, his breath frosting in the cold February air.

My heart dropped into the pit of my stomach and I tightened my grip on *dauda-dagr*. "What the hell are you doing here?"

Dufreyne smiled—his sharklike smile, not the bland one he used in court. "Why, hello to you, too, cousin."

"I'm not your cousin!" I spat at him.

"Tsk-tsk!" Removing one gloved hand from his coat, he wagged a finger at me. "And here I made the trip just to congratulate you in person."

I was confused. No decision had been reached in the trial yet, and from what I knew of Dufreyne, it didn't seem like him to accept a setback as a defeat. "What do you mean, congratulate me?"

"It was an outstanding effort," he said. "Really, it was. In fact, I was lucky to figure it out in time. But in the end . . ." Turning his hand over, he opened it to reveal the silver cross lying in his palm. Tendrils of smoke rose from it as it slowly seared a brand into the expensive leather of his glove. "Nice try."

I didn't say anything.

"It wasn't until this morning that it occurred to me to cook up a pretext to have a word with Judge Martingale in his chambers," Dufreyne continued conversationally. "That's when I realized that whatever you'd done to render him immune to my charms, shall we say, it was only in effect when he was on the bench. So I asked for a brief recess and had a look. That was quite ingenious, affixing it to the underside of his chair."

Ingenious, hell. It had been inspired by a prank Kim McKinney's brother used to play with a fart machine. I stared at the smoldering cross, thinking that should have been my first tip that this whole thing had been a very, very bad idea.

"Cat got your tongue?" Dufreyne inquired.

I pointed to the cross on his palm. "That's got to hurt."

"Not yet, but it will. Soon, if I don't do something about it." He bared his unnaturally white teeth in another feral smile. "I bet it didn't bother you one bit to hold this little charm, did it? Born of an innocent and all. But *you're* not so innocent, are you, Daisy?" He tsk-tsked me again, this time without the finger wag. "Calling in a bomb threat? That's a federal offense. Do you know what kind of sentence it carries?"

"No," I said. "Why would I?"

Dufreyne ignored me. "Ten years and a quarter of a million dollars." He paused, frowning. "I'll admit, I can't quite figure that part out yet. You had to have had help, and very sophisticated help at that. But no matter." He shrugged. "I'll save that for later. At the moment, I've far bigger fish to fry." His voice took on a low, velvety, reverberating note. "Once Pemkowet's affairs are settled, I'll make it a point to find out who your friends and connections are and *persuade* them to talk."

A wave of fury washed over me, lifting my hair, making it crackle with static electricity. "What the hell do you want?"

"From you, cousin?" Dufreyne asked, sliding his other hand from his coat pocket. "Nothing you're willing to give. Not yet, anyway. But here's what I think of your little town's magic." Stripping off his glove, he transferred the silver cross into his bare left hand and closed his fingers over it, closing his eyes with a slight wince. That sense of *wrongness* intensified as he concentrated hard. An acrid scent of hot metal arose, and molten silver dripped from his clenched fist, hissing as it puddled and cooled on the wet concrete.

I swallowed against the tightness in my throat, staring at him with hatred, filled with helpless rage.

"Ah, that's better." Dufreyne sighed with pleasure and opened his eyes, opened his hand to show me his unmarked palm. "See? All gone."

"Fuck you!" I said with impotent fury, tears stinging. "Fuck you and everything you stand for!"

"Do you know what's funny?" Daniel Dufreyne leaned toward me, his reek surrounding me. "What I just did? That's nothing to the power you stand to inherit." He snapped his fingers. "*Nothing*. You could reign over what's left of this mortal plane. All these petty pagan gods in their twilight years would bow to *your* will. And all you have to do is ask for it."

My right hand came up hard and fast, and I planted *dauda-dagr's* tip in the hollow of his throat. If we hadn't been in public . . . I don't know what I would have done. I honestly don't. Fear flickered in Dufreyne's eyes, a wisp of frost rising from his skin where the dagger's point dented it.

"Get out," I whispered. "Tell your master Hades that Hel's territory is *not* for sale, not at any price. And if he tries to take it, Hel intends to defend it with every weapon she has."

Backing away, Dufreyne raised his hands. "Oh, we'll see about that," he said smoothly. "And I told you, Hades has no interest in Pemkowet. By the time this is over, you'll wish he did. At least *Hades* is reasonable."

"Well, who does, then?" I shouted at him. "Goddammit! Who's behind Elysian Fields?"

Reaching behind him, Dufreyne opened the door of his Jaguar and eased himself into the driver's seat. "I'll be seeing you, cousin," he said before closing the door between us.

Seething with helpless anger, I watched him drive away.

Then I went inside and called Casimir. "We're in trouble."

# Forty-five

Two days later, the trial concluded. According to reports, the jury took all of about ten minutes to find in favor of the plaintiffs and award them the entire forty-five-million-dollar settlement.

Judge Martingale approved the settlement in record time, and gave the Pemkowet tri-community governments a hundred and eighty days to pay the entirety of this impossible sum.

It's not like the writing hadn't been on the wall for most of the trial's duration, but the verdict unleashed a firestorm of acrimony and recrimination. Residents of Pemkowet Township complained bitterly about the unfairness of being dragged into the lawsuit in the first place, and officials from Pemkowet and East Pemkowet pointed fingers at one another. Chief Bryant got his fair share of criticism, but the worst vitriol was reserved for Amanda Brooks, who in turn blamed her daughter.

Of course, everyone knew the entire trial was a farce and that in a sane world, the verdict would be overturned on appeal. But that's not what happened.

The town hall meeting—actually a tri-community meeting—that turned our lives upside down was scheduled on short notice to discuss the situation. If it hadn't been for Lurine, I'd have been in a state of near despair, but she remained surprisingly upbeat about the state of affairs, even after I confessed the whole fake-bomb-threat-slash-protection-charm caper to her.

"No offense, cupcake, but I really think your little coven could have come up with a less, um, dangerously illegal plan," she said mildly. "Don't worry about this Dufreyne and his threat. One way or another, I'll take care of him."

I eyed her. "Not that I'm entirely opposed to the notion, but is there a way that doesn't involve squishing him?"

Lurine shrugged. "Well, he's guilty of tampering with a federal jury, not to mention interfering with a judge. Now that I know magic will function in his presence no matter where he is, I'm sure I could persuade him it would be in his best interests to recuse himself from the case when it's appealed and let the legal process take its course. You should have told me sooner about hell-spawns carrying their own underworlds inside them," she added. "I could have paid him a visit weeks ago and laid this whole business to rest."

Oh, gah! Yes, I should have. I had a strong urge to stab myself in the eye with a fork. "It didn't occur to me."

"Sometimes the best defense is a strong offense, baby girl," Lurine said. "If you're going to protect this town, you might need to take the fight to your enemies instead of waiting for it to come to you. Right now, we just need to make sure Pemkowet's willing to go forward with the appeal. Once that's in play, I'll deal with Dufreyne."

"Are you sure you can handle him?" I asked. "After all, he's invoked his birthright."

Lurine gave me a sidelong look. "You don't think *my* powers of persuasion are a match for his?"

I flushed. "I'm just asking."

She laughed. "To be perfectly honest, I don't know. But don't worry. If I can't persuade him, I'll settle for squishing him."

It was a huge relief. Well, except for the part about the squishing. I hoped it wouldn't come to that. Mostly.

I felt guilty relying on Lurine to bail us out of a bad situation, but not as guilty as I felt about all my missteps along the way. Lurine was right. Instead of focusing on protecting the judge, I should have concentrated on attacking Dufreyne with everything at my disposal the minute he'd revealed himself as an adversary. It was the same mistake I'd made with Sinclair's mother last fall. I'd been too hesitant, too trusting in the advice and suggestions of others.

And, maybe, a little too absorbed in my own complicated love life. No more.

Along with reassuring the coven and the Scooby Gang that Lurine had promised to handle Daniel Dufreyne, I did a lot of thinking about what my role in fixing this mess ought to be. Acting in my capacity as Hel's liaison, I asked the board and council members for the opportunity to be the first speaker to address the town meeting. Although somewhat bemused, they agreed to it.

Pemkowet City Hall was packed to the rafters the evening of the town meeting. I have to admit, it was only the second meeting I'd attended. Mom and I had gone to one years ago, hoping it would be just like the popcorn-worthy town meetings in Stars Hollow on *Gilmore Girls*, but it turned out that the reality of municipal governance was a lot more dull and prosaic than it appeared on television.

Anyway.

The Pemkowet PD was providing security, including Cody, who studiously avoided looking at me when I arrived with Stefan. Members of the township board and the city councils were crammed shoulder to shoulder into seats at a long table at the front of the hall, with a podium and a microphone set up at an angle for residents of the tri-community area to address the room. The rest of us were crammed into seats facing them, latecomers packed into the standing-room-only spaces in the aisles and at the back of the hall. The furnace wasn't working properly and the place was frigid.

After the opening remarks, Jason Hallifax, the mayor of Pemkowet, called me to the stand.

"Good evening." My nerves got the better of me, and my greeting came out at a higher pitch than I'd intended. In the audience, Stefan met my gaze and gave me an encouraging nod. His pupils dilated

slightly, and I felt my anxiety abate as he drew on the connection between us. "I'd like to start out by apologizing to everyone here."

It got their attention. I saw my friends scattered throughout the audience frowning in perplexity, including my mom.

"As Hel's liaison, it's my job to enforce her order in the eldritch
community in Pemkowet," I said, my voice steady now. "And that includes protecting you from predators. I took down the Tall Man. I banished the Night Hag. But I failed to protect Pemkowet from Daniel
Dufreyne." There were murmurs of surprise. "We know in our hearts,
all of us, that that trial was rigged," I continued. "And some of you may
have heard rumors. Well, I'm here to confirm them. Dufreyne's a hell-
spawn, just like me. Unlike me, he was able to invoke his birthright
without breaching the Inviolate Wall. He has infernal powers, including the power of persuasion."

"How's that different from any other lawyer?" someone called, setting off a ripple of nervous laughter.

I ignored the interruption. "It's not that I didn't try to oppose him,
but the problem is that I didn't fight smart. I should have been shouting
his identity from the rooftops. I should have been meeting with our
legal team to figure out a way that we could pool our resources, eldritch and mundane alike, to expose Dufreyne for what he is, to negate
his influence. And I promise you, as we move forward with this appeal,
that's exactly what we'll do. And it *will* work."

There was applause as I took my seat.

The next speaker to address the room was Don Reynolds, whose
young son had been one of the Night Hag's victims. "Look, I've got a
lot of appreciation for what you do, Daisy," he said. "My boy sleeps
soundly at night because of you. But I'm concerned about throwing
good money after bad. We've already spent tens of thousands of dollars
in legal fees. What happens if you're wrong or you fail again?" He
shook his head. "If we appeal and lose, we're right back where we
started, only deeper in the hole. I think Pemkowet's tri-community
governments need to take a hard look at their assets, and figure out
how we're going to pay the damages."

There were some boos and hisses in the mix, but I was surprised at the number of people who applauded.

Over the course of the next half hour, various citizens spoke for and against appealing the verdict. A lot of people were just flat-out scared of the repercussions of losing an appeal, of the mounting legal fees.

The meeting had started at five thirty, and it was about a quarter past six when Lurine sauntered up to the podium. While the rest of us huddled in our coats to ward off the chill, Lurine was wearing a form-fitting sheath dress of black satin, a pearl necklace, and a pair of Louboutins with five-inch heels, and appeared oblivious to the cold.

Given that she regularly swam in Lake Michigan in midwinter in her true form, I suppose that wasn't a surprise.

A few men in the audience whistled as she adjusted the microphone. "Why, thank you, sweethearts." Lurine smiled. "Tell me, are any of you gambling men?"

"I'll take a gamble on you any day!" one of them shouted.

Her smile deepened. "Aren't you cute? Well, I like a good gamble from time to time myself. Now that I've heard both sides of the argument, *I'm* willing to gamble on a little thing I like to call the American justice system—not to mention my dear young friend Daisy—which is why I'm offering to underwrite the legal expenses of an appeal."

The hall burst into spontaneous applause.

"She waited long enough to make her offer," Stefan murmured in my ear, sounding amused.

I smiled. "It takes good timing to make an entrance."

"Thank you," Lurine said sweetly when the applause died. "Now, I'm confident that we'll win the appeal and recoup our legal fees in full, having had some experience in these matters, but . . ." She raised one hand. "In the *very* unlikely event that I'm wrong, I promise to personally spearhead the fund-raising effort to settle the damages. And I do still know a few people in Hollywood with deep pockets," she added.

More cheers erupted.

Lurine shifted to address the board and council members. "Now, just to be clear, *that* offer is contingent on your decision to appeal this ridiculous verdict."

"It's a generous offer," Mayor Jason Hallifax said sincerely. "I think I speak for all three municipalities when I say thank you, Ms. Hollister."

"Of course, you're very—" Lurine began.

At the back of the hall, the doors opened unexpectedly. A warm breeze swept into the room. It smelled like summer, like newly mown grass, like apricots ripening in the sun, sweet and golden and indolent. It was a scent that suggested an idyllic afternoon, dozing in a hammock in the deep green shade in the hottest part of the day, the sound of honeybees droning in the background.

I felt myself relaxing without thinking about it, the room's chill driven from my bones. Everyone did.

Well, almost everyone.

At the podium, Lurine stiffened, her gaze taking on a basilisk stare as she whispered something under her breath.

The woman escorted into the Pemkowet City Hall by a contingent of security guards in black jackets and trousers was, hands down, the most beautiful woman I'd ever seen in my life.

And based on the profound sense of *presence* that charged the summery air, a sense I'd never encountered anywhere but Hel's throne room in Little Niflheim, she was also a goddess.

A goddess, walking aboveground. That wasn't supposed to be possible.

A miasma of fruit hung in the air: apricots, nectarines, apples, pears, and plums, ripe and succulent. Sun-warmed grapes hanging in clusters on the vine. But there was another note beneath it, rank and poisonous.

Beside the goddess gliding into the hall strode Daniel Dufreyne, grinning like a shark.

I glanced around me, but everyone in the hall sat transfixed in their seats as the impossibly beautiful woman approached the podium.

Lurine's eyes flashed as she breathed a name, her voice filled with ancient hatred. "Persephone."

Persephone.

Duh.

That damned Dufreyne may have been splitting hairs, but he'd told the truth. It wasn't Hades who was interested in Pemkowet. It had never been Hades.

It was his fucking *wife*.

Standing on her tiptoes, Persephone whispered in Lurine's ear. Lurine shot me an anguished glance before closing her eyes and listening. After a long moment, she bowed her head in defeat.

"I'm sorry," Lurine murmured into the microphone without looking at anyone. "My offer is withdrawn."

I wanted to cry.

# Forty-six

Moving like an automaton, Lurine returned to take her seat beside my mother. Seeing her so defeated hurt me inside like I'd swallowed a mouthful of ground glass, and beneath the hurt was a building tide of anger.

"Daisy." Stefan touched my arm. "You need to keep your wits about you."

"I'm trying," I hissed at him. "But that's a goddamned *goddess* up there!"

"I know."

Any semblance of an ordinary town meeting had gone right out the window. With Dufreyne's assistance, Persephone's security brigade took over at the front of the hall, setting up an easel and propping a foam-board-mounted map of the Pemkowet area on it. It looked a lot like the map Lee had shown me months ago.

Throughout it all, the goddess herself stood with her hands clasped before her, gazing beneficently at everyone and no one.

I stood up. "Excuse me, Mr. Mayor," I said to Jason Hallifax. "But um . . . point of order? This is a town meeting for residents of the Pemkowet tri-community area. Are you and the other members just going to let a bunch of outsiders take over?"

The mayor of Pemkowet blinked at me. "Now, Daisy, you had your chance to speak. Don't be rude. Let's hear what Miss . . . Miss . . ." His voice trailed off as he turned his head to stare in adoration at the goddess. "Let's hear what *she* has to say."

There were nods of agreement all around.

"Thank you." Persephone's voice was soft and lilting, and when she spoke, there might as well have been a background track of birdsong and a babbling brook behind her. Her mouth was as lush as a ripe plum, and her faint Greek accent made her sound like Arianna Huffington dipped in honey. She looked all of nineteen or twenty, with exquisite features framed by shining brown hair in which gold highlights glinted, as though a private source of sunlight shone on her everywhere she went. "I wish to make you an offer. Mr. Dufreyne will explain."

"No," I said firmly. "Not him. No way."

Persephone turned her gaze on me. Her wide-set eyes were green, flecked with more shimmers of gold. She looked utterly beautiful and possibly a little bit insane. "You are the Norse Hel's liaison Daisy, are you not?"

"Yes."

Her ripe lips curved into a smile. "Daisy. I adore daisies. I understand that you are angry, but Mr. Dufreyne is not your enemy. He serves me through my husband, and I am here to do what is best for Pemkowet."

I glared at her. "By instigating a *lawsuit* against us?"

"Oh, but you wouldn't have listened otherwise, would you?" Persephone's voice took on a tone of reproach. "And you brought this on yourselves, did you not?" Heads nodded all around the room again. "I fear that Hel has not ruled you wisely," she said with regret.

"Are you offering to take her place?" I asked in a hard voice. "Because that's not up for negotiation."

Persephone's sun-flecked gaze shifted back to me. "It would be simpler if you allowed my representative to speak," she said plaintively. "Will you allow it if I promise his words will be mere words?"

I hesitated, then shook my head. "I'd like to hear it in *your* words."

She gave a delicate sigh. "Very well. Elysian Fields is prepared to offer fifty million dollars to purchase a large piece of property owned by the city of Pemkowet." A murmur of pleased surprise ran through the hall. Persephone glanced at Dufreyne, knitting her perfect brows. "That is enough to settle the debt that is owed, with additional funds to be shared for their trouble, is it not?"

He inclined his head. "It is, my lady."

"So you see," she said brightly. "It is the ideal solution. Everyone wins!"

"Not exactly," I said. "That's Hel's territory."

"No." Persephone gave me a rueful smile. "That is property owned by the City of Pemkowet. Yes, it has been occupied by your mistress for a hundred years, but the Norse Hel does not *own* it. I fear that is one of her more grave mistakes. Your mistress dwells in the days of yore, when her presence alone sufficed to make a parcel of land sacred and inviolable." She shook her head, and motes of sunlight scintillated all around her. "Those of us who endure live in a different world, and to survive, we must adapt."

My tail lashed. "To what end?" I asked her. "Your husband Hades's territory is in Montreal, and no god or goddess can rule over more than one demesne. So what do you want with Pemkowet?"

Persephone looked into the distance and smiled to herself. "I want a summer home."

I stared at her. "Are you serious?"

"Yes." Something subtle shifted in her expression, an ancient darkness surfacing behind her sunlit eyes. Suddenly Persephone looked nineteen going on ten thousand, and I thought about what I remembered of her story from Mr. Leary's Myth and Lit class years ago. Hades had abducted her when she was a maiden, and for the sin of eating six pomegranate seeds in captivity, she had been condemned to spend six months of every year in the underworld with him.

God, no wonder she was a little crazy.

"I want a summer home," Persephone repeated, her voice rising. The motes of sunlight surrounding her shivered and vanished with a sound like shards of crystal shattering. "A place to call my own. I have *endured* and *endured* and *endured*, and I want a demesne of my own!"

Beside me, Stefan rose. "Forgive me, Daisy," he murmured to me, his pupils swallowing his irises. "I cannot stay."

I couldn't blame him for being unable to handle a goddess's fury without ravening. "Go. I'll call you later."

"Oh, dear." Persephone watched him leave. "Well, you understand it wouldn't be *just* a summer home," she said to the hall at large. "I plan to build a resort. A very nice resort. Mr. Dufreyne, will you show them the plan?"

"Of course, my lady." Dufreyne swapped out the map of Pemkowet on the easel for another piece of foam board, this one with a plan depicting a prospectus for an elaborate resort named Elysian Fields. It included a twenty-story hotel with two restaurants and a nightclub, a marina, a golf course, a stable, and extensive riding trails winding through the dunes.

If you were willing to ignore the fact that it was in violation of pretty much every zoning ordinance in existence in Pemkowet, not to mention a dozen or so Department of Environmental Quality guidelines, it looked nice.

Oh, and it sat squarely atop Little Niflheim.

Persephone gazed fondly at it. "Lovely, isn't it? I think I could be happy there."

"Excuse me," I said incredulously, "but that is *Hel's demesne*. Why don't you go buy a piece of property somewhere else and start your own?"

She pursed her lush lips. "I'm afraid it's complicated. Technically speaking, I'm not an underworld deity, and yet my continued existence in the mortal plane requires that I be affiliated with an actual physical underworld. Hel's demesne has been consecrated by a hundred years of her presence," she said. "That's why I need it if I'm going to spend six months of the year here in Pemkowet."

It had all the simplicity of a child's logic: I want it, therefore it should be mine. "And are you proposing that Hel should share her demesne with you?" I asked quietly. "Or are you declaring war on her?"

"War!" Persephone's laughter was an enchanting sound. Dancing gold sparkles returned to her eyes. "What an archaic notion!"

"That's not an answer," I pointed out.

The scent of ripe fruit hanging in the air intensified. "Two deities from competing cosmologies cannot coexist in a single underworld," Persephone said in a calm tone. "Hel has relocated her demesne before. She may do so again."

"Hel intends to defend her territory," I said. "Which means you *are* declaring war."

"Of course not." She gave me a beautiful smile with a large dose of crazy in it, the motes in her eyes sparkling manically. "Hel's decisions, including her failure to establish a legal claim to her demesne, are not my responsibility. I'm merely making a generous offer to purchase this property and build something wonderful on it, something that will benefit *all* of Pemkowet and generate a great deal of tourism. You'll vote on it tonight, won't you?" she added to the council members. "You see, I can't stay. I'm not supposed to leave Hades until spring. I had to get special dispensation to be here today, and I'd really like to return with an answer."

Jason Hallifax glanced at the members of the city council. "Oh, I think we can do that, can't we?"

"Are you out of your minds!" I shouted at them. "No! You can't make a decision like that on a whim! You need to have a . . . a referendum, or a—"

"You know, I think we've heard enough from you, pretty Daisy," Persephone interrupted me. She made a slight, graceful gesture in my direction. "Let's let others speak, shall we?"

It's never a good idea to annoy a goddess. Especially a crazy one. Persephone might not have Hel's ability to stop a mortal heart with a thought, but my tongue froze to the roof of my mouth. I could taste her power trickling down my throat, honey-sweet and poisonous, and gagged ineffectually on it. At the front of the hall, Daniel Dufreyne raised one manscaped brow as if to say, *I told you so.*

"I think this is a perfect forum to discuss Miss . . . Miss, um, Persephone's offer." The mayor of Pemkowet sounded like a man unsure whether or not he was dreaming. "Isn't it?"

"Well, it's the city's decision," said Cal Burns, who was the Pemkowet Township supervisor. "But I think as long as you stipulate that the proceeds would be used to pay the settlement, we're all in agreement that this is a fantastic way to resolve the situation." He glanced at Trudy Penrose, the mayor of East Pemkowet. "Wouldn't you say so?"

"Oh, certainly," she agreed.

I wanted to scream, but all I could do was make a strangled sound in the back of my throat, a process that threatened to tear the skin off my tongue.

This was worse, so much worse, than Dufreyne's influence. At least there were ways to ward against him. How the hell did you stop a freaking *goddess* from dazzling the residents of an entire town, a town she was basically blackmailing into giving her what she wanted?

"Is there further public discussion before we call for a vote on the offer?" Jason Hallifax asked. "Does anyone wish to address the council?" He cleared his throat, shooting a guilty little glance in my direction. "Anyone who isn't Daisy Johanssen?"

"I do." It was Cody, on security duty at the back of the hall. His voice was harsh, more than a hint of growl in it. He strode forward, and it was Persephone he addressed, not the council. "If Pemkowet becomes your demesne, and you're in residence for half the year, what happens during the other six months?"

"Why, I'll be with Hades, as always," she said in a wondering tone. "Where else would I be?"

"I don't *care* where you'll be," Cody snarled, and I would have cheered him if I could have. Apparently, werewolves weren't so easily dazzled. "What happens to the eldritch community in Pemkowet when you're not here?"

"He's right." In the audience, Sinclair rose. The beads on his short dreadlocks were stirring of their own accord, and he had one hand pressed to his chest where the protective joe-pye weed sigil was etched.

He sounded uncertain, but determined. "What happens to the nature fey and all the rest?"

Ah, God! I hadn't even thought that far ahead. Like the adage went, as below, so above. If Pemkowet didn't have a deity present in a functioning underworld for six months out of the year, for six months out of the year, the town would be mundane territory.

No fairies, no hobgoblins, no bogles.

No naiads or dryads, nixies or undines.

No werewolves, no vampires.

No Outcast.

No Lurine, who was silently seething in her seat. The entire eldritch community would be unhomed.

Persephone gave a delicate frown of consternation. "Well, I imagine some of them will become seasonal residents."

"What if that's not an option?" Cody said grimly.

Don Reynolds rose. "Look, as the father of a seven-year-old boy who was attacked by an eldritch creature, I have to say, I'm in favor of weeding out some of the elements in our midst."

"Some of those elements are our family and friends!" It was my mom who called that out, her voice shaking with anger. "You can't just banish them!"

At the council table, Jason Hallifax cleared his throat. "With all due respect, I think we have to make this decision based on the needs of the ordinary tax-paying citizens who elected us."

Casimir stood, resplendent in a tall beehive wig. "Who are you calling ordinary, *dahling*?" he asked in an acidic tone.

The discussion raged for the better part of an hour. I was surprised that Persephone didn't shut it down, but the longer it went on, the more people spoke in favor of accepting her offer, and the more they did, the more others began clamoring for the council to vote on it immediately.

In the end, they did. It was unanimous.

# Forty-seven

Once the vote was read, Persephone gave a cheery little wave in my direction, unsealing my tongue.

I felt like I'd been hit by a bus. Everything had happened so fast. I'd come into this town meeting prepared to argue for all I was worth in favor of a decision to appeal, and my world had been turned upside down.

Which had been the very first card in the reading Mom did for me on Thanksgiving; *El Mundo*, reversed.

It had made me shiver then, and it did now. And *La Corona*, wealth. Well, that had sure as hell come into play. Which meant *La Bandera* came next. The flags of war were waving.

The meeting was adjourned. Persephone gathered her entourage, preparing to depart. "I trust that you'll inform Hel that her demesne will soon belong to me," she said, gazing at me with sun-spangled eyes. "I'll return on the first day of spring to take possession of it."

I said nothing.

"Now you're silent?" Persephone laughed her enchanting laugh. "As you will, pretty Daisy. I will see you anon."

She left Daniel Dufreyne behind to discuss the details. No doubt he'd get whatever he asked for, which now seemed like the least of my worries. There was a knot of friends and family waiting for me by the doors, but I approached the council before joining my people.

"You have no idea what you've unleashed here tonight," I said to the mayor and the council members. "*No idea.*"

"We made the best decision we could for the community," Jason Hallifax said defensively.

"No," I said. "You just voted to put Pemkowet in the middle of a war between two elder faith goddesses, and if you think otherwise, you're delusional. Persephone's declared war, all right. She's just using money as her weapon." I glanced at Dufreyne. "Money and a rigged trial."

"Nonetheless, it was a fair offer," one of the other council members said. "And Persephone was right. Hel's relocated before. Why can't she just do it again?"

"You might advise her to make sure she has legal title to whatever property she claims this time," Hallifax added.

I stared at him in disbelief. "You seem to think Hel's going to act like an ordinary human being. May I remind you that she's a freaking *goddess*, not some delinquent tenant being served an eviction notice?"

The mayor looked apprehensive. "Well, you'll just have to convince her it's in everyone's best interest if she, um, relocates."

"I'm sure Daisy will do just that," Dufreyne said in a smooth voice, allaying the council's fears. He smiled at me. "Unless she has another solution in mind?"

I transferred my stare to him. "You'd like that, wouldn't you? That's been your endgame all along, hasn't it? Well, go to hell. I'm not breaching the Inviolate Wall just because your crazy-ass mistress wants a summer home."

He just smiled.

Turning on my heel, I went to join my mom and friends.

"Are you okay, honey?" Mom asked me anxiously. "She didn't hurt you, did she?"

"Fine," I said. "Just pissed." I looked at Lurine. "Are *you* okay? What did Persephone say to you?"

"Oh, she threatened me with a fate worse than death if I didn't get out of her way," Lurine said in a flat voice that didn't belie the fury simmering beneath it. "I'll spare you the unpleasant details. Unfortunately, she could deliver on it; or at least Hades could, and I have no reason to believe he wouldn't. Damned Olympians." She shrugged. "That's what comes of losing a war. I told you the children of the Titans got screwed. I'm sorry, cupcake. I truly am."

I shook my head. "It's not your fault."

"Hey, Daisy?" Lee interjected. "I don't mean to interrupt, but I think that, um, there's a frost giant outside waiting for you."

Of course there was.

"Thanks." I took a deep breath. "It looks like I've got to report to Hel."

To say that the Norse goddess of the dead was displeased with the news I brought her was an understatement.

A massive, massive understatement.

A short time after Mikill picked me up at City Hall, I stood shivering before Hel's throne in Little Niflheim while Hel stared into the distance, both eyes open and blazing. In the darkness, thunderclouds gathered around her throne. Deep beneath us, the earth rumbled with vibrations I could feel through the soles of my boots; above us, the beams supporting the ceiling of the abandoned sawmill creaked ominously.

I really, really hoped Hel wasn't going to bring the whole thing crashing down around us. Being buried alive would be a sucky way to die.

In the end, her gaze returned from the distance, as it always had. The earth stopped groaning and settled.

I breathed a silent sigh of relief.

"So," Hel said in her most sepulchral voice. "It seems I am mistaken, and the gods of yore may yet make war upon each other."

"Does it *have* to be war, my lady?" My voice sounded small and plaintive. "Please know I mean no disloyalty . . . but could you relocate Little Niflheim?"

Hel closed her ember eye and smiled gently at me with the fair side of her face. "I fear it is an impossibility, my young liaison. The work of finding *this* place, of the Norns nurturing the seed of a second Yggdrasil, was the work of many years. This is something the Greek Persephone well knows," she added. "She cannot acquire my demesne by dint of mere money." Her left eye blazed open. "To truly claim it as her own, she must end my existence."

I winced. "You know, it would have been useful to have that piece of information a few hours ago, when I was trying to persuade the council not to accept Persephone's offer."

Hel waved her right hand in a dismissive gesture. "You pitted yourself against a goddess bent on persuading mortals to accede to her will. That was never a battle you were going to win."

"So what happens now, my lady?" I asked helplessly.

"Now?" Hel smiled, and it was a terrible smile on both sides of her bifurcated face. "We prepare for war."

"As long as Yggdrasil stands, there is hope," Mikill said in his deep rumble. "Our fates are tied to the world tree. The hellhound Garm yet guards it. The frost giants will give battle. The *duegar* will take up arms."

"Consult this ledger you have created and seek out allies above the ground, Daisy Johanssen," Hel said to me. "Surely there are those among them who are willing to stand and fight beside us."

I nodded. "Is there anything else you would have me do?" A fearful thought struck me. "My lady . . . is *dauda-dagr* capable of killing Persephone?"

"No, my young liaison. It cannot slay a goddess." Hel's voice took on a note of kindness. "You have served me with valor and loyalty. I am sorry that your service has been thus rewarded."

My throat tightened. "So am I, my lady. This, um, war . . . exactly what do you think we're up against?"

"The Greek Persephone's weapon is wealth." Hel's nostrils flared with disdain. Well, the right one did, anyway. The left was pretty much just a blackened hole revealing the sinus cavity beneath it. "Her husband's wealth. It is my belief that she will acquire whatever mortal army such wealth can purchase."

I swallowed hard at the thought of frost giants and dwarves facing off against some sort of Blackwater-style mercenary army equipped with body armor and assault rifles. "I'll do my best, my lady, but . . . are you *sure* there's no way to avoid this?"

"Nothing that lies within my power," Hel said gently. "Unless the Greek Persephone relinquishes her claim, war will be waged."

"There are worse fates," Mikill added in a philosophical tone. "If it is the end we face, it is fitting that we face it in battle." He rubbed his massive hands together in anticipation. "And it will be an epic battle."

"Don't get ahead of yourself, okay?" I said to him. "I'm not ready to lose you just yet."

He laughed deep in his chest. "Nor am I ready to be lost."

"Glad to hear it."

Once my audience with Hel was concluded, Mikill drove me back home. After calling Stefan to touch base with him, I fired up my laptop and spent a couple of hours poring over the Pemkowet Ledger, making lists of members of the eldritch community other than the Outcast who might be willing to stand with the denizens of Little Niflheim and take on a crazed goddess and her probable mercenary army.

At least I knew where to start.

# Forty-eight

Before I could begin my recruitment drive, I needed to warn Chief Bryant about what was coming.

He heard me out with deepening dismay. "Goddammit. Goddammit!" He rubbed his chin. "And you're sure there's no way to prevent this?"

"Not on Hel's end," I said. "Can you talk the city council into reversing their decision?"

The chief hesitated. "Daisy, the problem is that there's not a lot of sympathy for Hel in town right now. Let's face it—you're talking about a deity no one but you has ever seen, a deity who has contributed nothing to the community in material terms. A deity whose inability to control the eldritch population has resulted in a considerable amount of pain and suffering."

"Oh, as opposed to a deity who deliberately *bankrupted* the community in order to get what she wanted?" I asked bitterly.

He frowned. "You have a point, but . . ."

I waited for the chief to finish his sentence, but he didn't. I guess he didn't need to. Even in her absence, Persephone's charm held sway. Yes, she'd bankrupted the community, but she was paying it back with interest. She could walk aboveground among mere mortals, she was beautiful, she brought sunlight with her, and she smelled like an orchard on a summer day.

Hel was right. This was probably a battle I was never going to win.

"All right," I said. "I'll try it myself. I just wanted to warn you."

"What are the repercussions for the community?" Chief Bryant asked.

"Of two goddesses going to war?" I asked. "Sir, I honestly have no idea."

"Daisy." He called me back as I was preparing to leave his office, his expression grave. "Whether you like it or not, Persephone *will* hold legal title to that property. And all I can do is uphold the law. I expect you to do the same."

I didn't answer.

I ran into Cody on the sidewalk outside the station. He looked like he hadn't slept since yesterday. "Daisy." He caught my arm. "I wanted to talk to you after the meeting, but Jen and Lee said you'd been summoned to Little Niflheim. What did Hel have to say?"

I told him about the coming war, then lowered my voice. "Where do you think the, um, Fairfax clan will stand on this?"

"I don't know," Cody admitted. "We were up all night talking about it, but at this point everyone's in a state of shock. This is our home! Generations of Fairfaxes have lived their whole lives here in Pemkowet!"

"I know." My eyes stung and I gave a choked half laugh. "How do you feel about Seattle?"

He shook his head. "Not good. This war . . . is there a chance we can win it?"

"Mikill said that as long as Yggdrasil's standing, there's hope," I said.

"I'll tell the clan," Cody said. "I'll let you know what they decide."

I nodded. "You should probably know that the chief warned me about upholding the law."

"Do you think he'll fire you for siding with Hel?" he asked.

I shrugged. "I think that come the second day of spring, he might not have any choice, but right now I can't afford to worry about it. By the way, if any of the guests from your mixer were planning to relocate, you might want to tell them to put those plans on hold."

"Good point." He paused. "For the record, I'm not seeing her."

"Who?"

Cody smiled wryly. "Stephanie. After her visit, we decided not to pursue a relationship. I don't know what to call whatever it was you and I had going on, Daise, but I'm not ready to move past it yet."

"Oh." I flushed. "And you thought *now* would be a good time to tell me?"

"No." He shoved his hands into his pockets. "Not really. Actually, it's a pretty terrible time. I just thought you should know."

I eyed him. "You know . . . never mind. Right now, I've got to go summon the Oak King."

I drove out to the meadow where I'd first encountered the Oak King and he had given me his token—the meadow where Sinclair and I had laid the remains of Jojo the joe-pye weed fairy to rest.

Everything was quiet and still. Although it was a few degrees above freezing, we'd had a blizzard the previous week, and the meadow lay under a thick coat of wet snow. I plodded through it, my footprints leaving deep, waterlogged impressions charting my progress across the landscape. In the center of the meadow, I fished out the Oak King's token, the silver acorn-shaped whistle I wore on a chain around my neck.

Setting it to my lips, I blew the whistle.

It had a high, clear sound that seemed to hang in the air long after I'd stopped blowing, echoes sounding through the trees.

I waited, trying not to think about Cody's revelation. I mean . . . Jesus! Seriously? That was one infuriating werewolf. What did that even mean, that he wasn't ready to move past our sort-of affair?

I'll tell you what: Nothing. Unless Cody was willing to defy his clan, it was just another version of the same I-want-you-but-I-can't-have-you dance we'd been doing for months.

Of course, if he did defy his clan for my sake . . . I'm not sure how I would feel about it. At least with Stefan, we'd gotten to a place where matters between us were clear and direct. Exhilarating, occasionally terrifying, but clear.

Anyway.

All thoughts of Cody, Stefan, and my overly complicated love life went out of my head the moment the Oak King appeared on the verge of the woods.

The Oak King wasn't a god, but he was eldritch royalty and he ruled over the nature fey in Pemkowet, which included the fairies who adored Sinclair so much, a phooka or two, the brownies and hobgoblins, and possibly others I didn't have recorded in my ledger yet. In appearance, he looked like a tall man crowned with antlers, brown-skinned and brown-haired, a long cloak hanging from his shoulders that looked like deerskin one moment and a garment woven of leaves and moss the next.

The meadow seemed to shrink as the Oak King crossed it, until he stood looming before me, his antlers silhouetted against the wintry sky, sorrow and foreboding in his dark eyes.

I knelt in his presence. "Your majesty."

"Rise, Daisy Johanssen." His voice was deep and hushed, like the stillness at the heart of an ancient forest. "It is not required that you kneel in my presence."

I stood, brushing the dampness from my knees. "I've come—"

"I know why you have summoned me, Hel's liaison." The Oak King met my gaze. "War comes to Pemkowet, does it not?"

"Yes." I shivered. "The Greek Persephone—" God, now I was doing it. "The goddess Persephone is establishing legal title to Hel's demesne and means to claim it as her own."

"Legal title." He echoed the words as though bemused by them. "That such a thing should come to pass."

"Hel has no choice but to stand her ground and fight," I said. "She seeks allies. And, um, you should know that if Persephone succeeds, she'll only be in residence six months out of the year."

"Yes," the Oak King said. "Her story is known to me, and I am aware of what her victory would betoken. My people and I would be unhomed." His gaze shifted onto the distance in that staring-at-the-unknowable way of deities and eldritch royalty. "If that be so, I fear that there may be no further sacred places in the world with enough wilderness left to sustain us," he murmured with regret. "Mortal cities have swallowed the demesnes of the gods. Even here, I am diminished, and our numbers dwindle. And yet it is the way of the world. Perhaps our time is upon us."

My tail lashed with anger. "So you're just giving up?"

Beneath the shadow of his antlers, his eyes glimmered like a deer's, dark and liquid. "No, Daisy Johanssen. I do but weigh a grave choice."

I thought about Jojo being cut down by the Tall Man's axe, and envisioned a horde of fairies with slingshots mowed down by gunfire. My shoulders slumped in defeat. "I'm sorry. You're right."

"Ah." The Oak King inclined his head toward me. "You think of the little one who sacrificed herself."

I nodded. "Hel thinks Persephone will raise a mortal army. With, um, state-of-the-art weaponry."

"The joe-pye weed fairy's sacrifice was valiant, but foolhardy," the Oak King mused. "It is tricks and mayhem at which the least of my subjects excel, not warfare. They may be of aid, but there are others more suited to battle."

A spark of hope kindled in me. "Others who could help?"

"It is aid that would come at a price, Hel's liaison," he cautioned me. "It is the Wild Hunt of which I speak, immortal riders who strike terror and madness into the hearts of mortal men. The Wild Hunt owes true allegiance to neither the Seelie nor the Unseelie Court, but there is a bond of long standing between us. They will answer my summons. But once unleashed, the Wild Hunt cannot be constrained until a day and a night have run their course. Not even by me."

"But you could unleash them on Persephone's troops?" I asked him.

A cold breeze sprang up, stirring the Oak King's cloak. It rustled with a sound like dry leaves rattling in the trees. His dark eyes gleamed, and it was a hard gleam now. "Yes."

"Your majesty . . ." I paused. I'd read a lot of fairy tales in my life. "If I ask this of you in Hel's name, will I have cause to regret it?"

"It is possible, Hel's liaison." There was still a sense of deep quietude to his resonant voice, but it was a different hush—a cold midnight hush, the hush a rabbit might hear before the owl struck on silent wings, leaving nothing but bloodstains on the snow. "It is *always* possible. Do you ask it?"

I took a breath. "I do."

"Then it shall be granted." The Oak King smiled, and there was a joyful wildness to his smile. "I do not wish to fade and vanish without striking a blow against the men who come with iron weapons to destroy all that is wild and free in this world. I do not wish to accede without a whimper to the whims of a goddess who uses such men and their weapons to her own ends."

"I'm guessing she wasn't always that way," I murmured.

"No." He shook his head. "I do not believe it to be so. But it is so now." Reaching out, he laid a strong, sinewy hand on my shoulder. "Tell your mistress Hel that I will join her forces. Tell her that the Wild Hunt will ride on her behalf."

"Thank you, your majesty," I said. "I will."

Once more, the Oak King's antlered crown dipped toward me. "I will see you on the battlefield, Daisy Johanssen."

Shit.

This was getting real.

# Forty-nine

I spent the following weeks marshaling forces to fight a war.

A *war*.

"You know that the Outcast stand beside you, Daisy," Stefan said to me in an unofficial war council meeting. "We will do what we can."

"I'm thinking we need weapons, big man," Cooper said bleakly. "*Real* weapons. Firepower, do ye ken? Not just swords and the like."

"Which you wouldn't use unless it was necessary to defend your lives, right?" Oops, wrong question to ask one of the Outcast. "Or, um, the lives of your comrades?"

"If there are mortals on the battlefield, we will do our best to prevent casualties, but you are speaking of war, Daisy." Stefan nodded at Cooper. "Look into it."

"I will."

I didn't ask for details. I didn't want to know.

It did give me ammunition—no pun intended—to meet with the mayor and the city council in a last-ditch effort to get them to back out of the deal with Persephone. The good news was that I was able to get through to them. Confronted with a scenario of warring goddesses and the eldritch population giving battle to a possible mercenary army, they finally realized the magnitude of their decision, and that they might really, really have cause to regret it.

The bad news was that they'd signed a binding agreement with penalties that would send the town and the tri-community area straight back into crippling bankruptcy if they tried to get out of it. That's what comes of letting a hell-spawn lawyer with powers of persuasion handle the paperwork.

"It would destroy the entire community, Daisy." Jason Hallifax looked sick. "Literally. And I'm sorry, but I'm not convinced that isn't a worse outcome. I mean this war . . . it only affects the eldritch, right?"

"I can't say that for sure. Definitely not if Persephone brings in her own private militia," I said. "If Hel's right, we're talking about ordinary human mortals. Do you want *their* deaths on your hands?"

Marian Warner, one of the council members, shook her head. "No one wants anyone's death on their hands, Daisy, but we have to act in the interest of the community, not the members of some hypothetical militia."

The discussion went on a lot longer, but in the end, the result was the same. It still wasn't a battle I was ever going to win.

The galling thing was that if *I'd* had powers of persuasion, I could have gotten them to change their minds in a heartbeat. Actually, if I'd had powers of persuasion, none of this would have happened in the first place. I tried not to think about that, but it was hard. God, I was just so sick of being so fucking *helpless*! It didn't seem fair that Persephone or Hades, whichever one had done it, could basically commission a surrogate mother to get knocked up by a demon to breed the living embodiment of every lawyer joke ever written, and that Dufreyne could claim his birthright and wield power with impunity, when all I was trying to do was keep the peace and protect my community.

And it didn't seem fair that I had to live with the knowledge that power was mine for the asking when I needed it the most. Power; *El Mano* in my mom's reading. My greatest desire . . . and my greatest fear.

All I had to do was break the world to get it.

Needless to say, my nightmare returned during the days leading up to the vernal equinox. More often than not, I woke up sweating with terror, the crack of doom ringing in my ears.

Meanwhile, the deal went through, and Elysian Fields officially claimed ownership of Hel's territory.

But at least my recruitment efforts were paying off.

When I paid a visit to the House of Shadows, for the first time in our acquaintance, Lady Eris treated me as an equal, possibly because she was well and truly pissed off at the notion that her vampire brood would have to find a new haven.

"We have made our home here for more than fifty years," she said grimly, holding audience in the ballroom. "Abiding by Hel's order and dwelling in peace alongside mortals and immortals alike. We will not be forced out of our home at the whim of some obsolete goddess."

Dwelling in peace might be a bit of an exaggeration, but I wasn't in a mood to argue with her.

"Of course, any aid we might provide must be given by stealth under the cover of night." Lady Eris gave me a cunning sidelong look. "Hel's liaison, you speculate that Persephone's army will be composed of mortal humans. Do we have your mistress's permission to treat them as lawful prey?"

A soft sigh of indrawn breath went around the perimeter of the ballroom, where the members of her brood were watching and listening.

"Ooh, I've never had the chance to drink a mortal dry!" Jen's sister, Bethany, whispered with creepy delight.

"No." I held up my rune-marked left hand. *El Mano*. I pushed that thought away. "Sucking blood and enthralling mercenaries against their will, yes. But they probably have no idea what they signed up for. So no drinking dry, not unless your own lives are, um, at stake. Agreed?"

Lady Eris—I still had a hard time wrapping my head around the fact that *Eris* was actually her real name—rolled her eyes. "Agreed."

The same sentiments were echoed throughout the eldritch community. No one wanted to be unhomed.

"I've got nowhere else to go, mamacita!" Skrrzzzt said in a plaintive tone when I brought a six-pack out to the abandoned Presbyterian camp to talk with him. He gestured around with one thorny, long-fingered hand. "I mean, look at this. A bogle needs a proper haunt. I've got over a hundred acres here! You think I'm going to find a hundred-acre haunt in a major metropolitan area?"

"There's Central Park in New York," I said. "That's huge, right?"

The bogle snorted. "If you think there's an acre of Central Park that hasn't already been claimed, you're kidding yourself."

"I just want to be sure you're making the right choice," I said. "I don't want you to feel pressured because we're friends."

"Friends." Skrrzzzt mulled over the word, then spread his leathery lips in a gaping smile. "Hell yes, we are!" He chugged a beer. "You can count on good ole Skrrzzzt. I'll be there."

"Okay," I said. "I'll put you down for the night brigade."

He shot me an offended look with his molten-lava gaze. "What, you think I'm not good enough to fight in the light of day?"

I was confused. "I thought bogles only came out at night."

Skrrzzzt waved a dismissive hand. "Yeah, that's a personal choice. I'm not a freaking vampire, mamacita! Hey, if you'll give me a lift, I'll introduce you to a couple of trolls who live under a bluff down on the lakeshore."

I recruited the trolls, who were large and shaggy, and appeared to relish the idea of a good fight.

I recruited my mom's neighbor Gus the ogre, who was equally large and imposing and equally ready to give battle. "Anything for you and your mother, Daisy," he said in a voice like rocks grating, squaring shoulders the size of boulders and baring teeth like, well, smaller boulders in a terrifying grimace. "And this is *my* home, too!"

My mother was less sanguine. "I don't like this, honey," she said to me in the kitchen of her double-wide. Her blue eyes were troubled. "It scares me. It scares the hell out of me."

"Me, too," I admitted.

She searched my face. "Are you *sure* there's no way to stop this?"
*You have but to ask . . .*

I shuddered. "I'm open to suggestions. Got any?"

"No," Mom said in a rueful tone. "It's just . . . this shouldn't be your fight, Daisy."

"It shouldn't be any of our fights." I rubbed my tired eyes. "But I'm Hel's liaison. I accepted that responsibility."

"You didn't have any idea it would lead to this," she said quietly.

"No," I said. "I don't think Hel did, either. I don't know if anyone did. Maybe the Norns."

"As in the Norn who told you the fate of the world might hinge on your decisions?" Mom asked. "The Norn who told you to trust your heart?"

*El Corazón*, my heart.

"Yep."

"And what does your heart tell you?" she asked.

I sighed. "It tells me I can't back out of this responsibility. Especially not now, now that I've recruited practically the entire eldritch community. Other than that, nothing."

Mom kissed my forehead. "Keep listening."

# Fifty

The Fairfax clan were the last significant members of the eldritch community to commit to the battle.

Cody stopped by the police station on his day off to tell me. "We're in," he said briefly. "Elders and adult singles only. No teenagers, no parents with small children."

I nodded. "That's more than fair. Does, um, that mean you're including yourself among the fighters?"

"Yeah." He raked a restless hand through his bronze hair. "You know, I was always afraid I'd have to make this choice someday. But one of the reasons I became a police officer was to be in a position to protect my clan." He fished his badge out of his coat pocket. "Right now, I can't do both. I have to choose one or the other. And I choose my clan."

I raised my eyebrows. "You're turning in your badge?"

Cody shrugged. "Better than waiting to get fired for disobeying orders, don't you think?"

"Not really," I said. "I was going with the whole 'it's easier to ask for forgiveness than permission' thing."

Cody gave a humorless laugh. "Yeah, well, if we lose this war, I won't have a home to return to, so the job doesn't really matter, does it?" He shuddered. "God, it's scary, Daise! Where would we go? You heard the wolves at the mixer. They've barely got room to breathe. The world's getting too small for us."

"I know," I whispered. "Believe me, you're not alone. It's all that I've been hearing out there."

Chief Bryant opened the door of his office and poked his head out. "Oh, good. Fairfax, a word? You, too, Daisy."

Exchanging uncertain glances, Cody and I entered his office.

"Have a seat." The chief gestured to a pair of empty chairs across from his desk, settling his bulk into his own chair. He laced his hands across his ample belly, regarding us with his heavy-lidded gaze. "You know, I've been thinking about that mermaid we rescued last summer. You remember the one?"

As if anyone could forget. "Yes, sir," I said.

The chief cleared his throat. "Recent events have made it easy to, ah, lose sight of the fact that the nonhuman members of the community deserve the protection of our fine department, too." He raised one thick finger. "Now, my hands are tied. The law is the law, and I'm sworn to enforce it." Swiveling in his chair, he glanced at the calendar on the wall behind him. March 20, the first day of spring, was circled in red marker. It was three days away. "But I'm thinking it's for the best if the two of you are put on administrative leave for the rest of the week."

"So you're saying . . . ?" I let the question dangle.

Chief Bryant leaned back, his desk chair creaking. "I'm saying I'm on your side, Daisy," he said quietly. "There's nothing I can do to help you, but I'll try to stay out of your way as long as I can. And if Pemkowet survives this war, you'll have jobs to come back to."

It mattered more than I would have expected. A ragged half sob of gratitude escaped me. "Thank you, sir!"

Rising from his chair, Cody extended a hand across the chief's desk. "I won't forget this."

Chief Bryant clasped his hand. "See that you don't, son."

Three days.

*Three days.*

Crap, they went so fast.

The news of the impending battle had spread throughout Pemkowet, and the mood in town was strained and sober. The initial exhilaration that Persephone's offer had evoked had given way to a horrified seller's remorse at the realization of the repercussions. Everywhere I went, people asked me what I thought was going to happen, and all I could do was say I didn't know.

In an effort to get insight from the one person who might, I visited the library and asked the Sphinx for advice, but all she did was stare at me with those odd, luminous brown eyes of hers until I began twitching my tail with discomfort, at which point the Sphinx informed me that she'd already given me all the counsel I needed.

Right. Learn to see with the eyes of the heart. *El Corazón* again, no more helpful than before.

In a surprising show of support, Amanda Brooks agreed to let Hel's ragtag army set up a base camp on the old Cavannaugh property, the wedge of undeveloped land adjacent to Little Niflheim that had been in her family for generations. Between the lawsuit and the purchase of Hel's territory, Dufreyne hadn't bothered to pursue the acquisition of the Cavannaugh property, no doubt confident that Amanda would be willing to accept a much lower offer once her slice of untrammeled wilderness was overshadowed by a hulking resort complex.

I hoped that was a decision he'd have cause to regret.

If nothing else, the campsite gave us a great vantage point. We set up our operation on a long ridge of dune dotted with cottonwood trees and gnarled jack pines, high above the basin from which Yggdrasil II emerged to pierce the heavens and tower above the landscape. The formidable figure of the hellhound Garm appeared and disappeared as he patrolled the area in a tireless circuit, padding on paws the size of tractor tires. Garm glanced up a few times when Stefan and I first scouted the place, but apparently it was at enough of a remove that the hellhound would tolerate our presence.

Hel's army was a motley crew. Members of the Outcast arrived on modified dirt bikes and ATVs, armed with assault rifles; members of the Fairfax clan churned across the sand in Jeeps and pickup trucks, armed with hunting rifles and camping gear.

My bogle pal, Skrrzzzt, arrived on foot with half a six-pack of beer, armed with a baseball bat and a deck of playing cards. He got a game of poker going with Gus the ogre and the two trolls, who arrived armed with clubs. Mrs. Browne arrived armed with a broom and a basketful of fresh bread and pastries.

There were a number of hobgoblins who arrived and promptly disguised themselves as shrubs, so I never did get a head count.

There were fairies who came and went on whirring wings, scouting and reporting—Ellie the hellebore fairy, and some of the early spring flower fairies, crocuses and snowdrops and delicate blue hepatica.

The sight of so many members of the eldritch community in one place was wondrous and amazing. It made my heart ache with love and terror, because so many of them looked so goddamn vulnerable.

The campsite wasn't without its tensions. As the leader of the Outcast, not to mention a six-hundred-year-old knight, Stefan had assumed command of the operation, which didn't sit well with the Fairfax clan. With less than twenty-four hours before the first day of spring was upon us, those tensions erupted.

"I don't care how many battles you've seen—you can't tell a man to lay down his gun!" Elijah Fairfax snarled at Stefan. "And you sure as hell can't tell a wolf pack how to *hunt*!" Other members of the clan uttered low growls of assent.

Stefan's eyes glittered. "The only access road across Hel's territory leads them there." He pointed to the far side of the vast bowl. "And right now, we don't know for a surety what kind of army we're facing. We don't know whether you'll be of more use as humans or wolves."

"He's right," Cody said unexpectedly. "If we cache our weapons in the woods behind their lines, we can shift, retrieve them, and flank the enemy."

Cody's uncle rounded on him. "You'd take orders from a ghoul over the head of your clan?"

Cody stood his ground, his upper lip curling. "I've had a bellyful of your orders, Uncle Elijah," he said grimly. "But that's got nothing to do with it. This isn't a hunt and it's a hell of a lot bigger than any police action I've seen. It's a goddamn war, and Ludovic understands tactics."

"To a point. No one has ever seen such a war." Stefan deferred to me. "Hel's liaison, ultimately the choice of who commands here is yours."

God, that was a responsibility I didn't want. I looked back and forth between Stefan and Cody. "Can the two of you work together?"

Stefan inclined his head to me. "Yes."

"It wouldn't be the first time," Cody reminded me.

That was true. I owed my life to the two of them working together. "Co-commanders, then." I turned to Elijah Fairfax and the other were-wolves. "And we can't afford any of that hierarchical bullshit. Not now. I don't care if Cody's not the head of the clan. He's right. You're not hunting deer on the back forty here. Cody's a trained cop with good instincts, and I want you to follow his orders. Understand?"

Elijah muttered something into his beard.

I laid my hand on *dauda-dagr*'s hilt. "As Hel's liaison, I'm asking you a question. Do you understand?"

His eyes flashed green. "Yes."

I relaxed. "Good."

"Daise?" Cody cleared his throat. "Speaking of Hel, it would be really helpful if we knew what Little Niflheim's plans were so we could coordinate with their efforts. Can you find out?"

"I planned to make the same suggestion," Stefan agreed, glancing toward the basin. "It is difficult to know how we may proceed while the hellhound menaces friend and foe alike."

It was a good point.

"I need to pick up a few things from home," I said. "If Hel doesn't summon me herself, I'll request an audience."

It was Cooper who gave me a ride back to my car, which was parked on the unpaved access road that led to the old Cavannaugh property. I held tight to the sissy bar affixed to the back of his dirt bike as we jounced over the loose, sandy terrain. "Go and fetch what you need, m'lady," he said to me, pulling over and nudging the kickstand down with one heel. "I'll wait here for you."

In my apartment, I retrieved the iron casket containing scales of bark from Yggdrasil II that I'd stashed in the top shelf of my bedroom closet. Mogwai wound around my ankles, purring loudly. I have to admit, being back in my apartment felt familiar and comfortable and safe. There was a part of me that wanted to stay, to lock the door, hunker down, and let the battle take place without me. Mom was right. This shouldn't have to be my fight.

Except it was.

I filled Mogwai's bowl to overflowing with kibble. Since cell phone reception was sketchy out in the dunes, I took the opportunity to call Jen and tell her how much I valued our friendship, and ask her to take care of my cat if anything happened to me.

I called Chief Bryant and asked him to tell people to stay inside and off the street tomorrow, because I didn't know what might happen if or when the Wild Hunt was unleashed.

And I called my mom and told her that I loved her.

After that, I grabbed an extra sweater, stripped one of the pillowcases from my bed, and drove back to meet Cooper.

# Fifty-one

Cooper eyed me. "What's the pillowcase for?"

"Truce flag," I said briefly.

He raised his fair brows at me. "You think to bargain with the goddess Persephone herself, then?"

I shook my head. "I think to *beg*, Cooper. It's the only move I've got left."

His pupils dilated. "Sure, and you know that's not true. If *I* had your leverage, I'd bargain."

"How?" I challenged him. "And for what?"

"How?" Cooper gave a bleak laugh. "Don't ask me, m'lady. I thought to drive a bargain on the gallows, but the divvil himself wouldn't have it. But for what?" His ancient eyes gleamed in his narrow seventeen-year-old's face. "Me, I'd just like a chance to grow to a man's full stature."

"I know," I murmured.

Cooper gunned the dirt bike. "Hold tight."

By the time we returned to the campsite, it was late afternoon on what was technically the last day of winter. I was hoping that some of Persephone's forces might have moved into place in advance of her arrival, which would have given us the opportunity for some fey-style sabotage and vampiric terrorism in the middle of the night, but our scouts were reporting everything was quiet.

The campsite looked great, though. When I'd left, it had been nothing but a few tents pitched below the denser cover of a stand of white pines, with a path leading to the lookout point. In the hour I'd been gone, Mrs. Browne had transformed the campsite into something from the set of a Peter Jackson movie, the aboveground equivalent of a hobbit hole. Churned sand and pine mast had been swept smooth, obliging branches woven into snug little shelters. A teakettle hung from a spit above a lively campfire, whistling a merry tune.

"Here ye go, dearie." Mrs. Browne handed me a steaming mug of tea. "It'll warm your bones."

She was right. It tasted of ginger and cinnamon, and it spread a pleasant warmth all through me. "Than—" I caught myself before thanking her. Brownies had very specific rules governing their magic. You can't ask them for assistance, and it's dangerous even to thank them for it. Compliments were okay, though. I smiled at her. "It's delicious, Mrs. B."

If Mrs. Browne had been human, I would have said she flushed with pleasure. "Oh, it's nothing, nothing at all," she said modestly before bustling on to another chore.

Even if we did have a much nicer place to wait than anticipated, the waiting made me antsy.

I talked to my co-commanders, Stefan and Cody, about my plan to approach Persephone under a flag of truce and beg her to call off the war.

Unsurprisingly, neither of them approved.

I listened patiently to their arguments, the gist of which was that it was a pointless risk, dangerous and unlikely to succeed.

"You might be right," I said calmly. "In fact, you probably *are* right. But I'm doing it anyway."

Stefan's jaw was rigid with tension. "I'm tempted to forbid you," he said in an ominous voice. Beside him, Cody uttered a low growl of agreement.

Great, the two of them had found common cause. "I have to try," I said. "What kind of liaison would I be if I didn't at least *try*?"

Cody and Stefan exchanged a glance. "Then I will accompany you," Stefan said in a quieter tone.

"No." Cody shook his head. "I'll go."

I raised my voice. "We can't spare either of you! Hell, we can't spare anyone. I'll go alone."

They didn't like it, but in the end they agreed.

I didn't have to request an audience with Hel that evening. The sun had barely sunk behind the dunes in the west when Mikill's dune buggy roared out of Yggdrasil II's entrance and charged up the side of the basin, skidding a little in the loose sand as it crested the rise.

"Daisy Johanssen." The frost giant's voice was somber. "I am bid to summon you to an audience with Hel."

I got in the buggy. "Let's go."

It was unnerving to think that this might be my last visit to Little Niflheim; the last time I sent Garm bounding into the darkness after a loaf of bread; the last time Mikill warned me to keep my limbs inside the vehicle during the descent; the last time we spiraled down into the frigid cold, Mikill's dripping beard crackling with frost as it stiffened.

When we reached the bottom, I found that the *duegar* were nowhere in sight, but the streets—well, the one, anyway—of Little Niflheim were lined with spectral figures—ghosts, but more misty and insubstantial than those I'd encountered aboveground, many of them clad in attire that hadn't been in style for, oh, a couple thousand years.

None spoke, but all watched our passage.

"Who are they?" I asked Mikill in a hushed whisper. "What are they doing here? And where are all the dwarves?"

"The *duegar* prepare for battle. These are the dead of Niflheim." Mikill pulled up before the abandoned sawmill and cut the engine. "Tomorrow may be the end for all of us, Daisy Johanssen. The dead are here to bear witness."

I swallowed. "Oh."

As always, Hel sat upright on her throne. Both her eyes were open and blazing, but this time there were no thunderclouds gathering around her, no rumblings from the deep, no scary creaking overhead.

There was only a waiting silence fraught with a sense of foreboding that made the icy air feel thick and heavy in my lungs.

I went to one knee before her throne and bowed my head. "My lady."

"Rise, and tell me what passes aboveground, my young liaison," Hel bade me. I obeyed and she listened to my report, nodding with approval from time to time, especially at the mention of the Wild Hunt. "Yes, the immortal hunters who strike terror into the hearts of men are known to us from days of old. You have done well."

I cleared my throat. "My lady, may I ask what Little Niflheim plans in terms of battle?"

The left side of her face formed a grimmer rictus than usual. "Where the roots of Yggdrasil will bear it, the *duegar* lay traps beneath the shifting sands. The hellhound Garm will defend the world tree with his last breath." Turning her head from side to side, Hel acknowledged the three frost giants flanking her throne, and Mikill standing nearby, with a brief dip of her head.

"If Garm should fail, the four of us shall take his place," Mikill said in his quietest rumble.

"So . . . just to be clear, as far as Garm's concerned, there's no, um, cease-fire on the whole friends-versus-foes front?" I asked. "You can't teach him to, say, recognize your allies?"

A slight furrow etched the fair right half of Hel's brow. "The hellhound Garm will attack anyone who approaches the world tree, yes. Such is his immortal nature and purpose, which cannot be altered. Thus has it ever been, and thus shall it ever be. Is that what your inquiry was intended to discern?"

Crap. I suppose some supernatural Cesar Millan training techniques were too much to hope for. "Pretty much, yeah."

Hel closed her ember eye and gazed at me with the lambent one. "The world tree's roots are deep and vast. I shall remain here, pouring all the strength that is in me into them. For so long as this second Yggdrasil stands and the Norns may nourish its roots from the sacred spring, Niflheim endures. *I* endure."

I nodded. "So we defend Yggdrasil at all costs."

"Yes."

"Okay." I took a deep breath. "My lady, you should know that I plan to approach the, um, Greek Persephone under a flag of truce tomorrow, and beg her one last time to call this off."

Oops.

Hel's left eye opened, glaring with hellfire and fury. "You mean to *beg*?" Yep, there were those trembling rafters. "*Beg*? In *my* name?"

My knees were knocking, but I held my chin high, an answering anger stirring in me. "Yes, my lady. I do. But not in your name. You named me your liaison, and as such, I represent not just you but the entire community of your demesne, eldritch and mundane alike." I gestured overhead. "You're talking about my friends, my family. If we fail on the morrow—" God, again with the archaic language. "If we *lose* tomorrow," I said doggedly, "it doesn't just mean the demise of Little Niflheim. It means the destruction of my entire community. It means the loss of one of the few remaining places in the world where magic exists with space to roam free and wild, not dying a slow death in crowded cities. So, yes, I'm willing to beg on behalf of my people. *All* my people." I took another breath and exhaled, turning my hands palm outward. "What else do I have to offer other than my pride?"

Hel kept glaring.

Mikill approached the throne and murmured into Hel's ear. She closed her eyes and listened.

Mikill stepped back.

"Forgive me." Hel opened her lustrous right eye. "Betimes it takes the tender heart of a mortal to remind us of our duties." She bent her gaze on me. "I cannot bow my head to the Greek Persephone and beg for mercy. That is not the way of gods and goddesses. But I give you my leave to do so on behalf of your community."

I stifled a sigh of relief. "Thank you, my lady."

"Is there aught else?" Hel inquired.

I shook my head. "No, my lady."

The Norse goddess of the dead beckoned. "Then kneel before my throne one last time, Daisy Johanssen, and receive my blessing." As I knelt before the throne, Hel rose and laid both hands upon my head:

the fair white hand and the withered black claw. She spoke words that tolled through the depths of Little Niflheim in a language I didn't recognize, and I felt the power of her blessing settle into my bones, as deep and strong as the roots of the world tree, and as cold and crystalline as the waters of the sacred spring that nourished them.

With that, I was dismissed.

Mikill drove me back through the transparent ranks of the watching dead. Thinking about what had transpired, I asked him to slow down and stop for a moment as we approached the Norns, engaged in the endless chore of drawing buckets from the spring and watering Yggdrasil II's roots. They paused in their labor, but none of them spoke.

"Um, hi," I said awkwardly to the youngest Norn, the one who'd laid the soothsaying on me in the first place. "I just wondered . . . that thing Hel just said about the tender heart of a mortal . . . that wasn't what you meant when you told me to trust my heart, was it?"

After a moment's hesitation, the Norn who looked like a maiden gave her head an infinitesimal shake. The Norn who looked to be about my mom's age laid a hand over her heart, and the oldest Norn, the Norn who looked like a kindly grandma, pressed one silver-taloned finger to her lips.

All three of their misty, colorless eyes—well, all three Norns, all six eyes, you get the idea—began to shine with a bright white light, like those freaky angel schoolboys in "Total Eclipse of the Heart," which happens to be one of my mom's favorite music videos from her tween years.

"The Norns can reveal no more, Daisy Johanssen," Mikill said quietly. "Not without breaking the skein of time."

I waited until we emerged under the starlit sky to ask him a question. "So . . . what happens if the skein of time is broken?"

"The entirety of existence would unravel," he said in a matter-of-fact tone.

"The *entirety* of existence?" I echoed.

Mikill gave me a brief glance. "Yes."

"So what happens to the Norns if Yggdrasil falls?" I asked. "And what happens to the skein of time if the *Norns* pass?"

"It is as I have said. If Yggdrasil falls, it is the end for all of us." Mikill gunned the dune buggy up the steep slope of the bowl. "I believe it is unlikely that the passing of the Norns would break the skein of time," he shouted above the roar of the engine. "Even they are but one thread in it." As we hurtled over the crest, he downshifted and lowered his voice. "Although I may be mistaken," he added thoughtfully. "It is a deeply entangled thread."

Wolves swarmed out of the darkness, their eyes reflecting green in the dune buggy's headlights. Seeing it was us, they backed away. I stared at Mikill. "You believe it's *unlikely*? You may be *mistaken*?"

"Only the Norns know for a surety, Daisy Johanssen." Mikill put the buggy in park, letting the engine idle. "And they cannot say without—"

"Without breaking the skein of time," I finished for him. "I get it." I didn't know whether to laugh or cry. "No offense, but this would have been useful information to have earlier, Mikill."

"I did not realize you lacked it," the frost giant said simply. "Nonetheless, you possess it now."

"Yes," I said. "Yes, I do."

Mikill held out one massive pale-blue hand, gazing at me with his slush-colored eyes. "I wish you good fortune on the morrow."

I clasped his ice-cold hand. "And you."

# Fifty-two

It was quiet at the campsite.

There was no sign of the various trolls, ogres, and bogles. Stefan and Cooper were sitting and talking beside the campfire, which had burned low, but the rest of the Outcast had bunked down for the night. All of the Fairfax werewolves except Cody scattered after my return and headed for whatever dens they'd made for themselves, having relegated their camping equipment to the Outcast.

With wolf-Cody trotting at my side, I joined Stefan and Cooper.

"Do we have a strategy?" Stefan glanced up at me.

"Sort of." Mrs. Browne's teakettle was still whistling softly on the spit above the embers. I unhooked it and poured myself a mug of tea, then sat huddled on one of the surprisingly comfortable benches Mrs. Browne had fashioned out of deadfalls. "We need to protect Yggdrasil at all costs."

"And the hellhound?"

"Will attack friend and foe alike," I confirmed. "If Garm falls, four frost giants will take his place. The dwarves have laid traps beneath the sands. Oh, and there's a slight possibility that if we fail and the Norns perish, it will break the skein of time, and the entirety of existence will unravel." I blew on my hot tea. "I don't suppose either of you were aware of that particular fact?"

Stefan's incredulous stare probably looked a lot like mine had. With his nihilistic streak, Cooper looked less shocked, but apprehensive. The unraveling of existence sounded a lot like the eternal void of non-existence.

Cody . . . Cody's ears were pricked forward attentively, but I couldn't tell what was going through his wolfy head or how much he understood.

"No," Stefan murmured at length. "I was not aware."

Cooper gave a humorless laugh. "It's funny, innit?" he said. "This war . . . when you asked us to fight it, big man, I thought, why not? We all did. Loyalty's important to our kind, and win or lose, the Outcast would survive."

"According to Mikill, the broken-skein-of-time scenario is considered *unlikely*." I sipped my tea, eyeing Cody. "Would you care to shift and join the conversation?"

Cody laid down in the sand and rested his long muzzle across one foreleg. Apparently not.

I couldn't blame him. Right now, I'd rather be a wolf, too.

"This changes the stakes," Stefan mused. "Forgive me, Daisy. I was wrong to attempt to dissuade you from approaching Persephone."

I took another sip of tea. "She's a little nuts, Stefan. Do you think it will make a damn bit of difference to her?"

"*I* think we'd best pray it does." Cooper got to his feet abruptly. "And fight like blazes if it doesn't. All right, then. Since there's nothing else for it, I'm off for my bedroll." Following his lead, Cody rose smoothly and loped into the dark woods. I gazed after him, wondering what that was all about. Maybe it was easier for Cody-the-wolf than Cody-the-human to see Stefan and me together.

"Do you think Cody understood what we were talking about?" I asked Stefan.

He shook his head. "I cannot say, but we will speak on the morrow."

I moved over to sit beside him. "How likely do you think *unlikely* is?"

Stefan put his arm around me, and I nestled against his side. "I do not know the answer to that, either, Daisy."

We sat like that for a while, watching the shifting play of light and shadow in the dying embers.

Stefan pressed a kiss against my temple. "I would like to hold you in my arms tonight, Daisy, but I do not think it wise."

Neither did I, for a number of reasons. "I know."

"There will be other nights, Hel's liaison," Stefan said with a firm surety I wished I felt.

Leaning over, I kissed him. "There had better be."

I wasn't sure I'd be able to sleep that night with my mind reeling as it was, but as soon as I crawled into my old sleeping bag, nestled in a cozy woven shelter that Mrs. Browne had made for me, I was out like a light.

I had the nightmare, though.

Once again, I broke the world.

This time the familiar nightmare was mixed with images of the universe unraveling like a tapestry and laced with snippets of conversation echoing through my unconscious mind. I awoke to overcast skies, the smell of bacon frying, unexpected visitors, and the sense that I'd forgotten something important.

The bacon—bacon and eggs, actually—was courtesy of Mrs. Browne, who was hunkered by the campfire, a long-handled cast-iron skillet in one hand and a spatula in the other. Household brownies were one of the few fey who didn't abhor the touch of iron.

"Good morning, dearie!" she greeted me cheerfully, sliding a pair of perfectly cooked sunny-side-up eggs onto a tin plate, deftly snatching a few pieces of bacon from the skillet to accompany the eggs. "Eat hearty, child. 'Tis a big day today. No utensils, I fear, but there's trenchers of bread over yonder," she added.

Skrrzzzt ambled over with an empty plate and a hopeful look in his magma-glowing eyes. "Any chance of seconds, Mrs. B?"

Mrs. Browne whacked his hand with her spatula. "Leave the rest for the mortals, greedy-guts!"

Glancing around the campsite, I saw a dozen members of the Fairfax clan, now in human form, attacking plates of bacon and eggs with hunks of crusty bread. "Where did all this food come from?"

Mrs. Browne patted the picnic basket beside her. "Why, I brought it, dearie." She gave me an indulgent look. "Some things are bigger on the inside, you know."

I smiled at her. "So I've heard."

At that moment, we heard an uninvited vehicle approaching from behind our campsite. I wouldn't have thought a stretch Hummer limousine was actually capable of off-road travel, but damned if that wasn't what was making its way through the woods and across the dunes toward us.

For a few heart-stopping seconds, I thought it must be an ambush. Since the law was one of the tools Persephone had used against us, we'd assumed she would abide by it and that her attack on Hel's demesne would take place on property that was now legally hers. But no, it was too slow and clumsy an approach for an ambush, and the Outcast and the Fairfaxes had the Hummer surrounded in an instant. Stefan yanked the driver's door open, and the driver came out with her hands up.

"Oh, for goodness sake!" Lurine emerged from the rear of the giant limo. "We come in peace, sweetie."

Not just Lurine, but my mom, Jen, Lee, Sinclair, Stacey, Casimir . . . crap, the whole coven, my entire Scooby Gang, and a few other people, too.

"No," I said without thinking. "Oh, no, no, no!"

"Look, I know what you're thinking, Miss Daisy." Casimir came toward me, hands spread wide in a placating gesture. "But we might be able to help. With the whole coven here, we can cast a protection spell over the basin."

"Against a goddess?" I shouted at him. "Are you out of your mind?" I gestured toward my mom, Jen, and the others. "And what the hell are *they* doing here?"

"No one expects the protection spell to hold, Daisy," Mom said quietly. "We're here to bear witness."

"To bear—" It was what Mikill had said of the dead. I stared at my mother, at a loss for words.

"They're here under my protection, Daisy," Lurine announced. "I promise to keep them safe."

I transferred my stare to her. "Aren't you under the threat of a curse worse than death? And how are you going to keep them safe if Persephone brings a goddamn private *militia*?"

"I'm not intervening in the battle, cupcake," Lurine said. "But Persephone can't deny me the right to defend my friends."

"We'll retreat if we have to." It was Dawn Evans who spoke—Dawn Evans, who I realized had been driving the behemoth. She lifted her chin as I shifted my stare to her. "Ah told you ah drive a mean Humvee."

I shook my head in dismay. "I don't understand. Why?"

Dawn exchanged a glance with her husband, Scott, who had a hunting rifle slung over his shoulder. "What your mom said about bearing witness? She's right," he said simply. "And at least there's two of us here know what we're doing when it comes to a war zone." Lurine gave him a significant look and he flushed. "Or, um, three, I guess."

"Daisy, I have a feeling it's important," Sinclair said soberly to me. "I don't know how or why, but you need us here."

I turned around and walked away. My co-commanders Stefan and Cody—the latter back in human form—fell in beside me.

"It's your call, Daise," Cody said. "But if it were up to me, I'd send them away."

"I heard that!" Stacey shouted behind us. "You can't send us away. This is my family's property!"

Ignoring her, I walked farther down the path to the basin until I could see Yggdrasil II's immense trunk looming through the trees. El Arbol, the Tree.

"Do you think the young sorcerer may be right?" Stefan asked me in a quiet voice. "That their presence serves a purpose?"

I gazed at Yggdrasil II. "I don't know. But down in Little Niflheim, the dead have gathered to bear witness. Maybe it's fitting that the living should bear witness above. Especially if . . ." I glanced at Cody. "Did you catch that whole possible-unraveling-of-existence bit last night?"

"Yeah." He blew out his breath. "We understand things differently as wolves, but I understood it, all right."

I came to a decision and returned to the campsite to address my friends and family. "There's something you should know—" I began.

A snowdrop fairy burst into our midst, hovering on quivering wings, her head crowned with delicate, drooping white petals. "The invading goddess approaches!" she shrilled, pointing toward the north, just as we'd expected. "Half a league yonder! Her forces come in haste bearing cold iron!" The fairy shuddered with profound distaste. "Many vehicles and many men!"

Shit.

Cody and his relatives were already stripping in preparation to shift and take to the wooded dunes where they had their weapons cached. Belatedly, I hoped they'd remembered to cache spare clothes, too.

"Daisy!" Cooper called to me, straddling his dirt bike. "If you're going to get into position to meet Persephone, we've got to move *now*!"

"Never mind," I said to everyone. "I don't have time to explain. Stefan will do it if he can. Just know . . ." My voice caught in my throat. "Just know I love you all a lot, okay?" In that moment, I didn't even care that I'd included Stacey Brooks in my declaration.

"Daisy—" Mom began.

I shook my head at her. "I'm sorry. I've got to go."

Stopping briefly at the cozy nest Mrs. Browne had made me, I snatched the pillowcase I'd brought from home and shoved it in the pocket of my black leather jacket, then climbed onto the back of Cooper's bike.

We roared around the rim of the massive basin, fishtailing in the loose sand. It would have been a spectacular view if I hadn't been in a state of near shock. The lean forms of wolves streamed ahead of us, vanishing into the trees.

I was on my way to beg a demented Greek goddess for mercy, try to avert a war, and possibly the end of the entirety of existence.

And I was scared out of my fucking wits.

# Fifty-three

Cooper dropped me off on the far side of the rim. In the vastness of that space, he and his bike looked small as he made his way back to camp. Across the basin, our forces looked insubstantial as they spread out along the crest. Even the hellhound Garm didn't look that big from this vantage point.

Hell, everything looked small in the shadow of Yggdrasil II, standing as tall as a skyscraper. It seemed impossible that anything could possibly threaten it with serious harm.

Then again, a lot of people had felt that way about the World Trade Center. I shivered in the dank March chill, feeling very small and very alone.

I didn't feel alone for long or chilled, for that matter. A gust of warm wind carrying all the lush green and rich golden promise of summer with it announced Persephone's arrival. It soon mingled with the stink of diesel fumes as a long line of armored SUVs emerged from the crude access road that cut across Hel's territory. The snowdrop fairy hadn't been kidding. There were a lot of them.

I turned my back on the basin and Yggdrasil, facing the vehicles and raising my pillowcase over my head, holding it taut with both hands.

And yes, I felt pretty damn stupid doing it.

The SUVs fanned out and halted, disgorging dozens and dozens of men in high-tech black body armor, helmets and face masks rendering them anonymous. As one of them opened the passenger door of the lead vehicle and assisted Persephone out of it, the clouds parted overhead, sunlight spilling over the dunes.

Somewhere in the basin below, Garm let loose an uneasy howl.

"My lady Persephone!" I shouted, my arms trembling. "I'm here under a flag of truce. Can we talk?"

She looked mildly annoyed, but she nodded at the mercenary assisting her. "Bring her to me."

Two mercenaries escorted me to the goddess. The rest worked industriously at unloading arms and equipment I couldn't even begin to identify from the vehicles and setting it all up along the edge of the basin.

"What do you want, pretty Daisy?" Persephone looked me up and down. "As you can see, I'm quite busy. Also, you're trespassing," she added. "Though I'm willing to overlook it just the once."

"I've come to beg," I said simply.

She brightened. "Oh, well, then! Go right ahead."

"Please don't—"

With a faint scowl, Persephone flattened one hand, and I was driven to my knees in the sand as though struck by a pile driver. "You said you came to *beg*, pretty Daisy. Do so."

A rill of anger ran through me, but I quashed it mercilessly. I'd spoken bold words to Hel about offering up my pride, and I needed to make good on them. Gazing up at Persephone, I clasped my hands together. If it was begging she wanted, it was begging she would get. "Wise and beautiful goddess, I humbly implore—"

Her scowl deepened. "Don't make a mockery of it. Just speak from the heart, Daisy."

Out of the corner of my eye, I caught sight of Daniel Dufreyne emerging from one of the vehicles, his long coat and business suit contrasting incongruously with the armor-clad mercenaries. Bowing my head, I squelched another surge of anger.

In front of me, one delicate, sandal-shod foot tapped the sand impatiently beneath the hem of a diaphanous gown. "I'm waiting."

I looked up at Persephone's beautiful face. "Please don't do this," I said. "If you claim Hel's demesne, you'll be destroying a place I and many others call home. The world is growing too small. For many of the eldritch, there's nowhere left for them to go. And my lady . . . there's a chance that you could break the skein of time if you kill the Norns. There's a chance that you could unravel the entirety of existence. So I'm begging you, on behalf of everyone and everything that I hold dear, please, please don't do this."

Persephone's expression turned thoughtful. "How badly do you desire this boon, pretty Daisy? Would you be willing to renounce Hel's service for mine?" She stooped before me, her face close to mine. Her warm breath smelled of honey and pomegranates, and motes of sunlight danced around us both. "Would you renounce your family and friends, all that you hold dear, everything you've ever loved, and pledge yourself to serve me, and me alone?"

Somewhere in the background, Dufreyne coughed.

Blinking away tears, I whispered, "Yes. If that's what you require, my lady, yes."

"Let me consider it." Persephone tilted her head, sunlight pouring down the shining curtain of her hair. "No."

"My lady—"

"You haven't been listening to me," she interrupted me, holding up one finger. Hectic glints of gold shimmered in her eyes. "*I want my own demesne!*"

Emphasizing her point, Persephone jabbed me in the chest with her finger, driving the breath from my lungs and sending me flying backward, over the rim of the basin. It felt like I'd been hit by a truck. I tumbled head over heels down the steep slope, scrabbling at the loose sand, my chest heaving in a futile effort to suck in air. Below me, Garm gave a full-throated howl and headed for the slope.

Crap, no!

I managed to break my momentum. Breath or no breath, I scrambled up the face of the dune. There was shouting at the top. Someone grabbed me by the collar of my jacket and hauled me over the crest.

"You're welcome, Daisy," Dufreyne's smooth voice said.

I spat sand out of my mouth and drew in a wheezing breath redolent with his wrongness. "Fuck you!"

"You might want to cover your ears," he advised me.

Someone shouted, "Fire!"

I clapped my hands over my ears and whirled just in time to see one of the mercenaries launch a rocket-propelled grenade from a long tube over his shoulder at the charging figure of Garm, halfway up the slope and no longer looking anything less than massive.

My throat closed, but the missile veered unexpectedly away from the hellhound, exploding on the east side of the basin in a geyser of sand. Garm paused with an uncertain whine to gaze in the direction of the explosion, slobber dripping from either side of his jowls.

The mercenary examined the sight on his launcher. "What the fuck? Sorry, my lady," he added.

Persephone's dainty nostrils flared with disdain. "Mortal magic." She waved one careless hand like someone whisking away a fly, and there was a tinkling, splintering sound as the coven's hastily performed protection spell shattered. "There." She pointed across the basin toward our encampment, then rounded on me. "What manner of forces have you mustered?"

"Go to hell," I spat at her.

"No matter." Persephone tapped her lush lips in thought. "Send half your men to root them out," she said to the commander of the mercenaries. "Give no quarter. Meanwhile, proceed here as discussed and prepare the drones."

He saluted her. "My lady."

"Reload and fire on the hellhound," she said to the mercenary with the RPG. "Your missiles will fly true now."

After that, a lot of things happened, all of which I watched with helpless horror.

Garm was the first casualty. He'd padded out of range to investigate the explosion, but a couple of Persephone's men clambered down the dune to lure him back, shouting and waving. A convoy of ten SUVs was halfway around the rim of the basin, under ineffectual fire from the hunting rifles of members of the Fairfax clan attempting an ambush, when Garm came roaring back and charged the slope, yellow eyes blazing.

The first missile took him square between his glowing eyes, but Garm's skull must have been made of something denser than bone. It took a second missile to finish him. With a plaintive whine, the hellhound twice the size of a VW Beetle lay down in the sand and breathed his last.

Tears streamed down my face.

Across the basin, a lone figure stepped forth from a stand of cottonwood trees, a crown of antlers silhouetted against the sky. The convoy halted. The Oak King raised a horn to his lips and blew.

It was a wild sound, high and eerie, flung up into the cloudless sky. The sky echoed it back.

Clouds began to gather, dark and dense.

The Wild Hunt had arrived.

Spectral riders on spectral horses, they slanted down from the sky toward the convoy. Their leader had the face of a skull, its eye sockets filled with shadows and unholy glee, a gilded crown fused to his bony head.

The convoy scattered in terror, SUVs jolting west across the sandy terrain, plunging east into the basin. Some vehicles froze, armor-clad men spilling out to run on foot in a blind panic. With a rolling thunder of ghostly hoofbeats and a cacophony of horns, the Wild Hunt gave chase to everything that fled, wheeling and dividing in the sky above them.

"Hold fast!" Persephone shouted, her voice ringing with fury. "They cannot harm you!"

Maybe she was right, although I had my doubts—the Night Hag had killed poor old Irma Claussen with sheer terror—but there were other combatants on the field now. In the basin, a sinkhole opened up beneath an SUV, miring its rear half in the sand. Knotty figures of *duegar* emerged from hidden burrows, swarming the vehicle. Mikill and the other three frost giants strode forth from Yggdrasil II's entrance, armed with shields and battle-axes.

Across the basin, the eldritch entered the fray, Stefan and the Outcast leading the charge over the rim on dirt bikes, Gus the ogre and others following on foot. In the dunes to the west, I could hear sporadic gunfire and the yipping and howling of wolves on the hunt. Some of the Fairfaxes must have decided to give chase as wolves.

"Never mind." Persephone turned her back on the battle to address her mercenary commander. "The sooner we take down the tree, the fewer casualties. Are the drones ready?"

He looked pale and unsure. "Yes, my lady. But—"

Persephone laid one hand on his arm, gazing into his face. "But what?"

The uncertainty in the mercenary commander's face vanished, giving way to adoration. "Nothing, my lady."

Drones.

It hadn't registered when she'd said it before. The equipment the mercenaries had set up along the rim, tubes with tripod legs . . . those were *drones*. As in remotely controlled unmanned missiles, the kind of things the U.S. military used for terrorist strikes and God knows what else.

"No," I said in unthinking denial. "Oh, God! Please, no."

Everyone but Daniel Dufreyne, who arched an eyebrow in my direction, ignored me. The commander barked orders about securing the perimeter, and a contingent of mercenaries peeled off and spread out behind us.

"Launch the bird!" the commander shouted.

One of the tubes spat out a missile, its wings snapping open in midair. It looked more like a child's toy than a deadly weapon as it soared over the basin toward Yggdrasil II. Even the viewfinder the mercenary used to guide it reminded me of something from a vintage toy store. It was the real deal, though.

"Remember, it's just like bull's-eyeing womp rats in your T-16 back home," the commander joked.

"Roger that," the mercenary with the viewfinder replied without looking up.

The drone soared over the basin, over the combatants, who paused uncertainly to look up.

It soared straight into Yggdrasil II's entrance.

"It's pitch-black in there," the mercenary operating the drone complained. "I can't see—"

There was an explosion somewhere in the sands deep beneath us, and Yggdrasil creaked and groaned in anguish.

"No," I whispered.

The mercenary glanced up from his viewfinder. "Don't think I got all the way down to the roots."

"Don't worry," the commander said. "You'll get her on the next try."

"No!" I flung myself at the mercenary before he could fire a second drone, knocking over his launch tube. Hands dragged me away. "Look at this!" I shouted at Persephone, gesturing at the basin. The Wild Hunt had abandoned the battlefield and was receding toward the west in pursuit of their victims, the sounds of their horns fading as they ran their prey to ground, but battle was raging fiercely below us. The mercenaries who hadn't fled before the Wild Hunt were scrambling to find solid ground, leaving their mired vehicles and regrouping in tight clusters. They shot at the eldritch with frantic abandon, assault rifles sounding in staccato bursts.

I saw Stefan's second lieutenant, Rafe, go down in a hail of bullets, his ATV rolling over as his blood spattered the sand; and I saw Rafe reincorporate in the blink of an eye, crawling behind his fallen vehicle and reaching for his weapon while Stefan covered him.

The frost giants laid about them right and left with their battle-axes, bullets ringing against their shields. One of the mercenaries let out a terrible scream as a frost giant's axe sheared through his armor to sever his left arm at the elbow, blood spurting.

This was what war looked like.

The *duegar* swarming from beneath the sands sought to drag Persephone's troops back toward their root-laced burrows.

The mercenaries fired on the *duegar*. They fired on the surprisingly ferocious hobgoblins who scuttled into the fray, fighting tooth and nail. Even as I watched, a mercenary with an assault rifle blew away a hobgoblin, only to be struck down from behind with one blow of Gus the ogre's boulder-size fist. One of the trolls went down like an avalanche under a barrage of gunfire.

I felt sick. "How can you *do* this?"

"Do you jest?" Persephone's face was alight with happiness, beautiful and dreadful. She laughed, opening her arms wide, and sunlight radiated all around her. "I've never felt so alive!"

"You could destroy *everything*!" I said helplessly. "Are you willing to take that chance?"

"Oh, I suspect the Norse Hel is merely trying to frighten me. But if I'm wrong . . ." She tilted her head and gazed up at the sun, eyes filled with bliss. "It will have been worth it for this moment."

"Launch the next bird!" the commander ordered.

The second drone took out Mikill. The frost giants had realized the threat the little remote-controlled airplanes presented to Yggdrasil, but they were clever enough not to tip their hand. At the last instant before the second drone dove into the vast opening, Mikill lunged in front of it, his huge form exploding into a million shards of pale-blue ice. Another frost giantess stepped forward to take his place, raising her battle-axe to strike the next drone.

I was shaking with fury, too sick for tears.

"Let's get another bird in the air," the mercenary commander said, gazing through binoculars. "Take this big fucker out with an RPG, then send the bird through before another one blocks the egress."

Wave after wave of helpless rage washed over me. My hair rose, floating on the charged air. The military equipment began to tremble. I let the fury come, let it rise to a crescendo.

If it exploded the ordnance atop the rim and blew us all to Kingdom Come, so be it. Hell, I hoped it would.

"Oh, I don't *think* so!" Persephone said in alarm. She blew softly in my direction, a breeze of nectar surrounding me.

My fury remained unchanged, but the charge in the air dissipated, my hair settling.

Dufreyne smiled, dusted his lapels, and mouthed something at me, echoing my father's voice in my head.

*You have but to ask.*

I gazed at the chaotic skirmishes taking place in the basin, trying to see with the eyes of my heart. I saw Cooper take a bullet to the head, vanish for an instant, then reincorporate and return fire. I saw Skrrzzzt and Mrs. Browne fighting back to back, laying about them with a baseball bat and an enchanted broom. Somewhere deep below us, Hel sat on her throne, pouring the last of her immortal strength into Yggdrasil's roots.

"Third time's the charm," the commander said in a brisk tone. "Let's do this! Launch the next bird."

The distant figures of my mother and my friends were clustered on the far side of the rim, bearing witness to the imminent death of a goddess and the end of Pemkowet as we knew it, maybe to the end of existence.

My heart ached for them, ached for us all.

My heart, that thing I was supposed to trust, was telling me one thing, and one thing only.

I couldn't let this happen.

Dropping to one knee, I drew *dauda-dagr* and began etching a sigil in the sand.

# Fifty-four

"Daisy, *no!*"

I heard Stefan's faint shout of alarm in the distance and ignored it. His dirt bike roared toward the slope, faltered at the sound of gunfire, then roared again. I concentrated on finishing the sigil to summon my father.

Persephone grabbed me by the hair and yanked me to my feet, causing me to drop *dauda-dagr* in the process. "What have you done?" she demanded.

I didn't answer.

She scuffed out the sigil with one sandaled foot. "Well, it's undone now, pretty Daisy."

I could still see the traces of lines I'd drawn glowing faintly in the sand, the sight filling me with a dizzying blend of horror and disbelief. "No, I don't think so. You can't erase what was etched in earth with iron that easily. What was done is done."

Behind us was more gunfire.

"Shoot the ghoul's legs out from under him!" Dufreyne shouted impatiently. "Stop *killing* him!"

"Stay out of this!" Persephone whirled on him. "Stand down!" she ordered her men. "Let the Outcast approach!"

And then Stefan was there, his hands gripping my shoulders. His motorcycle jacket was ragged with bullet holes, and I wondered how many times he'd died just to get to me. "Daisy, do not do this thing." There was only a razor-thin line of blue around his pupils, but he wasn't ravening. Not yet. "Let me help."

At the sight of his face, something clicked inside me, and I understood. I understood what my heart and my half-remembered dreams had been trying to tell me. There was a way through this . . . maybe. At least there was hope. That had been the last card in my mother's reading. *La Estrella*, the Star—one last faint glimmer of hope. I tried to pull away. "Stefan, no. I *have* to do this."

Stefan shook his head, fingers digging into my shoulders. "No, you don't." He drew on the connection between us, draining my horror and fury and resolve. "It's all right, Daisy. I promised you. I won't let it happen."

"Stop!" I begged, shoving ineffectually at him with my empty hands. "I know what I'm doing!"

Stefan kept draining me, and I realized I should have kindled a shield, realized I no longer had the strength to do so. It was happening all over again. The razor-thin line of blue was vanishing.

In another few seconds, Stefan would be ravening. I caught my breath in a broken sob as terror blossomed and faded inside me. In another few seconds, I would forget what I'd intended to do in the first place.

Out of the corner of my eye, I saw a lean streak of tawny-gray fur launch itself at Stefan, taking him down with a silent snarl. Man and wolf tumbled and grappled in the sand.

"Shoot the wolf!" Persephone ordered.

"No!" Dufreyne countermanded his mistress, turning on the reverb. "Everyone hold your fire!"

Someone got a shot off before his powers of persuasion took effect, a lone crack of gunfire.

The wolf yelped in pain and shifted. Cody lay naked on the sand, pressing his hand to a wound on his side, blood spilling through his fingers. "Whatever you've got to do, just do it, Daise," he said in a ragged voice.

A few yards away, Stefan was climbing arduously to his feet, grimacing and clutching his shoulder.

I wished I'd had more time—time to explain, time to seek advice, time to think this through. A month, a day, an hour . . . hell, even five minutes would be a gift. But time was something I didn't have. In the space of a few heartbeats, Stefan would be on me again, and this time, he *would* drain me. Persephone wouldn't allow Dufreyne to interfere again. She would make sure it happened. She'd let Stefan drain me until I was an empty husk, no longer a threat to her plans, and then she'd order her troops to launch the third drone; and if that one didn't succeed, another and another, until Yggdrasil's mighty roots were blasted and destroyed, and Hel and the Norns with them, and a tangled thread in the skein of time was broken, and the entirety of existence might or might not unravel.

All I could do was trust my heart, no matter how much the prospect of what I was about to do horrified me.

Closing my eyes, I held the image of the sigil in my mind and spoke the words I'd never thought I'd say. "Belphegor! Father! I invoke my birthright!"

The ground beneath my feet trembled.

My father's face swam in the darkness behind my eyes, dipping toward me. His eyes were as black as my own, and long curved horns jutted from his temples. *Daughter, you have done well.*

Power filled me.

It didn't happen slowly like it had in my dream. It came all at once in a rush, exploding outward from the center of my chest. Brightness ran through my veins, and I blazed like a noonday star.

I opened my eyes.

No one had moved. Stefan looked at me with a profound mixture of pity and regret, then turned away, averting his face. Almost everyone else, even Persephone, gazed at me with fear and awe. Dufreyne was grinning with unholy glee, and I understood that he'd spoken the truth. I could taste hellfire and brimstone on my tongue, and the taste of it was sweet. With the full power of an apex faith at my command, I could bend even a goddess to my will.

I could bid the mercenaries to lay down their weapons; I could order the fighting to cease. I could banish Persephone. I could protect my community, everything I loved, and never, ever have to feel helpless again.

It was a glorious feeling.

But it came with a terrible price.

As it had in my dream, a clap of earsplitting thunder sounded as a jagged crack tore open the sky above us. Men fell to their knees in the sand, crying out in terror and covering their ears. In the basin, all fighting came to a halt. Atop the rim, only Persephone, Dufreyne, Stefan, and I remained standing. I wondered if my mother was standing or kneeling on the other side of the basin. I wondered if she'd turned her face away from me, too.

A clarion trumpet blast sounded a call to arms, and golden radiance a thousand times brighter than sunlight spilled through the crack in the sky.

There was darkness, too—darkness shimmering like a doorway over the dunes, and I saw in it my father, Belphegor, and a legion of demons behind him. Apparently the gates of hell couldn't be flung open wide until the gates of heaven were, which was a good thing, since I hadn't considered the alternative.

On the ground, Cody gazed at me with half-lidded eyes, his gaze steady. The sand beneath him was dark with blood and his breath was shallow, but at least he was still breathing.

I clenched my fists, feeling the leashed lightning in them, and lifted my face to the sky. "Look, I'm willing to take it back!" I shouted to the heavens. "But I want to bargain!"

"You can't *take it back*!" Daniel Dufreyne said incredulously, rounding on Persephone. "Can she?"

"How should I know, traitor?" Her tone was cool. "Mayhap she can. She has not yet used the power she invoked."

I waited.

Nothing happened.

"Come on!" I shouted. "You bargained with Abraham! You had big plans for him, remember?" I gestured all around me. "You can't tell me *this* is your last, best plan for humanity! You can't be finished with us yet, God. There's got to be more." I took a deep breath. "*Tikkun olam*, right? Give us a chance to repair the world! Give me the chance to mend *my* world!"

Stefan turned back toward me, a look of realization dawning over his features.

Overhead, the golden brilliance intensified, narrowing to a shaft, and then a single point blazing across the sky, falling toward us like a meteor.

It was an angel.

It was a motherfucking *angel*.

It didn't look like any painting of an angel I'd ever seen, at least from what I *could* see. Its face was almost too bright to look at and its hair streamed like fire. It was at least three times the size of a tall man, and it had six wings that shifted in constant motion, wings covered in a myriad of golden eyes that opened and closed ceaselessly. I don't know if this makes any sense, but the angel looked like the word *glory* made incarnate, and if I hadn't been filled with infernal power, I'm pretty sure I would have been gibbering on the ground.

The angel bent its radiant face toward me and spoke in a voice that rang like giant chimes. "*You presume much.*"

It was a simple statement of fact, no judgment or anger in it. Somehow that chilled me more than anger would have. "I know."

A dozen golden eyes on its nearest wing regarded me. "*What is it you seek?*"

The mind does strange things under duress. I had a horrible urge to answer with a quote from a Monty Python movie, and fought the desire to burst into hysterical laughter.

Or hysterical tears. I was close to either.

"I want to save Little Niflheim," I said. "I want Hel's demesne to be protected in perpetuity. I want mortality and a chance for redemption granted to the Outcast, and whatever . . . whatever loophole or crack that they fell through in the first place closed forever."

Several golden eyes closed. *"Once the Inviolate Wall is restored, heaven can grant no such protection on the mortal plane."*

Holy crap, I was bargaining with God. "Okay." My voice was shaking. "But you can save Little Niflheim if I give back my birthright? And free the Outcast?"

Massive wings stirred the air and the chiming voice turned stern. *"With God all things are possible. But know that if you renounce this power, it will be forever. Do not think to seek a second bargain."*

A wave of exhilaration filled me. "I know," I said breathlessly. "And trust me, I won't. I promise. Does that, um, mean we have a bargain?"

There was a long moment of silence in which the angel became motionless. Radiance continued to blaze from its face and stream from its hair, but its ever-shifting wings had gone still, the multitude of golden eyes adorning them closing as it considered my offer and conferred with God.

All at once, every single golden eye opened. *"Yes."*

Although I didn't dare do it, I was torn between cheering aloud and bursting into tears of relief.

Turning to Persephone, the angel extended one hand. A shaft of illumination brighter than sunlight burst forth from its palm, bathing her in brilliance. *"The world is not yours to destroy, little goddess."* There was a gentleness to the chimes. *"Be healed of this madness. Renounce this demesne and return to your own."*

Persephone gave a choked gasp of assent.

The angel spread all six of its wings, and bright shafts of golden light arrowed from all of its eyes. *"All who were cast out of the fold shall be returned to it."* It folded its wings and bent its face toward Stefan, who was now kneeling in the sand. *"Spend your mortality wisely."*

"I will," Stefan whispered in awe, tears in his eyes.

I thought we were done with heaven's end of the bargain, but the angel wasn't finished. It turned to Daniel Dufreyne, and the stern note returned to its chiming voice. *"For your role in breaching the Inviolate Wall, the unholy birthright to which you laid claim is revoked."*

Be careful what you wish for, right? Dufreyne cried aloud in denial and loss, and there was no reverb in it. "No!"

The angel turned back to me. *"Now."*

I approached the shimmering doorway of darkness where Belphegor and the legions of hell awaited.

Belphegor's horns gleamed like obsidian. I could imagine the same weight on my brow. I could have manifested horns if I'd wanted, or a proper devil's tail, or wings like a bat. They were all just visual manifestations of the infernal power that blazed inside me, the power to compel multitudes.

The power that I was about to relinquish forever.

It was surprisingly hard.

It was also very, very unnerving to stand before my father, only a thin veil of darkness between us.

"Hi, Dad," I said with a facetiousness I didn't feel. "Sorry, I guess I must be a disappointment to you. Then again, I guess that's what you get for raping an innocent young woman. But you know what? There's something Mom always wanted you to know. When you chose her, you messed with the wrong girl."

Belphegor smiled, and it was a smile filled with an impossible mixture of cruelty and amusement. His voice echoed in my thoughts. *Daughter, you struck a bargain with heaven today. Whatever you are, it is not a disappointment.*

I really, really didn't expect to find that my demon father's approval warmed my heart a little bit.

I would think about what the hell that meant later.

"Okay." I drew in one last breath with brightness singing in my veins, reveling in the sensation for a few more precious heartbeats. "Father! Belphegor! I renounce my birthright, now and forever!"

The power left as abruptly as it had filled me, snuffed out like a candle flame. A cry of anguish I couldn't stifle escaped me. The doorway onto hell vanished, taking my father and its legions with it.

I gazed at my hands, weak and empty, before turning to face the angel. "It's done."

The angel's voice chimed over the dunes as it spread its wings, rising aloft. *"Farewell."*

It departed like a meteor in reverse, a shining figure arcing into the broken sky. One last burst of golden radiance emanated from the jagged crack in heaven's vault as the angel passed through it, and then the crack sealed itself and vanished.

The Inviolate Wall was intact once more.

It was over.

# Fifty-five

In the wake of the angel's departure, Persephone fell to her knees in the sand, burying her face in her hands and uttering a heartrending cry. "Ah, no! What have I done?"

Even with the devastation she'd wrought, I couldn't help but pity her. "You've made a terrible mistake, my lady," I murmured.

"Yes." Lifting her head, she gazed at me with sun-spangled eyes. "Forgive me, young Daisy. I will do what I may to rectify it. The title to the Norse Hel's demesne shall be restored to you."

Daniel Dufreyne cleared his throat. "You're under no legal obligation—"

"Be silent!" Persephone drew herself upright, regal and shining. "Call a cease-fire. We shall withdraw from the battlefield. Bid your warriors to retrieve their wounded and dead," she said to her mercenary commander. "I will make restitution to their families."

The commander bowed his head to her. "My lady."

"May I point out that the company we contracted signed a release indemnifying—" Dufreyne caught her glare and fell silent.

As long as they were leaving, that was good enough for me.

I retrieved *dauda-dagr* and found Stefan at Cody's side, pressing a bandanna against his gunshot wound. "How is he?"

"Weak from loss of blood," Stefan said. "But I think the bullet passed through cleanly and struck no vital organs."

"How are *you*?" I asked.

Stefan paused. "The wolf has done some damage to my shoulder, but it will heal. Beyond that, I do not know how to answer you, Daisy," he said simply. "Except to say that I am very, very grateful."

"You took one hell of a risk today, Pixy Stix," Cody whispered with the ghost of a smile. "Holy shit! I'm just glad the world's still standing."

Tears stung my eyes. "Oh, shut up and save your strength, will you?"

Cody closed his eyes. "Okay."

If war was chaos, the aftermath wasn't a lot better.

The mercenaries packed their gear and retrieved their fallen comrades with unnerving efficiency, or at least all of their comrades that they could find. The Wild Hunt was still out there giving chase to those who had fled the battlefield in the initial panic. Horns echoed faintly in the distance, a reminder that there were things in the world that, once unleashed, no one could take back. Field medics administered first aid to the wounded, and a few motionless figures were hustled quickly out of sight. There would be no final tally of the casualties until the next day dawned.

The gnarled figures of the elusive *duegar* scurried around the woods and dunes, gathering deadfalls and loose branches, heaping a cairn of dry wood over the massive corpse of the hellhound Garm in preparation for a funeral pyre.

There would be no pyre for Mikill.

All that was left of the frost giant I'd come to consider a friend was shards of ice melting into the sand.

There had been other losses.

The surviving troll sat slumped on the blood-soaked sand, mourning for his fallen mate. The indeterminate number of hobgoblins had lost two of their brethren.

Skrrzzzt's baseball bat was in splinters and he'd lost an arm. "No worries, mamacita," he said to me in a weary voice after trudging up the slope of the basin to join us. "It'll grow back in time."

Mrs. Browne was miraculously unscathed. I'd known brownies were tough, but that broom of hers must have had some serious mojo in it. She examined Cody with a critical eye and summoned a number of spiders to spin a bandage to bind his wound. Which, yes, ew, but at least it stanched the bleeding. "Ach, this one will live, all right." She thumped his chest with one knotty fist, causing Cody to grimace. "Got a fine, strong constitution, he does."

There were no further casualties in the Fairfax clan, who'd played a canny game of cat-and-mouse—or werewolf-and-mouse—with the mercenaries in the dunes. And of course there were no casualties among the Outcast save for their immortality, although a number of them had sustained nonfatal injuries that could no longer be eradicated by dying and reincorporating.

It made them cautious, something they hadn't had to be for a very, very long time.

With the aid of Gus the ogre, we got Cody loaded into the back of his cousin Joe's pickup truck and covered with a blanket, then made the trek back to our campsite on the Cavannaugh property.

What do you say to the people you love when you've just come within a hairsbreadth of unleashing Armageddon? Now that it was over, I was dazed and exhausted, and I didn't have the faintest idea. No one did. We just gazed at one another in silence.

It was my mom who broke the silence. She opened her arms, tears in her eyes. "Oh, honey!"

That's all she said, but it was enough.

I walked into her embrace, feeling her arms close around me. Mom hugged me hard, and we stayed that way for a long time.

After that we set about the business of breaking down the camp. The Fairfaxes hauled Cody off to Doc Howard to get patched up, and a number of the injured, now-mortal Outcast, including Stefan, followed suit.

Cooper wasn't among them. He'd managed to avoid injury after his last reincorporation.

"So you did it, m'lady," he said to me. "You used your leverage after all."

I nodded. "How do you feel?"

"Strange to meself." Cooper gazed into the distance. "My beast's been with me for so long, I don't quite know what to do without it."

"Are you sorry I did it?" I asked him.

"Never!" His gaze returned to my face. "Don't mistake me, Daisy. I'm grateful beyond words. But it's going to take some getting used to."

I held out my hand to him. "Well, if there's anything I can do to help, I'm here for you."

Cooper regarded my hand with habitual wariness, then clasped it firmly. "Been a long time since I've held a lass's hand without thinking to feed on her," he mused. "It feels good."

I tightened my grip on his hand. "I'm glad."

Before we departed the campsite, Persephone paid us a visit. She emerged from an SUV that halted some forty yards away, carrying my pillowcase in one delicate hand. It was an incongruous sight.

Accompanied—at her insistence—by Lurine, I went out to meet with the goddess on the rim of the basin. Persephone still looked pretty stricken, and Lurine's presence didn't help, but my pity only went so far. I raised my eyebrows at the pillowcase. "You really didn't have to return this."

Persephone summoned a faint smile, only a hint of its former dazzle in it. "I thought it best to approach under a flag of truce." She glanced at Lurine. "Forgive me for my threat, sister."

Lurine folded her arms. "I'm no sister to you, Olympian whore."

"Do not be cruel." Persephone twisted the pillowcase in her hands, a pleading look on her face. "You know I had no choice in that matter."

Right, six pomegranate seeds had condemned her to her fate. "Does Hades even know what you tried to do here?" I asked.

"Yes." Persephone tilted her head, sunlight shimmering on her hair. "My husband loves me, you know, even if I have chafed against the ties that bind me to him. I believe Hades hoped that if he gave my madness free rein, it would run its course. And in a way, it has come to pass."

"At a hefty price," I said.

The goddess looked down, then back up. "Yes. I wish to assure you that there will be no further repercussions. The men who were slain or wounded . . . all fatalities and injuries will be reported as the result of a covert military operation." Another faint, rueful smile. "The lawyer Dufreyne spoke the truth. They signed away many rights."

"I bet."

"If others . . ." Persephone paused. "If others are found to have perished at the hands of the Wild Hunt, contact Mr. Dufreyne. He will arrange for their retrieval."

Huh, so she was keeping Dufreyne in her service. Maybe it wasn't her decision, since Dufreyne was on loan from Hades. I wondered if he'd find it trickier to transport dead mercenaries and military-grade weaponry without his powers of persuasion. I hoped so.

Then again, he did have a goddess in his corner. "Okay."

Persephone gazed around the dunes. "It is a beautiful place. I am sorry I thought to despoil it."

"Yeah, me, too," I said.

"I will donate it back to the city of Pemkowet," she said. "With a stipulation that it may never be sold without the Norse Hel's approval. I hope that may help make amends."

I didn't say anything.

The goddess sighed, a sound like the summer wind rustling through leaves in an orchard. She handed me my pillowcase and turned to go. "Farewell."

"Wait," I said. Persephone glanced back at me. "Look . . . what you said about wanting your own demesne, about never having felt so alive . . . I understand it. You got a raw deal. You've *had* a raw deal for millennia. For six months out of every year, you've felt helpless and powerless. I've felt that way for months. I'm pretty sure an eternity of it would have driven me crazy, too."

"And yet you relinquished the power you claimed today," she murmured. "You relinquished it willingly."

"It wasn't easy," I said honestly. "Even with the fate of the world at stake."

"I am grateful for your understanding." The goddess Persephone gazed at me, her eyes filled with sunlight and green growing things. "The Norse Hel is fortunate to have you, pretty Daisy," she said. "I will remember this. When I return to my husband's demesne, I will spend my season of freedom seeking companions such as you, loyal and true of heart. Mayhap it will ease my path when the cold months of autumn and my return to the underworld come."

My throat tightened a little. "Good luck with that, my lady."

Persephone inclined her head. "Thank you."

With that she left, taking the summer's warmth and the scent of sun-warmed fruit with her.

Lurine and I watched her go, the armored SUV vanishing in the distance. In the basin below us, the *duegar* set fire to Garm's pyre, and smoke billowed into the sky. Almost all the other eldritch had departed. Only the lone surviving troll sat motionless beneath Yggdrasil II's shadow, gazing at the flames.

"You're awfully quiet," I said to Lurine.

"Oh, that silly little bitch Persephone got me feeling sorry for her." Lurine put an arm around my shoulders and gave me an affectionate squeeze. "But she's right, cupcake. Hel's lucky to have you."

"Barely," I said. "It was a near thing. And what I said to Persephone . . . I meant it." I shuddered. "It was hard."

"I know, baby girl. I know it was. But you did it." Lurine gave me another squeeze, then released me. "Let's go home."

# Fifty-six

The next day, I reported to Chief Bryant.

In addition to the casualties on the battlefield, three mercenaries—and seven head of cattle—had been found dead, run ragged until their hearts stopped. At least there were no human civilian casualties. For once, people had heeded my advice and stayed indoors, avoiding the Wild Hunt.

"I don't quite know what I'm supposed to do about this, Daisy," the chief said when I'd finished, drumming his thick fingers on his desk. "How do I even begin to investigate?"

"With all due respect, sir, I don't think you do," I said quietly. "These weren't homicides. They were casualties of war."

Chief Bryant regarded me. "I'm not sure the law appreciates that distinction."

I shook my head. "I don't know what else to tell you, sir."

In the end, he let it go.

I don't think it was easy for him, and I'm pretty sure it involved a call from the private security company that Persephone had contracted. I felt guilty knowing that the families of the men who'd died would never know the truth; but then again, maybe it was better that they didn't. Especially the men who died in terror and exhaustion beneath the onslaught of the Wild Hunt.

It's hard to say.

One thing was for sure—those deaths were on my head, and I knew it. I'd done my best to prevent this war from happening, but I'd given the Oak King the go-ahead to summon the Wild Hunt. And if I had it to do over again, I'd make the same decision. Those mercenaries had been ruthless and efficient. If the Wild Hunt hadn't thrown them into chaos at the outset, the battle might have been over before it began.

And there was always that chance that the entirety of existence would have unraveled if they hadn't. So yeah, I was willing to bear that burden.

The mood in town was one of cautious relief. After our debriefing, the chief released a statement announcing that all paranormal hostilities in Pemkowet had ceased and that Persephone had had a change of heart and decided to donate the property back to the city.

Of course there were rumors and gossip—and the issue of whether or not to appeal the settlement was renewed—but for the most part, everyone was glad to have things back to normal.

Well, as normal as they ever got in Pemkowet.

Although that wasn't entirely true. Word got out about a convoy of Fairfaxes and Outcast converging on Doc Howard's clinic after the battle. Between that, Cody's challenge to Persephone at the town meeting, and generations' worth of mysterious wolf howls in the wilderness, enough people finally put two and two together that the Fairfax clan was officially outed.

It went over surprisingly well. Despite their clannish ways, the Fairfaxes were well liked, considered to be solid citizens and good neighbors, so if they were werewolves, werewolves must be okay.

And of course everything had changed for the Outcast.

I had dinner with Stefan at the Market Bistro a few days after the epic battle. It felt strange to sit across from an ordinary—well, not ordinary, a formerly immortal Bohemian knight was never going to be *ordinary*—mortal man instead of a supernatural predator. Strange to know that Stefan could no longer read my emotions like a book, strange not to be able to gauge the extent of his hunger in the waxing and waning of his pupils.

Hell, speaking of hunger, it was even strange to see him eating and drinking with genuine relish.

Stefan even looked different. The pale sheen of otherness was gone from his skin. He looked younger and more relaxed than I'd ever seen him, laughing at my account of how peeved the vampires at the House of Shadows, especially Bethany Cassopolis, were to have missed the entire battle.

"So how is it?" I asked him when we were lingering over after-dinner drinks. "Being mortal again?"

"It is difficult to put into words," Stefan said slowly. "Every day, I feel as though I am discovering the world anew."

"And that's a good thing, right?" I asked.

"For the most part, yes." He inclined his head. "I regret that I can no longer provide solace to those in need, such as the residents of the Open Hearth home, but to be free of the endless hunger . . ." Stefan took a deep breath and released it. "It is as though a great weight has been lifted from my soul." His expression turned grave. "Forgive me for not trusting you atop the dune, Daisy. I was wrong to attempt to stop you."

Yeah, we hadn't talked about that yet.

I shook my head. "No, you were right. You didn't know what I was doing. *I* didn't know what I was doing."

"You did, though," he said.

"Not until I saw your face," I said. "That's when I understood. If you hadn't tried to stop me . . . I don't know."

Stefan's brows rose. "If you had not yet thought to attempt to bargain with God, why did you begin the ritual?"

"The Norn told me to trust my heart," I murmured. "And all my heart was telling me was that I had to stop what was happening."

We sat in silence with that for a moment. I thought about the fact that now that Stefan was mortal, we could actually have a normal relationship. I could fall asleep in his arms. We could raise a family. We could grow old together.

It felt strange to think that, too.

I didn't have the chance to think it for long.

"There is something difficult I wish to say to you, Daisy," Stefan said in a somber tone. "You have been an unexpected delight in my life, and I will always cherish those memories, as I will always be grateful to you for restoring my mortality. But I think the time has come for us to part ways."

"What?" I stared at him. "Are you *breaking up* with me?"

"You're not truly in love with me, Daisy," Stefan said gently. "Nor I with you. How long do you think it would take us to discover that this violent attraction we have felt no longer exists now that I am free from the curse of being Outcast? How much our passion was fueled by danger?"

"That's not fair!" I protested. "Stefan, you have to give us a chance! At least we have one now."

"And then there is the matter of the wolf," he continued.

"My feelings for Cody—"

"I know what you feel for Cody," Stefan interrupted me. "And I know what he feels for you. Atop the dune, he did not hesitate. Against all reason, he trusted you." He rubbed his shoulder. "I bear the mark of his teeth in my flesh as a reminder," he said wryly. "I am quite sure that wolf is in love with you."

I was silent.

Stefan swirled the port in his glass. "You know I am right, Daisy."

"It doesn't change anything," I murmured. "I'll never be a suitable mate."

"I think you may find that the wolf is ready to make that determination for himself," he said. "You should go to him."

I gazed at Stefan. "You seem awfully sure about this."

He smiled a little. "I am."

"What about you?" I asked. "What will you do with your life?"

"Oh, I plan to travel." He raised his glass and sipped his port. "For all that I have lived in this world for centuries, there is so much of it I have not seen, having been tied to places with an underworld. I would see the rest of it. And I would return to places I have been to reunite with old friends. Those of us who have been Outcast for so long may help each other learn to live in this new world."

"So you'd just totally abandon the life you've built here in Pemkowet?" I said. "Forever?"

Stefan hesitated. "I cannot say. That life has changed. But a piece of my heart will always reside here," he said. "And a part of you will always reside in my heart."

So there you have it.

That was that.

I hashed it out with Jen the next night over pizza and beer, after making her promise that no matter what, the evening wouldn't end in drunken texting.

"I can't believe you're still holding that against me," Jen complained. "Okay, so how *do* you feel about Cody? Is the hot ex-ghoul right? Are you in love with him?"

"I don't know," I admitted. "I mean . . . Cody confuses me. He *annoys* me. That whole back-and-forth, dithering I-want-you-but-I-can't-have-you business is seriously annoying."

"Yes, it was," Jen agreed. "But what if he really *is* ready to choose you over his clan?"

"It's not like he's said so," I pointed out.

Jen shrugged. "He's recovering from a gunshot wound, girlfriend. Cut him some slack. Also, as far as Cody knows, you're still with Stefan. Maybe he's honoring the Bro Code."

"Maybe he should have tried to fight for me," I countered.

"*Maybe* that's exactly what he was doing when he charged through a line of heavily armed mercenary soldiers to take a bite out of the hot ex-ghoul so you could go ahead and very nearly bring the end-time upon us," Jen retorted.

She had a point.

So I paid a visit to Cody the next day.

Cody was convalescing at home, and he greeted me at the door in a pair of faded jeans and a threadbare flannel shirt, his face brightening at the sight of me. "Hey, Daise! Everything okay?"

"Yeah." I felt awkward. "I just wanted to see how you were doing."

"Good." Hoisting his shirt, Cody showed me the white bandages wrapped around his torso. "My sister-in-law Jeanne changed the dressing this morning. She says it's healing cleanly. Can you come in for a minute?"

"Sure." I followed him into the house.

"Can I get you anything? Beer? Glass of water?"

I shook my head. "I'm fine."

Cody padded into his living room on bare feet, turning off the football game on the television. "Sorry, it's a bit messy in here," he apologized, folding the hideous orange and brown crocheted blanket that lay crumpled on the couch, then straightening a stack of DVD cases sprawled across the steamer trunk that served as a table. "I've just been holed up watching TV and videos."

"That's okay." I sat on the couch. "You're entitled. Not the *Saw* movies, I hope?"

He grinned. "No. God, no. Once was enough. But I watched the whole *Fast & Furious* franchise."

"Figures," I said.

Cody eased himself onto the couch beside me. "Don't knock them until you've tried them, Pixy Stix."

"Cody . . ." I hesitated. "Why did you do it? Attack Stefan, I mean?"

He looked away. "Are you asking me to answer for my wolf? I'm not sure I can, Daise."

"Did your wolf even know what I was *doing*?" I asked.

Cody gave a slight shrug. "Is he okay? Ludovic? I know I drew blood."

"Stefan's fine," I said in exasperation. "He's fine and he's mortal and he broke up with me, and *you're* not answering my question."

He stole a glance at me. "He broke up with you?"

"Yes," I said. "Stefan Ludovic and I are no longer together. Now, will you please tell me what I want to know?"

Gazing at the ceiling, Cody blew out his breath. "You want to know why, Daise? It's because it's not just *this* shape that has feelings for you. It's all of me." He looked directly at me, a hint of phosphorescent green flashing behind his topaz eyes. "That's what I learned out there in the dunes. My wolf? It chose you, too. And yes, it knew what you were doing. We knew. *I* knew."

"Jesus, Cody! I could have destroyed the world," I whispered.

Cody nodded. "Yeah. But maybe a world where I couldn't have you wasn't worth living in anyway. Anyway, you didn't. I trusted you, okay? I promised you, no matter what, I'd always have your—"

That's all he got out before I grabbed his face in both hands and kissed him, long and hard and deep.

It felt good.

"Ow!" Cody winced. "Stitches."

Oops. I wasn't quite sure when or how I'd straddled him. "Sorry."

His hands caressed my back. "It's okay. Totally worth it."

Settling onto Cody's lap, I gazed down at him. "What about the clan?"

Narrowing his eyes, Cody smiled up at me. "The clan can go fuck itself. How's that, Pixy Stix?"

I smiled back at him. "Not bad."

# Fifty-seven

It's funny how things turned out.

If real life was like a fairy tale, Stefan and I would have had the happy-ever-after ending, since all the obstacles that divided us had been magically swept away.

Cody and I . . . not so much.

For one, the Fairfax clan was furious over Cody's decision, although they did stop short of ostracizing him. Apparently I'd gained some serious clout in the process of saving Pemkowet by almost destroying the world; which was ironic, since that leverage was gone forever. But the fact that I'd been willing—or crazy enough—to do it in the first place had earned grudging respect.

Eldritch and their love of hierarchy. Go figure.

And then of course there was the fact that Cody and I were what we were: a hell-spawn and a werewolf. For the rest of my life, assuming we stayed together, I'd lose him to the full moon once a month. Cody would spend his life never knowing what it was like to hunt with his mate beneath the full moon. As far as we knew, having kids wasn't an option.

Maybe it wouldn't work in the long run. Who knew? There were no guarantees.

And yet being with Cody felt right.

No regrets, though. If Stefan and I hadn't had our affair, I'd always have wondered what it would have been like. And frankly, the highlights had been pretty mind-blowing. I didn't feel like a schoolgirl with a crush around Cody anymore. I felt like a grown-ass woman with some pretty strong ideas of what I wanted out of a relationship, in and out of the bedroom.

Along with sorting out my love life, I spent my time updating the X-Files and the Pemkowet Ledger, and assessing the damage the war had wrought in both the mundane and the eldritch communities.

I reassured everyone I encountered in town that the war really was over and that the Wild Hunt wouldn't return.

I hung out with Skrrzzzt, drinking beer and playing *Battleship*, complimenting him on the emerging regrowth of his arm.

I tracked down the hobgoblins' den—my status among the fey had risen, and an obliging snowdrop fairy led me to it without a single insult—to offer my condolences.

I sat in silence with the surviving troll, whose name was Blunthuf, grieving for the loss of his mate.

The one thing I didn't do was visit Little Niflheim. I didn't know how badly the interior of Yggdrasil II had been damaged by the drone strike, and I didn't want to intrude while the world tree was healing.

Hel always knew where to find me. She would summon me when she wanted me.

Persephone kept her word and deeded the property back to the City of Pemkowet with the stipulation that it could never be sold without Hel's explicit approval. Not only that, the contract included a provision stating that Hel's liaison be granted oversight of the territory and paid a monthly stipend.

It wasn't a huge amount, but it was enough to pay my rent and bills, and even set a bit aside for a rainy day . . . and actually, for me, that *was* huge. For the first time in my life, I opened a savings account.

The tri-community councils and boards held a second town meeting to decide whether or not to appeal the decision in the lawsuit. Now that the community was flush, Lurine declined to repeat her offer to underwrite the legal costs of an appeal. Unsurprisingly, the members of our local governments decided that a bird in the hand was better than two in the bush, and voted to quit while they were ahead, using proceeds of the sale of Hel's territory to pay the damages and split the extra five million dollars among them.

Too bad.

Among other things, it meant that the legal precedent of holding mundane authorities accountable for the actions of the eldritch would stand. I hoped we wouldn't have cause to regret that someday.

It was a balmy spring evening, a month after the war, when Hel finally sent for me. Spring had been especially early and lush in Pemkowet that year, perhaps because of Persephone's brief presence there. The grass was turning green and there was a haze of budding leaves on all the trees. The woods were filled with trillium and sunny yellow dandelions dotted the meadows. Gardens rioted with daffodils, hyacinths, and tulips, front yards blazed with azaleas blossoming in a multitude of hues—coral, scarlet, fuchsia, hot pink, orange, yellow, and white.

In fact, I was at Cody's, standing in his front yard in the soft twilight and discussing planting some azaleas there when the dune buggy pulled into his driveway.

It made my heart ache to see a frost giant—actually, it was a frost giantess—who wasn't Mikill climb out of the buggy. It had always been Mikill who'd come for me.

"Daisy Johanssen," the frost giantess boomed, raising her left hand to reveal the rune etched on it. "My name is Geirdís. I am bid to summon you to an audience with Hel."

I held up my left hand in acknowledgment. "I'll be right with you. Cody, can I borrow a warm jacket?"

Geirdís waited patiently, dripping onto the gravel drive while Cody ducked into the house and grabbed his fleece-lined Carhartt jacket for me.

"You look like a cheerleader wearing her boyfriend's varsity letter jacket," he said, adjusting my zipper. "There's a pair of work gloves in the pocket."

Standing on tiptoes, I kissed him. "Thanks."

Geirdís wasn't much of a talker. Mikill hadn't been, either, but I'd gotten used to his silence.

"Do you have the loaf of bread for—" I broke off my sentence as the buggy jolted over the dunes. No, of course she didn't have a loaf of bread for Garm. Like Mikill, Garm was gone.

"The hellhound's spirit roams the sands," Geirdís said quietly. "It may be that we will catch a glimpse of him."

We didn't, though. A few minutes later, Yggdrasil II's opening yawned before us without a ghostly hellhound in sight.

Geirdís didn't warn me to keep my limbs within the vehicle during the descent. I'd never needed Mikill's reminder, but it was ridiculous how much I missed it. Tears froze on my cheeks as we descended.

Close to the bottom, the smooth spiral ramp veered into an unexpected jag. A massive chunk of the inside of the trunk was missing, leaving barely enough to rebuild and allow the buggy to pass. A second, more accurate drone strike would have taken out the heart of Yggdrasil II's vast canopy of roots.

It had been a near thing.

I shivered and fished Cody's work gloves out of the pocket of his jacket, my hands swimming in them.

Geirdís parked the buggy and ushered me into Hel's presence. Hel sat on her throne, flanked by the other two surviving frost giants, and the old sawmill was packed with *duegar*.

They bowed to me.

I mean *all* of them bowed to me, not just the dwarves. The frost giants bowed. *Hel* bowed.

Okay, it was a seated bow, but still.

"Daisy Johanssen," Hel addressed me, straightening on her throne, gazing at me with both eyes. "Niflheim and its denizens are much in your debt. Forgive me for not summoning you sooner to give thanks."

"That's okay," I said faintly. "I'm sure you had a lot to do."

"Yes." Hel's ember eye closed, her luminous fair eye regarding me with concern. "Are you well?"

My heart contracted in my chest at her question. It's funny, but no one else except my mother had thought to ask me.

Was I?

For the most part, yeah. I'd faced my worst nightmare made flesh, invoked my deepest fear and my deepest desire. I'd broken the world and bargained with heaven to mend it.

Most of me was profoundly grateful that I'd never have to worry about it happening again.

A little part of me missed it, and mourned for the power I'd renounced.

And it probably always would.

"Yes, my lady," I said to Hel. "I am well."

Hel inclined her head to me. "I am pleased to hear it, Daisy Johanssen."

There was a bit more to the audience, but not much. I explained about Persephone donating the legal deed to Hel's territory to the City of Pemkowet, including the stipulation about selling it and the provision for a monthly stipend to be paid to me. All of that met with Hel's approval.

"You have done well, my young liaison," Hel said to me in formal dismissal. "May your valor bring peace and security to my demesne for many years to come."

The *duegar* and the frost giants murmured in agreement.

I hoped it would.

When Geirdís and I reached the base of the world tree and the sacred spring, I made her stop the buggy and I hopped out.

The Norns paused in their labor to regard me.

"Hi," I said. "It's me again. Daisy. And I'm sorry, but I have to ask." I filled my lungs with a deep breath and expelled it in a nervous gust. "The risk I took . . . Was it worth it? Because it was an *awfully* big risk. I mean, we're talking Armageddon here, right? I just want to know. If Yggdrasil had fallen and you three, you Norns, had perished, would it really have broken the skein of time? Was the entirety of existence at stake, or was this just a way to preserve your, um, particular cosmology?"

One by one, the Norns shook their heads at me, refusing to answer. I would never, ever know for sure.

Never.

Goddamned soothsayers.

"Okay," I said. "Never mind. Forget I asked, okay?"

The Norns nodded in unison, returning to their wooden buckets, drawing water from the spring.

Maybe it was true; maybe it wasn't. Hell, Janek Król had believed my existence was a sign that God had forgiven the Outcast, and damned if they didn't have a second chance at redemption now.

Maybe that had been the divine plan all along. Maybe it was the only way it could happen.

I'd even made my mom's teenage fantasy come true. In the end, I'd made the choice she'd dreamed of . . . and my father, Belphegor, knew he'd picked the wrong girl to mess with when he chose her.

The world was still here and Yggdrasil II was still standing. Life in Pemkowet would go on for all of us.

Whatever the truth might be, I'd just have to live with it.

And I was pretty sure I could.